Blessed Shadows Dark and Deep

Michael Staton

Blessed Shadows Dark and Deep

By ten o'clock sunlight had burned away the fog cloaking the fields in front of A.P. Hill's breastworks. Blue-Bellies moved parallel to the Rappahannock, then right-faced toward Richmond Road. Booms erupted. On the extreme right of the Confederate line, two Virginia mobile artillery pieces, each harnessed to their team of six horses, wheeled down Prospect Hill. Bouncing, sliding, the caissons and gun carriages kicked up dirt, stubble and foliage. They creaked and groaned as they dashed toward the Blue-Bellies. Yankee twelve-pounders fired at them, their shells missing. Juddering to a stop, the gun crews unlimbered the rifled Blakely and twelve-pound Napoleon. With Yankee Springfields and artillery firing at them, the Virginians coolly loaded and primed their pieces. Black-powder smoke rings spewed from the barrels. The air thundered; Union infantry scattered like tumbling bowling pins.

"Sweet Jesus those men are brave!" Daniel exclaimed. "Twenty men against the entire Union army."

"More like a Blue-Belly regiment," Kenny retorted dryly, then grinned. "Still impressive I must say."

A cannonball rumbling across the ground smashed into the Blakely, splintering a wheel and gun carriage. Its barrel lay on the ground, muzzle half-buried in the dirt. Horses went down; shrieking; they struggled to rise. Two gunners lay unmoving in pools of blood, rammer and wormer splayed on their legs.

"Daring yes, but it's time to withdraw," Bill said, amazed that two field pieces were holding up the Yankee offensive.

Blessed Shadows
Dark and Deep

Michael Staton

A Wings ePress, Inc.
Historical Romance Novel

Wings ePress, Inc.

Edited by: Jeanne Smith
Copy Edited by: Joan Powell
Executive Editor: Jeanne Smith
Cover Artist: Richard Stroud

All rights reserved

Wings ePress Books
www.books-by-wings-epress.com

Copyright © 2017 by Michael Staton
ISBN 978-1-61309-664-2

Published In the United States Of America

Wings ePress Inc.
3000 N. Rock Road
Newton, KS 67114

Dedication

My favorite English teacher at Fort Frye High School, June Berkeley, inspired me to chase after my dreams of becoming not just a newspaper reporter but a fiction writer crafting novels as well. I dedicate *Blessed Shadows Dark and Deep* to you, Mrs. Berkeley.

One

A Civil Brawl

A breeze blew through the open windows of the Stamford Print Shop, providing relief from the sweltering late-July heat. Sixteen-year-old Bill Stamford offered a beaming smile to the fortyish woman buttoned up in an austere summer dress as she strode up to the counter. Not entirely unadorned, Bill realized. A miniature Bonnie Blue Flag lay pinned to Julia Dickson's bodice.

"Good afternoon, Mrs. Dickson," Bill said, relocating the novel he'd been reading to a shelf below the countertop. "How can I help you?"

Hair nearly invisible beneath a gray bonnet better suited for 1840, not 1861, the woman dug into her handbag and emerged with a sheet of paper swathed with intricate handwriting. Handing it to him, she said, "Kenansville sure could use an afternoon shower." She wiped a gloved hand across her forehead, soaking up beads of sweat. "Love the smell of hot lead in the wintertime, not so much in July."

Mrs. Dickson's pronunciation of her words was as meticulous as the writing on the paper. Bill glanced at her neatly spaced, perfectly drawn rendering of an enlistment poster. "This is the prettiest thing I've seen all day, except for you, Mrs. Dickson."

"I'm way too old for sweet talk, Bill Stamford." Mrs. Dickson's lips refused to quiver with amusement. "My husband plans a big blowout for the Duplin Rifles. A band, picnic, ice cream, games for the kiddies. The Second North Carolina Regiment needs more men, so we're going to recruit for Company C, our own Duplin Rifles. Mr. Dickson will take the recruits to meet up with Captain Kenan." Hand perched against her upper lip as if she intended to share a secret, she whispered, "I'd normally forbid it, but it's for the cause. There'll be a kissing booth, but only for boys who have signed their enlistment papers. Girls from the Female Seminary will man it."

Bill suspected his face must be redder than a Duplin Roads tomato. He fought to keep an outburst of giggling bottled in his throat. Taking a deep breath, he let it out slowly, then said, "Every Duplin grandmother will be praying for your soul."

She finally laughed. "Chaste kisses. You're going to get one, aren't you, Bill?"

He shook his head. "I'm just sixteen. I'll be seventeen on September twenty-second, so it'll be fourteen months until I can enlist. Momma won't allow me until I turn eighteen. I'm not going to buck her."

"Icie Belle's a hard-nosed woman," Mrs. Dickson agreed. "She's raising three fine children in you, Mark and Laura. I have to admit I didn't realize you were just sixteen. You look older."

"I know. A few grandfather types have scolded me for not being in the army." Bill shrugged. "We don't have an artist to reproduce your drawings of a band and soldiers marching, but we do have woodcuts just as good. I'll bring the proof to your house in two days so you can make any changes you want, Mrs. Dickson."

"Your papa courted me in our younger days, before Icie Belle won his heart. I know he'll do a wonderful job. What do I owe, Bill?"

"Two dollars for twelve posters. Enough to blanket the town." He deposited the bills in the cashbox as soon as she paid.

"Will you be a volunteer, Bill? Not for the army, but for the picnic." Mrs. Dickson patted Bill's hand. "You can captain one of the children's games... maybe shuttlecock."

"I'd love to do it. It's a game boys and girls can play together." He waved goodbye as she beelined for the front door. When he heard the door shut, he took a final look at Mrs. Dickson's mockup and pigeonholed it in the to-do box. The poster needed some jasm. He rested his thumb under his chin and wrote down some headline suggestions. *Repel the Invader*. That was catchy. In seventy-two point type, it would grab attention; the kissing-booth girls would do the rest. And below the Second North Carolina Regiment, the words *Thunderbolt of the Confederacy*. If Mrs. Dickson didn't kill the kissing booth, she'd not kill those two advertising gimmicks, Bill figured.

Slipping his fingers under the novel's back cover, Bill set the book on the counter. He'd left a bookmark between pages sixty-two and sixty-three of James Fenimore Cooper's *The Last of the Mohicans*. As he rubbed a finger along the bookmark's edge, Bill heard his papa amble into the front office.

"Someone escaping the heat? Or did we get some business?" Clarence Stamford slapped his son on the back.

Even teenage girls considered Clarence a handsome man. In his early forties, Bill's papa parted his coal-black hair in the middle, a look that gave him a distinguished appearance, like a railroad president. With a clean-shaven face and slim figure, Clarence could pass for a man in his early thirties, since he'd yet to start turning gray. Even in his farmer's shirt and railhead-striped work pants, he made women play vainly with their curls as he addressed them at the counter.

Bill retrieved Mrs. Dickson's poster order from the workbox and handed it to Clarence. "Looks like the Duplin Rifles are taking advantage of the whipping we gave the Yankees at Manassas. One of my school's trustees, James Dickson, is going to do some recruiting for them. All day Saturday, August 10, on the courthouse lawn."

Clarence looked up from Mrs. Dickson's dummy sheet. "James and Captain Kenan are longtime chuckaboos. They attended Grove Academy together." Grinning, Clarence eyed the ceiling. "It's hard to tell if the blowout's for recruitment or an excuse for a rip-roarin' good time. Lord, help me keep my patience. Just one battle where both armies were ill-prepared, but the Yanks broke first. Now everyone thinks the war's going to be over in three months, and we'll be free of Yankee meddling. Bill, it'll be more like three years. With the North's industrial might, it's going to be a ruinous war even if we win the damn thing."

Considering all the Confederate portraits on the wall and the Bonnie Blue Flag flying above the print shop's front door, no one would ever suspect Clarence Stamford harbored doubts. Or maybe realistic expectations, Bill thought. His papa wasn't a man to get caught up in the turmoil of the moment. He prided himself on the ability to anticipate the consequences of political choices men made on the national, state and local levels. Bill had never bested him in chess. His father wasn't a stupid man; publicly he supported the war.

"Papa, I didn't know you courted Julia Dickson." Bill expected his father to flash surprise, then conceal it. He didn't. Instead, he crossed his arms and harrumphed.

"Julia Dickson talks too much." Clarence put the woman's drawing on the counter. "Yes, I courted her. We were never serious. I admit we did share some spirited kisses and did the bear. When your momma and her family moved down from Ohio, my heart only had room for one woman."

Bill nodded. "I know you love Momma. I just find it funny you courted Julia Dickson. I don't think she ever fancied stylish hair. She's always wearing an ugly bonnet."

"She wasn't always so old-school, son."

"Obviously not, considering the kissing booth." Bill pointed to the mockup and the paragraph announcing the kissing booth. "See it, Papa?"

"I do now." Clarence actually giggled. "Honestly, I'd have never expected a kissing booth on a poster from the Dicksons. War makes for strange bedfellows." He tapped his finger along the top of Mrs. Dickson's drawing. "I don't see a work order."

"Whoops." Bill smiled sheepishly. "Forgot. Again."

Clarence tore a work order from its stack and slid it to his son. "No skimping on details. I'll probably have Dale Winland do the typesetting."

Dale was the shop's apprentice, and lived in an attic room in carpenter Ben Ezzell's farmhouse just outside Kenansville. Twenty-one years old, the Burgaw native from neighboring Pender County had been mulling joining up, maybe as early as the upcoming ice-cream social. If he did, he'd leave one person in a quandary, his sweetheart, Susannah Lelly, daughter of one of the town's lawyers, Isaac B. Lelly. She'd hounded him to do his military duty, yet she was a weeper, so Bill knew Susannah would blubber when Dale climbed aboard the Wilmington and Weldon train at Warsaw and headed north to drill, march and fight.

"I'd like to do the typesetting for Mrs. Dickson's posters," Bill told his papa. "I've some ideas for woodcuts and banners."

"Okay, but you need to fill out the work order." Clarence put a lead pencil in his son's hand. "Get in the habit, even though you'll—"

The bell above the front door rang. Both expected a customer to step into the print shop. Instead, Bill's best friend sauntered in. Charlie Kurtz settled his buttocks on a stool, then dropped a cloth bag onto the mahogany countertop. There was a solid thump when the bag came to rest.

"Fixin' for a game of marbles, Billy Boy?" Charlie splayed his elbows on the countertop, and gave Clarence a hopeful look. "If your papa agrees."

A scrawny lad, Charlie barely topped five-foot, three inches, yet never backed down from a heavier, taller bully. Crowned with a head of uncombable red hair, Charlie seemed to draw unruly girls who liked sharing kisses in woodsy places. Hands stippled with freckles as numerous as those on Charlie's face opened the bag. Soon two of his fingers held a ceramic marble decorated with four-leaf clovers.

"Go ahead, Bill, take a break," Clarence said, his manner easy going. "I'll man the counter. No more than three games, though. Then back to work." As Bill and Charlie stepped toward the front door, Clarence shouted, "How many posters for Julia?"

"A dozen, Papa." Bill opened the door. "Don't give Mrs. Dickson's job to Dale. I want to do the typesetting."

"Then you need to get back in here soon. Just a few games, remember?" Clarence dismissed them with a wave.

Bill stopped unexpectedly in the doorway. Charlie banged into him. "Oh, can I take the *Richmond Dispatch* with me, Papa? I want to read its account of Manassas to Charlie."

"Sure," Clarence said, nudging the newspaper out from one of the counter shelves. He held it up, and Bill quickly had the newspaper perched between his arm and ribs.

They liked playing marbles in the alley between the print shop and Stephen Graham's law office. Bill dawdled, slipping into the alley's shadows. He planted himself on the bench underneath the print shop's storefront window. Wedging himself in a corner spot, he stretched his legs and, enjoying the smells of petunias and zinnias blooming in planters, opened the *Dispatch*.

Bill read the lead and the next four paragraphs, then Charlie interrupted. "They ran lickety-split all the way back to

Washington? I thought the fellas up North were made of sterner stuff." Charlie kept shaking his head.

Bill expounded, "The correspondent says Yankee civilians drove their buggies to the battlefield to watch the fight and do some picnicking. They got caught up in the stampede. Papa says the Yanks will fight better next time. They realize it's not a lark."

"I've cousins livin' up in Pennsylvania," Charlie said, still shaking his head. "They're good people. They'd not run."

"Me too, Charlie. My momma's from a little town in Ohio… Arkona. Her people aren't cowards." Bill couldn't hold back a laugh. "Obviously, none of our relatives are in that Yankee army."

Playfully punching Bill's shoulder, Charlie said, "None of mine. Yours? I'm not sure."

They wrestled on the bench for a few seconds, then separated, out of breath, both giggling like five-year olds.

"With the Yanks in Washington licking their wounds, we sure won't see any of them marching on Kenansville." Bill smiled at the silliness of his words. Why would any Yankee general want to capture Kenansville?

The town had grown tremendously in the last twenty years, but held no military value. Like all Southern towns, folks traveling to Kenansville first saw its church steeples jutting above the trees. One carpenter, Joseph Carr, had built more than twenty houses on streets radiating out from the courthouse square. These homes, the courthouse, city hall, and St. John's Masonic Lodge were built in the Greek revival style. More than once, Bill had heard Wilmington folks refer to Kenansville as "that dashing little town with the fine schools." Not many towns with just six hundred people sported two schools with statewide reputations… Kenansville Female Seminary and Bill's school, Grove Academy.

As the Bonnie Blue Flag flapped above him, Bill gazed across the street at the remodeled courthouse with its new third story.

In just over a week, the courthouse lawn would be a fizzing place with band music blaring, old men tossing horseshoes, kids racing in burlap sacks, kissing-booth girls smooching boys bound for the Duplin Rifles, and everyone eating fried chicken and apple pie. The courthouse had been Kenansville's *raison d'être* for the first half of the 19th century. Now the Wilmington and Weldon Railroad powered growth. The line didn't pass through Kenansville, but that didn't spell economic doom for the county seat. The Teachey depot lay nine miles away; the Magnolia depot, eight miles, and Warsaw station, six miles. The railroad meant rapid, cheap transportation for Kenansville's farmers who needed to get their turpentine, lumber and cotton down to Wilmington's bustling port. All Bill had to do was look left and right at the grand homes and see the railroad had brought prosperity.

"Yanks are going to want to capture Wilmington," Bill muttered, sitting straighter on the bench. "They won't stay cooped up in Washington forever. They could march through here on the way to Wilmington. Just because we aren't a military target doesn't mean the war won't come here. I'd hate to see the courthouse and the houses burned."

"You really reckon Yankees could come through here?" Charlie sounded doubtful.

"They can't let the seaport and the railroad supply our armies in Virginia." Bill glanced at the newspaper on his lap. "Momma and Papa say I can't join up until I'm eighteen. But I'm feeling stubborn as a mule, Charlie. I wish I could enlist at the picnic next month."

"What picnic?"

"Big doings on Saturday, August tenth, at the courthouse. Mr. Dickson's helping Captain Kenan muster more men for the Duplin Rifles. Fried chicken, ice cream and, believe it or not, a kissing booth. Join up and you'll get a kiss from a Seminary girl."

"No way." Charlie rolled his eyes. "Kisses got to be sneaked. Ain't goin' to happen no how. Their mommas will have a hissy fit."

"Mrs. Dickson guarantees it. We're doing up a poster for her, and it includes the kissing booth."

"That's why you want to join up. You're after sugar from one of them Seminary girls."

"No how! If I tried to join up and wrangle a kiss, Momma and Papa would lock me in my room until I turn eighteen." Bill held the *Dispatch* up to Charlie, pointed at an advertisement for a Wilmington shipper. "Let's slink away to Wilmington and do it. We'll lie about our age."

Charlie shook his head. "I ain't goin' till I get drafted. No volunteerin' for me. Why are you even askin'? You know how I feel about this war."

Charlie's family hailed from Asheville. Mountain folks were mostly struggling farmers with crops on hillsides and in the creek valleys. A man could walk for a day and never see a slave. Men and women like the Kurtz family didn't much care for Tar Heel planters with their cotton and rice fields that stretched to the horizon and their addiction to slavery. And they sure didn't like getting dragged into a civil war hatched by planters. A job at the Grove Academy brought the Kurtz family to Kenansville, but they remained mountain rebellious through and through.

"Aye, I know, Charlie, and I agree with you." Bill folded the newspaper and laid it on the bench between them. "Papa says we're in the industrial age; slavery's a dying institution."

Charlie harrumphed. "Then why does your family have two slaves?"

Bill's ears perked. Boisterous voices, down at the intersection of Duplin and Seminary streets. One in particular, fifteen-year-old Ezekiel Merritt, barked drilling orders to three other boys, all shouldering wooden muskets: Ezekiel's younger brother, fourteen-year-old Sam Merritt, and two beefy thirteen-year olds, Frank Taylor and Ethan Wagner. They marched toward the print shop.

Azure blue for most of the day, the sky had turned dark just as Bill and Charlie exited the shop. As Bill eyed the marching foursome, the clouds parted and a sunbeam encased Ezekiel in an orb of light. He looked like an angel. That was an odd sight indeed. In spite of his biblical name, Ezekiel was a bully. Singing, Ezekiel blared, "We're goin' to drown Old Abe in Grove Creek. Sing, boys. We're goin' to drown Old Abe in Grove Creek."

"Shush!" Bill said tersely to Charlie. "Can't be bashing slavery when those rowdies can hear us."

"I ain't shuttin' up for no one," Charlie shouted above the singing. "Screw slave owners! Screw the Peculiar Institution!"

"Column right, march!" Ezekiel shouted. "We're goin' to drown Charlie in Grove Creek." A few steps short of the print shop's bench, Ezekiel yelled, "Halt! You're a damned traitor, Charlie Kurtz! A yellow-belly coward!"

Brother Sam taunted, "Your momma's nothing but a three-penny upright. A bangtail!"

"Bangtail! Bangtail!" Frank and Ethan hollered.

Scrambling to his feet, Charlie barreled into Ezekiel and drove him into the cobblestones. Straddling Ezekiel, Charlie drove his fists into the ringleader's face, bloodying the teenager's nose and lips. Howling, arms raised, Ezekiel blocked some of Charlie's punches but not enough to save his face from further damage. "I'll kill you," he wailed. "Kill... kill you!"

Bill blurted, "Charlie, stop! You're going to—"

Sam bashed his rifle against Charlie's back. Stunned, Charlie groaned and slumped against Ezekiel. Arms bulging, Ezekiel tossed Charlie aside and rolled atop him. Charlie did nothing to stop the punches raining down on his face.

Grinning madly, Sam raised his play rifle as if he intended to smash its butt against Charlie's head. Bill bounded from the bench and slammed into Sam, knocking him into his brother's legs. Stumbling, Sam toppled onto Ezekiel and Charlie, then scrambled toward his fallen rifle. Bill grabbed it first, hurled it away from the brawlers. Breathing rapidly, everyone's screams and shrieks pounding his ears, Bill reached for Ezekiel's toy gun.

Ethan's gun crashed against Bill's arm. As if God had dropped a bucket of paint on him, Bill saw everything in front of him turn red. Then he felt the pain, as if it had charged the air around him. He broke into a cold sweat. Any movement of his arm sent jolts of pain searing through him. Ethan raised his gun to hit Bill again.

Near the fighting boys, a buggy squeaked to a stop. "Confound it, hooligans!" The buggy's door opened. Dr. Chauncey W. Graham, a Grove Academy trustee, stepped down onto the cobblestones. "Stop the fisticuffs immediately! Don't make me say anything further!"

On his knees, Ezekiel whirled at the sound of the doctor's voice. Shockingly, a white halo surrounded the boy, so brilliant the nimbus consumed Bill's red dots of pain. Bill had seen a halo only once, when he was ten. It encircled a playmate, a young cousin, as the two of them prepared to climb a tree in their granddaddy's front yard. She fell, and a day later died. He told his momma and papa, and they called in the Reverend James Sprunt, who conducted an exorcism. There'd not been a reoccurrence until this moment. Bill swallowed hard, forcing the bile back down his throat. He expected Ezekiel to die, maybe within the hour. *Lord, take this burden away. Drive this vile thing out of me!* Six long years! Maybe if he prayed and prayed it wouldn't happen again.

Eyes huge at the sight of one of the town's most eminent governing fathers, Ezekiel and his gang fled as the annoyed doctor watched. "Explain yourselves, Charlie Kurtz and Bill Stamford." The halo burned more intensely as Ezekiel and the others disappeared behind one of the town's mansions.

Charlie wobbled to his feet and wiped a hand across his bloody mouth. "Ezekiel called me a traitor. Then Sam called my momma a bangtail. I had to fight, sir."

The doctor nodded. "Your momma's a sweet lady. I'll talk to their father. I expect Sam will apologize to your momma." He stepped closer to Charlie and grasped his rumpled vest, spotted with blood spatters. "Son, everyone in Kenansville knows how mountain people feel about secession and the eastern planters, but you need to keep your talk confined to your father's parlor. You can't fight every boy in town."

Charlie grimaced. "I got my licks in today. That's enough."

The print-shop door whined open. Bill's father stood on the plank sidewalk, hands pressed against his hips. "I step to the back to run the press for a few minutes and all hell breaks loose." Clarence fixed his harsh gaze on Charlie. "Those kisses you steal will dry up, Charlie Kurtz, if you don't watch your tongue. Better to keep quiet and keep those kisses coming, yes?"

Charlie grinned. "Since you put it that way, sir, I'm all for slavery and sweet kisses."

Stupidly, Bill braced his hand... the one connected to his hurting arm... against a cobblestone and tried to rise. Pain throbbed through his body, and he collapsed to his knees.

Charlie looked aghast. Clarence and the doctor raced to Bill's side. Doctor Graham examined Bill's arm, gently probing the bones. "It's fractured," Doctor Graham said matter-of-factly. "We'll get you home and get that forearm set and in a sling."

~ * ~

Six weeks... that's the time it took for the bones to fully heal. Bill stayed housebound for a week, not wanting to risk reinjuring it. Charlie came by every afternoon and said he'd not got into further fights. Bill never did do Mrs. Dickson's poster, and stayed away from her ice cream social. Thirty boys joined Company C, some as far away as Beulaville and Teachey-Duplin Roads. In late

September, Bill took off his sling and began working in the print shop as if he'd never been bashed by the rifle's butt.

Ezekiel died a day after the halo manifestation. Drowned in the Pollock swimming hole north of Kenansville. Bill said nothing to his momma and papa about the halo. Instead, he prayed every night that his Lord and Savior would keep him free of future manifestations.

Two

A Boy's Quickening Heart

Bill spied her from across the Grove Presbyterian churchyard, filling her plate with fried chicken, potato salad and black-eyed peas. The raven-haired girl, curls spilling from beneath a flowery hat, dipped her finger into a cake's chocolate icing. The sight of her tongue licking a glistening finger set Bill's heart fluttering. At that moment, he determined he must meet the lass, and with luck court her.

She'd never been to one of the soirees parents held for the Grove Academy boys and the girls of the Kenansville Female Seminary. Until this last day of summer 1862—two days before his birthday—he'd never seen her at a church gathering. She could have been at Mrs. Dickson's ice-cream social back in August 1861, but Bill wouldn't have known. He was cooped up in the house recovering from his broken arm. Most of the girls wore brown and purple day dresses with polygon embroidery patterns, appropriate for a fall social. The brunette refused to acknowledge the end of summer, instead wearing a light blue cotton dress with lace frills, silk-embroidered roses, and a beautiful smile. Inhaling a determined breath, Bill stepped toward the table where she'd just sat with a middle-aged gentleman and two older women.

Perhaps it was the stern look on the man's mustached face that made the other boys at the party shy away from her. If Charlie had been along, he wouldn't have been deterred, but would have flitted around her like a bee humming around roses. Where was Charlie anyway? He hadn't been to Bill's house for Saturday breakfast, something Charlie rarely missed. And now he'd passed up the picnic and its covey of pretty girls. With so many boys in the Southern armies, there wasn't much competition for slip-into-the-woods kisses.

At the buffet tables, Bill filled a plate with fried chicken, potato salad, black-eyed peas and one other item the raven-haired lass had dodged— corn on the cob. Duplin land grew corn, but not as good as out in the Midwest. Normally, it was fodder for hogs, but with the new Confederacy at war, folks were glad to eat it. Seventeen months into the war, the Yankee blockade was taking its toll. The food on the tables looked mouthwatering to Bill. The soiree could be the last hurrah for months, if not years.

The spot next to the girl remained open. A boy with a pronounced limp and a small plate of ice cream, Owen Beveritt, headed for the seat. Bill increased his pace, hoping to outrun Owen, but wavered. A race to the chair, crowding out a boy with a limp, would look unseemly, especially at church. Ten feet from the girl, a stooped, bearded man rested a hand on Owen's shoulder. Reverend Sprunt pointed to a nearby field where boys and girls prepared to play a game of croquet. The iron rings had been driven into the ground. Mallets were perched on shoulders. Drawing closer, Bill heard the reverend say, "Owen, I've told 'em to delay startin' so you can join in."

Join in, Owen, Bill thought. *Look at all those pretty girls with mallets.* Bill brushed up against the vacant chair at the table, just inches from the girl and her flowered hat. He regarded the older man directly across from the girl. Probably her papa. "May I join you, sir?"

"You may," the gentleman with an Old Dutch beard said. "Please, Becky, scoot your chair over to give the gentleman more room."

Turning, Becky inclined her head and eyed Bill. She proffered a sly smile, as if she knew why he'd chosen the spot next to her. "I'm at a disadvantage, sir," she said, her voice silvery. "You know my name. I don't know yours." As lady-like as possible, she nudged her chair slightly, taking care not to display her lacy underthings.

"Bill. Bill Stamford," he replied as he set his plate on the table and seated himself.

A hand clutching a plate of ice cream appeared between Bill and Becky. "I've two heapin' scoops of ice cream," the Reverend Sprunt said cheerfully. "Miss, may I offer them to you, before the ice cream melts?" The pastor put it on the table between Bill and Becky. "Its previous owner decided to play croquet."

"Thank you, Pastor," Becky replied. "It looks delicious."

The Reverend Sprunt laughed gaily. "Sadly, you'll have to eat out of order, my dear, else the ice cream will melt before you've finished the fried chicken and potato salad."

"I've no problem eating the ice cream now," Becky said, amused. "Perhaps my new friend Bill will help me?"

Bill unwrapped a cloth napkin, revealing silverware, then picked up a spoon and sailed it toward the ice cream. He stopped inches short. "Ah, you must know I love ice cream."

"See, already we have something in common." She glanced up at the preacher. "Thank you, Pastor."

"Later, you two young'uns should join the others playin' croquet," Reverend Sprunt suggested.

Bill liked the pastor's advice. The perfect way to spend more time with Becky after they'd finished eating.

She took a bite of the ice cream, then shared a glance with Bill. "Your turn."

He dipped his spoon into the cold dessert and let it glide down his throat. "Thank goodness Reverend Sprunt thought to have an ice house built. Nothing like ice cream on a warm day."

A mid-afternoon sun ruling in a nearly cloudless sky made for a perfect picnic day. Not so perfect, though, for eating ice cream before it melted. "Yummy," Becky exclaimed. "You must be a Kenansville boy. I don't get over to Kenansville much. The farthest north we get is the North East Methodist Church, three miles from Father's house. Aunt Susan lives up the street"— Becky nodded toward the lady sitting next to a woman who looked like Becky, except grayer and with wrinkles—"and she said the picnic would be a hog-killin' good time." She grinned.

"Was she right?" He took another swallow of ice cream.

"So far." Becky shifted and her dress brushed his leg, rustling so loud the man across the table frowned. "Oh, I'm sorry," she said innocently.

He could feel her crinoline. The touch... amazingly sensual. His soldier was hollering: It's time for some tupping. Bill had heard Old Man Donaldson refer to baby-making as tupping. Except Donaldson wasn't looking to cojoin to make kids. He wanted some rapture time. Bill became a drill sergeant, ordering his soldier to stand down. Reluctantly, it did so. "I'll leave the last of the ice cream to you," he told her. "You're from Teachey?"

"Duplin Roads. My father's the senior trainmaster at the Teachey Depot. A five-minute buggy ride from our house to the depot, rain or shine." She gestured to the older gentleman across the table. "My father, Louis Powell. To his right, my mother, Diana Powell, and to his left, my father's sister, Pauline Hall. My little sister Nan's back in Duplin Roads staying the night with a playmate."

Bill pushed his chair back and stood. "Pleasure to meet you, sir, and the fine ladies." He bowed as Louis stood and shook Bill's hand.

"Please sit, Bill," Louis said, resuming his seat. "I won't mince words. Why aren't you with General Lee? You look at least twenty. Look around you. The men your age are gone. Who's left at this picnic are boys too young to serve and cripples like the one playing croquet."

Bill gulped. He should have expected the question. He knew he looked older than seventeen. "I'm just—"

Louis's gaze shifted to a spot just above Bill's head. A shadow fell across Bill, snaked across the table and darkened Louis's face. Shifting in his seat, Bill looked over his shoulder. His papa had risen from a nearby table and stood behind Bill.

"My son's just seventeen, sir." Clarence's tone was polite but stern. "His momma and I forbid him to join until he's eighteen. Bill was brought up right. He didn't run away to enlist, although I'm sure he thought about it. He'll be eighteen in two days. I expect he'll soon march in the Army of Northern Virginia."

"A birthday in two days?" Becky clapped, glee sculpting her mouth. "Father, we must hold a birthday party for him at our house. Please. Pretty please."

"Yes, we'll gladly fete the newest member of Lee's army." Louis reached across the table to shake the hand of Bill's father. "You're the newspaper editor, aren't you?"

"I am. Clarence Stamford, editor of the *Gazette* and print-shop owner. I've boarded the train a few times in Teachey. I may be coming by in the near future to ask you a few questions. Thinking of doing a story on how the railroads are holding up."

"I'll answer your questions the best I can." A faint smile tightened Louis's lips. "But I have to take care not to upset my bosses." He regarded Bill. "You'll be joining soon after your birthday, right?"

Bill sneaked a glance at Becky. *Darn, I've a chance to be with her again. Maybe there's a garden where we can hold hands... and Charlie's favorite pastime, kissing.* "Yessir, don't want to miss the war. The way the Yanks are losing, it could soon be over." Actually, he doubted the North would sign an armistice anytime soon. Eventually, they'd find a general as good as Lee. But he wanted Becky's father to like him.

"Lemonade or tea?" Becky asked Bill.

"Lemonade." He held out his tin cup.

"Keep the cup steady. Don't want any drops spilled." Her fingers rested against his as she poured the lemonade. "See! No spillage." She pointed toward her cup. "Tea, my drink of choice. I'm so glad we can celebrate your birthday. It's the perfect opportunity to get to know you better. And now that I know your father's a newspaperman, you intrigue me even more, Bill. Do you plan to follow in his footsteps?"

Bill craned his neck to see if his papa still lurked behind him. Thankfully, Clarence had returned to where Icie Belle,

Mark and Laura sat eating their picnic meals. Laura waved. "Maybe. Not sure. I like typesetting, creating posters. I'd love to do theatrical ones for Wilmington's Opera House. They'll someday be considered works of art... after we learn to use color. Just imagine... actresses like Laura Keene and Maggie Mitchell in bright colors."

Becky patted Bill's arm. "Slow down, mister. I can see you love the print shop. But what about the pen?"

He swallowed a spoonful of Julia Dickson's potato salad, more likely made by her darky cook Fatima. "A newspaperman? I'm going to give it a try. I've written some poetry and rib-tickling stories. Wilmington's *Daily Journal* printed two of them this year. So I guess I've a knack for it. Papa wants me to write a story about today's picnic. Duplin town tries to find a moment of joy in a year of casualty lists... that's the angle."

She leaned in and rubbed her shoulder against him. "Thought I'd see if I can't get some of that talent of yours to rub off. I love writing poetry. I've tried to write a story or two, but they ended up disasters."

He finished the potato salad and took a bite from one of the legs. "I hope you kept the stories. Sometimes if you wait a few weeks and take a second look, you'll find ways to improve them."

"I tore them up." Shrugging, Becky assumed a pained look.

"I wish you hadn't." He picked up the corn on the cob, nibbled, then returned it to the plate. Eating corn was way too messy when trying to converse with a lovely woman. "You could read it at that birthday party you plan for me."

Her eyes lit up. "What a splendid idea! I'll write a story and have it ready when you arrive." Her gaze swung to her mother. "I knew I'd find a man who loves what I love. If

Daddy introduces me to one more trainman, I think I'll scream."

"Everyone's a soldier nowadays," her father said drolly. "It's hard to tell the difference between a trainman, furniture maker and a literary man when garbed in butternut and shouldering a musket."

Food eaten, Bill pushed the plate away. Becky did the same, then tapped Bill's arm and pointed toward the croquet players. "I'm ready for a—"

Her mother interrupted, "You plan to run off with our birthday boy, eh?" Diana's eyes glittered with amusement.

"Just over to that field, ma'am," Becky replied, sliding her chair, again brushing her hoop against Bill's thigh. "I've never played croquet. I want to see if I'm a natural. Care to join me, Bill Stamford?"

Now she teased him. She knew he'd not let her wander far from his side. "I've played the game a few times, but I'm not very good," he said, his tone self-effacing.

"Oh, then I'll have to find another boy who'll teach me."

Bill shook his head. "I suddenly remember I once won a croquet tournament."

Becky gave him a sly smile. "I'll be a good student, I promise."

Both teenagers said "excuse me" to their elders, and headed for the croquet field. Bill offered Becky his arm, and she slipped her hand into the curve of his elbow. The chitchatting voices at the tables in the shade of the church faded; the croquet players' whoops rose as Bill and Becky approached.

Bill winced as he eyed the players. Tonya Wells steadied herself to swing her mallet, rolling a ball toward a ring. Next in line... Sam Merritt, and it summoned unwanted memories of halos and death, a little girl falling from a tree and Ezekiel Merritt drowning in Grove Creek.

"What's wrong, Bill?" Becky squeezed his arm.

"One of the boys playing croquet's Sam Merritt." Bill slowed their pace. "A year ago, I was in a fight with Sam and his brother Ezekiel. Broke my arm. The next day, Papa told me Ezekiel drowned in Grove Creek." He pointed to a stand of trees. Through peek-holes in the leaves, a ribbon of water gleamed.

"Well, we won't play croquet. Neither Sam nor you would enjoy each other's company." She nudged him to the right, toward men in red uniforms who were busily unloading musical instruments—flutes, clarinets, flageolets, snare drums, bassoons, trombones, violins and French horns. "That by far looks more interesting, don't you think?"

"You've convinced me." He patted her hand. She hadn't donned her gloves, so he enjoyed their skin-to-skin touch.

"Do you hope to be an author someday?" She rubbed against his side. Bill got a whiff of a sweet rose scent. He thought he'd passed through the celestial veil and walked on the gold streets of Heaven. "I don't mean short stories in the *Daily Journal*. Books. Novels, like that Englishman Charles Dickens and the South Carolinian William Gilmore Simms. I love Simms's *The Cassique of Kiawah*. You strike me as the kind of man who won't be satisfied until your books are the rage of Charleston and," she whispered into his ear, "New York City. You did barge right in and sit beside me." She giggled. "To hell with stuffy manners."

Damn, I like this girl. A rebel's heart... and in the right way. He too liked Simms's books, although he detested the man's over-the-top support of slavery. Of course, that wasn't something Bill shared with most others. Becky seemed like a kindred soul, but he'd wait until he knew her much better before broaching the subject of slavery. And like Charlie pointed out, Bill's doubts looked hypocritical, considering his father owned two slaves. Better to wrap himself in silence. Slavery: silence. Halos: silence. "To hell with stuffy manners," he echoed.

"You never answered. Do you want to write a novel?"

Bill draped his arm around Becky's shoulders, then withdrew it quickly, lest an older lady see his show of fondness and think it boorish behavior. "Really? I said nothing? I remember thinking *'yes'*."

She put his arm back around her shoulders. "It belongs there. Like books authored by Bill Stamford belong on library bookshelves. Right?"

"Becky, you're going to have the town's grandmothers in a tizzy. We're not even to hold hands until the sixth month of a courtship." He didn't remove his arm. "I can hear them now. 'You two are acting like Frenchies.'"

"Don't the old biddies read the casualty lists? Our boys are dying or getting maimed on battlefields. You're going to join up soon. Who has time for old-biddy courtship rules?"

"With a spirited girl like you encouraging me, how can I not write the next great Southern novel? For you, I'll give it a go." Bill caressed her shoulder, then let his arm.... the one he broke ...fall to his side. It tingled, nerves still healing after more than a year.

"You know how to say the right words." She walked a finger along his hand; only the most observant biddy would have noticed. "I've dreamed of being courted by a writer. And look... here you stand beside me. I'm not letting you get away."

The band men, all older than forty, took longer than expected to tune their instruments. They were too busy eyeballing Becky. No doubt a few wives would chastise their men later in their bedrooms. Bill whispered, "You've won some hearts, especially the conductor's. In a few weeks, I expect the band will perform a new song about a beautiful Duplin girl who won the love of a musician at a church picnic."

"Shame on you! He probably has a seamstress wife and six kids." No longer finger-kissing his hand, she playfully slapped it.

"Thirteen kids and a scrawny wife, bone-weary from caring for all those kids while he travels the county playing his trombone."

Becky slapped his hand again. "You're incorrigible." She laughed. "Do incorrigible men make good dancers? I aim to find out."

The band played after sundown. With candle-lanterns hanging from tree limbs, dancers formed quadrilles and danced to the commands of the caller, Doctor Graham. Bill would have preferred a polka or waltz, but those dances were too risqué. Instead, Bill and Becky hopped, whirled and promenaded, their moves choreographed by the doctor's calls. Bill found the calls hilarious and even hooted, drawing a curious look from Becky.

"A right and left around the ring while roosters crow and the birdies sing," the doctor hollered as the band played "Colonel Crockett."

Barely warmed up, Doctor Graham sang out, "All join hands and circle to the south, get a little moonshine in your mouth." That got a twitter from Becky and a girl nearby, Donna Schrader.

"Cat in the barn, rat in her mouth, grab your honey and head her south." The doctor reached into his coat pocket, pulled out a toy rat, and put it between his teeth.

"That's nasty," one of the dancing girls cried out.

Graham did a jig himself, then sang out, "Promenade and take that girl, take a little walk to the old corral."

The doctor winked at the dancers: "Swing that lady with a hole in her stockin', knees keep a knockin', petticoat a floppin'."

"You got a hole in your stocking?" Bill inquired innocently.

"Maybe you'll find out later," Becky said, not so innocently.

Graham pretended to play a fiddle. "Jenny is sweet, and Sally is a good'n, I want the girl with the tapioca puddin'.

"Ladies to their seats and gents all foller, thank the fiddler and kiss the caller." The doctor plopped down in the seat behind him and slapped his thighs.

Bill was ready for another dance. Not Becky. "I like the doc's suggestion," she said, a mischievous grin on her face.

"Huh?" Bill could sometimes be thickheaded.

"The old corral, silly."

"Oh, you want to take a walk." He chuckled. "For a nefarious reason."

"Too many people. I want you all to myself."

They made their way past what had been the croquet field, now in use for kids' footraces. Candlelamps dangling from poles lit the field, as did the full moon. Nearby, middle-aged men tossed horseshoes. The band struck up "Nelly Bly." Bill turned to look back and take in the moon and candlelit dancers.

"No! Always look forward." Becky tugged on his shirt collar. "Pretend I'm Little Red Riding Hood and you're my handsome woodsman. Into the woods we go." She pointed at the copse of trees and Grove Creek nestled within the leafy chestnuts and beeches.

He reached for her hand. Surprisingly, she jerked it away. "Little Red Riding Hood's obstinate?" he asked, puzzled.

"Not now. Later," she teased, her voice smoky.

Inside the trees, moonbeams flitted among the branches while the breeze ruffled the leaves. "Lordy, it's beautiful," Bill said in awe.

"More than me?" She took his hands in hers.

"Nothing's as beautiful as you, even Niagara Falls. Sweet heaven... I love the way the moonlight makes your straw hat glow." Bill reached for the hat. "May I?"

"You may."

He removed the hat, let it drop to the ground. Stepping closer, he ran his fingers through her curls and let them brush against her chignon. "Right now I'd give up my life to kiss you."

"You don't have to do that. But you may kiss me."

Bill stopped, his lips just inches from her face. Her breath tickled. She drew her hands around his neck, and pulled his mouth against hers. They hungrily kissed, then stepped back so they could rub fingertips over eyebrows and lips.

"God, I want you," he groaned.

"I wish I could let you have me right here. You know we can't." She pressed her bosom against him, slid her hands behind him and caressed his buttocks. "Let me show you how I like to be kissed." She gave him a staccato of barely touching kisses, then slipped her tongue into his mouth. "Now that's proper kissing."

"Is it possible to fall in love in one night? I think I did." He stroked her back.

"Yes... because I have." She sighed. "You really shouldn't come to my house until after you celebrate your birthday with your family. Let's do it on September twenty-third, a day later."

Of course, he agreed. Then he could have two birthday parties, and perhaps find a way to steal more kisses from Becky. Holding hands, they returned to the square dancing.

Three

A Friend Enlists

Bill seemed to float from his bedroom to the top of the stairs. As he descended, he bounced down the steps as if his feet had grown springs. And why not... he'd fallen in love with Becky Powell. Soon, he'd eat the first breakfast of the rest of his life... a life with Becky center stage.

Laura and Mark sat at the dinner table, their feet dangling above the floor. "Didn't think you'd ever come down," Mark clowned, digging his fork into cornbread soaked in sorghum syrup. "Miss Becky Powell must have tired you out."

"Tired him out? How?" Laura asked, her mouth filled with cornbread pancakes as she petted the cat perched on her lap. Indy had once been Bill's cat, but now considered Laura his human.

"Don't pay him no mind." Malinda shook her finger in Mark's face. "Your sis's too young to hear such talk. I be understandin' your meanin', boy!"

Mark lowered his eyes, contrite, obviously hoping to avoid one of Malinda's smacks. Malinda had been the family cook and maid for as long as Bill could remember. He'd even suckled at her darky breast when an infant. His sister and brother had as well. Bill loved the plump, light-skinned Negress, her hair tied back in a chignon and swathed in a kerchief. He'd once heard his momma scold Malinda for dousing her hair in a mixture of lye, eggs and potatoes to straighten out the kinks. White women didn't have Malinda's problem; they wanted thick curls that fell in waves to their shoulders. They'd employ concoctions to make straight hair curl.

"I don't get the meaning," Laura complained. She took a sip of newly squeezed lemonade.

"And you won't till you be thirteen, young'un." Malinda crossed her arms over ample breasts, then glared at Bill. "And you'd better done nothin' to get that pretty girl big..." Malinda patted her belly.

Bill sunk into his seat. "No, ma'am. Just sweet kisses. I've been raised right by Momma and you."

"I hear she was the prettiest girl at the picnic, and that came from an expert... Miss Laura Stamford." Malinda patted Laura's chestnut hair. "Frankly, Bill, I'd given up on you ever findin' a darlin'. I guess'm it had to happen sooner or later."

The bread, bacon and cornbread pancakes were already on a plate waiting for Bill. With Malinda judging him, eyes like an eagle, he lowered his head and prayed, then spooned her breakfast into his mouth. "Sumptuous, Miss Malinda. The blockade's really starting to hurt, yet you keep our bellies happy."

"I make do." Malinda shrugged. "Your papa's at the print shop doin' print magic, then he's goin' to the church to do deacon work. He said to get your rump down to the shop, or he just might be forgettin' to get a birthday gift."

Bill scoffed down the last of the bacon rashers and cornbread pancakes, and headed for the entranceway. Hand on the doorknob, he turned and shouted, "Momma at the shop too, Malinda?"

"No. I reckon she's at Fred Smith's farm gettin' canned strawberries, enough for a birthday pie." Malinda lunged across the table and reached for Indy, who'd leaped from Laura's lap to poke his nose in his human's breakfast. "Scat! Scat, wicked boy!" The cat sprang to the floor and flew toward the stairs.

Outside on the front walk, under a gloomy gray sky, Bill bumped into two people... Malinda's husband Wilson, the family's butler, gardener and stablekeeper, and Charlie, hoping to do some mooching.

"Any cornbread pancakes left?" Wilson patted his belly. "Been groomin' Peanut and puttin' a new wheel on the buggy. Ya're goin' to need it when we drive up to Warsaw to catch that train, the one takin' you to your sweet thing's bosom." He winked.

"Sweet thing?" Charlie said, his voice incredulous. "Lordy, Bill, what's you been doin' while I was out of town? You can't be girl-sneakin' without me."

"Wilson, you're getting me in trouble with Charlie," Bill complained good-naturedly. "Now I've got to explain Becky to him before he starts gossiping and makes her a saloon girl down on Wilmington's Front Street." Bill immediately knew he'd made a mistake.

"Oh, sir, things are terrible there," Wilson lamented.

"Yellow fever's killed nearly everyone," Charlie added, scowling. "A cousin, Douglas Banks, died a month ago. He was a stevedore hired to unload blockade runners. He's a long ways from our beloved Smokies, buried in a mass grave in Oakdale Cemetery."

"I'm so sorry, Charlie." Hands fisted in frustration, Bill pounded them against his hips. "I'm a nincompoop. It's not like I don't know yellow fever's raging in Wilmington. Been a wildfire for several months now."

"Child, we're sixty miles away," Wilson reminded Bill. "Easy to slip the mind at this distance. Especially when a girl's tuggin' on a boy's heartstrings."

"I've got to hear about this lass of yours." Charlie headed for the front-porch steps.

"I'll tell you, but only if you walk with me to the print shop." Bill jogged toward Lodge Street. "Papa's expecting me." He eyeballed Wilson. "Better hurry. Mark's got quite the appetite for cornbread pancakes."

Right palm to his forehead, Wilson gave Bill a Confederate salute, bounded up the steps and into the house.

"Wilson's salute is quite appropriate for the news I've for you, Billy Boy." Running hard, Charlie caught up with his friend. "I done joined the Army of Northern Virginia. Company G, Eighteenth North Carolina."

Bill pressed his hands against Charlie's shoulders. "What? I thought you were going to make them draft you?"

"I've a plan," Charlie explained, stepping back. "I'm a smart man, ain't I?"

Bill cocked an eyebrow. "Sometimes. Mostly. Not sure about this time. Go on. Explain."

"I know I'll be goin' in as a private, but I don't intend to stay at that rank. I figure I'll get promotions, end up an officer by the war's end."

"You can't get into fights. Brawlers don't become captains." Bill shook his head. "I can't imagine what you were thinking."

"Thinkin' smart, Billy Boy." Charlie stooped and picked a swamp sunflower blooming along the front walk. "Your slave, Wilson, keeps this yard lovely. Do you reckon Wilson and Malinda will be tendin' to you after the war?"

Bill glanced at the street to make sure no one walked nearby. Loose talk about the evils of slavery could get a couple of teenagers tarred and feathered. The street was deserted. "What did you do? Join the Union Army? To free our darkies?" Bill let his face bloom into a smile. "I know we've discussed this before. Papa and I expect the politicians in Raleigh and Richmond to bark like rabid dogs at any talk of freeing the darkies. But they don't want to lose the war. And they don't want our slaves running north and helping Lincoln beat us. Old Abe's raising what the North calls colored troops, darkies who want to fight for their freedom. Better to have them free and in our armies than in theirs and shooting at us. Our politicians will come around, Papa says. I just pray they don't wait until the Yanks are entrenched around Richmond and it's too late."

"Bill, I aim to be a captain or higher, and if I survive, I'm goin' to become a politician." Charlie smelled the sunflower's petals. "If the Confederacy wins, I'll be sittin' up in the House in Richmond makin' sure our *former* slaves get a fair shake. I'm sure there will be some firebrands who want to turn back the clock. We can't let that happen. We must make sure our Southern flowers bloom for whites and colored folks. Not darkies. Colored folks or better yet, proud black men."

"And, God forbid we lose this war, then what, Charlie the flannel-mouthed politician?"

"Then I help North Carolina get back into the Union, win a seat in the U.S. House, and do what I said I'd do in Richmond, except it'll be in Washington. I'm joinin' to stop the South from committing suicide." Charlie blew on the sunflower, sending the petals tumbling through the air. "What are you doin', Billy Boy? Just enjoyin' the smell of Wilson's green-thumb magic? Or are you intendin' to tell your papa it's time to free Wilson and Malinda?"

Bill grimaced, not at Charlie's words, but at the fact that Wilson and Malinda were still slaves. His papa planned to free them, but doing it was always something left for some time in the future when emotions weren't always boiling. His papa had told him more than once, "It isn't so easy, son. Freedom will probably get them killed, the print shop burned and maybe my death. I'll free them at the right time." Bill had a sinking feeling... there'd never be a *right* time.

"Charlie, I tell him all the time. Papa promises he will. I guess it won't be until the Yankee army's only a few miles away and they can safely reach it. Papa's a cautious man, especially when it doesn't take much persuading to incite a mob."

The front yard was stunning, especially when fall plants like swamp sunflowers bloomed. Halfway to the house, the flagstones branched around a terracotta fountain of children, umbrella above their heads. A yellow birch overlooked the yard to the teenagers' left. A red cedar and a flowering dogwood shared lawn space to the fountain's right. Carolina roses, swamp sunflowers and brilliant rhododendrons lined the walkway up to the front-porch steps. Royal ferns grew in front of the porch's latticework. If his papa couldn't free Wilson and Malinda immediately, maybe he could pay them a decent wage so they'd have spending money. Yes, he'd corner his papa at the print shop and suggest paying them a stipend. One problem... inflation bloomed brighter than the swamp sunflowers. Confederate dollars wouldn't buy Wilson and Malinda much.

"Billy Boy, keep talkin' to him," Charlie stressed, dropping the sunflower stem. He laughed. "You keep pesterin' him enough, he'll free 'em just to shut you up."

Bill turned toward the street, tossed words back toward Charlie. "He's not the type to be pestered. Then again, it wouldn't hurt to try."

They headed down Lodge Street toward Seminary Street. "Oh, when I was joinin' up, I told Lieutenant O'Rourke about you, Billy Boy." Charlie earned a stern stare from Bill. "Told him we do everything together. I can't imagine shootin' a Yank without you by my side takin' a bead on one. I don't want the lieutenant thinkin' I'm a liar, so you'd better pay him a visit."

"Damn it, Charlie!" Bill stopped alongside the street, hands on his hips as two buggies wheeled past. "Don't tell me you went into Wilmington to enlist. Not with yellow fever putting people in Oakdale Cemetery."

Charlie grabbed his arm. "Come on. Nothing to fear. I went to Burgaw. Lieutenant O'Rourke set up shop in the lobby of the hotel down from the depot. I signed up while sitting in the handsomest chair ever made. Leather, deep cushions, softer than a fat woman's buttocks. Burgaw's twenty miles short of Wilmington. With an arm amputated after the Seven Days battles, O'Rourke didn't want to tempt fate." Charlie looked at his vest watch. "Bill, it's almost time for church. Maybe we should forget the shop and head there."

"I'm in trouble."

"Just tell your papa we were discussin' weighty matters." Charlie grinned.

"Aye. I'll be sure to tell him how you've been weighing in on the proper way to free Wilson and Malinda."

"Ah, let's change subjects." Charlie gave Bill's back a roguish slap. "This lass of yours…"

"Becky." Bill punched Charlie in the arm. "The girl I'm going to marry."

"Whoa! Marry? How long have you known this girl, Billy Boy?"

"Since yesterday." Bill raised his palm to stop what he figured would be a flood of words from his friend. "The time's not important, not when it's ordained. I saw her sitting with her family at Saturday's church picnic. I've seen plenty of pretty girls and thought, 'I'd like to get to know her.' With Becky, there was no debate. I determined I was going to sit next to her and let God's plan bring her into my arms."

Charlie said nonchalantly, "Hopefully, the chair next to her was empty."

Buggies were crowding Seminary Street, townspeople and countryfolk on the way to Kenansville's churches, forcing Bill and Charlie to walk on the grass. "It was. A sunbeam illuminated it, as if God instructed me to sit by her." He exaggerated, but really did think it was love at first sight. Even the Reverend Sprunt had stopped Owen Beveritt from sitting in the chair, instead sending him off to play croquet. Bill saw that as predestination, since the pastor intervened, not an ale-loving farmer. And in a peculiar way it did make sense, since God had already burdened him with halos. Still, with enough sincere prayers, maybe he'd not see another. "So I sat beside her... and several hours later we were kissing on the bank of Grove Creek under a full moon. I'm meeting her again on Tuesday. Going to her place in Duplin Roads. She's giving me a birthday party."

Puckering his lips, Charlie whistled. "So you reckon you're in love? I hate to disillusion you, Billy Boy." Unexpectedly, he rapped Bill in the groin. "That's your steed givin' you orders."

Sprinkles squirted from the gray sky as Bill and Charlie walked up the steps into the church vestibule. With his hair getting damper by the second, Bill couldn't help but think of the front-yard fountain and the umbrella above the children's copper heads. Statues were more prepared than him.

Four

A Roundabout Excursion

The author of a story should never do its typesetting, Bill decided as he stood at the print shop's composing table. On deadline, Bill had to resist an urge to rewrite his account of Saturday's church picnic. Oh, how he wanted to make his story perfect, but doing so would delay the evening's press run. Broken deadlines meant unhappy merchants. Readers would open their newspapers and see the sales advertisements too late. Bill wouldn't disappoint his papa.

Even with deadline pressure rattling him, Bill managed to get everything into twelve paragraphs without having to cut anything—a comment from the Reverend Sprunt on how well-behaved people were at the square dance; a thank you by the reverend to the congregation's cooks; a rundown of the footrace and croquet winners, and a review of the summer dresses worn by the girls. Hands down, Becky Powell wore the most beautiful dress, the story noted.

He struggled to keep his concentration focused as he typeset the piece, probably the last he'd do for many years. Later in the week, after Becky's party, he intended to join Company G of the Eighteenth North Carolina, a Wilmington regiment that needed an influx of men after the summer's battles. His stomach churned, heavy with Malinda's pound cake and its brandied strawberry mélange icing. Bill battled second thoughts. A year ago, Duplin's boys marched to war stirred by Sir Walter Scott's tales of gallant knights... and all of them willing to die for the Southern Soul. Bill failed to bottle a horrific thought: What if the next halo shimmered around his own body?

"I can't stand this any longer," Clarence growled, backing away from an adjacent composing table. "I hate typesetting casualty lists. I have to walk away for a few minutes or go mad. Care to join me, Bill?"

Left unsaid... Clarence might someday typeset his own son's name.

Outside on the bench, Bill savored the touch of sunlight on his face. After Sunday and Monday's rains, it was good to see blue sky, or at least patches of it among the billowing white clouds. "I'll soon be drafted anyway, Papa. With volunteering, at least I get to choose where I go. I don't want to end up fighting in Tennessee and Mississippi. Just sorry it has to be so soon after meeting Becky."

Clarence lit up a pipe and puffed. "Enjoy your time tonight with her, son. I got it from good authority that a two-layer White Mountain cake will be waiting for you. Not sure if there will be eighteen candles, though." Clarence reached into his pants' pocket and looked at the watch he'd bought in Wilmington before the war. "It's just after ten. I told Wilson to have the buggy here by eleven."

Bill loved the smell of his papa's tobacco but hated smoking. He'd tried it once and got sick. "Papa, you've told Wilson and Malinda they're going to get their freedom, right?"

"I've given them the papers, Bill. Wilson has them stored in a lockbox in their bedroom. I'll help them get into Yankeeland when it's the right time. I just don't know when that will be. Got to watch and be ready."

With no one else near the print shop, Bill and his papa didn't need to worry about eavesdroppers. "I didn't know about the freedman papers."

"I just did it."

Bill stood, hands on his hip. "Charlie says we should pay Malinda and Wilson so they have spending money. He calls it a goodwill gesture."

"Does he now?" Clarence grabbed the bench's armrest and braced himself as he rose. "Getting old," he grumbled. "The littlest things make me tired. Bones complain even on a warm day. I'm glad Charlie's your friend. He's right, of course. Paper's just paper. Now a small salary, that'll make the freedom papers real for Wilson and Malinda. Tell Charlie I'm going to do it. But make sure he knows not to go bragging to others. Don't need the town riled up. Doesn't take much to get people doing stupid things."

"I know you don't want to get back to those casualty lists, but I need to finish typesetting my picnic story," Bill said, heading for the door. "I want to have it done before Wilson gets here."

The shop's apprentice, Dale Winland, arrived punctually. Dale glanced over Bill's shoulder at the picnic story. He giggled as he slapped Bill's shoulder. "I see Becky gets top billin'."

Bill nodded. "She'll always be top billing."

The front-door bell rang. The three swung around toward the sound. Wilson had arrived. Just before the door closed, Bill caught a glimpse of Peanut and the buggy parked at the curb.

Clarence fixed his gaze on the apprentice. "I'm leaving you in control. Going to take Bill to Warsaw to catch the train. If I'm not back by closing, crank up the press. You're ready to handle the *Daedalus* all by yourself."

Dale's eyes widened. "Thank you, sir."

Bill typeset the last line and yelped a little cheer. "I'm done, except for proofreading."

"I'll proof Bill's picnic story, sir, and finish up those casualty lists," Dale promised. "The print run won't be delayed."

"Did I just hear I ain't takin' young Bill to Duplin Roads?" Wilson sidled around the front counter and made his way into the composing room.

Clarence put a couple of Confederate dollars in Wilson's hand. "I've decided to take Bill to the Warsaw train depot. Wilson, buy some roses for the yard. Whatever's left, get some rock candy for yourself."

A Mississippi-wide grin spread across Wilson's face. "I will, and some for Malinda, Laura and Mark as well." Wilson slipped the money into a pants pocket. "The road to Duplin Roads ain't practical, sir. A Hanson driver says a big ole sinkhole's blockin' traffic."

Clarence shrugged. "What do you say, Bill? Take the road to Warsaw and then the train to Teachey? There's a nice toy store in Warsaw." Clarence winked.

"Little Treasures. You must plan some early Christmas shopping."

"Indeed. A Montanari doll for Laura and some doll dress patterns that Icie Belle and Laura can sew together. I'll stay overnight in the depot's hotel. In the morning, you can take the train back to Warsaw, and we'll head home." Clarence winked again. "We'll hide Laura's Christmas presents in the boot."

After a short detour to the house to pack a carpetbag for the overnight stay at Becky's, Bill and his papa were soon on the road to Warsaw. Just beyond the town's most prominent house, the Owen Kenan mansion, Clarence gestured to pastureland west of the road. "At the courthouse, I saw a most intriguing land sale. Wilmington's Louis Froelich now owns three acres of road frontage."

Bill swept wind-tousled bangs out of his eyes. "Froelich? Name sounds familiar."

"He owns the sword factory in Wilmington. The man lost dozens of workers to yellow fever. I hear he fears another outbreak next summer."

"Lordy! You're saying he's moving his sword factory to Kenansville?"

Clarence swiped at an annoying fly near his face. "That's the rumor. As soon as Mayor Whitehead verifies it, I'll write a story."

Bill laughed sourly. "I was going to say it would mean a job boom for Kenansville, except all the men have gone to war." He sighed. "So slaves will supply the muscle."

"Nothing new. They're working at the ports, mines and railyards."

As the houses along the Kenansville-Warsaw Road thinned, Clarence urged Peanut into a brisk trot. Although not as busy as the days before the war, the road remained well traveled by a hotchpotch of day trippers in buggies, carriages and carts. While prewar business had dwindled, war-related commerce had picked up. The cotton in wagons went into railcars, transported to the Wilmington port, and loaded aboard blockade runners. Weapons, uniforms, salt pork, cornmeal, desiccated vegetables and dried beans were conveyed in railcars from Duplin's depots up into Virginia to Lee's army. Bill could soon be eating desiccated carrots and dried beans. He gagged at the image of the wooden-looking cubes. Like chewing on splinters.

Bill took a sidelong glance at his papa. Things had turned out grand for both of them. His papa got to do a bit of Christmas shopping while Bill would get to spend the night at Becky's house. And no buggy ride back to Kenansville in the darkness. Even with a partly cloudy sky and the moon rising after sunset, few would venture forth on a country road after nightfall. In Wilmington, gas-lit streetlights shone sufficiently to let Hansom cab and carriage drivers make their way from the opera house and restaurants to people's homes. Except for the kerosene lamps and candles in people's houses, Kenansville remained dark at night, and the countryside between Duplin's towns even darker. Only an emergency would send a man onto a country road at night.

Clarence nudged Peanut closer to the edge of the road to give a Wilmington and Weldon cab room to pass.

Bill stretched his leg, dangling it outside the confines of the buggy. "Papa, I just realized this will be the first time I'm on my own."

"You're eighteen now and about to join the army. Finding your way back to Kenansville should be much easier than capturing Washington, D.C." Clarence chuckled and Peanut snorted as if the horse found it funny, too.

"So here's the deal, Papa. I'm going to put the cost of a train ticket to Warsaw on your running tab with the railroad." Now Bill did the laughing.

"Deal accepted. I said it yesterday. Need to say it again. Happy birthday, son. That new wallet I got you... do some sweet talking tonight, and get Becky to give you a lock of hair. Make sure she perfumes it. Keep it in this locket." Clarence fumbled in a pocket and withdrew a round locket with a fancy B engraved on its cover. "The wallet has a pocket made special for lockets. When you wish you were in her arms, open the locket and smell her hair."

On the outskirts of Warsaw, Bill and his papa passed a detachment of Colonel Thomas Claiborne's cavalry troopers encamped in farm fields peppered with tents, there in case Union forces in New Bern, seventy miles away, went raiding. The cavalrymen squatted around campfires eating an early-afternoon meal.

Bill harrumphed as he considered Raleigh's calamitous response to Union General Burnside's spring offensive in the Tar Heel State. "Ridiculous having Federals so close to us. Thank God Governor Clark lost the election. Bungling politician!"

Clarence eyed Warsaw's steeples and bell towers. "With Zebulon Vance the new governor, I think Warsaw and Goldsboro should be safe. Vance is a soldier. He knows what he's doing." He sighed. "Burnside has been good news for Wilson and Malinda, though. With New Bern, Morehead City, Beaufort and Washington in Yankee hands, their North Star hangs right over us. It's tempting to help them head for freedom, but seventy miles is a scary distance. On sleepless nights, I don't want to blame myself for their deaths."

In Warsaw, fine two-story houses with rounded corner towers and columned porches bordered College Street. Most were new, built within the last fifteen years, their owners employed by the railroad. Just beyond Front Street, the depot stood at the intersection of College and Railroad streets. Like the houses they'd just passed, the depot had been built in the last decade, a stick-style frame building with board-and-batten siding and a gabled slate roof. "I sure hope the Yanks don't go venturing out of New Bern. I'd hate to see the depot burned down." *Lordy, I'm turning glum. Can't be acting this way when I'm with Becky. It'll make her fret more about me joining up.*

"Lots of depots will burn before the war's over," Clarence said resignedly. "In the South and up North, too."

Bill and his papa stabled Peanut, and then ate at the Whistle Stop Café. The owner, Mrs. Lucy Tower, owned a farm outside Warsaw, so had access to meat, grain, eggs and sundry vegetables. They ordered fried chicken with peppered gravy, sweet potatoes, corn, butter beans and tea. Fortified by Lucy's cooking, Bill went across the street to the depot, bought a ticket, checked in the carpetbag, and waited for the two o'clock train to signal its arrival from Goldsboro with steam-whistle blasts.

"Kind of antsy, aren't you, Bill?" Clarence slapped his knees and chuckled. "I know you don't think I was ever young. Every girl I courted I was spoony over. I was quite the rake when it came to a proper bit of frock. Kissed them and left them... except for your momma." Clarence leaned against the bench's backrest and tucked his hands behind his head. "Be a gentleman, but do find a way to take her outside for a walk. A little hand holding and a kiss or two... they're good for the soul."

"That's my intention, Papa. A walk and a kiss to tide her over until I come marching home." Bill glanced at the depot's grandfather clock. "The train's running late."

Sometimes Bill's thoughts terrified him. He'd actually known Becky for just one day. But those kisses they shared... they were so exquisite, and Bill wanted more. He was getting crazy thoughts. Imaginings of how Becky would look without her clothes—skin as fine and pale as porcelain, forehead barely bussed by a late-afternoon sun, slender hands with delicate fingers whose nails could make love to a man's chest and nether regions.

Scooting forward, Clarence stood. "Got to see a man about a horse." When Bill's father returned, he stopped at the ticket window where he chatted with the clerk for a few minutes. Later, Clarence plopped down beside Bill and breathed a weary sigh. "The telegraph lines are all abuzz. Lee's retreating into the Shenandoah after a battle in Maryland. A place called Sharpsburg. The casualty lists are going to get longer."

"Damn! Sorry for the profanity, Papa."

Clarence shrugged. "You're eighteen. Lee retreating out of Maryland is worth a couple of damns."

"We needed to whip them, then march on Washington and force Lincoln to recognize the Confederacy. Just like you say, we could then fight the Richmond politicians and drag the South into the nineteenth century like other civilized countries. England, France, even the North, all know the future smells of factories and working men of all colors earning a fair wage."

"You and I and even Charlie... that's how we think," Clarence said thoughtfully. "Most of our neighbors think the darkies are not up to snuff. Expect granting them freedom will come with a price—a return to Africa."

"Wilson and Malinda are smarter than most of our neighbors." A train whistle sounded, heralding Bill's train. "Pay them a decent wage, educate their children, and they'll do fine."

Five

A Romantic Birthday

Carpetbag in hand, Bill strolled onto the loading platform. Brakes squealed as the train came to a juddering stop. The conductor helped a soldier missing a leg hop down onto the platform. A wife in a flowery summer dress and a bonnet festooned with silk roses rushed up to him, trailed by a boy and three girls. Her lips pressed against his mouth, her hunger for him palpable. The youngest child, the boy, wrapped his arms around his daddy's leg. The corporal mussed his son's hair while he kissed his wife. His daughters stood back, tears flooding their cheeks.

Bill recognized a few Warsaw businessmen who'd advertised in the *Gazette*. He didn't know the soldier, but understood he'd witnessed unrestrained joy and relief.

"God, I wished Lee had won at Sharpsburg," Clarence said, caressing his son's shoulder. "This war would soon be over."

Bill took a step up into the passenger car the wounded soldier had just left. He whirled and waved to his papa. "But then I'd not be able to prove my courage," Bill said, louder than he intended.

The corporal turned. "Courage don't save a man from the surgeon's saw."

The conductor led Bill to a window seat. "You joinin' up?"

"In a day or two." Bill took a long breath. "Figure I'll soon be bound for the Shenandoah Valley."

The train whistle blew and the locomotive lurched forward, chugging noisily. His papa ran alongside the car, shouting, "You've nothing to prove, Bill. Nothing."

The wood-fueled locomotive, the *Doodlebug,* pulled eight cars—a baggage car, two passenger carriages and five freight cars filled with cotton and bourbon bound for Wilmington and a blockade runner. Bill sat in the second carriage toward the back, a soldier without his right arm in the row immediately to his front and a businessman for the Appomattox Locomotive Works behind him. Nearly three-quarters of the men in the carriage were convalescing soldiers, almost all lacking an arm or a leg. Some would detrain at Duplin and Pender depots, but most would file down the steps at the Wilmington station.

The soldier in front of Bill, a private, turned in his seat and draped his remaining arm on the backrest. "Goin' to Castle Hayne to kiss my sweetheart, then marry her," he told Bill, delight in his voice. "The war's over for me. The bullet that got me at Second Manassas, it's the last one I'll ever have to worry about. Now I pray the rot don't set in."

"I'm headed to Teachey to see my darling before I join up," Bill explained. Against his will, he kept sneaking glances at the fellow's stump. Lordy, he hoped he wouldn't be riding a train home after his first battle, a leg or arm left behind in Virginia. "I just heard there was a big battle up in Maryland, lots of casualties. I guess they're going to need me really fast."

"At least winter's comin'," the private pointed out, sweat glistening on his forehead. Outside, an overcast sky meant a mild temperature even inside the carriage. The mending Butternut shouldn't be sweating so badly unless he was battling a foe different from Yanks... infection. "You'll be buildin' a hut with a fireplace, not out marchin' and freezin' to death." He wiped his gray kepi across his forehead, eliminating some of the sweat. "Beware, recruit, fevers and flux come a lookin' for green young'uns like you. Don't come back to your darlin' in a box."

"I've seldom had colds or the flu," Bill said, laughing off the soldier's warning. "I've got a sick-proof body."

"Don't brag too much, Hayfoot. War has killed kings and emperors."

Lulled by the humming of wheels on the track, Bill stared out the window. Before the war, a locomotive like the *Doodlebug* averaged twenty miles per hour. Nowadays, with the war nearly eighteen months old, locomotives struggled to maintain half of the earlier speed, and travel at night was near-impossible. The *Gazette* teemed with stories of derailments, and sometimes injuries and even death to soldiers. Bill's train stopped once near Magnolia, waiting until slaves repaired track on the verge of separating. Once the track was fixed, the *Doodlebug* clacked into Magnolia.

On the town's outskirts, slaves were hammering, bolting and sawing, building the Wilmington and Weldon's new maintenance yard for repairing locomotives, carriages and freight cars, and for storing rails and crossties. Next to the yard, a sea of tents speckled what had been farm fields. They housed four companies of infantry, a battery of artillery, and the Seventh North Carolina Cavalry. Farther into Magnolia, streets branching off from Railroad Street hosted new houses... large edifices with towers, porches and gables.

The train stopped and let off a wounded soldier, this one from the other passenger carriage. A leg and an arm gone, he was lifted down to the platform on a stretcher, and then trundled away in a wheelchair by his wife and children. The private in the seat in front of Bill didn't say anything as he watched the wheelchair-bound soldier disappear into the depot. He just shook his head slowly. Wrapped in blankets, even though mid-September, the soldier in the wheelchair seemed only days from death. Lowering his head, Bill said a prayer for him and his family.

No halo flames sparked around the quivering soldier. Did it mean he'd not die? Or God was proving fickle? Bill had seen only two halos in his life – one when ten and another a year ago. With so many wounded on the train, a few should be encased in halos. When it came to his so-called gift, nothing made sense. Better not to think about it, he decided.

No one from Magnolia boarded the train. No flagman appeared to flag down the *Doodlebug* in Rose Hill, so the locomotive and its cars clattered along the tracks, almost two hours late to Teachey. Bill glanced at his pocket watch... almost six o'clock. Twenty minutes until he'd see Becky waiting for him on the platform. *Holy moly... I've barely thought of her since we left Magnolia.* Bill's belly roiled and not from the swaying motion of the passenger carriage.

He'd been bombarded by the nonstop natter of the one-armed soldier. In a few months, would he be one of the invalids riding the *Doodlebug* back to Warsaw? Bill pushed the thought from his mind, replacing it with the way Becky looked in the woods near Grove Creek on Saturday night, just before they kissed.

He didn't see the Teachey depot until it appeared in his window, the loading platform almost filling the entire window. No Becky, though. Just a darky in a Wilmington and Weldon uniform standing beside a luggage cart, ready to unload Bill's carpetbag as soon as the *Doodlebug* stopped. Maybe she'd be in the depot's waiting room?

No Becky in the waiting room either. Smothering his disappointment, Bill retrieved his carpetbag.

"Sir?" A slave's voice, remarkably cultured, yet the accent was unmistakable.

"Yes?" Bill regarded a middle-aged darky wearing yellow wool pants and a red vest, a straw hat atop his clean-shaven head.

"Mister Bill Stamford?" The darky bowed.

"Yes. I've come to pay my respects to Miss Becky Powell."

"I be your driver, sir. A buggy's waitin' for ya." He reached for the carpetbag. "Let me have that bag, sir."

The walk wasn't long to the depot door. The Teachey station was half the size of the Warsaw and Magnolia depots, although similar in construction. The driver helped Bill into his seat, then untied the reins from a hitching post and climbed aboard. Spinning around to nod at Bill, the darky said, "Name's Jacob, sir. Becky's been doing nothin' but spoutin' your name all day. Ya're goin' to like your cake."

"Can't wait to taste it, Jacob."

The Powells' driver flicked the reins. "Ho, Applejack, away we go."

Jacob and Applejack gave Bill a sunset drive to Duplin Roads, a crossroads community not yet large enough to earn the title *town*. A new family had just moved to Duplin Roads, according to Jacob, and so the place consisted of nine families, including the Powells. In the lengthening shadows, Bill counted seven farmhouses and two Queen Annes, as well as a general store, grain-feed store, shoe shop, tavern and a gristmill on Paget Branch. If folks wanted to worship, do some banking or get their horses shoed, they hitched up their buggies and went to Teachey.

To pass the time, Jacob shared a local legend. An ornery bear attacked one of the earliest pioneer families. It ripped the door off the hinges and lunged at the family cowering behind the overturned trestle table. Growling, leaping from the cabin loft, their dog Boomer lit into the startled bear and sent it scurrying into the woods. For the rest of his life, Boomer ate with the family at the trestle table and always got to sleep on the bed with the husband and wife, or so Jacob claimed.

Jacob pulled into a cobbled drive and stopped next to a brick sidewalk that led to a white two-story house, its key features a ground-floor wraparound veranda and a corner tower that incorporated an upper-story porch. Bill had seen similar houses in Rose Hill, Magnolia, and Kenansville. The style exuded sophistication.

Jacob started to step down to help Bill from the buggy. "Don't bother, Jacob. Go ahead and take the surrey to the stables," Bill spoke up. "Wish me luck with Miss Becky."

"You won't need no luck with her, sir. She be taken with you. That's plain to see."

Bill lurched back from the front-door knocker, the fanciest he'd ever seen and the scariest. *Becky's papa should take it down and mail it to Lincoln. The sight of it would kill him on the spot.* A John Marley ghost knocker, mouth open, screaming in torment. Likely Becky had convinced her father to purchase it. Either that or the father had a fondness for Dickens.

Laughing at his reaction, Bill gripped the knocker and whacked it twice. Far sooner than Bill expected, a servant in a butler's livery opened the door. "You're expected by the young miss, Mister Stamford. Please come in and share in the Powell family's hospitality." Stepping away, he motioned Bill into the grand reception hall. Charlie's house would fit inside, with space to spare. Mounted bear, elk, deer and bison heads adorned the walls. Whole stuffed animals—mountain lions, gray and red wolves and even a peregrine falcon—were displayed in stalking or hunting positions atop marble end tables.

"Mister Powell awaits you in the parlor," the butler said politely as he led Bill past the staircase and its alabaster statue of a Greek maiden carrying an oil lamp.

Inside the parlor, chock full of couches, chairs and marble tables crowded with glass oil lamps and bric-a-bracs, Louis Powell rose from an intricately carved high-back chair and greeted Bill. "Ah, here at last. It pains my heart to see the trains running later and later, but that's war." He shook Bill's hand. "We try to keep the locomotives in running order and the tracks maintained, and I think we do a good job. Still, the schedules are impossible to meet."

"I'm just glad seats are still available to civilians." Bill glanced around at the overabundance of upholstered chairs. "Buggies and wagons are fine for around Duplin, but not down to Wilmington and up to Goldsboro. If we can't ride the trains, it'll be like we've suddenly woke up in 1820."

"Sit on that burgundy couch, Bill." Louis lit the kerosene lamp on the stand next to couch. "Becky will be down soon.

I expect she'll want to share the couch with you." He smiled. "My wife did the same when we were courting."

"Courting?" Bill said, thinking aloud. "You'd be okay with me courting your daughter, sir?"

"Yes, but when the war's over." Louis reached for a decanter of white wine and a long-stemmed wine glass. "It's Muscadine wine, made right here in Duplin. A nearby vineyard." He poured the wine and handed it to Bill. "You have my permission, but now that you're eighteen you have a duty to fulfill."

"I've a good friend who just joined the Eighteenth North Carolina. Charlie Kurtz. He told the recruiter I'd be joining later in the week." Bill forced out a half-smile. "Can't let Charlie head up to the Shenandoah without me."

Louis laughed. He swept back his brownish gray hair as if he knew it had shifted and revealed his bald spot. "Buddies got to stick together."

Bill heard light tapping of feet descending the grand stairway. "Stick together? What are you and my *friend* Bill plotting, Father?" At the base, visible from where Bill sat, Becky and her mother Diana emerged into view.

At the sight of the women, Louis and Bill stood. "A bit of patriotic fervor, Daughter." Louis took a sip of Muscadine and set the glass on the table.

"No patriotic fervor allowed tonight." Becky promenaded into the parlor. "Right, Mother?"

"We discussed this earlier, darling," Diana said patiently. "Tonight's for eating a special meal and birthday cake. No politics, General Lee or the army. Have you broken our agreement?"

The older gentleman took a step toward his wife; Bill approached Becky.

"Sorry, dear," Louis apologized. "It won't happen again. But I can share this news. Bill planned on joining later in the week, but he'll have to do it tomorrow." Louis patted Bill's arm. "Sorry, I never got a chance to tell you before the women interrupted. Your recruiter, Lieutenant O'Rourke, is a good friend of mine. I know for a fact he and his recruits—including your buddy Charlie—will be aboard the early-bird train heading north. You're going to have to get on that train with them if you're going to join this week."

"Bill won't get a chance to say goodbye to his family." Face white with consternation, Becky removed her satin gloves and reached out to Bill.

He took her hands, felt the touch of her fingers. "It's not as dire as it sounds. Papa took me to Warsaw to meet the train. He's staying overnight and planning to shop for my sister Laura in the morning. I'll get a chance to see him. He'll have some hard explaining to do to Momma. And I'll have to write a long letter to her in a day or two. I wish I could make a quick visit home and then catch up with O'Rourke."

"Can he, Papa?" Becky cast a hopeful look her father's way.

"I wouldn't take the chance. You know how undependable rails are, Bill." He shrugged. "You need to catch the lieutenant's train in the morning and not leave anything to chance."

Chance? What chance did folks with halos have? He couldn't leave his future in the army up to chance, yet he had no idea how to cope if he witnessed another halo. *You mentioned a terrible word, Mister Powell.*

"I'll sign up aboard the train in the morning." He shook his head. His momma would be so mad at him. Bill could try to downplay it, but he knew her. She was a Northerner; she hated the war.

Becky brought Bill's hands up to her lips and kissed his fingers. She glared at her father, who wore a censorious look. "Say nothing, Father! He's going to war while you play with your trains." Sighing, she grumbled, "I'd like to ride my horse up into Virginia and give General Lee a tongue lashing for how he treats mothers."

"A general like Lee who must give orders that kill and maim men… he has come to accept the scars in his heart." Bill led Becky to the couch and stood back as she raised her dress slightly and sat on a cushion. She leaned forward, lest her hem fly upward and reveal her underthings.

"Oh, I wish I hadn't sat. I've something to show you." Rising, she rushed past the stairway, heading for another room. Soon, she returned with an armful of papers. "I've written a short story, *A Wife's Lonely Fears*. I'll read it in the music room after I play some tunes at Father's request. If you like the story, I'll try the *Daily Journal* again. Second time's the charm, eh?"

Bill nodded eagerly. "I can't wait to hear it."

Leaning over a side table, she shuffled the pages into a neat stack and tucked them under an arm. "Nan's in the music room. She's too shy to come in here. Once she gets to know you, she'll talk your head off, Bill." Hand raised, she gestured for Bill to follow.

Inside the music room, Nan, maybe eight, sat on the floor in a hoopless dress, playing pickup sticks. She looked up as Bill strode into the room alongside Becky, and turned as scarlet as the color of the couch near the piano. "Oh, there you are," Nan stuttered, then giggled. She looked like a smaller version of Becky, the same raven hair, the same jade-green eyes. "Becky, he's so handsome. Please marry him. Then we can have a double wedding."

Bill knew he looked baffled.

"My brother Howard's engaged to be married. Howard's with the Twentieth North Carolina, Confederate Grays.

When he re-enlists, he'll get a furlough, and they'll get married. For poor Nan it can't happen fast enough. The child loves pomp and circumstance." She settled on the piano bench and set the story beside her.

Scurrying, pickup sticks in her hand, Nan plopped on the couch without any effort at dignity, then moved her dress so Bill would have space to sit. "So are you going to marry her?" she queried.

"Hush, Nan! Your sister's about to play," her mother hissed, chastising the girl.

Louis and Diana sat in chairs in front of the cold fireplace.

Fingers dancing along the keyboard, Becky played three songs, singing the words to "Secession Grand Marc," "I Know a Pair of Hazel Eyes," and "Happy Land of Canaan." Anytime Bill went to a young lady's party, he'd hear the songs, sometimes played with accompaniment by other instruments like the harp, sometimes only the piano. All the girls sang; it seemed to be a requirement of their mothers.

"She's good," Nan whispered, "but I'm going to be better."

When the last note faded, Becky pushed back the bench with her red shoes, rose to her feet and turned daintily. With the moon ruling in the sky outside the windows, two kerosene-fueled lamps provided the interior light. Their tawny glow on Becky's face and on her silk evening dress proved alluring. Bill took his first guileless look at the dress, which revealed enough of Becky's neck and upper chest to make Bill hope he was indeed the boy who would marry her—and soon. He didn't want another man in her marriage bed gazing at her naked body.

She sauntered to the couch and stopped inches from Bill's knees. One of her shoes perched atop his left boot. Nan's eyes grew wide.

"Bill, may I read my story to you? And you better say you like it."

Bill never got a chance to answer. Becky's mother declared, "Later. Now it's time to eat. Our cook, Andalea, just signaled me."

The plates on the dining-room table were heaped with enough food to feed the Army of Northern Virginia. Turkey and pork on silver-plated trays. Steaming porcelain bowls filled with dressing, okra and tomatoes, black-eyed peas, collards, butter beams and sweet potatoes. A blue-and-white gravy boat containing pepper vinegar turkey gravy, and beside it a pan of cornbread. And for dessert, pecan pie and a White Mountain cake with eighteen homemade candles. Sitting down between Nan and Becky, Bill stared at the emperor's offerings. His mouth watered, unsure which fare to partake of first. To be able to put together such a feast at a time of war, Becky's father had to be far more than a stationmaster, perhaps he was a vice-president-in-training.

"We'll not eat another feast like this until the war's over," Louis announced, his eyes fixed on Bill. "All this food has been prepared by Andalea in your honor, Bill, at the orders of my elder daughter. You're a lucky man."

Bill swung his gaze from Louis to Becky, whose green eyes glittered in the soft light of the dining room's lamps. "I know. I'm a lucky man."

Louis nodded to his younger daughter. "Nan, please say grace."

The eight-year old steepled her hands. "Lord, bless this food and keep our soldiers safe. And bless my sister's new beau, and watch over him as he prepares to join my brother and General Lee up in Virginia. Amen."

"Amen," everyone chorused.

"Dig in, Bill," Becky said. "Let's see what kind of man you are. A pork man or a turkey fella?"

Everyone laughed as Bill took slices from the pork and from the white meat of the turkey.

"A two-meat man!" Louis remarked, reaching for the sweet potatoes. "I'd expect nothing else from one of General Lee's boys."

Bill ladled and spooned the darky cook's offerings onto his plate and bowl, and soon the taste of roast pork tenderloin seasoned with rosemary and garlic teased his taste buds.

Over the next hour, Bill ate two helpings, and as he wiped his face with a linen napkin and rested his hands on his belly, he knew the meal he'd just eaten was as good as any served at Delmonico's in New York City.

Reaching across the table, Becky's father handed a matchbox of Swedish phosphorus matches to her, and she lit the cake's candles. "Make a wish," she told Bill.

He did... that the hands of the grandfather and mantel clocks slow and this night go on and on and on. Then he blew out all the candles.

"Your wish will come true," Nan exclaimed. "What did you wish for?"

"He can't say," Becky jested. "Then the wish won't come true."

Becky sliced the two-layer cake into sixteen slices. Bill got the first one. Flitting his gaze from Becky to her mother to Andalea, Bill savored the taste of almond in the cake and the orangey tang of the powdered sugar icing. "Wonderful," he told Diana and Andalea.

"What about me?" Becky declared, laughing. "I chose the cake. Had a hunch you'd like it."

Bill sampled the pecan pie, and then Becky slid her chair back and rested her hands on the table edge. "I'm going to steal Bill away from all of you for a few minutes. Going to the veranda so I can read my story to him."

"But I want to hear your story too," Nan grumbled.

Standing, Becky draped her hand on Bill's shoulder. "And have you laugh at me?"

She led Bill on a maze-like journey through the house. Through the reception hall into the music room to retrieve *A Wife's Lonely Fears*. Then back into the reception hall with just a glance at the library as she prodded him into the sitting room.

"I thought we'd step out onto the veranda from the music room." Bill tilted his head, a tad confused.

"Not going out onto the veranda. Going to outsmart my sister and any other sneaky souls." Becky stroked his arm. "Going to have you all to myself."

Inside the sitting room, she lit a cranberry kerosene lamp with a marble base and brass stem, and proceeded out onto the back porch. She plopped into the swing and didn't care that the hoop flared upward, revealing stockings and the hem of her crinoline. Giving him a come-hither smile, Becky patted the seat beside her, then set the lamp on the porch floor.

He looked at the sitting-room door. "So you think we're safe?"

"For a while. They'll think we decided to take a walk." She rolled her eyes. "Except Nan. She'll probably find us. Little stinker."

Sighing, Becky snuggled against him. "I've been waiting all night to spoon."

"May I?" Bill shifted his face close to hers.

"No one's stopping you."

He cupped her chin and kissed her, let his lips linger against hers for a pregnant moment; he counted his heartbeats... four.

Gently, Becky pushed his face away. "Behave yourself. And anyway, it's time to read."

She lifted the first page of *A Wife's Lonely Fears* from her lap and let the lamplight illuminate it.

Her sparkling eyes meeting his, Becky straightened her back, slim and tall, and began to read.

"The coming of war shocked Avis Russell. Avis never mulled politics, never listened in on the arguments and passions of 1861 that consumed her father and his friends, never cared much for elections and speeches. Only her coming marriage mattered. Not until later did it dawn on her that she'd have to wave goodbye to her brand new husband as he marched off to places with names like Manassas and Malvern Hill. Of course, Avis played the role of the patriotic Southern woman, waving a Bonnie Blue Flag as each new regiment boarded the trains for the trips north into Virginia. Even when he returned from battle, walking on crutches, his right leg missing, she waved a small flag. She wanted him to know his sacrifice wouldn't be in vain..."

When Becky finished, she shuffled the papers and set them on her lap. "It's awful, isn't it?"

"Lordy, no! It should be published." Bill grimaced. "But it'll take a brave editor to do it."

"That's my fear as well," Becky said in a quiet voice, not quite trembling but nearly so. "An editor may blanche when he reads Avis's words at the end of the story: 'Who'll be left to celebrate victory besides us women if all the men are in graves or relegated to rocking chairs?'"

"Have you let your father see this?"

"Oh, no! He'd hate it." She relaxed her head against Bill's shoulder. "He just doesn't understand how a woman could be broken by this damned war. I may not send the story to the *Daily Journal*."

"You don't see into his heart, Becky. Your father's a very stoic man. He just won't voice his doubts." Bill kissed her cheek, then glided his mouth to her lips.

"I don't think I ever told you." Becky stroked his leg… over and over, a hint of what would someday come if he earned a *forever* promise from her. "My brother Howard's with the Army of Northern Virginia. His fiancé, Sally Somersett, is terrified he's going to get hurt. Like my Avis, Sally loved watching Howard march off to war. She waved General Lee's battle flag. I heard her shriek to my brother, "Bring me a Yankee scalp!"

"I assure you, Becky, you won't get one from me."

Pinching his arm, she chided, "You better not. Then I might not let you court me." Again, she pinched him. "Humbug! I wish you could wait a couple of months. I want to get to know you better. Holding your hand and kissing you are much better than writing letters."

"Wait for me, Becky. I'll court you so well your toes will curl."

"You're so funny, Bill Stamford. Yes, I'll wait for you. And write you a letter every day. Maybe two."

"One a day will do." He fingered her short-story manuscript. "You can keep me up to date on your efforts to find a publisher… if you decide to risk your father's wrath. And you can tell me about picnics and dances, but not about any guys filling up your dance card."

"Just you." She kissed him with her tongue, probing past his lips to touch the roof of his mouth. "I'm such a hussy. I'll go with you to the depot in the morning. And I'll give you the best kiss since Cleopatra kissed Mark Antony. It has to be the best; its memory has to keep you warm during those cold Virginia nights. I hear it even snows." She straightened her dress and rose, then offered her hand. "We should return. They're probably in the parlor deciding who should come out here and chase us into the house." She giggled. "Old folks don't trust teenagers."

Later that night, on the way to where he'd sleep, Bill savored the back-porch memories, just as he'd savored the myriad smells and tastes of his second birthday dinner. The butler led him upstairs to a bedroom filled not only with an ornate bed, dresser and armoire fit for King Louie XIV, but two couches, reading chair, secretary desk, and a cupboard filled with a boy's toys. *This is Howard's room*, Bill thought as he settled onto the bed.

Too wound-up to sleep, Bill nevertheless extinguished a kerosene lamp on the toy cupboard, stripped to his waist-high long johns and slipped between the satin covers. His head resting on a pillow, Bill watched moonlight slither past the curtains and illuminate wallpaper that featured sailing ships and Revolutionary War soldiers.

He clenched his fingers in the bedspread folds. There were sounds beyond the closed door… adult voices fading, a child's voice giggling. A door opened, then closed. Bill tensed. Not just any door. His door. The floor creaked. Loud and ghostlike. A silhouette in the shadows, someone stood near the entryway. The figure moved toward the bed. A nightrobe swished. A voice, barely above a whisper: "I had to kiss you goodnight."

Bill too spoke in a whisper: "I can't believe you came here. Madness! If we're caught, there won't be a courtship."

"Hush! You're leaving for the army. We don't know what will happen." Her meaning was clear… he could die. She'd been doing oodles of thinking about the war; her short story reflected that fact. "I want to say goodbye a lover's way." Becky disrobed, let the nightdress puddle beside her bare feet. She raised the bedspread and blanket, and shimmied into bed beside him. Only her thin underthings separated him from those areas he wanted to touch.

"Oh, God, Becky! I've dreamed of this, yet I'm terrified. Your father."

"He and mother are on the other side of the house." Her voice sounded a tad irritated. "And they're half deaf. If anyone hears us, it'll be Nan." She slid closer, so close her orangey breath stroked his lips and nose. "Touch me."

Cuddling against him, Becky took his hand and rubbed it against her chemise, the linen barrier separating his fingers from her bubbies. He felt them beneath the soft fabric. "Oh, sweet Jesus, I want to kiss them!" he whispered, then groaned.

"Yes, please... my nipples. And the areolas."

"Aureola?"

Becky giggled. "No, silly. That's a circle of light around someone holy. A halo. I mean an areola, the circle around a woman's nipple."

Aureola? That's what he'd seen around his cousin and around Ezekiel, and both had soon died. Halos. Now also aureolas. He'd no longer call them halos. Henceforth, they'd be aureolas.

She arched her body; her other hand finessed the chemise up her legs and past her hips to her belly. Moaning, she tugged his long johns down to his knees. Fingers caressing the back of his neck, she rubbed her fairest flower against his loins.

Bill was a virgin, but not a naive one. He'd heard tales of how men and women joined in amorous congress. Or in the case of Charlie, prigging or tupping. "Lordy, you're torturing me, Becky."

Creaking sounds... loud, more than one. In his arms, Becky's body turned rigid. He felt like he held a bundle of wood boards, not a warm, breathing girl.

"What's that?" She pressed her hands against his chest and rolled away from him.

"Noisy floor. Nothing to worry about." He stretched out a hand to caress her cheek, but she slapped it away.

"The house's not that old." Her breath rapid, she threw back the covers and rose to a sitting position. "We're being foolish. If Father finds me with you, I'm ruined."

"I hate it, but I understand." No flood of bliss this night. Bill kissed the back of Becky's neck. "I don't think we were being foolish. Just in love."

She rose from the bed. "We'll have our flood of bliss, but when it's right." Donning her robe, Becky listened at the keyhole and then slipped out the door.

Upset stomach growling his frustration with the night's outcome, Bill turned over onto the feathered pillow beside him. It still held her imprint... and her scent. He wanted Becky Powell, not war. But he'd not have her at all if he let the lieutenant's train head back to war without him.

Six

A Train Trip to War

Becky and her family went with Bill to the Teachey depot, leaving at seven in the morning to make sure he caught the train from Wilmington. Bill had hoped it might be just Becky and the slave Jacob. Not a frustrating journey though, not with Becky's shapely softness pressed against him. She sat quietly while Nan chattered as the buggy rolled and shuddered on the road to Teachey. "You're going to write to me, aren't you, Bill?" Nan jabbered. "Not just Becky. Me too! I'll write and tell you all that happens at Rockfish Girls Academy. Even the boys who want to hold my hand. Ugh!"

"Nan!" Becky chided. "Quit fibbing. Eight-year olds don't hold hands."

"I'm not fibbing. A boy named Johnny wanted to hold my hand. I bit his fingers."

"Bit? We need to call you Mad Dog Nan." Becky chortled.

Nan joined in. "Mad Dog Nan? I like that... I really do."

They arrived well before the Early Bird Special. Of course, the locomotive ran late. Becky took advantage, holding Bill's hand.

A slave sweeping the waiting-room floor bowed to Louis and Diana. "Mornin' Mister Powell and the missus. Goin' to be a fine day, I be predictin'. I heared the telegraph man say the train be delayed by bad rails."

"Thank you, Tandey." Louis turned to Bill and Becky, sitting together on the bench, fingers entwined. "Sorry. Going to be a long delay. Looks like you could have eaten a better breakfast."

"The eggs and bacon were quite sufficient, sir," Bill explained. "And truthfully, I'm still stuffed from last night's dinner."

"Maybe the lieutenant will return to Virginia on another day." Becky's eyes brightened as she spoke her words. "Who wants to wait for hours until the slaves fix the tracks? Perhaps we'll have Bill as our guest a little longer."

"Doubtful," her father countered. "Bad rails are normally found by the locomotive engineer. Sorry, Becky, your beau will join the army today. Lieutenant O'Rourke's on the train. I'll check on how the repair work's progressing."

Louis ducked into the ticket office, also the telegraph's hidey-hole. A few minutes later he re-emerged, the corners of his mouth tucked with a puckish grin.

"Papa?" Becky's cheery look melted.

"The repair crew's foreman said the track's negotiable as long as the locomotive keeps to a crawl. They'll repair it after the train passes. It'll be here in forty minutes. The lieutenant's aboard."

Becky clutched Bill's arm. "I'm holding onto to you for dear life, sweetheart."

Sooner than he wanted, Bill heard the blasts of the steam whistle. He leaned his head against Becky's shoulder. "These last twenty-four hours have been the best of my life."

Seventeen months before, in the springtime of 1861, the locomotive chugging into Teachey had sported patriotic colors. Now the paint had faded, strips peeling from the boiler and the cab, more evidence the Wilmington and Weldon struggled to maintain its stock. Its name printed on the locomotive's nose—*Black Hawk*—could barely be seen. No longer flying down the track, the *Black Hawk* crawled.

On the loading platform, Becky kissed him brazenly, ignoring two older ladies wearing day-dresses fashionable in the 1840s who eyed the couple as if they were destined for the fires of hell. Becky's mother and father probably disapproved as well, but masked their emotions.

As Bill took a step onto the passenger carriage's stairs, he felt a hard tug on his left arm. He turned.

"I hear mini-balls sound like bees," Becky said, her fingers kneading his coat sleeve as the locomotive hissed. "Don't let any sting you. I want you back whole." She climbed onto the first step and again kissed him full on the mouth. "Momma's going to say I'm a mollisher."

"Mollisher?" He didn't want the embrace to end.

"A girl who likes to hug and kiss boys way too much." She caressed his lips where hers had just touched. "Watch out for those buzzing bees... the metal kind. I love you."

They waved to each other as the *Black Hawk* chugged away, creeping toward Rose Hill and Magnolia at a bone-breaking speed of ten miles per hour. Like the train he'd ridden to Teachey, the *Black Hawk* pulled a mix of cars, two passenger carriages and eight boxcars filled with supplies bound for Virginia. Bill didn't see any officers in the carriage he'd boarded. Gritting his teeth to smother a case of the nerves, he headed for the other carriage.

He'd no sooner passed through the vestibule into the next carriage when a familiar voice rang out, "Billy Boy!" Springing up from his seat, Charlie waved his arms. "Come to say goodbye, eh?"

Weaving in the aisle, hands gripping the backs of seats on either side of him, Bill retorted, "Nope. Come to join up."

Charlie chortled. "Lordy, Bill! She gives you a birthday party, and you up and leave her cryin' at the depot. What she do? Put poison in your cake?"

Bill rolled his eyes. "Don't act innocent, Charlie Kurtz! You volunteered me to Lieutenant O'Rourke." He sighed. "You've an ally. Becky's father knows the lieutenant. Laid the law down to me. If I hope to court her, I better join the Eighteenth. So here I am."

"Well, I hope you at least got to tickle her ripe fruits, Billy Boy." Charlie earned some laughs from other recruits, all still dressed in their civilian garb.

Grimacing, Bill countered, "Charlie, Becky's wife material. Please keep the talk civilized."

Up at the front of the carriage, concealed by the hulking body of a recruit with long blond hair tied in a ponytail, an officer rose and turned stiffly. "I keep hearing my name," said Lieutenant Jamie O'Rourke, who wore a striking uniform, no doubt made by a Wilmington seamstress, maybe one of his wife's household slaves. Even his slouch hat looked spotless. "What's the commotion?"

"No commotion, Lieutenant, sir," Charlie replied, his manner apologetic. "Remember my friend who I said would probably join up?"

"Yes, I recall our conversation, Private Kurtz." The lieutenant eyed Bill. "Your friend?"

"Yessir." Charlie play-punched Bill in the arm. "Another boffin for you."

"Bill Stamford, sir." Bill straightened his spine. "Son of Clarence Stamford, publisher of the *Duplin Gazette*, owner of the Stamford Print Shop. A patriotic son of the South."

O'Rourke gestured to the twenty-seven recruits in the carriage car. "All these men are patriotic sons of the South." The lieutenant limped along the aisle to Bill and held out his hand. "Lieutenant Jamie O'Rourke, Company G of the Eighteenth North Carolina, Lane's Brigade, Army of Northern Virginia's Second Corps." He slapped his bum leg. "Took a miniball at Malvern Hill. Brother's a surgeon who studied in Vienna. He came up to Virginia after the battle and saved my leg. The army's saw-boys wanted to cut it off. If you're ever in such a fix, remember that bromine and iodine will do wonders."

"So I've heard, sir," Bill said, nodding. "Dr. Iuppenlatz is a friend of my father's."

"I know the fine doctor. One of Wilmington's best. Indispensable during the recent epidemic." O'Rourke pushed his hat back from his eyes. "You're from Duplin. Why do you want to join a New Hanover company?"

Bill grinned at Charlie. "He's the reason. We're comrades-in-arms."

The lieutenant shrugged, hands outspread. "It's unorthodox, but what the hell. We're all fighting the same egg-sucking Blue-Bellies. Take a seat, Bill. When we get to Warsaw, I'll sign you up and swear you in."

Bill did find a seat. Toward the back beside one of O'Rourke's recruits. The fella moved so Bill could sit next to the window. "I hate to make you move, friend," Bill said in a sociable manner. "You're more than welcome to the window spot."

"No thanks." The recruit, an older man with a balding head of night-sky black hair peppered with gray speckles, yawned. "Slip in there next to the window. I'm going to nod off. Didn't get much sleep last night."

Bill settled in, elbow resting on the windowsill. With the train moving at a crawl, Bill got long looks at the Duplin countryside. No one flagged down the train in Rose Hill, so the *Black Hawk* chugged on for Magnolia. Perhaps a bit faster than a crawl, maybe a toddler's walk. Less than a week until the official start of autumn, but the sun still shone like it had forgotten the month... July, not September. Blue sky on the pine-tree horizon and an even darker blue at the top of the window. He perched his head against the glass... warm, like a summer day. Christmas was only three months away, but it seemed an eternity from where Bill sat in this slow-moving train.

In Magnolia, the *Black Hawk* picked up three passengers, one bound for Faison and two for Goldsboro. Between Magnolia and Warsaw, small farmsteads of no more than a hundred acres speckled the countryside along with their shotgun clapboard houses. In the fields, middle-aged farmers in sack coats, button-down shirts and straw hats harvested vegetables. From inside the train, Bill found it difficult to discern what kinds of vegetables. Could be turnips, squash, green beans, or cucumbers. Sometimes the men harvested alone, sometimes with the help of one or two slaves. Once or twice he saw a farmwife and kids harvesting. No young farmers, though.

The *Black Hawk's* steam whistle announced its Warsaw arrival. As the locomotive braked to a whiny stop, O'Rourke limped back to where Bill sat. "I'll sign you up in the depot, Stamford. It's a dinner stop. Locomotive's taking on water and wood."

Outside on the loading platform, Bill found his papa waiting for him. He introduced him to the lieutenant. "Ah, the newspaper man and printer," O'Rourke said, shaking Clarence's offered hand. "Which do you prefer?"

It hardly took anytime for Bill's father to answer. "Printer pays the bills. The newspaper's for love."

Inside the depot, Clarence stood beside his son as Bill signed the paperwork, then raised his right hand and repeated the recruit's oath: "I, William Stamford, do solemnly swear to support and defend the Constitution of the Confederate States against all enemies, foreign and domestic; that I will bear true faith and allegiance to the same; and that I will obey the orders of the President of the Confederate States and the orders of the officers appointed over me, according to regulations and the Uniform Code of Military Justice. So help me God."

O'Rourke shook Bill's hand. "Welcome to the Eighteenth's Company G and the Army of Northern Virginia, Private Stamford."

"Thank you, sir." Actually, Bill wasn't thinking of his life in General Lee's Army, but of Becky back in Duplin Roads and the sweet cuddling he'd shared with her the night before. Months, maybe years, separated him from more of her kisses.

Charlie slapped Bill on the back. "Well, we're goin' to war, Chuckaboo. Side by side. And a fifty-dollar bounty to boot. You'll be able to buy your sweet Becky a ring."

Unsurprisingly, Charlie bummed a free meal, sitting with the lieutenant, Bill and his father at the nearby restaurant, the Whistle Stop. The other three carried on a lively discussion of how newspapers were covering the war, especially the editorials. Not Bill. With Becky fresh in his mind, memories of the unwelcome aureolas always a threat to disturb his sleep, Bill found his mood growing darker. He finished up the last of his simple meal of chicken fried steak, field peas and greens, and briefly fixed his gaze on the lieutenant and then Charlie. *When will a damned aureola flare around one of them?* Bill scowled.

Later, after Bill hugged his father goodbye and headed up the steps into the passenger carriage, Charlie turned, and studying him, said whimsically, "Why the scowl, Billy Boy? Save that for the Yanks. It's mean enough to kill."

Next stop, somewhere in the Shenandoah Valley.

Seven

A Dreary Drill Field

A blustery October wind mauled the curls peeking from beneath Bill's slouch hat as he and the other recruits lined up on the drill field. His wretched uniform itched worse than a bad case of poison oak. Fleas and lice homesteaded on the uniform and his skin... and he'd only been in the army a few weeks. Lordy, he hated it, but at least a cloudless sky provided enough sunshine to dry the sweat on his face. Most folks loved October with its flamboyant trees popping with color. Not Bill. He hated the unpredictability. One day, summer-like rays lulling farm fields and village squares. The next, dark clouds of sleet pelting those same fields and squares. For Bill and the other soldiers of Company G, such fickleness made camp life one of grimness. The weather seemed especially fickle at Bunker Hill in the lower Shenandoah Valley. The wind danced a devil's jig.

For the veterans of the Eighteenth, time in camp offered a chance to heal physically and mentally after Second Manassas, the Seven Days campaign and Antietam. Far too many friends no longer shared campfires. The regiment had lost half its numbers since leaving North Carolina in the spring.

Eyeing the ragged line of recruits, the drill sergeant, Brunswick County's Frank McKinney, growled, "Y'all's fodder, boys! For the souls lost in the Seven Days battles and Sharpsburg." He stepped up to a recruit, a stick-thin fellow with a pimply face and niggardly beard, and poked him in the chest. "Hold that musket like you're a soldier, not a plow boy doin' some huntin'! Stand tall!"

"Yes sir," the strawfoot wheezed.

The sergeant harrumphed. "Y'all wouldn't be here if not for the threat of conscription. And the bounties. You'd rather be hidin' behind your momma's apron or under your wife's bed."

Maybe some, Bill conceded, but not Charlie and him. Neither joined due to conscription. Charlie thought volunteering was the quickest way to become a politician and help shape the South's future after the war. For Bill, he could only court Becky if he joined the army. So here he stood in the chilly wind, teeth chattering, listening to a sergeant tell him he was fodder for the Confederacy.

McKinney's raw voice shattered Bill's thoughts like grapeshot shredding a battle line. "They're sendin' us cumberworlds. Bunch of useless dalcops. Let's see if this day's salvageable."

McKinney loved pain, even his own. While nearly all men in the Eighteenth sported beards, some quite long, he shaved every morning with cold water. He refused to look disheveled. A day ago, Bill heard Charlie joke, "McKinney eyes a louse, and the critter dies on the spot."

Breathing hard, McKinney stomped along the line, eyeing each recruit. "Oblique march! Into line of battle! Halt! First row kneel! Prepare to fire!"

The sergeant called out the commands for loading and firing muskets and rifles. One recruit, a thickheaded redhead from Wilmington, forgot to pull out the ramrod. "Damn fopdoodle!" McKinney bellowed. "Take the damned ramrod out of the barrel, loiter-sack!"

Composure shattered, the offending soldier sagged as he withdrew the ramrod. Thankfully, they drilled without black powder and mini balls. If the fopdoodle had shot the ramrod across a battlefield, he'd not be able to load any more mini balls. The redhead, a fellow named Tim Donahue, had worked in Wilmington's CSA Arms Factory. Besides swords, he made guns, but hadn't actually fired one. His hunting forays never ventured beyond hunts for Water Street's prostitutes.

The sergeant growled, "We're goin' to keep doin' the drills 'til y'all no longer make mistakes. Mistakes kill soldiers. Dead soldiers win battles in Hell. Not on sweet Virginia soil."

The recruits had been drilling for a week. They were getting better, their formations more cohesive, their loading and firing crisper, but Donahue still annoyed the sergeant. A slow learner, he struggled to get things right, like he saw the world differently from everyone else. He could hardly read, said he saw words backwards. Charlie wanted to bust up the fellow's face, but Bill knew the redhead tried his best and so stood up for him.

"One more time! The loadin' and firin' steps. We're goin' to do it like true Tar Heels, not New York Irishmen." Again,

McKinney yelled out the steps. This time everyone, even Donahue, properly loaded and pretend-fired their guns. "Competence!" McKinney yelped a rebel yell, soon joined by the recruits. "Dismissed!"

Beyond a gap in a split-rail farm fence, a sea of scruffy tents lay between Mill Creek and a broad expanse of trees, mainly red and chestnut oaks. Bill hadn't seen the sun in days. A dismal sky laden with a thick soup of gray clouds shrouded the camp and the drill grounds.

Boots crunching stubble, Bill and Charlie stepped through the gap and headed for their tent, more than two hundred yards away. Their frosty breaths blazed the trail through a city of white canvas, not winter quarters of laid-out streets and huts belching chimney smoke. Off toward the oaks, the smoke from hundreds of campfires veiled a plantation mansion known by locals as the John Boyd House. Beyond, the crossroads town of Bunker Hill sprawled at the confluence of Mill Creek and Torytown Run. Veterans wagered they'd soon get orders to build the huts, and their temporary stay at Bunker Hill would last into early 1863. Like others in the camp, Bill had heard that Lee was waiting to learn if Union General George McClelland would risk one more movement south before the cold and snows made marching impossible. Bill could almost taste that order, like chicory coffee heated on a hut's fireplace grill. Bona fide bunks and a table, and Charlie was real good at furniture-making.

Near where Bill and Charlie ambled, soldiers rolled dice or sat at tables playing card games. A chaplain frowned at the gamblers, but said nothing. In the war's younger days, he would have overturned the table, much like Jesus did to the moneychangers.

Aureolas—the lack of them—suddenly popped into Bill's mind. Dozens of soldiers perched around campfires, and not one wore a damned aureola. He'd lacked time to think about them. Drilling consumed the daylight hours, and at night he collapsed into a near-coma sleep, too weary to ruminate over the things. "Hear all the coughing?" Bill stopped walking so he could listen better. "This is a sick place."

"I'll never go to a hospital tent." Charlie grimaced. "All the veterans say you don't come out alive."

Then why no aureolas? There should be one or two, if the aureolas foretell imminent death. A Bible verse he memorized in Sunday school came to mind: "As the heavens are higher than the earth, so are my ways higher than your ways and my thoughts than your thoughts." *I won't complain if you don't bedevil me with another one until I'm eighty, Lord.* Bill resumed walking.

Beyond the card sharps, he spied his home-away-from-home. Bill and Charlie bunked under a canvas shelter, better than a lean-to but hardly a full-fledged tent. Two next-door veterans, Kenny Morgan and Daniel Livingston, had shown them how to tie each end of the shelter to a bayonet fixed into the ground. Some preferred fence posts, but the veterans always got first dibs.

Charlie knew how to snag new friends, like a pretty lass at a dance getting her card quickly filled with the names of her admirers. On one of his jaunts through camp, Charlie returned with two Union rubber blankets captured at Sharpsburg. Perfect ground cloths. The canvas shelter was cozy; a grumbler might say cramped. Just the day before, Charlie had complained, "Only a dog could crawl under it and stay dry." With the way the sky looked, the two would soon see if their shelter could stop the rain.

One of the company's sergeants, Jerry Barnard, thought recruits adapted faster to army life with veterans as neighbors. Kenny and Daniel had fought in the summer campaigns—the Seven Days battles and at Sharpsburg. They'd re-enlisted after their three-month musters were up, and now were in the war for the duration, or as Daniel put it, "Until Hell freezes over."

Folding stools were arranged between Bill's tent and the veterans' full-fledged tent, Yankee contraband claimed by Kenny at Sharpsburg. Daniel and Kenny were seated on two of the stools, Daniel reading his Bible, Kenny whittling a tobacco pipe. The campfire looked inviting to Bill, who planned to perch on the edge of a stool and warm his hands, then pluck a crinkled letter from his shell jacket's breast pocket and read it for the umpteenth time. He needed his hands to be warm, lest he drop Becky's letter into the fire.

Once seated, Bill hovered his hands over the flames, then nodded at Kenny's whittling project. The veteran had shaped the pipe into a woman's face.

"Your wife? Carrie?" Bill flexed his fingers, letting the flames' heat nibble at them.

Kenny shared a glance with Charlie and both chortled.

"No, not the wife." Kenny tapped his groin. "My toffer for joinin' giblets. Some serious groin rubbin'."

Daniel glanced up from his Bible. "His hedge whore."

Bill sighed. He'd been getting quite an education since arriving at camp, especially the crude slang for conjoined lovers.

Charlie jabbed a hand toward the oak trees. "He's been meetin' this Carrie in those woods for some tupping." With one hand he formed a loose fist and with the other jammed a finger through the side opening over and over again. "Storm of heaves in the leaves. A naked woman and leaves... the perfect combination."

That seemed reckless to Bill, especially in a corps under the command of a straightlaced Presbyterian, General

Thomas Jackson. But the chaplains were turning a blind eye to the card playing and the dice rolling, so maybe the giblet couplings were a necessary evil. But if they weren't...

"Be careful sentries don't see you." Shaking his head, Bill slid his hand inside his shell-jacket pocket and caressed the letter.

Kenny shrugged. "They don't care. Probably do it themselves. Carrie and me... we're more worried about feral pigs interruptin' us."

Withdrawing the letter, Bill gently unfolded the paper. He'd looked at it so many times he worried it might tear along the creases. Kenny was welcome to his Carrie; Bill intended to save himself for Becky. Her penmanship was immaculate, the inked words carefully crafted to reassure a man who might be away from her arms for months, maybe years. He read the most vital paragraph: "It's so wonderful to read how much you miss me, sweetheart. Just like you, I promise to stay faithful. Only your lips will ever kiss my lips, my breasts, my lady parts. I promise my virginity to you, Bill Stamford. Now look what you made me write. I will have to sneak this letter past Father. I can't chance him or Momma getting a look at it. Love you, darling boy. Your forever girl, Becky."

After he read her letter the first time, shortly after being outfitted for his uniform, he'd pulled out a sheet of paper and a pencil from his haversack and written: "I arrived safely at the army camp. The new uniform scratches. Learning how to drill and fight as a unit. Not done any fighting yet, but that doesn't bother me. When the drill sergeant yells 'you're dismissed,' all I can think of is how wonderful you smell when you're close to me. And I can't wait until I can resume our courtship. Don't tell anyone, but I just kissed this paper. Put your lips against it, and you'll get my long-distance kiss. Your sweetheart, Bill." He'd carried it to the mail tent next to the plantation house, bought a stamp, and bid it farewell.

Bill glanced beyond the mansion, expecting to find Bunker Hill obscured by the smoke from the campfires. Instead, a shift in the wind had blown it away from Torytown Run and Mill Creek. The wind swirled leaves and dust among the steeples of the Christ and the Presbyterian churches, and the waterwheels of a woolen mill and gristmill. Carrie was probably from Bunker Hill. The war had made girls like Carrie more adventurous, more reckless. Bill wondered if she would come to regret her woodland frolics.

Kenny stopped sculpting his pipe and scrutinized Bill as if able to read his mind. "Carrie lost her husband at Second Manassas. She's lonely. Likes being held, her bubbies kissed. I oblige her every Sunday night if it ain't rainin' or too cold."

Folding the letter, Bill returned it to his jacket pocket. "Sounds are different at night. Sentries might get scatter-nervous and shoot you two."

Kenny snickered. "The sounds lovers make... day or night... they don't change."

Daniel closed his Bible, smacking the pages together, like a mini-thunderclap. "Kenny, if you survive this war, you're going to have to look your wife in the face, the mother of your children, and know you betrayed her."

Grimacing, Kenny packed his carving knife and half-done pipe in his haversack and picked up the coffee pot from a grill nestled above the fire. Pouring chicory coffee into his tin cup, he took a swallow. "Just as you said, Daniel, if I survive the war. Hells-bells, I'm not even fearin' battle right now. The flux and camp fever liable to kill me first. I'm goin' to get some tuppin' while me and my Johnson can stand upright. And anyway, my wife ain't ever goin' to know."

"But you'll know, Kenny." Daniel slithered his Bible into his haversack, then dropped the bread bag to the ground. "Big doings tomorrow, some Second Corps maneuvers. Marching in time, wheeling to meet a flank attack, falling in and out of battle lines. Sergeant McKinney gonna let you parlor soldiers join us?"

Charlie shook his head. "The sarge said nothin' about it." He punched his fisted right hand against his left's open palm. "Not too long ago, Daniel, we'd be rollin' on the cold ground exchangin' punches, but I swore I'd be a proper soldier. I'll overlook that slur on me and Bill's honor."

Daniel nodded solemnly. "Better get used to it, Charlie. When you've faced Yankee hornets and not run, no one will ever again call you a parlor soldier."

Bill shifted the conversation. "I've my doubts about all this close-order drill. No doubt proper back in the days of Napoleon Bonaparte. Now I'm not so sure. Papa's a newspaperman. I do a heap of reading. Those Frenchies fought with smoothbores. Sadly, some of us still do, but not the Yankees. They're shooting at us with rifles. Much greater range. I bet we won't be using the damned battle formations in a year."

"Maybe, virgin." Daniel coughed, then again and spiraled into a hacking fit, turning him red. When he could breathe again, he managed in a raspy voice, "I like knowing my buddies are next to me."

"I *am* next to you," Kenny told Daniel. "And I'm sayin' you need to go to the hospital tent. Your cough's gettin' worse."

"No!" Daniel eyed their skillet hanging from a tent pole. "Too many go there and die. Cook the four of us dinner, Kenny. I've heard all I want to hear about hospitals."

Standing, Kenny grabbed the skillet. "It's probably just a nasty cold. Seems like the ones having the runs and the coughin' fits are the virgins. Just not use to camp life, I guess."

Daniel's cough made Bill think about his aureola musings. So far only two, and they were years apart. He feared that would soon change. Yet none so far in a camp filled with sick soldiers. *You're driving me crazy, Lord. I don't like rolling your dice.*

Bill suddenly felt a prickle in his throat. He swallowed extra hard, hoping to remove the itch with the mucus. *Damn! Can't afford sniffles now.* He admitted it was odd getting the throat itch just after Kenny mentions that recruits are most susceptible to the camp maladies. *Is all this hospital talk turning me into a swooner, always thinking a sneeze will lead to ague, consumption or the bloody flux?* All through childhood, Bill was one of the kids who never got sick. He cleared his throat. The tickle was gone.

Eight

Railroad Track Shenanigans

The fire burned so hot Bill stepped back until he no longer felt like the skin on his face might melt. "Hate to see track destroyed like this," he told Charlie. "A real shame. Maybe a Union raiding party will do the same to the Wilmington & Weldon at Magnolia or Warsaw."

Leaning on a crowbar's handle, Charlie blew on his fingers to warm them, then shrugged. "Pure enthuzimuzz. Look how much fun the boys are havin'. Better than back at our tents freezin' to death." He slipped the bar under a rail and tugged, loosening it.

Nearby, within shouting distance, Daniel overheard their conversation. Shouldering his crowbar like he would a rifle, he took a short break, joining Bill and Charlie. "It's got to be done. Can't let the trains run men and supplies with impunity. They're aimed at us, remember?"

Bill pried at the other end of the rail Charlie had loosened. "I know. I'll do what I have to do. I grew up in a county filled with Wilmington and Weldon depots. Even rode one of their trains to meet the woman I'm going to marry."

As Charlie continued prying, spikes broke and the rail on his end wriggled free. He wiped forehead sweat with the brim of his hat. "Holy-moly, Billy Boy! You just met her. You'll meet a dozen girls before you find the right one."

Bill jimmied his bar until his end of the rail popped loose. He kicked a cross-tie spike toward a large pile of ties burning brighter than a Kenansville barn he'd once seen go up. The Eighteenth's men were tossing rails atop the bonfire. Breathing heavy, he crouched, catching his breath. "Nope. Going to marry Becky. It's prophesized in my bones." He laughed. And in another area of his body.

Kenny swung around, ready to resume rail demolition, then abruptly turned back to Bill and Charlie. "Forget her, Bill. Plenty of girls in Bunker Hill with a proper bit of frock."

"Just not for me, Kenny. I'm a caged fellow. I don't want to fly free." Bill grinned. "Unless it's down Becky's bosom."

The hard work of tearing up rails warmed Bill and gave him an odd perception of summertime. But a glance upward revealed otherwise. A mostly dark overcast, hinting at a cold nighttime rain a few hours away. Just two weeks old, November 1862 had proved to be a rain-drenched month. Bill half-expected to float away along with his shared tent. So while the railroad-track work was grueling, at least no rain or sleet. All in all, well worth a small thought sent heavenward: *Thank you, Lord, for small mercies.*

Just days after General Lee promoted Stonewall Jackson to lieutenant general with command of the Second Corps, the devout disciplinarian sent eight thousand infantrymen on a raid to destroy a thirty-five mile stretch of the Baltimore and Ohio Railroad. Colonel Lane gave the order, and the brigade marched to Martinsburg, a pro-Union city.

Shopkeepers, grocers, blacksmiths, printers and railroad men had been gallingly silent as the Confederate troops marched toward Martinsburg's railyards. Although the temperature hovered just above freezing, women had rolled down second- and third-story windows and waved the Stars and Stripes. The men on the sidewalks might have been silent, but their glares had been colder than the afternoon temperature. Even waist-high boys and girls had aimed hateful stares at the Butternuts.

The Confederates had heated the place up, angry flames lighting the sky above Martinsburg. They burned bridges, the B&O's engine house, machine shops, half-round house, and the ticket and telegraph offices. Bill and the other Butternuts had marched through Martinsburg singing "Bonnie Blue Flag." He'd raised his voice, "... our rights were threatened, the cry rose near and far, hurrah for the Bonnie Blue Flag that bears a single star..."

That had been two days ago. Now they were tearing up track as they marched toward Harper's Ferry. They'd been setting fires and bending the rails since Berryville. Twenty-six miles all told. Another three days and they could return to their camp at Bunker Hill. Bill scanned the rail bed to his rear and then fixed his eyes frontward. An unbroken line of fires illuminated the bellies of clouds sharing a sliver of early-evening sky with a waning-crescent moon.

A derisive voice punctuated the ongoing daydreams inside Bill's head. "Hey, Bill, quit the woolgatherin'," Kenny yelled, one end of a rail balanced on his shoulder. "I could use some help!"

Hastening toward Kenny, Bill grabbed the other end. They lugged the rail to the closest pile of burning ties and tossed it atop other rails being licked by the flames. Later, Bill and Kenny wrapped rails around tree trunks. "Stonewall's neckties," Kenny clowned.

A shot rang out. A ball whizzed by Bill. His shell jacket tore at his shoulder. He expected to feel a sharp pain, seeping blood warming skin. He felt nothing.

"Get down, damn it!" Charlie tugged on Bill's pants, clutching fabric at the hip.

I've been shot! Damn! Bill eyed nearby soldiers. Not one aureola. *I'm in a war, and no aureolas. Lord, you're confusing me!*

All around Bill, the soldiers crawled on their bellies, eyes darting side to side, searching for the sniper.

"Over there!" Kenny screamed, gesturing toward the railroad bed. It made a natural breastwork, and veterans knew how to seek cover.

Grimacing as his slouch hat fell beside him, Bill dropped to his knees, then flopped onto his belly. He reached for the tear in his shell jacket, but Charlie was quicker. Charlie's fingers wiggled through the tear. Bill gritted his teeth as pain seared his shoulder. He thought the worst... soon another arm would end up in a trash heap.

Charlie laughed. "Barely a drop of blood, Billy Boy. Stop being a baby."

Crawling closer, Daniel heard Charlie's droll words. "You're no longer a parlor soldier," Daniel said, then whistled a long sigh.

A sergeant, Jerry Barnard, crawled along the railroad bed behind the Eighteenth's soldiers, exhorting: "Get ready! Time to flush him out, give him a third eyeball."

"I love turkey shoots," Kenny muttered.

To Bill's front, skirmishers, their rifles raised and ready to shoot, quick-stepped toward a copse of trees nearly stripped of their red and yellow leaves. "Up boys! Stretch those muscles." Barnard rose and crested the railroad bed. He pointed toward the coppice. "Forward!"

Another shot resounded, this one aimed at the advancing skirmishers. It missed.

Toting an ancient hunting musket, a boy, no more than ten, darted from the cover of a birch. Dressed in farm clothes and a straw hat, the lad sprinted toward a ramshackle barn. Bill's thoughts raced: *Sweet Lord! Don't shoot him!*

Charlie brought his musket up to firing position, the butt against his cheek. "Don't fire," Bill screeched. "You'll hit a skirmisher." Bill slapped at the rifle's barrel, but no shot roared.

"God, Bill! I ain't a fool." Charlie kicked dirt at Bill's legs.

Skirmishers dashed after the boy. The fastest, a fellow who'd won footraces in camp, tackled the lad near a stone fence. The boy's hunting musket and the soldier's Springfield went flying, smacking dirt on the other side of the fence.

On all fours, the boy scrambled away, but the Butternut had him by the seat of his pants, yanking the youngster back toward him. The soldier flung him over his knee and spanked him. The kid wailed as if he'd been stung by a swarm of bees. Another skirmisher flung the boy's musket against the wall, splintering it. "Damn Rebs!" the boy whined.

The gun-wrecking skirmisher shoved the boy toward the barn and adjacent farmhouse, both on a ridge a quarter-mile away. "Skedaddle! Go home to Mommy!" The soldier kicked the boy in the rump. As if shot out of a cannon, the kid hurtled the wall and sprinted toward the barn and farmhouse.

Arms crossed against her chest, the boy's momma waited on the front porch. When he lurched up the stoop, she seized him by the ear and dragged him into the house.

As the advancing Eighteenth came to a disorderly halt, Kenny rested the butt of his musket against the soil. "What the hell! This is Virginny! They're damned Unionists and traitors. Even their little 'ums are mean cusses."

Bill and Charlie exchanged glances. "Just like the mountain folk of North Carolina," Charlie said in a matter-of-fact tone. "I expect these Old Dominion mountaineers will soon secede from Virginia."

Bill stared at the deserted porch. "Even more important we tear up the track. Lots of rails left for making Stonewall neckties. The faster we get it done, the sooner we get back to camp."

Nine

The Ice March

General Jackson's orders went out to his corps commanders. They passed them down to their brigade commanders, who explained them to the regimental commanders. At the bottom of the feed trough, the company's officers and sergeants carried them out. And men like privates Bill Stamford and Charlie Kurtz learned they'd not build huts and settle in for the winter. Instead, they prepared to march southward.

Mid-November... a time to hunker down, snuggle in a hut wrapped in blankets, stay dry from ice, sleet and snow. Except mid-November 1862 would be a time to prepare for battle, Bill realized when he heard Sergeant Barnard's orders.

Charlie liked to walk from campfire to campfire and jaw with men from other companies. On November 20, he shared a humdinger of a rumor with Bill. "Lincoln relieved McClelland a week or so ago. Burnside's commandin' the Blue-Bellies. The new commander's hot to sneak off on a flankin' movement and sit pretty between us and Richmond. He thinks he's goin' to win a great victory for egg-suckin' Lincoln." Charlie squatted before the fire newly stoked by Bill and warmed his hands. Once the sun set in mid-November, the temperature quickly plunged.

The dusk sky, gray and gloomy as always, looked ominous, a drenching inevitable. "Terrible time to march," Bill observed. "Yanks are crazy."

Piqued by Bill's words, Kenny ambled to the campfire. "Ground's hard. Burnside's got a head start. Lee must catch up. When he does, he'll make Burnside look like a fool. We're goin' to beat the Potomac boys again."

Huddled on a log before the fire, Bill scratched at the beginnings of a beard. With all the drilling and other soldierly stuff, it'd gotten too dang-fangled hard to shave. He decided he'd prefer to comb out whatever lice homesteaded in his new beard. Maybe he'd let it grow to his belt buckle. Like Charlie and Kenny, Bill took pride in his looks. Since returning from Stonewall's necktie party, he'd started using a baby-sized mirror to gaze at his whiskers. Yep, he'd not think of trimming until the hairs tickled his belly.

Bill resettled his buttocks on the log. "At least it'll mean the end of drilling. We're getting better, don't you think? Even the redhead Donahue?" He regarded Charlie.

"Yep, Donahue's doin' his right-face, forward-march drills like a professional." Charlie laughed. "And if Redhead's legs don't get too wobbly at the smell of black powder, he'll be able to load and fire his musket. But it's not what I reckon; it's what percolatin' inside Sergeant McKinney's head." Charlie reached for the coffee pot and filled his tin cup with the genuine stuff liberated by Kenny from a Bunker Hill citizen eager to make money. Kenny paid with stamps. Charlie took a sip. "Damn good! What was I saying? Oh, yes... McKinney. Sarge must reckon school's out and we're ready for college."

Kenny plopped down on a rickety stool and poured another cup. "Won't be so easy doin' these drills on a battlefield with mini balls whizzin' by and cannonballs bouncin' at your legs." He raised his cup to his mouth and groaned with pleasure, then pretended to be a sergeant. "Left wheel! I said left wheel! Get back here, Private Charlie! No running to the rear!"

"I ain't no coward!" Charlie bolted to his feet, hands fisted, his face a mask of rage.

"Calm down!" Bill whacked the back of Charlie's leg. "Remember your reason for joining? Kenny's not calling you a coward. He's calling us fresh fish. We haven't been shot at yet." Bill chuckled. "Well, a ten-year-old did shoot at me. But that doesn't count."

"I'm just joustin', Charlie." Kenny turned at the sound of a tent flap whooshing, then swiveled his gaze back to Charlie. "If it becomes bad enough to run, I'll be ahead of you."

Charlie nodded, sipped more steaming-hot coffee, and returned to his seat. "No hard feelings."

Toting a camp stool under his arm, Daniel unfolded the contraption and sat next to Kenny. "Burnside, eh? I know an A Company sergeant, a fellow from New Hanover. He too knew Burnside. Met the Yankee general in the 1850s when Burnside was treasurer for the Illinois Central. Interestingly, McClellan was president of the line."

Kenny's coffee smelled nearly as nice as Becky when she crawled into bed and snuggled beside Bill. Unable to resist, Bill plucked his cup out of the bread bag, Kenny's word for haversack. Soon, the real stuff glided down Bill's throat. "The sergeant's keeping strange company for a New Hanover man."

Daniel shrugged. "Not really. The sergeant's originally from Illinois. Married a New Hanover girl and moved to Wilmington. He's an in-the-trenches railroad man, an engineer. Got a job for the Wilmington & Weldon. If we ever hijack a train, he's the man to climb into the locomotive."

Charlie fed a log to the fire and stoked the flames to reheat the pot's lukewarm coffee. "So what does your A Company sergeant think about his friend Burnside?"

Daniel couldn't get his hands to stop waltzing on his lap. Mulling Charlie's question, he explained, "Burnside won't be as cautious as McClelland. That's good for us, he believes. Thinks Burnside's in over his head commanding an army. The next week or two should be interesting."

Bill raised his cup for a toast, earning puzzled looks. "Well, that explains why we've gotten these marching orders. A toast to a thorough whipping of Burnside and his Blue-Bellies."

As if at a Louis Powell dinner party, Bill fancy-danced his cup against Daniel's and shuddered as if he'd been jolted by a closer-than-comfortable lightning strike. White flames so bright Bill had to look away capered around Daniel. Maybe Daniel, Kenny and Charlie thought he'd seen a ghost. Bill wished he had. No, not a ghost. Something else far too familiar to Bill and his terrified soul. Another damned halo... no, Becky had a new word. An aureola enveloped Daniel from his boots to the crown of his head. Bill lidded his eyes, and when he risked opening them after long, scary moments, the flames were gone. Expecting he looked pale as a corpse, Bill breathed deeply to calm his nerves and proceeded with the toast as if he'd not almost crapped his pants. "And here's to good marching weather and blue skies."

"Blue skies, good marching weather and a sound thrashing of the Blue-Bellies," Daniel said, finishing off his coffee. As Daniel coughed, Kenny and Charlie made their toasts.

Kenny slid the coffee pot to the edge of the grill he'd purloined from an abandoned Yankee camp. "Sun's down. Goin' to cook dinner, if anyone's game."

"What's on the menu, chef?" Charlie slapped his stool's armrests in anticipation.

"The stuff we've had since gettin' back from the necktie raid, like we've had for weeks and weeks." Kenny rolled his eyes. "Salt pork, desiccated vegetables, cornmeal and more of this first-rate Yankee coffee. Goin' to turn it into a pork-and-beans stew."

Jackson's Second Corps spent the rest of Thursday, November 20 and Friday, November 21 cooking rations and preparing for the march. Always a stickler for prayers, the devout general must have been wondering why his godly request for good marching weather wasn't answered. Just after midnight on Saturday, as sleet battered his frozen body, Bill packed hardtack, bacon, desiccated vegetables, cornmeal, and chicory coffee in his haversack. With the rubber ground cloth unfurled, he arranged his blanket and tent canvas atop it, then rolled them up and tied the ends together with a leather strip. He draped the bedroll across his body, and with his tin cup, plate and frying pan jangling, stepped into the marching columns. Soon the men of A.P. Hill's division, including James Henry Lane's Brigade, were marching south up the Shenandoah Valley Turnpike in columns of four.

"Goodbye, my sweet toffer," Kenny said, his voice jaunty as he took a look back at Bunker Hill. "May you have a long life with a lovin' hubby and lots of little ones."

Bill tapped his inside jacket pocket, felt the crinkly paper, Becky's letter. She could have lots of little ones too, as long as he was the father. He allowed himself a private smile.

Bored, Daniel tried to spur some chitchat. "Lordy, the valley's beautiful." He pointed toward a farmhouse barely visible through the fog and sleet. Beyond the homestead, the fog curled among the shadowy peaks. In the fence-bordered fields, a mist slunk low and furtive, like barn cats stalking mice.

No one felt like gabbing, so silence greeted Daniel's efforts. Guilt ate at Bill as he tramped through the sleet-and-rain mixture, listening to it splatter on his slouch hat, shell jacket and anywhere skin peeked through. Daniel could very well be dead in a day or two. Bill chewed on his lower lip, struggling with his dilemma. Warn Daniel about the aureola? Or keep silent? Bill kept his thoughts to himself.

In the summertime, thousands of marching soldiers would have kicked up a dust storm, torturing men in the rear. No dust on this Saturday morning, not with the clouds retching sleet as the Butternuts slogged south on the turnpike. Ice and a swirling wind gnawed at Bill's face. The wintry misery should consume his thoughts, yet unbidden aureolas and an image of a broken young girl... they wouldn't stay buried in his head where they belonged.

Tears mixed with the sleet on Bill's face as he looked down at his boots splashing water up from the planks. Against his will, Bill's mind returned to an earlier time, when he first saw an aureola.

~ * ~

Bill had been happy to take the short buggy ride to Castle Hayne and his granddaddy's farm. He loved his Granny Stamford's apple cobbler and mince pie. Bill would sometimes eat so much he'd get a bellyache so bad he'd get a serious case of the moans. The visits to the Castle Hayne farm meant get-togethers with a cousin, Jenny, a wild tomboy. Jenny and Bill were foreordained pals from the moment they were born. They loved playing marbles, and on this particular visit it was no exception. He'd been concentrating on shooting one of his cat's eyes, his concentration only focused on the marble lodged between his thumb and index finger. Bill flicked his thumb… the shot slapped marbles outside the line drawn in the dirt. Grinning, he cast a triumphant look at Jenny. An aureola surrounded her. It didn't scare him. He thought it beautiful, white flames frolicking around her like fairies in the nursery books his momma read to him. She giggled when he shared his vision with her, snorted that he was full of cow manure. "Smells like it too," she'd joked, then dared him to climb the yard's elm.

Urged on by Jenny, Bill climbed so high she looked tiny back on the ground. "I can climb higher," she taunted. Bill refused to go higher, the limbs were too flimsy. The aureola had vanished when she began her climb, slithering up limb by limb, a human monkey. Soon, she clambered past him.

"It's too dangerous, Jenny. Stop!"

Suddenly, a splintering sound, agonizingly slow at first, then sickeningly fast. A limb cracked, and she fell screaming. Jenny's head smacked one of the larger branches below him. Then silence, except for the nauseating thud when she hit the ground.

Granddaddy Stamford took Jenny up to one of the farmhouse bedrooms where she died before the Wilmington doctor could get to Castle Hayne. Granddaddy advised Bill to come into the room and say goodbye. He held her cold hand and kissed her cheek.

~ * ~

Bill hadn't seen another aureola until Ezekiel's… and now this one that had wrapped around Daniel like a lover. *Sweet Lord, why me? What am I supposed to do?*

Bill heard a groan, then a splintering sound, and Charlie's frantic voice. "Look out!" A shadow passed across Bill's face as Charlie jerked him away from a falling limb. The thick branch lay just where Bill had been marching.

"Lordy, that was close!" Bill stared as icicles peeled from the bough and shattered against the planks. He'd heard such sounds before… whenever a breeze tousled a chandelier's crystals.

Charlie brushed ice from Bill's shoulders. "Damn, Possum! You've got to quit daydreaming, Billy Boy."

His mouth a sheepish smile, Bill nodded. Good old Charlie… he'd been the possum who'd got out his housewife kit and sewn the slash in Bill's shell jacket while an army doctor cleaned and bandaged the flesh wound. If seeing aureolas was God's gift to Bill, it was one he didn't want. Not if it meant that someone else would die without Bill able to do anything about it. Actually, he'd never tried to thwart an aureola. They terrified him; so did the thought of taming one. It was bad enough marching toward a battle; he didn't need to muse over things way too big for an insignificant man's mind.

"You're right, Charlie," Bill agreed, fingering his friend's mend job. "Daydreaming before a battle isn't a good thing."

The ice storm had devastated the trees. Ahead, limbs and the occasional trunk littered the turnpike, slowing up wagons, field artillery limbers and caissons. Bill's teeth chattered. Not as loud as the sounds his boots made as they slapped freezing water, but noisy enough for Charlie to eye him drolly. Sweet lord, how he wished an overcoat cloaked his shivering body. He knew he looked like a sourpuss.

Suddenly, Bill lost his footing, his boots sliding forward, his butt slamming planks. Charlie and Kenny went down too. Somehow, Daniel kept his footing. Invisible ice. Cursing, grabbing his rifle, Bill crawled beyond the ice, then scrambled to his feet. Winchester lay fourteen miles beyond Bunker Hill. An eternity, considering the way Bill felt. Tiny icicles dangled from his nose. His fingers tingled with pain. At least he had boots; some Second Corps men marched in their bare feet, their brogans or boots too tattered to bother wearing. He'd heard Kenny describe how Eighteenth soldiers at Sharpsburg stripped brogans off dead Yanks. Some took blankets, tent halves, overcoats, even coffee. War and deprivation make men do things they'd never do in civilian life.

Beside Bill, Daniel staggered and lurched to the edge of the turnpike. Legs wobbly, he collapsed to his knees, then fell back onto his buttocks. "Give me strength, Lord," he groaned, pounding the slushy ground.

Kenny reached out to help his possum to his feet. "We're almost to Winchester."

"Leave me. I'll catch up." Daniel coughed, initiating a fit that didn't want to stop. He visibly weakened as the hacking continued. Gloom clouded his face. He grimaced as the coughing finally subsided. "Need to rest. I'll be fine."

"You need to keep moving in this cold and sleet." Kenny seized Daniel's right shoulder, Bill the other. Together, they lugged him to his feet. Daniel quivered as they half carried, half dragged him toward Winchester. He too needed a frockcoat, just like all the soldiers needed them. The Army of Northern

Virginia's Quartermaster should be hung from the nearest chestnut tree, Bill thought as he reshuffled Daniel's weight.

Had Bill just decided to try to outwit the aureola? Maybe if they'd left Daniel behind, it would have claimed him. He really had no way of knowing. But Bill couldn't let Daniel sit in the freezing mud and suffer. He'd do his darndest to keep his new friend alive.

As noontime drew near, Winchester's steeples, chimneys and courthouse tower poked above the misty horizon. The sleet persisted as the boys marched into the town, pelting their hats and kepis... thump, thump, thump. Ignoring the ugly weather, patriots lined the sidewalks and crowded porches and balconies, cheering Bill and his fellow soldiers as they advanced through the town of four thousand people. Two middle-aged women wearing yesteryear's winter dresses waved miniature Bonnie Blue Flags from the plank sidewalk in front of a fancy mansion. Slaves held umbrellas above their heads.

"Those boys are freezing," one of the women said, her voice filled with anger. "Look, Gladys, they don't have overcoats and gloves."

"One's missing shoes, Sarah," Gladys said, clearly repulsed by the sight. "And another and another. What's wrong with Richmond?"

Nodding, Sarah exclaimed, "Oh my! Their fingers are so red. Those muskets must be biting cold." She turned to her house slave. "Scipio, go to the house and get as many mittens as you can."

"Yessum, mistress." Slip-sliding, Scipio beelined for the house, scuttled up the steps onto the wraparound porch, then darted through the front doorway. Moments later, Scipio and three other slaves were running along the columns handing out mittens to boys without gloves.

Teeth chattering, Daniel strained to fit his quivering fingers into a pair handed to him by Scipio. Finally successful, he clapped his hands together and coughed.

Bill seized Scipio's sleeve, preventing him from racing to other soldiers needing mittens. "Please, ask your mistress if she can spare a frockcoat for my friend. He's suffering so."

Daniel raised his newly gloved hand. "No, I don't need—"

Ignoring Daniel's protests, Scipio took off his coat and waved it in the soldier's face until he reluctantly took it. "My mistress has been good to me. She'd want me to do this fer ya."

Bill helped Daniel don the coat, even as the devout private grumbled under his breath. "Don't want to hear another cough out of you," Bill joked.

Daniel rolled his eyes as he smothered a cough.

The Eighteenth marched past burnt buildings, wood-and-brick casualties of past battles. While working in his father's newspaper office and print shop, Bill had read Richmond newspaper accounts describing the Kernstown and Winchester battles. With the railroads a staging point in the Shenandoah Valley, Winchester would likely see more battles before the bugles and guns grew silent. Already, it had changed hands several times, the shuttlecock of the Confederacy. For these Southern patriots, the war had a physical cost, unlike Kenansville. At the outskirts of Winchester, some townspeople braving the sleet stood in the yard of a church and sang "When Johnny Comes Marching Home." The boys of the Eighteenth joined in.

The Butternuts pitched their tents in the darkness with sleet pouring down on them. Bill and Charlie slept huddled together, sharing brittle warmth in the freezing cold. Nestling with Charlie wasn't all beer and skittles, not like sparking with Becky, but Bill would have slept with the devil to stay warm. Some of the men didn't bring their tents; they slept wrapped in their drenched blankets under a tree or bunched up against shrubbery, not even a rubber ground blanket beneath them. Bill didn't know what they were thinking... maybe they needed their mommas to shout out: "Make your bed! Button up your coat! It's cold and rainy outside!"

The new day brought relief from the sleet and rain, but wretched cold still gripped the land. Bill and Charlie packed the tent and resumed the march south to New Market, another town in the valley, surrounded by the Blue Ridge to the east and the Appalachians to the west.

At New Market, the Eighteenth turned eastward through the Luray Valley and Fisher's Gap. So far, the regiment hadn't come into contact with any snooping Blue-Bellies, and that was fine with Bill. He'd fight when the mini balls started flying, but he'd be happy if that didn't happen until spring. Unlikely, he knew. Why else send Jackson's famed foot cavalry on a dash south?

Charlie had heard a rumor. General Jackson wanted his corps to swing below the Rappahannock River near Fredericksburg. The columns were approaching Madison. That's about one hundred and thirty miles over the last eight days. To reach Fredericksburg would require another sixty-some miles of marching in vile weather. Their marching fortunes were about to change... and for the better. As they approached Madison Courthouse, they found Southern patriots selling moonshine whiskey, or bark juice, as Charlie called it.

The great majority of Second Corps officers turned a blind eye. Bill, Charlie, Kenny and even Bible-reading Daniel were grateful. The bark juice bulwarked them against not only the cold, but the hours of muscle-numbing marching as well. Some soldiers fell out to rest, stragglers who'd hopefully catch up before nightfall. One straggler from another company lay sprawled alongside the road, so drained he ignored the mud.

"You should buy him bark juice, Billy Boy," Charlie said playfully. "Probably bring his legs back to life."

"I'll get some… for us." Bill hoped he never reached the point where he couldn't keep up with his buddies. "That fellow can buy his own whiskey."

"You still reckon Becky Powell's worth this traipsin' through cold and sleet?" Charlie skipped for a short distance, as if a boy again. "Fine winter weather we're havin'. Nothin' like glorious sleet to keep a fella awake for some letter-writin' to his sweetheart."

Bill groaned. "Yep, glad I joined. I do get a bit perturbed knowing the buggers with the gold braiding have their darkies to pitch their highfalutin tents and wait on them hand and foot… when we're freezing."

Charlie grinned. "Now you're seein' my point of view." At a bend in the road, a farmer stood beside a rough-hewed table supporting bark-juice bottles that once held bitter-tasting medicine. "Goin' to get me a bottle. How about you, Billy Boy?"

"I'm worried about repercussions. General Jackson's about as devout as they come." Bill raised his head heavenward. "Devout Presbyterian. A teetotaler. A stickler for rules."

"The dice and the card playin' didn't stop back at Bunker Hill. I ain't worried about Stonewall. I'm more worried about this damned cold killin' me if I don't get whiskey in my belly." Charlie raised his voice and sang "Vive La Compagnie…" "Let every good fellow now join in our song, vive la compagnie! Success to each other, and pass it along, vive la compagnie!"

Bill had heard that Jackson and the Eighteenth's division commander, A.P. Hill, were feuding over perceived dishonor. The kind of feud that would leave a teetotaler like Jackson fuming if he heard of his army's dash for bark juice. Bill would risk Jackson's wrath… he wanted a drink in the most desperate way. Even more than the feel of Becky's lips on his mouth. He joined in with the singing.

"Swindlers!" Charlie harrumphed when he learned what the farmer was charging. "They shouldn't be charging soldiers. We're protectin' their butts."

Bill dug into his bread bag and waved a couple of Confederate dollar bills in the farmer's face. Soon Bill had the bottle tucked away in his haversack. "There's one thing all Americans agree on. Making money. No doubt Yanks too would grumble if this was Pennsylvania."

Charlie harrumphed some more, but paid the moonshiner for a bottle, then the two possums rushed back into the columns.

Four days later, the whiskey long consumed, they climbed a ridge and looked down on the waters of the Rappahannock sparkling in sunlight. They'd covered more than one hundred and eighty miles in twelve days, faster than the Yankees who dawdled, in no hurry to cross the Rappahannock. The boys figured they faced a battle sometime in the next few days. Bill found himself thinking like the great Jackson. *What will be, will be. It's all foreordained.*

Ten

Misery on the Rappahannock

In the early evening under a dreary sky, Bill hunkered on a log, his legs splayed toward the campfire flames. A candle in a bayonet jammed into the frozen ground provided enough light for him to write a few lines to Becky. A frying pan offered a solid surface for his pencil and paper. He chewed the end of the pencil as he considered the next sentences he wanted to write, ones that would touch her heart. Already, he'd written: "We're close to a battle. I've been doing a lot of praying. I want so much to get to know you better. I'll say it—even if your father reads my words—I want to taste your kisses, feast on your sweet bubbies. But if I don't get that chance, I want you to know that you'll be the last person on my mind when I take my final breath. I'm so cold. Day after day we have freezing weather. Hard times. We don't get near enough to eat."

Now he needed to tell her in a fairytale way how no other woman could ever compare to her beauty. "The veterans warn me not to think of your love when it's time for battle. It can get a soldier killed. I tell them, 'Hogwash!' My thoughts of how beautiful you look in your day-dresses are shields that protect me from Yankee mini balls. I carry your letter in my shell-jacket pocket against my heart. I love you so much, Becky. Please write to me. Your words sustain me. I'll write my last sentences in a few minutes. Our colonel approaches. I need to hear his orders."

Folding the letter, Bill slipped the paper into his jacket pocket along with the pencil. It was a snug fit since Becky's letter to him already occupied pocket space. A shadow flitted along the ground near Bill. He raised his head toward the sound of coughing... Daniel, still afflicted with his perpetual cold.

"I like that man. Doesn't keep us in the dark. A good company commander." Daniel rested a hand on Bill's shoulder. "He just talked to General Lane. Must be some important doings planned. Makes me nervous. Lane's only been brigade commander since Sharpsburg, since General Branch's death. Not tested. Fine regimental commander, though."

"Lane will do fine." Bill patted Daniel's hand. "That cough isn't getting better. Take care of yourself, Daniel."

Daniel hadn't died during the march. Maybe the cough would claim him. Jenny and Ezekiel... they died soon after the aureolas. Maybe the Lord was teasing Bill this time. Two weeks and still alive. A man could hope.

Lieutenant Colonel Purdie stopped at Bill's campfire. Rising, Bill saluted him. Purdie's presence drew soldiers from surrounding fires, who crowded close to make sure they heard his words clearly. "Major General Hill's staff meeting just ended," Purdie told everyone. "General Lane says we're to move to the land around Thomas Yerby's house. Belvoir, about six miles southeast of Fredericksburg."

"Battle comin', Colonel?" The question belonged to Charlie, who'd slipped between Bill and Daniel.

"Soon." Purdie acknowledged Charlie with a sharp nod. "We're to make sure Burnside can't cross the river near Yerby's house." Purdie glanced at a pocket watch visible in the fire- and candlelight. "Get what sleep you can. We'll march to Belvoir at four in the morning." A faint smile softened Purdie's face, stern below a marvelous crown of black curls. "Yerby's expecting us."

Once Purdie headed for his tent and the care of his darky servant, Bill plopped back down on the log. The orders weren't unexpected. "Six miles. I'm not sure I can walk half a mile. I should've waited and let the draft get me."

Charlie fiddled with Bill's shell jacket near the inside pocket. "Finish your letter to this Becky of yours. That should remind you why you didn't wait." Charlie still had some whiskey left, so he took a swig from his canteen. "Sleep by the fire, Billy Boy. That should warm those hurtin' muscles. Nearly two hundred miles. What's another six?"

Bill retrieved his pencil and the unfinished letter. "It's been so cold even the polar bears are complaining." He rolled his eyes. "And the sad part... I'm going to have to cuddle with you tonight to stay warm."

"Yep, it's too damned cold to even chew over the mess the Richmond politicians are makin'. We win the battles; they're goin' to lose the war." Charlie winked at Bill. "Cuddle, eh? The sacrifices I must make to stay warm and win the war."

Bill didn't feel much like writing flowery prose to Becky. She knew he loved her. He curtailed the letter with three short sentences. "Purdie just gave us our orders. Moving out in a few hours. Say a prayer for me."

Daniel looked over Bill's shoulder at the letter. "Tell her to say a prayer for me too."

Bill jerked at the sound of Daniel's voice. He eyeballed him as the man settled on a log before the fire. After the hours and hours trudging through the sleet, Bill could almost believe the aureola had never happened, a dream experienced while he slogged along in a daze. Except he knew otherwise. The aureola did flare around Daniel back at Bunker Hill. Just like Jenny and Ezekiel, except Daniel still lived, still defied what the aureolas predestined. Maybe the darkey's coat kept him alive? Maybe it just delayed his inevitable death? Bill didn't know what to believe.

Returning from a piss, Kenny warmed his hands at the fire. "We'll never get warm until we can build our huts and stoke the chimney fires. That ain't goin' to happen till we send the Blue-Bellies scurryin' back to Washington. Sooner the better. I'm goin' to build the warmest hut between Washington and the Rappahannock, sit in my chair and do some whittlin'."

Daniel steepled his hands. "I'll sit in mine and read Galatians."

At four in the morning, and the darkness still shrouding the land, they marched. General Lane was a punctual commander; he'd not risk annoying his boss, A.P. Hill. As soon as the brigade reached Yerby's Belvoir, the men dug rudimentary breastworks and waited for the Yanks to try to cross the Rappahannock. Just another day of cold beneath a bleak, gray sky.

The river was much deeper and the current faster than where the Eighteenth had forded it on the march from Bunker Hill. Charlie had been reconnoitering the other companies in the Eighteenth, even other regiments. He should have been the son of Kenansville's editor, not Bill, who couldn't keep his teeth from chattering. Between Daniel's coughing and Bill's talkative teeth, it sounded like an off-key Kenansville bandshell concert.

Unsheathing his bayonet, Charlie thrust the blade into the ground and scooped up the loose soil with his tin cup, helping Bill strengthen the breastwork in front of them. "Here's the scuttlebutt, Billy Boy. General Lee has us watchin' the river south of Fredericksburg to Port Royal. Longstreet's guardin' the high ground from Fredericksburg westward. That's thirty miles of riverfront. The Blue-Bellies are over there"—he pointed to the land beyond the far bank—"keepin' quiet. Why ain't they layin' pontoon bridges? Are we goin' to spend the winter starin' at each other?"

Many in Company G liked Charlie's gossip. Sometimes he was barely above a camp canard, a tall-tale spinner high on melodrama, low on truth. Gossip or intelligence, it gave the boys a glimpse of the bigger picture and conversation fodder on cold nights. Nothing could get privates and corporals riled up than a debate on the competence of generals.

Kenny rested his dirt-filled cup on top of the half-finished breastwork. "I expect the Yanks will come across soon. They're like a dog that keeps gettin' his nose mauled by the family cat. Worst possible weather for a battle, yet they'll attack. Burnside captured New Bern, so Lincoln must reckon he's the North's new Joshua."

Daniel gazed out at the river, cloaked in mist. "Lincoln's our best general. We should thank God for the North's voters. Burnside's the worst possible man for the job. Even a gal-sneaker like me knows Lincoln and the Yankee

Congress will recognize the CSA by Valentine's Day. Get ready for a victory parade in Richmond."

Bill harrumphed. "Everybody's been waiting for that parade since First Manassas. I expect we'll still be waiting in 1868. This is an endless war."

Relieved by Sergeant Barnard, the four possums retreated to a campfire to warm up and cook their rations. Frying pans and coffee pots emerged from bedrolls and soon Kenny squatted at the fire cooking salt pork, cornbread and desiccated vegetables, and heating up the chicory coffee. "Lordy, I fear my bones are goin' to shatter," he grumbled, watching the salt pork sizzle in the frying pan.

Bill stretched his arms, palmed his hands against the back of his head. "Going to see if I can find the mail wagon. Time to mail Becky's letter. I want her to have it… just in case."

~ * ~

Snow fell on December 5, four inches of the wet stuff. For Bill, who didn't think it could get any sorrier, the snow proved that life in General Lee's army could get much worse. Shivering, wobbly knees banging together, he knew the Blue-Bellies across the river were just as cold and miserable, but it didn't make him feel any better. Every Butternut between Port Royal and Fredericksburg was certain Lincoln's hordes would try to build pontoon bridges; they just didn't know where and when. The Yanks were exasperatingly slow, Bill thought, as he nestled behind the breastwork and gazed at the misty, snow-cloaked land… the trees, fences, the bramble bushes. Deceptively beautiful, it would turn deadly when the Blue-Bellies emerged through the mist.

Gripping a snowball, Phillip DeLuca, a Company B private, tried to instigate a regimental snowball war. He failed; nobody was in the mood. Even Charlie declined.

Perched beside Bill, Charlie eyed the fog twirls veiling the countryside between the Confederates and the Rappahannock. "God, I hope their fingers are fallin' off! What the hell is Burnside thinkin'? His people should be building huts, not tryin' to bridge the river and start a damned battle in the wintertime. Madness!" He kicked snow into the air and watched the flakes float groundward.

"Rest assured the Blue-Bellies are warm in winter overcoats," Bill said, letting his musket rest against the breastwork, the barrel too damned cold to touch. "Burnside's lousy at carrying out battles, but his quartermaster makes sure the Blue-Bellies are properly winterized. That's what the veterans say." Scowling, Bill eyed his boots, frayed, soles partly detached. He'd sworn he would never abscond with anything on a dead Yank. Now he wasn't sure. His belly growled. When was the last time he felt full? Three months ago at Becky's house after his birthday meal.

Soon after Sergeant Barnard freed them from manning their section of breastwork, Bill pointed toward the Yerby house off toward the horizon. "Let's take a walk, Charlie. I'm freezing. Got to get the blood circulating."

They slogged through snow, trudging through fields that in the summer teemed with corn and wheat. Near Yerby's outbuildings, Bill and Charlie trekked past orchards, snow clinging to limbs. Beyond, they wandered past slave shacks, their interiors dark. A gaggle of slave children wearing patched coats lobbed snowballs at each other. When they noticed the two soldiers, they fled into nearby woods.

Squatting, Charlie packed a snowball and chucked it at the fleeing children. "If abolitionists get their way, those slave kids will someday work in factories in New York City and Cleveland."

"Earning a real wage, eh?"

"Livin' in homes paid for in blood and sweat. Sendin' their kids to schools to get the education they weren't allowed. Not a bad thing, right?"

Bill nodded. "A good thing. You'll not find me disagreeing." Bill watched as the woodland shadows masked the kids. "Those fossil bones scientists are finding—the giant ones—they're called Dinosauria. Slavery's going to be just like those dinosaurs. The Romans had slaves. They also had steam toys, but no one turned them into something useful. It took the Brits to see the value of coal and steam power. The Yanks are forward-thinkers. They've greenbacks dancing in their heads. We Southerners... we got scared of our darkies, got myopic. Look at our railroads; they barely function. Even if we whip Burnside and capture Washington, I think slavery's days are numbered. Otherwise, we're doomed to stay a backward nation."

"You're finally makin' sense, Billy Boy." Charlie laughed. "If we weren't so self-righteous, we could learn something from the Blue-Bellies. Regardless, we Southern fellas are better joinin' giblets with the ladies."

Hardly noticing, they'd made their way past Yerby's ice house and overseer's cottage. Ahead, under yet another dark sky without stars or the moon, Yerby's mansion sparkled, candlelight flickering in all the windows. The snow blanket and the candlelight gave the gray mansion a magical look. The house and Massaponax Creek would make a splendid daguerreotype, Bill decided.

Near the mansion's colonnaded porch, grooms wearing blue frockcoats tended to officers' horses, leading them to the stables. The officers bounded up the steps and into the house, perhaps to give Stonewall an update on defensive artillery fortifications and Yankee troop movements. With smoke rising from chimneys, the parlor and other rooms were contentedly warm for the officers in sharp contrast to the snow and bitter cold at the breastworks. Seen through the window glass, officers accepted tea from pretty girls, who flitted fans as they flirted. A party, Bill surmised, annoyed at the splendidly uniformed buggers drinking tea while their men froze in the trenches. Tea, not liquor or wine. Bill didn't bother to smother a laugh. With Stonewall in command, no spirits for the generals, colonels and captains.

"Not much sufferin' here." Charlie puckered, as if he'd swallowed something sour.

Bill held a finger to his lips. "Watch your tongue." He pointed to officers on the front porch puffing on pipes. "Need to watch what we say. And not get any closer."

When the tobacco-smoking officers swung their gazes to Bill and Charlie, the two possums turned and headed back to the breastworks.

Charlie grumbled, "House slaves to serve their every need, then when they get back to their tents, their blackies ready to baby them. Lordy, I hate the gentry."

Eleven

A River Crossing

The land rumbled, like the low growl of a far-off thunderstorm. Bill craned his head above the breastwork, the wall of dirt piled high to stop cannonballs and mini balls. No lightning flashing inside black clouds. Instead, a mostly blue sky beneath farmland nearly free of a first-light mist. An unusual December so far. Snow a few days earlier, now melted on this bone-chilling morning, December 10, 1862. Bill looked forward to the afternoon when the temperature should climb into the balmy fifties. Except the Blue-Bellies had been noticeably noisy on the other side of the Rappahannock.

Near Bill, Captain John Poisson, a Wilmington shopkeeper before the war, made his way along the breastworks, chatting with the men. Noticing Bill's pensive expression, the captain remarked, "Yankee gunboats firing at D.H. Hill."

"That's a long ways away. Port Royal." Bill shook his head as if to clear cobwebs.

The heavyset captain with his head of storm-black hair chuckled, his coarse voice strong. "Pratt's Bluff, to be exact."

More rumbles prickled Bill's eardrums. "That's more than fifteen miles away, sir."

"You're right, Private. Fog in the mornin, warm afternoons." Poisson gazed skyward. "Weather's unusual. Sound's carryin'. That's why we're hearin' the big guns."

Charlie had been listening. "They're goin' to try to break through our lines up at Port Royal?"

The captain shrugged. "Maybe. Or tryin' to fool us, and the real attack's comin' here at Fredericksburg." Poisson moved on away from Bill and Charlie, then turned around. "We got to stay alert. Been heaps of commotion on the Union side of the river at Fredericksburg. Be ready, boys! Could be movin' out soon." He rambled away, chatting with more soldiers.

Charlie took a long, painful breath, then knitted his brow. "Looks like we might see the elephant tomorrow."

"Never liked circuses." Again, Bill took a quick look at the landscape to his front, listening for any sounds carrying across the river. The wind rustled weed stalks. A dog barked. Horses neighed. Artillery on Pratt's Bluff growled. Curiosity sated, he dipped his head below the breastwork's crown.

Chewing his lower lip, Bill glanced at Daniel. A snowstorm, sleet, and days and days of marching separated Bill from when he had seen Daniel's aureola. Now it seemed more a dream than something real, like Daniel's ongoing hacking. The cough could eventually kill him. So could the battle, whenever it happened. Bill peered along the breastworks at dozens of soldiers waiting for orders. Some would die in the days ahead... and not one aureola proclaimed their deaths. *What are you trying to tell me, Lord?* He returned his gaze to Daniel.

"Why are you staring at me?" Daniel challenged.

"Can't help it. You're by far the most handsome man in the Army of Northern Virginia. I got to keep Becky away from you."

"Just Daniel?" Charlie muttered, pretending outrage.

"Becky has girlfriends, Charlie." Bill snorted. "But they're the church-going type."

"There's always room for more than one woman in my heart," Charlie rejoined.

Kenny guffawed. "Since you're offerin' your sweetheart's girlfriends, I'll take one."

Smothering a giggle, Bill produced a respectable representation of an incredulous look. "But I thought you loved your Bunker Hill widow woman?"

"I've a wife back in Whiteville." Kenny rested a hand against his heart. "Goin' to return to her lovin' bosom, lads. If some damned Blue-Belly don't put a mini ball in my brain in a day or two."

Daniel scratched at his shoulder. Probably lice. "You're too ornery to die in this war."

Charlie ribbed, "Too ornery and a cunny chaser."

Smirking, Kenny shot back, "Not once I get back to my Whiteville nightingale."

With sunset approaching and the temperature plunging, Sergeant Barnard sent men to relieve Bill and his chuckaboos. They headed for their lean-tos and cold campfires, except for Charlie. He beelined for A.P. Hill's left flank where it linked with Longstreet's line, which overlooked the steeples of Fredericksburg. He hadn't gossiped with men from that section of the line.

"Don't get yourself captured," Kenny warned good-naturedly, a grin on his weary face.

"Too fast for the Blue-Belly slowpokes," Charlie joked as he double-stepped away. "I'll be a hundred years old before they build those pontoon bridges."

~ * ~

Charlie returned, hardly able to contain his enthusiasm, to share the latest gossip. Even before he warmed his hands over the flames, he plopped down on his knees and blathered, "Longstreet's ordered Barksdale's brigade into Fredericksburg to make the Yankee crossing a living hell. General Lee must reckon they'll start coupling the pontoons soon." Charlie grinned. "You scared, Bill?"

Gritting his teeth, Bill fed more logs into the fire, raising the heat to the coffee pot while chasing away the evening's chill. "No time right now." *Lord, forgive my lie. And keep my fears at bay.*

Charlie filled a cup of chicory coffee. His hands quivered as he held the cup in front of his face. "I'm too excited to be scared. That make sense? Maybe after the battle."

The half-moon hung in the night sky, sharing the darkness with stars and a few slow-moving clouds. Barely a breeze stirred the land this December night, just two weeks until Christmas. The moonlight shined on a landscape thinned of trees around Yerby's Belvoir Plantation. Bill heard the distant sound of axes biting into trees, soldiers taking them down for firewood. The noise would get more ferocious when General Lee's boys whipped the Blue-Bellies and were finally allowed to build winter huts.

Daniel sipped coffee. The hand grasping the cup's handle was rock steady. "At Gaines Mill, I realized I was firing into the air, not even close to any Blue-Bellies. So jittery I didn't even think to aim. Charlie, the battle's going to be the most exciting and the most terrifying thing that has ever happened to you. Just remember not to leave your ramrod in the barrel. Shoot straight, and you'll do fine."

Kenny added, unusually serious, "We're always scared. We do our duty, stand with our possums."

Bill kept checking his pocket watch. It gave his fingers something to do. The latest check? Three in the morning. No one slept, not with Charlie's news that Barksdale's brigade had taken up sniping positions in Fredericksburg. He waited to hear shell fire. Nothing. The gunfire from the Union gunboats downriver at Port Royal had died down hours ago. Incredibly, many old-timers were sleeping in their blankets, nestled close to campfires. He heard Tar Heel drawls as flames crackled. Not one glowing aureola swaddled a soldier. The enigma perplexed him. If an aureola foretold death, many of those soldiers should shine with aureolas. Bill shrugged away his frustration. Sometimes it was easier to just say: *Thy will be done.* And wait.

Soon, the moon dipped below the horizon, followed by the first tendrils of mist lit by starlight. Bill slipped away to the lean-to and returned with his blanket. At a nearby campfire, an insomniac wrote a letter as his buddy snored. Perhaps a letter from his heart to his wife and children? Bill heaved a sigh that drew looks from Daniel, Charlie and Kenny. No doubt the letter lacked any mention of slavery or states' rights. He couldn't stop yawning. His head slumped. *Don't think about the coming fight. Think about Becky's bubbies. About how sumptuous Malinda's strawberry...*

Cannon fire shocked him awake. Four raucous booms echoed across the landscape. Not from Port Royal. Not this time. These originated in Fredericksburg, six miles away. The campfire's flames had died down, but enough light remained to spur Bill to dig out his watch. The clock-face read five in the morning. Bill had managed two hours of sleep. Nonetheless, he knew he'd not be sleepy on this day, December 11, 1862.

Across the Rappahannock, the barrels of Yankee cannons flashed. Invisible to the naked eye, cannonballs arched across the dark sky, their destinations the businesses and homes of Fredericksburg's citizens. *Burnside, burn in hell*, Bill thought. *Bastard! He's attacking innocents.*

More barrel flashes. Fiery mortar rounds, fuses burning red, rocketed across Fredericksburg's black sky, followed by thunderous explosions. Ravening flames leaped skyward above burning buildings; the ground beneath Bill rumbled. Stacked logs waiting to be fed into the campfire toppled. One jarred the coffee pot, nearly overturning it.

Further fire from the Yankee side of the river… no visible trails to mark the shrieks. Near the rooftops, grand flashes lit the sky. "Canister," Daniel growled. "Aimed at Barksdale's men… and anyone else out on the streets."

Soon, the Yankees and Confederates were exchanging artillery fire. As Bill hunkered in his blanket before the dying fire, he scratched his nose, and detected the stench of gunpowder and burning wood. Shuddering, he thought of the mothers huddled in Fredericksburg's basements hugging their petrified children. *God help those poor people.*

He could put two-and-two together. No need for Charlie to go from campfire to campfire gathering gossip. Bill glanced at his friend, who lounged beside the campfire rubbing his eyes. Longstreet's men must have spotted Yankee engineers building those damned pontoon bridges.

"Feel the elephant rampaging, Charlie?" Bill stoked the fire, resurrecting the flames. "The earth's shaking."

"Rattlin' my bones," Charlie concurred.

Kenny finished off the leftover coffee, then poured water into the pot and stirred in chicory coffee before setting it on the coals. "Looks like the Yanks want to dance."

"Lord, protect my friends and comrades today… and always your will be done." Daniel unsteepled his hands and said, "Amen." Bill, Kenny and Charlie echoed Daniel's amen.

Soon, first light painted the sky. Gazing toward Fredericksburg, Bill couldn't see a thing. Fog cloaked the hilltops, farm-field stubble, the Massaponax, Prospect Hill, and the steeples and bell towers. Rising, he jumped up and down, warming himself. It helped for a few minutes, but then the cold clutched him again.

Between cannonball and shell shrieks and booms, Bill heard the cracking sounds of musket fire echoing across the farmland.

"Sounds like Longstreet's snipers found themselves some pontoon builders," Kenny quipped, then sampled his newly made coffee. "Wish I had the real stuff, but this will do. Don't hold back, boys. What we need now is hot, not good."

Colonel Purdie meandered among Company G's campfires sometime after eight o'clock, trumpeting news from General Lane. "Battle's coming." Voice sharp, he barked the words out in a *get-moving* manner. "Cook two days of rations; fill your cartridge box. Sixty rounds. Yanks want a fight." Then Purdie was gone, moving to other campfires to share General Jackson's orders.

Bill couldn't stop his hands from shaking. Soon, his whole body shook. *Lord, give me courage.* Frustrated, Bill tried to claw his fingers into the soil and failed. Too cold, too hard. Dampness and the mist penetrated to the bone.

Donning a mask of stoicism, Bill calmed his fidgeting fingers and stuffed cartridges into his sixty-dead-men box as the cannon fire at Fredericksburg abruptly grew louder, almost deafening. Triple the number of shells exploded above the town, raining fire on the buildings. Flames roared high into the air. The ground at the campfire grumbled, shaking Bill's toes and his knees.

"Looks like the Blue-Bellies are intensifyin' their fight," Kenny said casually, drinking coffee as he loaded his cartridge box. "I'd say our boys inside Fredericksburg are irritatin' their bridge-buildin' engineers, and it's hard to dislodge men hidin' in cellars." He grinned. "Loud enough for you, Bill and Charlie?"

Both nodded vigorously.

"That ain't loud," Daniel weighed in. "We've not heard the Second Corps' cannons."

Bill mulled aloud, "Sweet Jesus... I pray we've evacuated the citizens."

"Expect so," Daniel said as he scanned the firecracker sky above Fredericksburg. "General Lee's a good man. He'll look after them."

~ * ~

Hurry up and wait... that's how Bill saw the day. The raucous noise coming from Fredericksburg meant something was afoot, but that didn't mean the Eighteenth and the rest of the brigade were going to clank and rattle into battle lines. The battle for the Eighteenth turned out to consist of cooking rations, preparing cartridges... and waiting.

As the first pink of sunset mottled the sky, Charlie joked, "Looks like another night of snugglin', Billy Boy."

"I'd rather it be July and the sky be the one at Wrightsville Beach, but I guess I'm stuck with you, Charlie."

Bill refilled his coffee cup and drank. Reclining on his side, shrouded in his blanket, he closed his eyes and imagined Becky burrowed beside him, sharing warmth.

As the evening temperature plunged, Charlie tossed a couple of logs on the fire. Bill could feel the rejuvenated flames, the heat a pleasing caress to his face and hands. He opened his eyes. With daylight nearly spent, the Fredericksburg sky glowed ruddy red. The stirred breeze bore the smell of burning buildings and black powder.

Kenny cooked dinner for the four. More salt pork and desiccated vegetables for a stew. Always tasteless, this time it made Bill nauseous. They piled the campfire high with firewood so it would burn hot during the night. Bill lay on his back, looking up at the smoke-tinged sky, the smell foul, like he imagined hell. He must have somehow drifted off into sleep; how else could Sergeant Barnard's gruff voice startle him. "Up, damn it! We've a battle to fight." Hands cold and jittery, Bill somehow managed to extract his watch and read the face. A few minutes before five in the morning.

Darkness still cloaked the Yerby Plantation. Quickly, he and Charlie made chicory coffee and a breakfast of hardtack and desiccated vegetables. Bill felt the food writhing up his throat, but he forced it back inside his rumbling belly. Again, the sergeant's voice rang out: "You men who are barefoot. Stay put. You're excused from this battle. General Lee's orders."

Charlie pretended to pull off his boots, earning a rebuke from Bill: "Not funny!"

At six-thirty in the morning, the Eighteenth formed into column, and with the rest of the brigade, tramped toward the woods and fields around Prospect Hill.

Twelve

Baptism of Fire

As if Napoleon in a Meissonier painting, Colonel Purdie led the brigade away from their breastworks at first light. Bill made note since it could portend the start of his last day on Earth... Friday, December 12, 1862. With Purdie astride his Morgan mount, the brigade slogged away from the Yerby Plantation, boots and brogans vibrating the carriage bridge spanning Massaponax Creek. The men were eerily silent as they marched away from their smothered campfires.

Morning mist clung to the low lands around Prospect Hill, a miasma of smells... of charred wood, roof tar, flax-and-wool rugs and whatnot. Out of this gut-wrenching fog emerged refugee families making their way toward what Bill hoped were country homes of loved ones living beyond the reach of Blue-Belly guns. A good mile northwest of their old breastworks, Company G men passed a tent town of mothers, children and grandparents clustered around meager campfires, dazed eyes fixed on the soldiers. No cheers for them. Not one waist-high boy darted away from his mama to march alongside the Butternuts. No longer the summer of 1861.

As the sun rose above the treetops, the freezing temperatures began to rise, but not as fast as Bill wanted. It remained cold enough to snow. The Eighteenth's five companies snaked along in the middle of A.P. Hill's division. To the front or behind were Hill's other brigades... Anderson's, Garland's, Ripley's, Rhodes, and the artillery train. Jittery murmurs traveled like a wave rushing toward the sand dunes of Wrightsville Beach.

Charlie jabbed his hand toward a ridge blanketed in fog, except for its crest of skeletal trees. "See? Riders."

Trotting from the mist like King Richard the Lionheart out of a child's storybook were Stonewall and his staff, riding the hilltop, eyeing the land's layout.

"Damned fog makes it nigh impossible to see," Kenny grumbled. "But I don't need to see to know what they're lookin' at, boys. Stonewall's watching Hill place the division."

"Love to be up there with 'em seein' how we're goin' to fight the battle," Charlie said, regret in his voice. "Anyone know how to turn me into a fly so I can settle on Stonewall's shoulder?"

Visualizing Charlie as an insect perched on the general's shoulder turned Bill's thoughts to aureolas. He didn't know if he considered them magic. He couldn't control them, and he sure as hell didn't want to see one appearing around another friend... or even a stranger. Pulling a rabbit out of a hat... that was fun. Or making a beautiful lady disappear and then reappear. Knowing someone was going to die—Bill shuddered as he glanced at Daniel—withered the soul. Of course, others would die today, but he'd not seen aureolas around them. *The Good Book says turn my burdens over to you, Lord. I have. Take back your aureolas or at least tell me what I should do after I see one. Let the death happen? Try to prevent it? Learn to live with my frustration?*

Charlie smacked Bill on the arm. "Daydreamin' about Becky?"

"I'm always thinking about her, Charlie. You know that." A tiny lie, one that turned into a tidal wave of guilt. He should think more about Becky and less about aureolas. Going into battle, and he has to be reminded of Becky by Charlie. "She's the reason I joined up." Bill laughed. "Went to war so I could court Becky Powell." He knew it sounded ridiculous, but it had been the final kick in the buttocks that got him to sign the recruiting papers.

Along with Fredericksburg's stench, Bill sniffed something new, a hotchpotch of smells from the Massaponax and its banks of rotting vegetation. A stench but almost pleasant compared with the stink coming from the smoke columns rising in Fredericksburg. With Becky fresh in his mind, he thought of the rose water scent she bore when she crawled into bed alongside him.

The Eighteenth and the brigade's other regiments reached the hastily thrown-up breastworks of Texas General John Hood's troops at eleven o'clock and relieved them. They climbed a railroad embankment and settled in front of the tracks. Sergeant Barnard called the area Hamilton's Crossing, a hamlet that consisted of a Richmond, Fredericksburg and Potomac depot and the Forest Hill Plantation house. Inside woods bare of summer finery, Hood's men shifted left along the ridge, shortening Longstreet's line. The breastworks were little more than ditches.

"No protection!" Kenny moaned, loud enough that Sergeant Barnard overheard.

"Well, strengthen them!" the sergeant shot back.

The ground-hugging mist was lifting, revealing Blue-Belly breastworks near the confluence of the Rappahannock and Mine Run. Three pontoon bridges were visible, no longer veiled within the breeze-stirred whirls.

The higher the breastwork, the safer the soldier. Those had been the words of Sergeant McKinney on the first day of drill at Bunker Hill. So Bill set to work like a dam-building beaver. He stabbed his bayonet into the hard ground, loosening the dirt, then scooped it up with his tin cup. Inch by inch, Bill built up the breastwork's height. He took a breather and eyed other soldiers, including the former fopdoodle, Tim Donahue. The redhead sported a small axe he'd undoubtedly *borrowed* from a barn somewhere between Bunker Hill and Hamilton's Crossing.

The men only stopped to eat dinner and supper. By two o'clock, the breastwork stood two feet high. By five, three feet. When the three-quarter moon ruled high in the night sky, the dirt wall stood four feet high. Bill could fire his musket from behind it and know the barrier would stop oncoming mini balls.

With breastwork construction done for the night, Bill washed his tin cup and ate a snack of hardtack dipped in cold water. Charlie wandered the lines, visiting the Thirty-Third, Twenty-Eighth and the Thirty-Seventh. He returned angry as a hornet harried from a smashed nest.

Cursing aloud, Charlie leaned against the breastwork and glared at twinkling Yankee campfires along the Rappahannock. "The Blue-Bellies are slow, but they ain't stupid," he grated. "What the hell's wrong with A.P. Hill? He's left a gap in the marshes between us and Archer's people. Sweet Lord, Billy Boy! Them Yanks are goin' to flank us."

Bill burrowed his fingers through his thick beard. In the weeks since the train ride into Virginia, he hadn't bothered shaving. Too much trouble. "Lane's talked to Hill?"

Overhearing the conversation, Daniel added his input. "Hill can be obstinate. His feuds are fearsome."

Charlie nodded, his face a glimmer in the dim light. "Hill insists the marshes aren't passable. Says thaw ain't enough to cause the Blue-Bellies trouble."

Kenny looked up from where he stacked limbs for a small fire between the breastwork and the tracks. "Generals goin' to do what they want. Maybe it'll turn out Hill's right. He's West Point. Smart man except for his feuds. If not, we can pray a lot tonight, and tomorrow learn to fight in two directions." He laughed sourly.

One word jangled inside Bill's head: Prayer. Daniel prayed every night. Quite loudly, as if the noisier sound would speed the words past the trees, the moon and the stars to Heaven. Most of the men would pray tonight and write letters home... just in case. Bill planned to do the same. If he fell, friends would see that his letters would get to Becky and his family. For an instant, Bill thought of Daniel's aureola, then replaced it with another thought... the feel of Becky's breast as he crawled a fingertip along her areola. Smiling, he recalled his confusion between the two words... areola and aureola. What good did worrying do? Ultimately, God would prevail.

With the nearby flames providing a modicum of heat, enough to make the December night somewhat bearable, Bill leaned against the breastwork and closed his eyes. Unable to sleep, he could hear a concert of pencils scratching words onto letter paper. He opened his eyes, prepared to extract a pencil and paper from his jacket pocket. Instead, as if drawn to the sky, he looked up. For most of the past two weeks, the sky had been overcast or patchy with just enough openness to allow the moon to shine through. This night nothing interfered.

He awoke shortly before sunrise, his back stiff and still pressed against the breastwork, pencil and paper never extracted from his pocket. Next to him, Charlie snored. Down the line, some men were awake—like Daniel and Kenny—and others slept. At first light, Bill nudged his head above the breastwork. Mist clung to the land and the Rappahannock.

In the freshness of the cold morning, vestiges of smoke from Fredericksburg's smoldering buildings comingled with the Massaponax's swamp smells. One moment *eau de bonfire* offered up a moist, earthy smell, next Bill's stomach roiled. Some of those smells had once been people's houses and shops.

Colonel Purdie walked the Eighteenth's breastworks. "Smell the smoke, boys!" Purdie said, his tone hard. "We've a reason to kill wagonloads of Yanks today. Shoot true. Make 'em pay."

The boys cheered.

By ten o'clock, sunlight had burned away the fog cloaking the fields in front of A.P. Hill's breastworks. Blue-Bellies moved parallel to the Rappahannock, then right-faced toward Richmond Road. Booms erupted. On the extreme right of the Confederate line, two Virginia mobile artillery pieces, each harnessed to their team of six horses, wheeled down Prospect Hill. Bouncing, sliding, the caissons and gun carriages kicked up dirt, stubble and foliage. They creaked and groaned as they dashed toward the Blue-Bellies. Yankee twelve-pounders fired at them, their shells missing.

Juddering to a stop, the gun crews unlimbered the rifled Blakely and twelve-pound Napoleon. With Yankee Springfields and artillery firing at them, the Virginians coolly loaded and primed their pieces. Black-powder smoke rings spewed from the barrels. The air thundered; Union infantry scattered like tumbling bowling pins.

"Sweet Jesus, those men are brave!" Daniel exclaimed. "Twenty men against the entire Union army."

"More like a Blue-Belly regiment," Kenny retorted dryly, then grinned. "Still impressive, I must say."

A cannonball rumbling across the ground smashed into the Blakely, splintering a wheel and gun carriage. Its barrel lay on the ground, muzzle half-buried in the dirt. Horses went down; shrieking; they struggled to rise. Two gunners lay unmoving in pools of blood, rammer and wormer splayed on their legs.

"Daring yes, but it's time to withdraw," Bill said, amazed that two field pieces were holding up the Yankee offensive.

He suddenly realized what he'd just witnessed. Bile gurgled up his throat; he fought not to spew the food digesting in his stomach. Except for a smidgen wetting his lower lip, he managed to keep it churning in his belly.

The remaining piece continued to fire canister at the Yankees. Desperate to evade buckshot shell fragments raining on them, the Blue-Bellies sought natural cover, hollows in the land, fallen tree limbs, boulders, even the dead.

Bill—and most of the men in the Eighteenth—craned their heads above the breastwork to watch. Appalled, Sergeant Barnard screamed into Bill's ear: "Snipers, Stamford! Want a mini ball through your forehead?"

Bill flopped to the ground as if the sergeant's voice heralded lightning. Men within hearing distance dropped as well, then looked sheepish.

As detonations rumbled across landscape near the pontoon bridges, the sergeant's voice rumbled as well: "Canister's nasty stuff, Stamford. You could be out there gettin' splattered, not the Yanks." Barnard slapped the breastwork. "Think of this as your momma's cradlin' arms. They'll keep you safe as long as you keep your noggin down."

For an hour, up to nearly eleven in the morning, the Virginia artillerymen kept the Blue-Bellies pinned down, delaying Burnside's attack. Then the Yanks assaulted the exposed artillerists, forcing them to hitch their remaining piece to the horses and bolt back to Prospect Hill. They left behind the wrecked Blakely and dead horses, but not the wounded and dead artillerists.

With the Napoleon twelve-pounder ensconced back on the hilltop, Confederate artillery bombarded the Yankees. Curiosity egging him on, Bill peered above the breastwork. The Yanks getting showered with shells and cannonballs weren't breaking but digging in, not withering under the Butternut cannonade. They looked familiar. He'd seen illustrations of them in his papa's Northern newspapers. In the Army of the Potomac, they were famous for their fancy Hardee black hats.

"Black Hatters," Kenny said, eyeing the Union force, confirming Bill's suspicions. "The Iron Brigade, the best the Blue-Bellies have." He grinned. "We need a nickname."

Charlie returned Kenny's grin. "How about Iron Smashers?"

Even more Confederate batteries opened up, filling the air with jolting booms that rattled Bill's brains and splattered dirt on his slouch hat. The Yankees answered, their artillery fire even more thunderous.

"We're goin' to see the elephant soon, Bill," Charlie predicted, hands clapped over his ears. "My reason for joinin' up seems stupid now. I may not even have a future."

Bill squeezed Charlie's shoulder. "Of course, you do, friend. You do get beat up a lot, but like my watch, you keep ticking." And the aureola wasn't around Charlie. Bill glanced at Daniel, whose lips moved silently as if in prayer.

"We're close, really, really close." Kenny's voice quivered. "*Dyin'* close."

Dying close? Don't let yourself get spooked. Bill's hands shook like a short-haired dog out in snow. He tucked them between his legs. *Can't let anyone see me like this. Lord, be my fortress!* His stomach roiled. Pain shot through his abdomen. *No! I will be a man! I will walk beside the Lord's still waters. I will trust in him.* Slowly, the shivers subsided.

He'd joined so he could someday court Becky. Like Charlie's reason, Bill's now seemed silly. Others? Many had joined to repel the invader, some for adventure and glory… shopkeepers bored by their jobs, farmers' sons running away from the plow.

The hullabaloo seemed to last for hours. Actually, it was just noontime, one hour since the Virginians hightailed it back to Prospect Hill. The Yanks fired not just at the big guns on Prospect Hill, but at the breastworks at the railroad embankment. Not only solid shot, but bolts from rifled guns roared from cannon muzzles. Huddling behind the breastwork, musket cradled against him, Bill heard the *ripping* sounds of cannonballs speeding through the air. Sometimes he'd feel a thud as one careened into the breastwork and ricocheted. There was no peeking above the wall of dirt, not with the sky alive with booms and ripping sounds, as if a giant djinn with a nasty disposition and an enormous Saracen sword had decided to slash open the blue firmament. Sometimes he'd silently recite Psalms: *The Lord is my light and my salvation, whom shall I fear?*

Explosions rained shrapnel on the Butternuts huddled behind breastworks. A hundred feet away, shrapnel sprayed three boys: Mike Snyder, Ray Benson and Tim Donahue, the recruit who'd been Sergeant McKinney's whipping boy. They writhed in pain as buddies bandaged bleeding heads and shoulders with cloth torn from shirtsleeves. Grimacing, Bill turned away, not wanting to watch fellow soldiers struggle to tame their pain. Overhead, shells shredded nearby trees.

The artillery duel sputtered into silence. As men murmured prayers, Bill turned to his trusty doodad to control his nerves… his pocket watch. One o'clock, three hours since the two horse-artillery guns had opened fire on the Yankee troops advancing along the bank of the Rappahannock. Louder than the prayers, Colonel Purdie shouted, "They're coming! Fire at my order!"

"Good God, Billy Boy! You've got to look." Charlie had inched his head above the breastwork.

Snipers be damned, the temptation proved irresistible. Bill peeked. Thousands of Union soldiers were forming into double battle lines. Officers were adjusting the lines as if about to parade before a visiting king. Bill loaded his musket and perched it atop the breastwork.

Two divisions quick-stepped toward the Butternut front lines, officers leading on their mounts. The artillery guns stayed silent, both Confederates and Yanks. Bill bit his lower lip; the sting intensified his thoughts. *Sweet Jesus, I hope we're not out of shells.* His musket's stock felt cold against his cheek.

Grayback artillery officers' strident voices lanced the warming air. "Load guns! Fire by volley!" The voices echoed down the Butternut line like rippling musket fire.

Tongues of flame roared from the muzzles of dozens of cannons. Black-powder smoke roiled just beyond them, leaving a rotten-egg smell that irritated Bill's nose. Solid shot, shell and canister thundered toward the oncoming Blue-Bellies. The rounds shredded the battle lines. Arms, legs, heads flew in all directions. Blood spurted from wounds, pooling on farm-field stubble. The Yankees closed the gaps and advanced.

"Fire at will!" artillery officers screeched.

Boom... boom... boom. The sky filled with projectiles. Their arced flights seemingly ripped open the air above the battlefield. Once, on the long march to Fredericksburg, a fresh fish told Bill the shells sounded like horses whinnying. No neighs, the air shrieked with otherworldly sounds... *whir... whir... whir... sh... sh*. Demon laughter poured from rips in the air.

The shells and cannonballs shattered more bodies, and the Blue-Bellies closed ranks. Like watching fire ants attacking a tarantula, Bill couldn't turn his eyes away from the artillery fire's bloody work. Next to him, Kenny blood-curdled a scream, "Die, bastards! Every one of ya'll!"

Sunshine sieved through the thick black-powder smoke, shining on the Blue-Bellies so that the red circles on their hats gleamed. First Corps badges. *Of course*, Bill thought, bringing his loaded musket into firing position. Black Hatters were First Corps soldiers.

Captain Poisson strode along Company G's portion of the breastworks. "Fire in volley at command! Then fire at will!" Poisson slipped between Bill and Kenny, and trained his keen eyes on the Blue-Bellies who continued pressing forward through the hail of canister balls and shell fragments. Three hundred yards away. Well within rifle and musket range. "Fire!"

Bill pressed the trigger. A sheet of fire surged out the barrel. The recoil drove the stock's butt against his shoulder. A volley of a hundred or so muskets and rifles rattled his eardrums. His ears ringing, he heard a far-off voice yell, "Fire at will!"

Just like drill, Bill reached into his cartridge box and drew out a mini ball, bit into the paper cartridge, dumped the power charge down the muzzle, inserted the bullet, rammed it, placed a percussion cap on the nipple and fired, all in thirty seconds. Not bothered by the clamor. Or men shrieking and falling away from the breastworks, faces shattered, chests spurting blood. A hard-edged veteran, not a fresh fish, not a parlor soldier. Some men had their barrels aimed too high. They weren't hitting anything. Bill knew his mini ball tore into Blue-Belly flesh.

The smell of black powder permeated the battlefield, smoke so thick he swore he could pour some into a cup and take a drink. Bill kept firing, reloading the best he could without becoming a target. It was easier to reload standing up, but that meant increasing the odds of becoming one of the wounded or somebody's darling. The Union lines were thinning, many left on the ground writhing in pain or unmoving. Thinned… but not broken. *Crazy bastards. They just keep coming.*

Intent on stopping the charge to his front, Bill didn't sense the rising commotion to his right. "We've been flanked!" someone squawked. Other voices squealed, "Flanked!" And others, "They're in our rear!"

The Thirty-Third broke and ran. No orderly retreat. Men bolted. Beyond the Thirty-Third's breastworks, no sign of the Twenty-Eighth and the Thirty-Seventh. Instead, Yanks in a ragged battle line were charging. The Blue-Bellies poured enfilade fire into the Eighteenth.

"God damn!" Daniel bellowed.

Daniel never cursed. This was serious, Bill thought. The Yanks had charged through the impassable marsh and flanked the brigade.

Charlie looked wild-eyed at Bill, then darted his gaze to the Yanks—ones to his front, then those on the flank—over and over again.

Bill aimed his musket at the Yanks to his front, hesitated then swung his gaze to the Blue-Belly battle line on his right. The ones charging head-on, rushing his breastwork at a full run, they were just two hundred yards away. He fired, his aim still pegged on the flankers.

To Bill's right, several Confederates went down. On his knees, his hands quivering, Bill struggled to reloadand not give in to the panic gurgling up from his belly. A scared voice in his head begged: *Run... run like the boys in the Thirty-Third. Run or die!* Somehow, he kept his feet planted at the breastwork.

Eighteenth officers tried to bend the line at a ninety-degree angle so the men could defend their position from the front and the flank. "Bend! Bend, boys!" Poisson hollered, then collapsed, a mini ball in his shoulder.

More Blue-Belly musketry and rifle fire... from the flank, flashes followed by puffs of smoke and whizzing bullets. Daniel slumped, coming to rest on his buttocks. He gazed open-mouthed at his belly, blood leaking from a gut wound. His eyes fixed on Kenny. "Bad luck." Daniel pressed his hands against his stomach. Blood seeped between his fingers. Blunter: "Ah, shit!"

Charlie whirled around, sending his hat flying off his head. "Can't you see? Battle's lost. No use stayin' here." He vamoosed for the rear. All around Bill, Kenny and Daniel, Eighteenth men were fleeing.

"At least he kept his rifle," Kenny wisecracked.

"Go!" Daniel jabbed his arm toward the rear.

"Not without you, Possum." Kenny dropped to his knees beside Daniel.

"I'm a goner." Daniel again pointed to the rear. "Get before you're dead too."

"Yell all you want, Daniel. We're not listening." Bill clutched Daniel's left arm. "Grab his right, Kenny."

Bill looked over the breastwork. The Union boys were no more than twenty yards away.

Rifles strapped to their backs, arms wrapped around Daniel, Kenny and Bill hightailed for the rear. With Blue-Bellies so close, the possums could have been shot dead or captured. The Yanks showed mercy.

Confederate reserves from the divisions of Brigadier Generals Jubal Early and William Taliaferro parted to allow Bill, Kenny and their gravely wounded friend to pass through. Soon, Bill could hear the racket of musketry fire as the reinforcements counterattacked. Several hundred yards closer to Massaponax Creek, they found the Eighteenth and other regiments of the brigade. They were being reorganized by General Lane for a charge meant to seal the breach and salvage lost honor.

Colonel Purdie recognized the three, gestured toward the Massaponax. "Take him to the Yerby house. First aid station's there. Don't worry about us, boys. We're going to chase the Yanks clear to the Rappahannock." It was two-thirty in the afternoon, just ninety minutes after the Union infantry had begun their attack.

Thirteen

A Time of Suffering and Death

Bill sat cross-legged on the barn floor listening to Daniel's shallow breathing. Oil lanterns cast flickering light on Daniel's face so that the sweat on his forehead shimmered. A kerosene pall hung heavy in the air. Just five in the morning on December 14, the sun had yet to rise, and the temperature hovered near freezing. Bill wore his shell jacket buttoned to his chin, but he still shivered... and not just because he was cold. He felt helpless, doomed to watch a friend die.

Fifty wounded men from both Jackson and Longstreet's corps were spread out on the straw. The moaning men shared the barn with cattle and bales of winter fodder. So far, Bill had done an adequate job filtering out the moans, cries and the prayers. Earlier, those same cries had tugged at his heart, and he'd gone from soldier to soldier sharing water and whatever else they requested... reading a letter, shuffling a pillow, holding a hand. Now he heard only Daniel's tortured breathing.

Someone with a light step entered the barn, one of eight cowsheds on the plantation, all housing wounded Confederates. Bill looked up to see Julia Neale weaving among the injured. The Fredericksburg refugee checked the pulse of an unresponsive soldier, then shared a resigned glance with an attending officer. "Another for burial, Lieutenant."

Wearing an unnaturally white mob cap, Julia passed near Bill and the prostrate Daniel. "Please, Mrs. Neale, could you tell Doctor Straith my friend Daniel still lives? He said he'd be dead by midnight. If the doctor gives Daniel a chance, he'll be one of the doc's miracles."

Kneeling beside Bill, Julia unstrapped a canteen and dribbled water on Daniel's cracked lips. "I'm sorry. Gut wound. It's just a matter of time. Pray for a merciful death." She squeezed Bill's shoulder, then checked the remaining men, many dying.

Throughout the night, Bill had ministered to Daniel's needs, providing water, rearranging blankets to make him more comfortable, reading aloud from a Bible provided by Mrs. Neale. When Daniel was cognizant, Bill read from the eighth chapter of Romans: "What shall we then say to these things? If God be for us, who can be against us? He that spared not his own Son, but delivered him up for us all, how shall he not with him also freely give us all things?"

Bill refused to think about the aureola that had flared around Daniel, yet couldn't deny Julia's words. Daniel would soon die. He contemplated words he'd heard a poet speak:

Better angels of our nature
Stay awake now, you're in danger
The coming night is dark and deep.

If Bill could make the aureola into something he could hold in his hand, he'd hurl it into the Rappahannock and watch it sink like a sack of apples. As Julia left the barn, Bill caressed Daniel's forehead. "Go, my friend, go fly into God's arms."

Kenny had returned to the Eighteenth in the late evening to tell Colonel Purdie Bill would remain at Daniel's side and await his last breath.

Suddenly, Daniel awakened. Eyes huge and glowing, like the barn's oil lanterns, he gazed up at the ceiling beams, smiling as if greeting an old friend. His lips moved. "Bill, you should have told me about the halo." He closed his eyes, and took his last breath.

Straw clenched in his hands, Bill sat beside Daniel's body, stunned. At the end, Daniel had known. How? Daniel had seen something among the rafters, and said those damned words. Bill thought of Jesus in the Garden of Gethsemane: "My Father, if it is possible, let this cup pass me by." *Lord, please, no more aureolas. Let someone braver than me fathom your purpose and do your will.*

He glanced toward the barn door, now closed. Julia and her attendant were gone. He tugged Daniel's blanket up over his face. Rising, he headed for the barn door. Bill needed to find her.

Julia stood on the Belvoir's front porch chatting with a fellow helper, Carrie Morton, a neighbor of the Yerbys. Bill approached them. "My friend just died, Mrs. Neale. Would you happen to have some nails? A hammer? I'm headed to Yerby's sawmill to build a coffin."

The Fredericksburg woman hugged Bill. "I'll handle the details. Your friend will get a proper burial. Thomas's slaves have been building coffins for our dead. We've been given permission to inter them in a Confederate cemetery next to the city's burial ground." Bill felt the reassuring touch of her hands on his back, pats of caring and condolence.

"Thank you, ma'am." Bill bowed.

"One more thing, soldier." She looked at the other woman. "Mrs. Morton, I watched our private tend to his friend in that hellish barn. He has a way about him." Julia returned her gaze to Bill. "I'd like you to help us with the wounded in the house. Write letters for them, read to them, hold their hands, change their bandages. I'll let your brigade commander know I'm *stealing* you. Please. Do you agree?"

"I should return to my regiment. Daniel's gone."

"The battle's over, Private. You routed the Yanks." Julia gestured to a window that provided a view of the wounded jam-packed inside the Belvoir's parlor. "Please, we need you here. We're overwhelmed."

Bill chewed his lower lip, glanced toward friendly lines, then swung his gaze back to the parlor window. "So much suffering. Tell me how I can help."

"Wonderful. I'm going to put you into the able hands of my daughter, Franny." Julia led Bill into the house where they found Franny asleep on a mattress in the library, snoring softly among the shelves.

A table lamp glowed softly until Julia turned the wick up, brightening the room. Swaddled in quilts, Franny shifted on the mattress and rubbed her eyes, forcing herself to consciousness. "Oh, hello. Momma, you've brought a man." Franny laughed lightly. It sounded discordant in a house full of suffering soldiers.

The daughter swept back the quilts, revealing a prim brown cotton dress with a calico print stained with blood. A yellow Zouave jacket had helped keep her warm while she slept.

"Indeed, Franny," her mother answered. "A nice gentleman, one of A.P. Hill's soldiers, is here to help you minister to the wounded. Bill just lost his friend. When Bill's soldiering days are over, he'd be smart to become a doctor."

Franny rose smoothly to her feet, exposing shoes of blue cloth and black leather. "I remember you now." Her eyes settled on him as if he were the only person in the library. "I saw you in that horrible place. If anyone asked for water, you were there with your canteen. You didn't notice me... you were busy helping a soldier with a cramp."

Actually, Bill did remember her. Not her mother, but Franny... she'd given him the Bible. Strikingly beautiful in the lamplight of last evening and just as lovely in the morning, even with sweat-dulled golden hair that had tangled free of its pins. Franny stepped up to him and offered her glove-free hand for a handshake, just like a man would do. Momentarily startled, Bill recovered and awkwardly shook her hand. Her warm, soft skin sent tingles down his spine. Not as beautiful as Becky. Still, he'd surely enjoy her company for the next day or so.

Confound it! Daniel has barely taken his final breath, and here I am daydreaming about kissing Franny. Forgive me, Lord and Becky. And I've not once thought about Daniel's final words. He laughed sourly. *Too much turmoil.* She expected him to say something. *Don't sound stupid.*

"You're so kind, Miss Neale. I'll do whatever I can to assist you." He sounded so damned formal, but he had to if he intended to stay true to Becky. Even immodest thoughts were sins, the Rev. Sprunt had preached more than once... and Bill still had plenty of them in spite of his recent words asking for forgiveness.

Her bright azure eyes fixed on him, she stood so close he could see the pores on her face. Not soft skin as she should have had, but weatherbeaten with a touch of sunburn. She'd been out in the elements during daylight, a refugee fleeing the Yankee shells demolishing her city. No doubt her house had been reduced to burnt timbers and ashes.

"Let's go to work, Bill." Franny took his arm.

It was a whirlwind of a day. Faces of soldiers, some as young as Bill, blurred as more and more were brought to Yerby's Belvoir. The ones in the house were mostly officers who had a chance to survive. Almost all were amputees who needed bandages changed and wounds cleaned on a schedule. At first, he worked alongside Franny, but later she left him alone... until she touched him on a shoulder as he read a newspaper story to a soldier who'd lost both eyes. "You need a break, Private Stamford."

She took him to a guest bedchamber where Franny and her mother had been sleeping since fleeing the bombardment. He watched her light an oil lamp. There really wasn't a need for the lamp, not with the sunset colors of red and orange filtering past the curtains. "Miss Neale, I'm so sorry the war has done this to you and your family." He stayed near the door, made no move to close it.

"Miss Neale? Please! We've been together for hours." She gestured to the blood on her nurse's apron. "No need for formalities, Bill. Franny's my name." She sidled by him and shut the door. "Say it."

Shrugging, Bill smiled. "Franny. Always, it'll be Franny— Fredericksburg's Florence Nightingale."

Loose curls flipping, Franny shook her head. "You're the William Nightingale of Fredericksburg, Bill Stamford. You've a knack for nursing."

"My mother was a nurse in a Cleveland hospital before she married Papa." Bill turned at the sound of voices in the hallway. He knew his face wore a look of alarm.

"Don't worry." Snagging the lamp, Franny drifted to another door and opened it. A walk-in closet this time. "The wounded are all downstairs, except for General Gregg. They've turned the Yerby bedroom into a dying room for the general."

"We should really return downstairs." Bill stayed put, though.

What was wrong with him? Instead of flirting with Franny, he should be using these moments free of the Belvoir's chaos to ponder Daniel's last words.

"In war, we take risks, Bill Stamford." Franny moved sidewise so Bill could see the closet's interior. Not just clothes chests and shelves stacked with hat boxes and copies of *Godey's Magazine*, but several comfy chairs as well. "When I need to get away from the sadness, I shut the door, sit and remember the balls of 1860." With the lamp nestled next to a box of toy farm animals, she seated herself and gestured for him to join her in one of the other chairs. "Shut the door behind you, Bill. I swear this is the only spot in the house with some privacy." When he settled into the chair, she affectionately squeezed his kneecap. "Don't feel guilty. In ten minutes, we'll be back trying to ease the misery."

"I'm honored to be your newest friend, Franny. More than honored. You're a gift from God, given at a terrifying time." So much had happened in the last few hours. Joined in a friendship forged by the carnage of battle, Bill and Franny had comforted men fresh from surgery in Yerby's carriage house. When the chloroform wore off, a soldier first saw their faces—an angel with gold-spun hair and rose-pink lips, and a big brother the Grayback never knew he had. They were the ones who hugged him, who kissed his forehead moments after learning the surgeon's saw had claimed a leg or arm.

"You're a very sweet man, Bill." Leaning forward, Franny placed his hand against her cheek. "I'm normally not this forward. The war has done it. I've a fiancé with the Army of the Mississippi. So I'm a bad girl for engineering this private time with you. I don't care." She paused as if considering her words, then continued. "I really don't know anything about you, yet I feel like I've known you all my life. In war, a few hours equal a lifetime, eh? What were you doing before the war? What do you hope to do when we win our independence? Do you have a sweetheart?"

Bill laughed as Franny released his hand, allowing him to draw it back to his knee. "Take a breath, Franny. I don't know where to start." She sucked in a deep breath and smiled shyly. Bill grinned... shy? Franny was likely born with a tiny hand tugging on the doctor's beard. "I attended Grove Academy in Kenansville, North Carolina, during the day, and after school helped my papa in his newspaper office and print shop. So I'm a Tar Heel, Miss Franny Neale."

Franny clapped. "Ah, a budding newspaperman. If you weren't a soldier, you'd be covering the war for *Richmond Dispatch*. And I would have never met you, so I'm glad you enlisted, although sad you had to see your friend die in that horrid barn."

"Thank you, Franny." She was the jammiest bits of jam, a sweet morsel he'd need to be careful around. More tempting than homemade ice cream on a July day. "When this war's over and if I survive, I'll probably try to hire on at one of the Raleigh newspapers or maybe down in Wilmington."

"I'll pray every night that you'll get the chance."

"Most of us die of camp ailments." He nodded as Franny's eyes ballooned with doubt. "Many recruits end up sick, especially the ones from big cities like New Orleans and Charleston. I made it through the first few months of soldiering, so I figure I'm safe from a quick-step death as long as they don't force the blue-mass pills down my throat."

Lamplight glimmered on her face. "Blue mass?"

"Calomel. Compound of mercury and chalk. Army doctors love it. We get it for diarrhea, dysentery, typhoid fever and whatnot."

She rolled her eyes. "I was a student at East Tennessee Female Institute studying to be a schoolteacher, and I swear I don't know half of what you do."

Bill thought Franny exaggerated. She had far more smarts than him. He shrugged. "I read a lot."

"You should be a writer, an author." Her voice resounded with enthusiasm. "Your days at Fredericksburg—the battle, helping me minister to the wounded and dying—they should be turned into tales."

"Looks like I'd sell at least one book." Bill grinned.

"Oh, many books, I think."

Bill let his gaze wander to the shelves filled with slapdash hat boxes, clothes and toy chests. One chest had tipped over, spilling game pieces of Snakes and Ladders, tin Red Coat soldiers, and a doll. He laughed softly as he returned his gaze to the high-spirited girl. "This closet's filled with Yerby family history and one other item ...Franny Neale." He retrieved his watch from his jacket pocket. "We really should return to the first floor. Your momma may have already noticed our absence. She'll think the worse of me."

"You'll find that my mother isn't a prude. She encouraged me to show you the bedroom closet."

Bill rose from his chair. "Really? Your momma wanted you to trap me up here?" He wasn't quite sure why he hadn't mentioned Becky to her. Maybe he liked her flirtations, and didn't want them to end.

As if acknowledging defeat, Franny rose as well. "Now you're making me feel guilty for stealing some private time with you. Shame on you, Bill Stamford." Instead of opening the closet door, she stepped up to him, so close her bosom brushed against his chest. "I'm going to steal a kiss." Her fingers caressing his face, Franny pressed her lips against his mouth, and let her kiss linger. At first, he didn't return the kiss, but soon his lips sought hers eagerly. His will melted faster than a dusting of snow in April.

Sorry, Daniel. Your aureola will have to wait until I get back to camp.

"The sweetheart you didn't tell me about... she's going to have to share you." She kissed him again... and again. "I've never said this to anyone else. Before my fiancé left for the war, we had ourselves a storm of heaves. It was Heaven come to Earth. He's not here right now, but you are. I'm willing, Bill."

"I can't, Franny." Her scent of rose water, *Eau de Imperiale*, and sweat made him regret the words.

"I understand." Lamp held aloft, she led Bill through the doorway back into the main room. "Not today, but perhaps another day? Doing the bear, sneaking a kiss, sharing lovers' words, they're so important in these horrible days." They skirted the bed and paused by the door so she could return the lamp to the nightstand and extinguish its flame. As the room plunged into darkness, he heard her fingers scratching at the door leading into the hallway. The hinges squeaked and light again filled the room. As she stepped into the hallway, Franny reminded him, "On days like this, we all need to be loved."

At the top of the spiral staircase, they heard the moans of the wounded down in the parlor and in the music room. In the parlor, the curtains had been drawn and the lamplight dimmed. On couches and mattresses arranged on the floor, some of the men slept, hugged by the tranquility of the darkness. Cold air swirled into the parlor when orderlies swung open the porch door and lugged in a stretcher holding a soldier whose leg had just been amputated.

A weak voice: "Stamford? Over here." Bill turned to where his name had been spoken. The voice came from along the fireplace wall... Captain Poisson, minus his right arm, sawed off at the shoulder. He lay on a blood-stained mattress beneath a portrait of a planter, William Herndon who, according to Franny, had built the Belvoir four decades ago.

"See to your officer," Franny told Bill, then pointed to a woman in a bloomer Vivandiere dress and white apron. "That's Matilda Hamilton from a neighboring plantation. I'll get some more marching instructions from her." She squeezed his hand.

Bill squished through blood and knelt beside the captain. "Water, sir? Something to eat? I'll make a run to the kitchen."

"You're doing a good deed, Stamford." Poisson shifted on the mattress and scraped his stump against the wall. He bit down hard on his bottom lip, but a whimper still escaped. "Damn! Stupid of me!" He glared at the bloody bandage covering the new stump. "Don't want rot showing up. Arm's gone. Don't want to lose my life." Even in the shadowy lamplight, the look in Poisson's eyes begged for help. "Would you wash my wound? Change out the bandage?"

"Of course, sir." Bill had some forward-thinking ideas about wound care acquired from his mother and a close friend of his papa, Doctor Craig Iuppenlatz, who'd trained in Vienna and now lived in Wilmington. In the privacy of the Stamford home, the good doctor had often castigated American doctors for their antiseptic practices. Bill would do his best to keep the captain's wound from putrefying. Just as Doctor Iuppenlatz advised, Bill planned to wash the cleaning cloths and linen dressings in boiling water. Hopefully, he could get his hands on a bottle of bromine. Doctor Straith should have plenty. Army surgeons were using bromine and sometimes iodine to try to keep rot at bay. They really didn't understand the why behind their effectiveness. Just that they worked.

The captain eyed the blood-soaked bandage with distaste. "We regained our breastworks, even went farther. Nearly pushed the Blue-Bellies into the Rappahannock. Rotten luck, though. I really didn't want to give my arm to the cause." He laughed sourly.

"This won't take long, Captain Poisson." Bill patted the captain's kneecap.

Standing, hands steepled, Bill went out the front door onto the colonnaded porch, then headed to the adjacent kitchen, a one-room outbuilding with two cooking fireplaces. As he made his way along the gravel drive, the light inside the carriage house caught his eye. Doctor Straith stood at the makeshift operating table, sleeves rolled up to his elbows, his bare arms and linen apron smeared with blood. Saw held between his teeth, the doctor helped the attendants lift a pain-wracked soldier onto the table. "Momma! Momma!" the soldier cried out.

Bill found himself unable to look away from the grisly scene. Bent over the table, Straith sliced through the pants leg to get a better view of the wound. He motioned to an attendant stationed at his elbow, who administered chloroform and positioned the sergeant for the bone saw. "God, let me die. Sweet Lord, the pain! Momma, I need—" The chloroform did its merciful work.

Straith took the saw from between his teeth, wiped twice across his bloodstained apron. The cutting—brutally agonizing to watch—began. Two attendants kept the soldier firmly in place on the table. Bill swore he could hear the saw grinding through the bone, but that wasn't likely, not with the sometimes gusty wind and the prattle of guards, attendants and livery-stable slaves congregating near the driveway fountain. When the limb lay in a bucket, Straith looked around and shouted, "Next!" It took next to no time to take off a man's leg. Bill swallowed hard, stunned by the speed of the procedure.

Inside the kitchen, Bill explained what he needed to one of the cooks. She gave him a puzzled look. "What a cockamamie thing to do," the heavyset darky said, shaking her head, double chin jiggling.

"Not a time fer jokin', Tovah," the head cook scolded. "Get crackin' on what he needs."

Soon, a kettle of steaming water dangled above the flames in one of the fireplaces. His hands snuggled inside rubber gloves, Bill scrubbed bedsheets, tablecloths and linen rescued from Yerby's ragbag. As he dipped the cloth in the bubbling water, he recalled Doctor Iuppenlatz saying, "Wounds do better when the dressings are first washed in boiling water. I think the boiling water kills bacteria. I'm continuing the practice." And so Bill would as well.

Bill returned to the main house with a bowl of hot water, dry cleaning rags and linen dressings. First, though, he jawboned an attendant into giving him a bottle of bromine. Actually, Straith overheard Bill's pleadings and signaled the attendant to give Bill the bottle. The doings inside the house were so hectic nobody noticed him stepping through the hallway and entering the parlor.

"Sweet Lord, Stamford! I'd thought you walked to Richmond and back." Captain Poisson tried to laugh, but it turned into a moan.

"No, sir. Just tidied up these dressings and washrags. Doing what you asked. Making sure the rot doesn't set in on your stump." Bill arranged the linen dressings and cotton washrags on a nearby table, then showed the captain the bromine bottle. "Rounded this up for you. It'll stop decay."

Poisson frowned, then offered a painful grin. "I was hoping for a little alcohol. Not only good for the wound, but for the spirit as well."

"Grain alcohol would work, sir, but bromine's much better." Bill set the water bowl, washrags and the bromine bottle beside the captain, knelt and removed the blood-soaked dressing, a rolled bandage of what had once been clean cotton. Blood leaked at the sutures, not a flood but enough that a dressing would need to be changed more than once a day. Bill hoped the captain could soon be transported to a field hospital beyond the range of Yankee artillery.

"Morphine's wearing off," Captain Poisson rasped, then gritted his teeth. Every time a draft of cold air touched the stump, he grimaced.

Franny knelt beside Bill, a glass of well water grasped in one hand and a pill held in the other. "Opium," she told Bill, then helped Poisson take the pill. "Relief's on the way, Captain."

The wound had been packed with lint. Bill discarded the blood-drenched lint and soaked up any leaking blood with a wet washrag and then a dry one. He unstopped the bromine bottle and poured the liquid along the edges of the wound and at the sutures, then soaked up any driblets trickling onto Poisson's chest and belly. "Captain, if anyone else changes your dressing, make sure bromine is used. Scream bloody murder if they refuse. Insist they wash the bandages and washrags in boiling water." Bill applied the dressing and secured it with thread, which he knotted so it wouldn't loosen. Leaning back on his heels, he watched the captain's eyelids droop.

Poisson forced open his eyelids and regarded Franny. "Ah, Mrs. Neale's lovely daughter. You must be here for Stamford, not a dizzy-age fella like me. Thank you for your help, Stamford. I turn you over to this able lady." Relaxing, the captain began snoring.

Bill helped Franny to her feet. "With that wound, he'll soon be bound for Wilmington," he said, eyeing Poisson. "War's over for him. He'll soon serve in the Invalid Corps."

"Come the next century, old people's homes are going to be filled with aged men missing arms and legs." Franny took his arm and led him down the hallway into the library, illuminated by a single lamp on a desktop. Her mother stood at one of the shelves inspecting book spines. Julia turned toward the doorway when she heard her daughter's voice. "Mother, I brought him to you. He doesn't know yet."

"We have a special patient for you, Bill," Julia told him. "I was watching how the men enjoy having you read to them. You're quite good at it. I volunteered you to do more reading, this time to the general. He's upstairs, comfortable as we can make him."

Bill scratched his forehead. "General?"

Fourteen

A General Faces Death

Julia Neale extracted a book from the shelf she'd been examining. She handed it to Bill. "The Bible, printed by the Company of Stationers, 1671, London. I'd like you to read some scripture to General Gregg. He's up in the master bedroom."

"He's dying, Bill," Franny added.

Clutching Bill's elbow, Julia led him and Franny from the library to the spiral staircase and up to the second floor's master bedroom. The low voices and moans faded, replaced by the upper floor's creaking as they made their way to the bedroom. "We're keeping Maxcy comfortable, per General Jackson's orders," Julia said in a near-whisper. "He mentioned having someone read the Bible to him, some of the Psalms and the Apostle Paul's words about love and devotion. General Gregg never married, so he must be thinking of the sweetheart who never bore his name."

"I told General Gregg about you, Bill." As they passed the guest bedroom where Bill and Franny had shared a kiss, Franny gazed at its closed door and smiled wickedly. "The general's a firebrand, but as the end nears, he's having a softening of his heart. Not that he'd ever walk to Heaven alongside a Yankee. I told him you'd be perfect to read Edgar Allen Poe's poems and Paul Hamilton Hayne's sonnets. You've got a stage voice sweet as John Wilkes Booth."

Juliet interjected, "Maxcy is a cultured man, one of the best the South has to offer."

The master bedroom lay at the far end of the hallway next to a small office. Julia knocked on the closed door. Distinct footsteps, and then the door rasped open. A darky, his face weary and dirt-smudged, sighed upon seeing Julia and Franny.

Partly blocked by the darky, Bill nonetheless could see the room's French Rococo bed and a man blanketed in quilts, his head propped up by satin pillows.

"We've brought the writer, Andre," Julia said softly.

"Please come in." Andre shifted aside so the three could pass.

A hand-painted lamp of red roses on a mahogany side table cast a glow that left the cushioned chairs, divans and the bed in twilight. The general's face lay among the shadows, his features partly cloaked.

"Is he asleep?" Bill swung his gaze between Gregg's servant and the general. "I could come back rather than disturb him."

"I'm awake," the general inserted weakly. "Sleepy, but awake. I've been given an opiate for the pain. I'm not in the mood for Bible reading. I'll hear it from the Lord's mouth soon enough. Please, some of Hayne's sonnets."

Bill looked questioningly at Julia. "I'll need to go back to the library."

Franny turned toward the doorway. "I'll get one of Hayne's books. Please stay with the general."

"I'll come with you, daughter."

After the two women departed, Andre gestured to a green velvet chair next to the bed. "Please sit, sir. I'll move the lamp closer so you won't ruin your eyes." The slave, no more than sixteen, sounded amazingly articulate and not at all as Bill expected.

Bill sat in the chair, the large Bible perched on his lap; a moment later, the lamp rested on the end table beside him. "Thank you, Andre."

Some wouldn't have bothered saying thank you. Not Bill. His maternal grandparents were from Ohio. Cousins were serving in the Army of the Potomac. Once, when he was twelve, he'd taken the train up there and spent the summer with his Grandma and Grandpa Schumacher and his Northern cousins. Grandpa Schumacher had a butler, a darky named Cumberland Smith, who'd been paid a fair wage. Andre reminded Bill of Cumberland.

A few days earlier, before the battle, Andre's tasks were washing his master's clothes, preparing his food, brushing his uniform, polishing his swords and buckles, running errands, and tending his horse. Now Andre had another responsibility... tending to his master's death.

Sooner than Bill expected, Franny breezed into the bedroom with two books cradled in her arms. "Found some works by Poe and poems by Hayne." Arms extended, she offered them to Bill. Their fingertips touched, and a shock of pure carnality soared up his spine.

As if a spider had crept into his pants and bitten him on the buttocks, Andre sprang to his feet and took a seat on the floor between the divan and Bill's chair. Too big for the end table, the Bible ended up on the floor as well. Bill transferred Franny's two smaller books to his lap to hide his engorging loins.

"Please sit, Miss Neale," Andre insisted, patting the divan's armrest.

Franny nearly sat down, but then shook her head. Her blonde hair spun as she swiveled to return downstairs. "I can do more good in the parlor and the Great Room. Send Andre if you need me, Bill." She squeezed his shoulder.

A voice chirped from the bed. "Thank you, Miss Franny. I didn't expect to hear any Hayne poetry, but you made it happen. You're my sweet miracle."

"Thank you, Maxcy. I would bring Hayne in person if I could." She advanced to the bed and kissed the general on his damp forehead.

When Franny had gone, Gregg closed his eyes, and breathing weakly, said in a shallow voice, "Please read *The Shadow*. Speak up. I'm partially deaf."

Bill thumbed through the book until he found the poem, then read aloud:

The pathway of his mortal life hath wound
Beneath a shadow; just beyond it play
The genial breezes, and the cool brooks stray
Into melodious gushings of sweet sound,
Whilst ample floods of mellow sunshine fall
Like a mute rain of rapture over all....

When Bill finished, he sighed, then scooted forward in the chair. "Another, perhaps more romantic?"

"*Love's Caprices*," the general said, his tone sad as he lay on his back, head tilted toward Bill.

As Bill looked for the poem, Andre rose from the floor and settled in the divan. "A most excellent choice, Master," he opined.

Bill found the poem, and clearing his throat, began reading:

Come, sweetheart, hear me! I have loved thee well,
God knoweth. Through all these years my holiest thoughts,
Like those pure doves nurtured in antique temples,
Have fluttered ever round thine image fair,
And found in thee their shrine. No tenderest hope
Of mine, which hath not warmed its radiant wings
Within that heaven, thy presence, drank strength
And sunshine from it.

The general sniffled, as if fighting back tears. "I lost her to cholera just a month before our wedding. I hope she's the one who comes to get me."

The glow from lamplight surrounded a portrait of a young woman, like an aureola. The painting hung above the bedpost, as if looking down on the general. Bill wondered if the woman resembled Gregg's fiancèe. Probably not. Nonetheless, the image ensured his thoughts would keep coming back to the general's almost-wife.

Bill ran a finger along the Hayne book's leather spine, felt the lettering tickle the end of his finger. "Another poem, sir?"

"Later. I want to rest for a spell." The spell didn't last long, for he soon opened his eyes and trained his gaze on Bill. "Shot in the back. Near Prospect Hill. Where the Yanks broke through. Hit the spinal cord. No feeling at all. Now I feel a degree of reaction." Gregg rolled his eyes. "Hoped I would live. The surgeon said otherwise. Now we wait for the great mystery to be revealed."

"If you're able, you must tell me what you see at the end." Bill closed the Hayne book. "If I'm permitted to stay."

"What a splendid idea," Gregg said, then coughed and groaned. "Yes, you may stay. And yes, I will try to tell you. No promises, though. Perhaps God will forbid it." He glanced at the window curtain. A slightly open panel allowed moonbeams into the room. One found the general's face. "Please, Andre, close the curtain."

Andre had hardly closed the curtain panel when the door opened and A.P. Hill, the division commander, stepped into the room and approached the bed. Straightaway, Bill vacated the chair, thinking General Hill would want to sit close to his dying friend. Instead, Hill stood silently over the bed for five minutes, moist eyes fixed on Gregg, then kissed him on the forehead and left without speaking a word.

"General Hill was much too solemn," Gregg said, chuckling until pain transformed the laughter into a groan. "Decided not to ruin the moment by letting him know I was awake." He gripped the quilts as a spasm wracked his body. When it subsided, Gregg continued, "Stamford, right? Please get Doctor McGuire. I need a stronger dose of opiate."

Bill didn't know a Doctor McGuire, but after making inquiries learned he was the medical director of Jackson's Corps, Dr. Straith's boss. One of Straith's assistants took Bill to McGuire, who sat in a small candlelit tent writing reports. With Gregg's message delivered, soon Bill and Doctor McGuire were on the way to the Yerby house with the opiate syringe dangling from the doctor's hand. They returned to Gregg's room to find another guest hunched over the bed, the Second Corps Commander, General Thomas Jackson. "Please forgive me," Gregg kept saying, as if those were the only three words in his vocabulary.

Thoughts muddled, Bill gave Andre a serious, questioning look. Quiet as a church mouse, Gregg's slave sidled up to him and whispered, "The master quarreled with General Jackson. It's been eating at him and leaving a bitter taste. As you see, even your poetry didn't bring my master peace."

Jackson shook his head insistently. "I'm the one who needs your forgiveness, Maxcy. We are strong-willed men; in the heat of the moment, we say things we don't mean. Our friendship will forever endure. Death cannot end it, my friend. Let me ask you to dismiss this matter from your mind and turn your thoughts to God and the world to which you go."

Relief washed over Gregg's face. His eyes filled with tears. "I thank you. I thank you very much."

Andre dabbed his eyes with a sleeve. Bill, too, felt tears trickling down his cheeks.

Taking leave, General Jackson noticed the medical attendant, syringe in his hand. "I see you have work to do," he told Doctor McGuire, then turned back to Gregg. "My friend, the doctor is here to take away your pain until the good Lord comes for you."

Later that night, as the temperature in the room became noticeably colder, Andre stoked the hearth fire. With the cold chased into corner crevices, Bill read more sonnets to Gregg, and then Chaplin Monroe Anderson came into the room with General Jackson in tow. Trailing them, David Gregg McIntosh, a kinsman of Gregg's, claimed an armchair in one of those cold corners. Doctor McGuire returned too and stood silently beside McIntosh, hands clasped at his belly. He acknowledged Bill's presence with a nod. No one asked Bill to leave... yet.

In the grip of the opiate, struggling not to sink into sleep, Gregg said quietly, "Mr. Anderson, I would kneel if I could." He offered a torturous smile.

The chaplain read from his Bible, led everyone in the hymn "Rock of Ages," and said a prayer. General Jackson nearly made Bill leave, but Gregg intervened. "No, my friend, he has a peaceful voice, perfect for reading Hayne's sonnets."

After the service, with the room silent again, Gregg rubbed his eyes and said to Andre, "Stamford still here?"

"Yes, Master. Sitting on the divan. We didn't want to disturb you, Master."

"Good. I'm ready to hear more Hayne. Stamford, sit next to me."

As Bill read, the general fell asleep. Bladder complaining, Bill stepped outside and made his way to an outhouse, a three-hole brick affair. Done, he buttoned his fly and headed back to the house. Looking up, he saw a most amazing sight... the aurora borealis glowing in the sky, rays darting within the ruddiness. *God's aureola of fire*, Bill thought.

Once back in Gregg's room, Bill nodded off, and then—at about four-thirty in the morning according to his watch—he prepared to leave for good. "No. Please stay," Gregg insisted. "Your presence... it's reassuring."

Ten minutes later, Gregg's eyes suddenly opened and his mouth moved as if trying to formulate words. Nothing came out, though. Waved forward by Andre, who stood beside the bed, Bill joined the general's servant and waited for the man's soul to fly free. In the lamplight, Gregg stared wide-eyed out toward the window, as if he could see the heavenly river Jordan and departed loved ones waving at him. Still staring, Gregg mouthed distinctive words, "Wonderful gift. Halos of fire."

Startled, Bill choked on spit and stumbled away from the bed, right hand pressed against his mouth. *No, Lord! Do I have no say? I've pleaded, just as Jesus did. If you are willing take this cup from me.* Jesus had added a caveat: "Yet not my will, but yours be done."

Brigadier General Maxcy Gregg died at five o'clock in the morning on December 15, 1862.

Although Franny and her mother protested, Bill decided to return to the Eighteenth. He'd done all he could at the Yerby house. Time to return to the regiment and help man the breastworks.

Franny wanted to accompany him partway to the Second Corps' lines. Her fingers curled around his elbow. "I just don't want to let you go."

The pair made their way past the barren terraced garden. Come spring, the Yerby garden would bloom with flowers of every color. Staying to the winding drive, they strode past the carriage house transformed into a surgery building; barns and stables; the icehouse, and the caretaker's cottage. Beyond the outbuildings where moonbeams provided the only light, they passed a carriage road that led to Hunter's Lodge. At the juncture with a second carriage road, this one to the Hamilton Place at Forest Hill, they turned up the gravel path. Splotches of orange and pink, the first hints of morning, lightened the sky behind a forested ridge. A woodpecker hammered away on a nearby tree. An owl hooted, sounding like the bark of a dog.

Maybe a thousand yards down the carriageway, Franny stopped at a farm fence. She pointed, "Follow the field and you'll find your lines." She reached out and pressed her hands against his chest, her fingers entangling in the wool of his shell jacket. "I wish I could linger with you but it's North-Pole cold." She embraced him, hugging him tightly, and shared a farewell kiss. "If it were June, I'd remove your jacket, vest, and shirt and do some tactical maneuvering, soldier." She patted his cheek. "Maybe another time?"

After Gregg's death, Bill really needed her lighthearted-ness. "You don't give up."

"Because I think I see a breach in your willpower." She nuzzled against his face, her lips exploring his cheek and chin.

Unable to seal the breach, he sought her mouth, kissing her hungrily. When they stopped to take a breath, he managed, "You're better at breaching than Stonewall."

"I can't afford to dally, not with this war wrecking everything." Franny stepped back, played with the buttons on his jacket. "I overheard General Jackson talking to other officers. There's a truce. The armies are recovering more wounded and dead. Burial details are hard at work. Nightmarish work. Sweet Jesus, I hope they don't make you do any of this, not after all the help you have given us. I think the fighting's over. General Jackson says the Yanks lost twice as many men as us, and retreated across their bridges to lick their wounds for the winter. Again, I'm sorry you lost your friend, Bill."

"Thank you, Miss Franny Neale." This time he was the aggressor, taking her into his arms, kissing her mouth, neck and earlobes, running his fingers beneath her bonnet and through her hair.

Fifteen

Winter Bivouac on the Rappahannock

Bill lay on his bunk just before dawn, the rubber blanket beneath him thwarting the floor chill. Christmas was just one day away. Christmas Eve on the Rappahannock.

As the flames in the hut's fireplace capered and hissed like cats, he couldn't get the deathbed words of Daniel and General Gregg out of his head. They still rattled inside his brain, like marbles in a tie-sack. He'd never said a word about the aureolas to either man, but both mentioned them. Their words had not reflected his misgivings. They'd seen the aureolas as gifts, not a curse. But the devil could deceive the unwary, even the dying. Just three aureola visions in his eighteen years of life, but Bill feared he'd soon see another. The war made it inevitable. Maybe he could prevent the vision; he just needed to figure out how.

Reveille sounded, a raucous noise that sent Bill's thoughts on aureolas scrambling for cover. The three other men in the hut—Charley, Kenny and a recruit, Nathan Pacini—vaulted from their bunks. Soon, the four were assembled with the others of the Eighteenth for morning rollcall. No snow on the hard ground or dark clouds in the sky, but everyone still shivered and hungrily eyed their huts, wood smoke coiling from chimneys. Bill juddered when he heard his name called. "Present, sir." Frost tinged his breath as he plodded to the cook's hut to get the fixings for breakfast, fare not much better than what he had eaten on the march to Fredericksburg. Ersatz coffee, hardtack, desiccated vegetables and real bacon, the last bit supplied by the women of Fredericksburg as a thank you.

Bill had maybe two hours... until 10 o'clock... before he had to report for morning drill. Until then, he plopped his buttocks in a chair Kenny had made, and read a letter from Becky, turned fragile by his sweat, fingers, and snow. She'd perfumed it with *Kiss Me Sweetly* cologne. Bill breathed in the orange-blossom fragrance. Until he received this letter, he'd only gotten one from her since joining up. Now that Franny had meddled in his life, Bill found it annoying not to have a cache of fragranced love letters to remind him of Becky.

He liked how she started out the letter: "My dearest sweetheart." And the next words: "I've daubed the page with perfume and kissed the daubs. Now you can kiss the paper and know you're kissing where my lips touched. I've also applied the perfume to my breasts with thoughts of your lips on them. Oh, how I wish this war were over."

Her words were brazen, yet they reassured him: "Don't worry, my love. Father's away on business in Kenansville, and I will leave soon to mail this letter. I can be foolhardy as in I can't wait until you and I have our first Melting Moment. When I think of you, I become reckless."

Then, an apology of sorts for letting so much time pass between letters: "I know you must be angry with me for not writing more. Please forgive me. I've spent the last several weeks with a cousin at her Wrightsville Beach cottage. Sharon has been there since the yellow fever outbreak. The winter is cold here, starving out the fever, but her papa's too afraid to return to Wilmington. She begged me to come visit, and I couldn't say no to the lonely girl. There's so much sadness in New Hanover. Many of the fever victims were buried in a mass grave in Oakdale. I wish you were here to hold me."

Bill set the letter on his lap. *Forgive me, Jesus.* Traitorous thoughts percolated. Becky and Sharon… they'd been amassing beaus, filling their dance cards at cotillions, sneaking kisses with those duty shirkers while he helped bury good men in shallow Virginia graves. Well, that wasn't precisely correct. He'd handed out shovels to darkies who did the burying. Bill whispered aloud: *Becky's not been whooping it up at balls. Not in New Hanover where hundreds have perished in a yellow fever die-off.*

Becky shared what she'd been doing since she took the train back to Duplin Roads. Quilting socks and sewing a shirt for him, which she promised to mail with a package that would include secret items. He sighed. Maybe new long johns for when he drilled out in the cold and walked picket duty along the Rappahannock. Thank the Lord the Blue-Bellies had recrossed the river and cut the moorings to the pontoon bridges. He looked around the hut, happy to be warm as the fireplace crackled.

It was a fine hut in a fine winter-quarters camp, practically a town with streets and cabins, some built better than others. Putting together a winter camp was like a barn-raising—soldiers working together to put roofs over their heads, sometimes in bitterly cold temperatures, sleet or even snow. First a cellar dug two feet deep, then a five-foot wall of split-pine logs resting on the ground, held up by stakes. Flying squirrels in Confederate gray put up the roof, two shelter tents fastened together and stretched over a ridge pole between two stout uprights. Bricks from Fredericksburg's burnt buildings constituted the fireplace and chimney. To keep out the cold drafts, the boys made a proper door and caulked the walls with Virginia mud tough as dried spruce gum. With the Virginia winter sure to turn the ground into a quagmire, the Butternuts ditched around the hut and routed the water into the company gutter. With many soldiers under the weather and often silently mourning their dead comrades, the hammering and sawing took longer than normal, but the toasty warmth inside made the hard work well worth it.

Like Wilmington, the camp had its scourges. Ceaseless ailments were filling up the hospital tents and makeshift graveyards. Whenever Bill walked to drill or to the post office, he heard young soldiers coughing and quivering like old men. Some of the ground around the Belvoir was quite swampy; Bill wondered if that was the reason for all the sickness.

He slipped Becky's tattered letter into the haversack hanging from a nail fixed to the wall above his bunk. The bugle blew just as he closed the flap... time for drilling. Bill groaned. If he were still fifteen and back in Kenansville, he'd burrow deeper into his blankets. "The devil curse that bugler's lungs," he grumbled before he sprang to the floor. The drill grounds lay in fields between the camp and the woods, near the railroad tracks. They were so large A.P. Hill and his division staff could do brigade-size maneuvers. On Christmas Eve day, they'd being doing regimental drills.

Camp air throbbed with discontent, murmurs of anger. The men didn't want to drill on Christmas Eve. Nonetheless, Company G men shouldered their muskets and marched toward the drill ground to join the Eighteenth's other companies. General Jackson might be a Virginian, but in religious fervor he was puritan through and through. Idleness was the handmaiden of Lucifer, so the men drilled. Soldiers responding to sergeants' barked commands can't be rolling dice, drinking whiskey concealed in their canteens or sneaking into the woods to meet a fancy girl. Even Bill knew temptation... he couldn't resist Franny's lips.

The boots and brogans of Company G's men echoed on the cold ground like the matched steps of pallbearers conveying a corpse to its grave. Ragged soldiers with sunken cheeks, some coughing, men who wanted to be inside their huts, not headed for the drill field. Bill knew the temperature was on the rise; he could feel the kiss of sunlight on his face. At least he couldn't see his breath when he breathed.

The drills were punishment. That was the rumor. No Merry Christmas from A.P. Hill. Instead, chastisement for the brigade breaking in battle. For Hill, it didn't matter the boys had reformed their lines and routed the Yankees, regaining their breastworks and pushing the Blue-Bellies back toward the Rappahannock. Except for Charlie, the boys weren't in the mood for what they considered Hill's maltreatment. The general had ignored the warnings of his line officers that the so-called swampy land between brigades wasn't as swampy as he thought. Hill was the reason for the gap and the short-lived rout, not any shortcomings by the boys. Right then, Hill was probably smart not to make an appearance on the drill field.

Charlie stared straight ahead, poker-faced as he marched. That's the way he'd been since Bill returned from the Yerby plantation. If any expression snuck onto Charlie's face, it was guilt, and only for an instant before that deadpan look returned. Bill couldn't get his friend to open up about what had happened just before Daniel was shot. He tried, but Charlie would say, "None of your business!" Bill wanted to scream: "You're not a coward. Everyone ran!" The man beside Bill wasn't his happy-go-lucky possum buddy.

Once on the drill field, the officers of the Eighteenth put the men through drill. Marching in time. Wheeling to respond to a flanking attack. Falling in and out of battle lines. Over and over again. Finally, the officers dismissed them for dinner. The meal did little to slake the rumbles upsetting Bill's belly. When he returned to the drill field, the belly growled louder than before – and not just him. The thunder of hundreds of bellies out-boomed the yells of sergeants and officers, or so it seemed. If Bill weren't so weary, he'd have laughed.

Later, after final dismissal, the bunkmates retired to the hut. Candlelight flickered on the walls as Bill leaned back in one of the hastily built chairs and watched Kenny whittle a thick stick of scrap chestnut. He carved furiously, his knife slicing slivers the way a fat rich man devours a Delmonico steak. Bill didn't think Kenny fashioned a pipe or an Indian. On the contrary, his friend likely carved nothing but his frustrations. Kenny's mind needed something to focus on besides Daniel's death, and now that *something* lay scattered on the floor, a hundred slivers that could have been an Indian maiden or even a sculpture of Daniel's face.

A candlelamp hanging from a wall peg provided light as Charlie lay on his bunk reading a book. Not any book. The Bible. Appropriate for Christmas Eve. But Charlie? He should have been skulking through the nearby woods, carrying out a rendezvous with one of Fredericksburg's sweet-kissing bobtails. Instead, he apparently thought reading enough scripture might cleanse the sin of cowardice. Bill grimaced and sighed. Charlie never had run from a fight... not until Fredericksburg. Hopefully, Charlie would work it out before his conscience made him do something stupid on the next battlefield, something that would get him killed.

The newest man in the hut, the recruit Nathan, reached into a small chest at the foot of his bunk and drew out a Chuck-A-Luck game, three dice and a tin cup. He sat on the dirt floor and eyed Kenny. "Looks like you done kilt that piece of wood," he told Kenny. "Want to do some wagerin'?"

Kenny scratched his nose. "Oh hell, why not? You roll first, Fresh Fish."

Bill couldn't quite get the fascination some of the boys had for gambling. In Chuck-A-Luck, players placed bets on the numbers they thought would show up on dice rolled from a cup. For some, if they weren't drilling or eating, they were rolling dice.

"What do you want to wager on?" Nathan looked around the hut, focusing on Kenny's bunk and a chest he'd built to hold his possessions. "How about that quilt you borrowed from the Yerby house? I'll put up the winter coat Ma made for me."

Kenny nodded. "Agreed. Each time one of us rolls and gets within one of the predicted numbers, he receives the point total of the roll. First to one thousand points wins. Rules okay with you?"

"Agreed. I'm goin' to enjoy your quilt." Nathan dropped the three wood dice into the tin cup and handed it to Kenny. You go first."

Kenny settled into a kneeling position. Before rolling, he retrieved a pencil and paper to keep score. "The coat's goin' to keep me warm on nights when I go huntin' bubbies to kiss." He shook the cup and let the dice roll along the ground.

Bill turned away from the game. He couldn't complain too much about gambling… the dice were keeping Kenny from obsessively dwelling on Daniel's death. A draft slithered between logs, scuffed his face and found pathways to his chest. He scooted to the edge of the chair and knocked on Charlie's bunk. "We should do some new chinking between the logs. Right now we're wasting fireplace heat."

Face still expressionless, Charlie set the Bible aside, then swung his legs so they dangled off the bunk. "Okay." Standing, Charlie jerked his head toward an unexpected sound from outside—musical instruments being tuned.

Bill grinned. "Sounds like we're going to have a Christmas Eve concert after all."

"And maybe some preachin'," Charlie said in his new voice, detached, cold.

The cannons and muskets had barely ceased firing. Battle burials were less than a week in the past. Disease and the quickstep were scourging the winter camp. No one felt like celebrating Christmas. They preferred brawling and gambling, not singing carols. So A.P. Hill had canceled the concert. Bill swung his gaze to Kenny, who set the cup on the dirt floor and darted for the door, followed by Nathan. At least two gamblers preferred Christmas carols.

"Looks like the guitar and banjo pickers of Rodes Brigade ain't listenin' to General Hill," Kenny said, opening the door. "No bah humbug. We're goin' to have us a singalong."

"The chinking can wait, Charlie." Bill slapped his friend on the back. "Let's do some wassailing."

Hundreds were gathered on the drill field when the first strains of "God Rest Ye Merry, Gentleman" floated across the frigid air to Bill's ears. They stood solemnly, most singing. Some wore frockcoats, others were draped in quilts and blankets, silhouetted by lamplight and a quarter moon. Bill had forgotten to bring a blanket… not Charlie, who shared his with his friend. The warmth of the wool blanket felt heavenly to Bill as he tucked his hands inside his pants pockets and sang. As the music faded, there were shouts of "Hallelujah" and "Amen."

One of the banjo pickers yelled out to the soldiers, "Here's an old Frenchie tune. Please, some mercy for us. We've not had much time to practice playin' it, boys. Too busy dodgin' cannonballs and bullets." Chortles rolled across the crowd like swells on the ocean. "It's called 'Angels We Have Heard on High.' Pardon the rough spots."

The soldiers gave them a pardon… and lots of "Hallelujahs" and "Amens" and even a few rambunctious rebel yells. Bill glanced at Charlie. Tears rolled down his face.

"This is how Christmas Eve should be," Bill told Charlie. "Sure glad Rodes' band decided to buck Hill. Wouldn't have been right not singing carols."

"God and sinners reconciled," Charlie said, his voice cracking with emotion. "He forgives."

Next, the band played an 18th century Irish tune, "Come Thou Long Expected Jesus," a song Bill vaguely remembered hearing in the Grove Presbyterian Church when a child.

And so it went well into the night, soldiers swaddled in frocks, quilts and blankets, the wintry cold kept at bay, singing carols, their minds remembering Christmases of home, forgetting the war for a few hours. "Angels from the Realms of Glory," "Good King Wenceslas," "Hark! The Herald Angels Sing," "Joy to the World," and lastly "Jingle Bells."

While the soldiers clapped, Chaplain Monroe Anderson walked up to the string band and shook hands, then addressed the crowd. "Let us remember those who died in the recent battle and in earlier ones and those lost to sickness, all celebrating Christmas this year in Heaven and singing God's carols. Please pray with me." As the chaplain prayed aloud, music drifted across the Rappahannock... more Christmas carols, coming from a Blue-Belly brass band.

"Bastards!" The voice dripping venom belonged to Nathan. "We should drop some artillery shells on 'em. They can sing carols for the devil. Damned invaders!"

"Hush!" Bill hissed. "It's Christmas, right? Songs of peace... for at least one night."

"You're right," Nathan grumbled. "But I don't have to like it."

No Northern Lights to usher in Christmas day. Instead, a bland quarter moon still shone in the Christmas Eve night sky when the last notes of the Union band faded, and Bill, Charlie, Kenny and Nathan strolled back to their hut. No one spoke, although nearby soldiers clowned around as if churchgoers who'd just watched a pageant and not the survivors of a battle. Bill inclined his head toward the laughter, trying to learn what they found funny. Unexpectedly, a hand tapped his shoulder. The chaplain shadowed him. "Sir?" Bill said neutrally.

"You've gained an admirer, Private Stamford." Chaplain Anderson handed him an envelope. "From its style, I'd say it's an invitation to a New Year's ball at the Forest Hills plantation. I've a similar one. I apologize for glancing at the envelope. I noticed the sender's name. I do believe we both know her... Franny Neale."

Bill stumbled. The chaplain and Charlie caught him before he fell to his knees. He'd thought their time together a never-to-be-repeated happenstance brought on by the stress of nursing all those mangled men. He rubbed the coarse ink on the envelope's front. That made it seem more real. *Sweet Lord... she wants to see me again.* "I can't go. I'm not an officer."

"Balderdash! A Neale woman wants you there. That outranks any colonel or general. You will go with me." The chaplain harrumphed. "I assure you, friend, I'll have you cleared by A.P. Hill himself to attend the ball."

Bill swallowed hard, glanced at Charlie, no longer morose but grinning stupidly, obviously enjoying his friend's discomfort. "I've nothing to wear."

The chaplain scrutinized Bill's ragged uniform. "I can fix that shortcoming. You'll be properly attired, Stamford. You'll look so pretty you'll blind Franny with your splendor." Anderson saluted Bill as if he addressed a general, not a lowly private. "No excuses. One of the Hamilton buggies will pick us up at the Yerby house on New Year's Eve, six o'clock. You should show up at four in the afternoon. I've plans for you, Stamford."

Sixteen

Orders to Delouse

Bill went to the cook's cabin. Charlie tagged along. The disposition of Bill's buddy had noticeably improved since the Christmas Eve concert. Still, there were times when Charlie's bad day in the breastworks would burrow again into his mind, and he'd walk the camp's streets with his shoulders drooped… like now.

"I thought you said God had forgiven you, Charlie," Bill told him, tone tinged with annoyance. "No need to mope."

"I know." Charlie nearly walked into interlocked muskets stacked in front of a hut. "But on some days"—he gazed skyward at a bleak sky that threatened rain or even snow—"it scares away everything else in my mind."

"Most of the division ran, Charlie, but the boys reorganized and charged. They sealed the breach and chased the Blue-Bellies to the Rappahannock. You were with them, right?"

"Yep." Charlie grimaced. "But I left Daniel, you and Kenny in the lurch. I knew Daniel had been shot and yet I ran. That's hard to live with." He shuddered.

Inside the cook's cabin, Bill glanced at the raw food—predictably salt pork, dried beans and dessicated vegetables—that would become a respectable stew. He turned to Charlie. "That's between you and God, and He's always in a forgiving mood. As to Kenny and me, we're not holding it against you. We know it could be one of us with a bee inside our pants and doing some skedaddling the next time General Lee bloodies Burnside's nose. The lily-livered things men sometimes do are just unexplainable. When mini balls fly thick as hornets, we must try to do right."

Outside again, icy sprinkles splattered Bill's face as he toted the foodstuffs toward their hut. All of a sudden, a blanket of ice slid from the roof of a nearby hut and shattered on Bill and Charlie's heads and shoulders.

"Damned ice feels like mini balls." Bill's best possum brushed the sleet from his nose and cheeks.

Bill fought off the urge to hug Charlie. He definitely didn't need mollycoddling. "I'll take slush over real mini balls. No marches and battles until July. I'm not itching to give up our warm hut."

Grinning himself, Charlie shot a frisky look toward his friend. "I know why you want to stick around Fredericksburg, and it ain't 'cause of our hut." He hummed the first stanzas of "When the Corn is Waving, Annie Dear."

"For you, Billy Boy, it ain't Annie. It's Franny. Just one day to go, and y'all be off to your New Year's Eve ball."

"I'm not sure I'm going."

"Of course, you're goin'. I'll hogtie you and help the preacher drag you there, Billy Boy."

"I'll feel guilty the whole time."

"Becky?"

Bill nodded. "I'll be a damned scoundrel."

Charlie stabbed his arm toward the hospital tents. "Those men over there coughin' their lives away would give anythin' to be in your boots. Sweet Jesus, Billy Boy! This time next year you could be dead! Grab life, grab some lovin'. Don't be a fool. Go dance with the bit of frock."

Another avalanche of sleet and snow pelted the two as they threw open their hut's door and darted inside. Shivering, Bill tossed his shell jacket atop a chair and sidled to the fireplace where he stacked the foodstuffs on the mantel and let the flames warm him. He was soon snug as a bug.

"Well, look what the bear dragged to our front door," Kenny joshed as he sat on his bunk whittling a block of wood that looked like it might turn out to be an Indian. "A couple of no accounts."

"Thought you meant a couple of darky-lovin' Yanks." Nathan plucked a mouth harp from a pocket. "I'm sure lookin' forward to puttin' some mini balls between the eyes of a bunch of Lincoln-lovin' bastards."

Kenny harrumphed, then groaned. "Another fresh fish braggin' before he's had to duck a bouncin' cannonball." He nodded toward Bill and Charlie, still warming up before the fireplace. "The blowhards... they always end up absquatulatin' just before battle. They get big gray ears and turn into hospital rats. You the sickly type, Nathan?"

Nathan's face reddened. Veins at his temples throbbed. "I ain't no coward, not like that skinny runt of a man." Ensconced in a chair, his feet propped on another, Nathan jabbed his hand directly at Charlie's back.

Whirling around, Charlie growled like a big cat about to pounce. Bill shifted to block him... too late. Charlie dodged

Bill's arm, and rushed the recruit. He bulled into the Sunday soldier, overturning the chair, ramming Nathan against the wall. A snowfall of chink flakes floated to the floor, sparkling in lamplight. Astride Nathan, the recruit's arms pinned, Charlie rained punches on his bunkmate's face.

Puffing hard, Bill grabbed his friend's sleeve and hair, and yanked him off Nathan.

"Let 'em fight, Bill," Kenny said, still whittling. "The parlor boy needs a lesson in manners."

Charlie twisted around, right hand fisted and ready to swing at Bill. He tried to stop his arm, and while his efforts slowed the haymaker, Bill's chin still felt the sting. "God, Bill, I'm sorry." Charlie's face soured into an *oh-shit* look.

While Bill rubbed his chin and glared at Charlie, Nathan leaped at his attacker. Nonchalantly, Kenny launched a kick and sent the recruit sprawling. "Damn! One of the chairs is broken. I worked too damn hard buildin' them."

Bill stepped between the fighters. "Save it for the Blue-Bellies!" Again, he glared hard at Charlie. "Remember the scripture you've been reading, Possum. Whoever shall smite thee on thy right cheek, turn to him the other also." Bill picked up the mouth harp and handed it to Nathan. "Looks like a dog chewed on you, Fresh Fish. Head over to the hospital tent and get patched up. Keep your mouth shut over how it happened."

Nathan nodded. "Took a nasty fall in the mud."

"That'll work," Kenny opined, resuming his whittling.

As the door slammed behind the departing recruit, Charlie righted the undamaged chair and plopped down on it. He looked at his bloody knuckles. "Overreacted a bit, didn't I? Probably end up cleaning latrines."

Kenny chuckled. "Half the army's cleanin' latrines."

"Nathan still believes the politicians' balderdash." Bill dropped onto Nathan's bunk. "We just want to get home in one piece, not end up in some God-forsaken field."

Putting away the whittling knife and half-done Indian, Kenny ambled to the fireplace and picked up the foodstuffs. "At least you didn't ruin our supper," he muttered, then began to prepare the pork stew. "Won't be long, and I'll have vittles for our breadbaskets."

Bill looked skyward as if seeking God for guidance. He didn't expect any, not with the way the aureolas worked... so unpredictable and sphinxlike. "Guess Nathan will never again insinuate you're a coward, Charlie."

Charlie shook his head, sighing. "I would've beaten him to death if you hadn't stopped me."

Nathan hadn't returned by the time the others finished eating their share of the stew. He undoubtedly paced the winter camp in the snow and sleet trying to make sense of what had happened to him, Bill figured, sipping chicory coffee almost too hot to taste.

"I've a surprise for you, Bill." Kenny stood from where he'd been kneeling at the fireplace. "Goin' to spring it as soon as I get the fire tidy."

Bill rolled his eyes. "Surprise? I don't know if I want a surprise from you, Kenny. Could be dangerous."

"I know about it," Charlie conceded, then swallowed the last spoonful of his stew. "Miss Franny will be glad we did it."

"You both vouch I'll survive this surprise?" Bill opened the door. A few flurries fell, but no sleet. The light of thousands of candlelamps in huts and cabins let him see Nathan's fresh bootprints in the dusting of snow outside their hut.

"Going to take a jaunt to the cook's cabin." Kenny elbowed Bill aside and closed the door. "Ready for some lice killin' and skin soapin', Bill? But not before I have another cup of coffee. The opened door let in way too much cold air."

Nathan still hadn't ventured back to the hut when the others, armed with a candle-lantern, skated their way to the cook's kitchen well after nine o'clock. No moon, no stars, just a measly few flurries swirling around them. And no lock on the door, so they easily stomped their way into the cabin, even though the cooks had long retired to their huts. The cooking fires had been doused, leaving the interior tomb cold. Working diligently, Kenny and Charlie soon had fires glowing in the hearths. Bill sat near the flames enjoying the warmth, while Kenny and Charlie carried buckets to nearby Deep Creek. Once back with their filled pails, Kenny and Charlie gestured for Bill to stand up. "Uniform off!" Kenny commanded in his best sergeant voice.

"Cabin's still too cold," Bill protested halfheartedly.

"Remove everything, soldier!" Kenny barked. "Even your long johns."

Kenny dumped the pails of water into five kettles dangling above the flames.

Actually, in spite of his griping, Bill was pleased to see Kenny and Charlie enjoying their prank… and not thinking of all the what-might-have-beens. What if A.P. Hill had closed the gap? What if the Blue-Bellies hadn't breached the line? What if the Yankee bullet had just grazed Daniel or not struck him at all? Instead, they were thinking: How can I make Bill's life a living hell?

Well, to start with, making him undress in front of them, their mischievous eyes fixed on him. Bill started with his boots. Next, his shell jacket, followed by his vest and shirt. More: pants, wool socks, even his battered slouch hat. The fireplace light cast him in a soft amber glow.

Kenny pressed his arms against his chest. "Off with the long johns."

Bill wriggled out of the underwear and stood before them as if he were Julius Caesar regarding the barbarian Gauls.

Kenny chortled. "Your Franny will like what I'm seein', Bill Stamford."

The shell jacket held by his fingertips, Charlie dropped the garment into a simmering kettle and beat it with a plunger. Charlie grumbled, "The cold kills us, but nothin' seems to hurt the lice critters, except boilin' water. Die, bastards!" The buggers, some of the boys called them graybacks, floated in the mini-maelstrom.

"Bad night in Fredericksburg," Kenny joked. "Lots of girl lice mournin' their dead men."

Kenny and Charlie spent nearly three hours delousing Bill's clothes and blankets. While the clothes dried on a makeshift clothesline near the fireplace, Kenny ground up eight garlic cloves, hand-brushed them into a bowl and added two teaspoons of lime juice, creating a varmint-killing paste.

"Into your hair, Possum," Charlie demanded.

Grimacing, Bill obeyed, smearing the paste throughout his hair... head, groin and armpits.

"Tiny coffins for you, little Graybacks," Kenny sniggered.

Bill hand-checked his clothes. Still damp, even the long johns. "Someone needs to come up with an invention that dries clothes in thirty minutes."

Kenny leaned against the log wall and eyed Bill as if ogling a New Orleans mollisher. "This Franny's goin' to like you unrigged. I've a lass in Fredericksburg who likes my nebuchadnezzar and twittle-diddles. Can't keep her hands off them."

Again, Bill brushed his hand against the shell jacket, then his shirt. Jacket, still damp; shirt, dry. "I'm just going to dance with her. She's the kind of woman generals marry, not for the likes of me. Without this war, she'd not give me the time of day."

Charlie cocked an eyebrow. "You better look again at that invitation, Billy Boy. She's game for an engagement with her cloven inlet. You'll be doing far more than dancin'."

Glad they were no longer focused on Daniel's death, Bill nevertheless didn't like where their minds had gone. The war had dragged gentlemen's minds into the gutter. "Just dancin', Charlie. Her momma will keep a close watch on us, I'm sure."

Yawning, Bill finally got to don his varmint-free clothes. He headed for the door when Kenny hollered, "Wait! One more secret." Kenny reached into a pants pocket and emerged with a red-tinted bottle. "*Eau de Cologne*," he announced proudly. "My Fredericksburg darlin' swears your Franny will love smellin' the cologne. Use lots of it tomorrow before you go. Guaranteed... your Franny will be draggin' you to the greenhouse garden."

The streets were quiet, the night sky clear when they walked back to their hut. So quiet they could hear their boots squish in the ankle-deep snow. Or so Bill thought until he heard coughing from one hut, and then another. Soon, he realized the hacks came from nearly all the huts in the vicinity. Near them, a soldier, his pants down below his buttocks, darted through a hut's doorway and scuttled for the closest latrine.

Only one window glowed with candlelight and that was Bill's hut. Nathan had returned. They found him sitting on his bunk, his back resting against a pillow braced against the wall. He'd nearly let the fire go out. Shadows played across his face, but the damage could still be seen... a dressing across his forehead, a black eye and a busted lip.

His good eye stared into the shrunken flames. He tried to rise from his bunk, groaned clamorously and collapsed back against the pillow.

"I need to have my say first," Nathan spoke up, his socked feet quivering. "I want to say I'm sorry, Charlie. I'd no right to say those things. I've been told I'm a blabbermouth. I don't expect to be forgiven. That's okay. Just so you know it'll never happen again." Nathan laughed sardonically. "I told 'em I had an *engagement* with one of Fredericksburg's doves, but the terrible weather ruined our plans. On the way back to camp, I smashed into a tree darker than the sky." He shrugged. "They didn't call me a liar."

Bill shoved Charlie forward. "Your apology accepted, Nathan. I got a hair-trigger temper," Charlie said, then gave his version of a sour laugh. "It weren't a fair fight the way I ambushed you. We can fight like boxers if you want."

"Naw. I hurt too much." With his split lip, Nathan's effort at a smile looked grotesque. "You gave me a good lesson in manners."

Once out of his clothes, except for his long johns, and in his bed, Bill discovered he couldn't sleep. Thoughts of Franny pestered him. The bottle of *Eau de Cologne* rested on the floor next to his bunk, so close he could touch the cap. He knew if he daubed it on his body after sunrise, it meant he wanted to spend the evening with her... and with it all the complications, their clothes no longer on their bodies, hands caressing skin, kisses over intimate areas. *Dear Lord, save me from myself.* He sighed. More likely she'd notice a cavalry officer with a curling mustache and abandon him.

~ * ~

New Year's Eve day went excruciatingly slow for Bill. He couldn't keep his hands away from his pocket watch. The more he looked at its turning hands, the slower they seemingly moved. Time crawled. Only when he drilled did he ignore his vest pocket. When officers dismissed the Eighteenth in the late afternoon, Bill raced to the hut to run a comb through his hair and dab *Eau de Cologne* on his neck, cheeks, armpits and chest. He thought about applying a spot or two to his groin area but vetoed the idea. Ten steps away from the hut, he realized he couldn't feel the weight of straps against his shoulders. No knapsack. Frustrated, eager to get to the Yerby house, he returned to the hut, crammed the cologne bottle, comb and a shaver into the knapsack and slung it over his shoulders. He left the hut just as Charlie approached, toting a bucket of swishing water.

"Billy Boy, good luck with the dance... and your proper bit of frock." He set the bucket on the ground, grabbed Bill's shoulders and playfully kissed him on the cheek.

The *old* Charlie had definitely returned. Bill did worry, though. Now his friend would probably fight to the death before he'd do any hightailing to the rear. Bill kept those inner thoughts to himself. Instead, he pretended to punch his friend in the gut. "Looks like you've a serious case of the gigglemugs."

Halfway along the camp street, sprinkles began falling. Warmer than the day before, so no snow. He'd prefer the snow. Better than slogging through mud. *Balderdash*, Bill thought, although meaner words ricocheted through his mind. With the sprinkles threatening to become a hard rain, it meant Bill would be soaked by the time he got to Belvoir.

The ground rumbled. Bill turned toward the sound and a side street that led to the carriage road to Belvoir. A team of horses and its Brougham buggy sloshed to a stop where the camp's street joined the carriage road. Once ensconced inside the buggy, Bill shook the chaplain's hand.

"Afternoon, Reverend Anderson. Sure glad to see you. Thought I'd be walking to the Belvoir in the pouring rain." Bill's buttocks sank into the seat's rich upholstery.

"Couldn't leave the Nightingale of Belvoir out in a drenching rain." Anderson kept a firm grasp on Bill's hand. "Your admirer gave me strict orders. Don't let you get soaked and risk a cold or worse. Thankfully. I'm here just in time." Anderson released Bill's hand, then looked up at the carriage roof, making a racket as the rain pelted the metal.

"Nightingale? I see Franny has been busy extolling my limited nursing talents." Bill sighed.

"Odd, I know," Anderson said, his voice lighthearted. "She was very impressed with how attentive you were to all your fellow soldiers' needs. I know General Gregg's loved ones and friends were grateful for your presence." The chaplain flicked raindrops from Bill's shell jacket. "Your idea of using steaming-hot water to clean dressings and washrags... where did that come from?"

"Papa's got a doctor friend who studied in Europe. Some forward thinkers believe steam's the way to go. Papa's friend says pus is bad for the wound. With so many dying, there was nothing to lose. Captain Poisson? He's doing alright?"

"The captain's recovering nicely, thanks to you." Anderson wiggled his nose. "Did you do some colognifying, Bill?"

"I overdid it?"

"Maybe a tad. We'll fix that when we reach the Belvoir."

"Fix? Sounds like something I won't enjoy." Bill rested his head against the cushioned backrest.

"Franny will. In fact, she made me swear to do the *fix*." He laughed evilly.

At Belvoir, the chaplain ushered Bill into the same upstairs bedroom used by Franny and her mother while they stayed at the mansion. Inside, two darkies, girls no older than fifteen, poured buckets of steaming water into a metal bathing tub. Hands at his side, Bill stood beside the exquisitely made bed and couldn't draw his eyes away from the walk-in closet where Franny had first kissed him.

"Out of your clothes!" the chaplain barked.

Bill squinted, confused. "I'm clean, my uniform's clean. No lice as far as I can tell."

Anderson pointed to the tub where the darkies had just finished filling it. "Hardly. But I promise you will be. Leave the clothes on the floor, not the bed. And get in!"

Slithering out of his uniform duds and long johns, Bill climbed into the tub. The girls had stoked the fireplace flames, yet the air remained noticeably cold, so Bill slid beneath the hot water. With their bosoms noticeable through their drab gray dresses, Bill wanted his ballocks submerged, especially since the chaplain was just a few feet away. One of the girls, the taller, skinnier one with her hair partly covered by a turban, skipped out the door, leaving the shorter, light-skinned one behind.

"Scrub him, girl!" His arms crossed against his chest, Anderson watched the girl scour Bill with a sponge and a large bar of lavender-scented soap.

Bill hadn't smelled anything as nice since he'd lain beside Becky. *Damn rotten time to think of Becky.* His stomach twisted with guilt. Two women on his mind... was that so bad? He'd have a good time—no, a splendid time—tonight, Bill promised himself.

Her breasts hanging over the edge of the tub, the girl scrubbed his back in a grueling, circular pattern, over and over again. "That's enough!" he protested. "You'll scrape my skin off."

"Keep at it, girl. And do his hair," Anderson said briskly. "Mister Stamford, you're going to smell so heavenly every girl at the ball will want to dance with you."

The girl's bosom brushed against Bill's shoulder, a delightful sensation. "Sir," she addressed the chaplain, "should I coat him with the concoction now?"

"Concoction?" Bill's voice quivered with trepidation.

The chaplain patted the girl on the back. "A special brew Sabra's momma distilled, guaranteed to kill every louse on your body."

"But we killed them already." Bill coughed roughly when soapy water poured into his nose and mouth.

"Those critters are harder to kill than a Yankee cavalryman." Anderson picked up a towel from the bed. "But I'm going to get every one of them before I let you near Franny."

"Lordy, terrible smelling stuff!" Bill's thumb and forefinger held his nostrils shut.

"Field slaves concocted the potion. Buggers drop dead within a mile." Sabra grinned, revealing pearly teeth. "Even flies and fleas give up the ghost." She smeared the limey mixture into his hair, her fingers massaging his scalp. He thought she let it soak in for way too many minutes.

"Any flames coming out of my head?" Not that hot, Bill knew, but hot enough for him to squeeze his thighs.

"Don't be a baby!" Sabra chided. "Head sinkin' time, Soldier Boy." She pushed him under the water. He ingested more soapy water, and when he broke the surface, had a small coughing fit. His eyes burned... but not so bad he couldn't see the look of concern on her face.

"I'm fine," he assured her.

She stuck a finger in the water. "Bunch of dead Yankees floatin'."

"Can't believe there were so many buggers still in my hair."

"They're stubborn critters." Anderson unrolled the towel, a sign for Bill to rise out of the water. "Last night they probably hopped from your bunkmates to you. Poor Franny got them bad when she helped nurse the wounded. Don't want her tussling with them again."

Bill said nothing. He didn't want her troubled by lice either.

Sabra toweled him off under the watchful eye of the chaplain, who chased her away once Bill was dry. With one more duty out of the way—Bill shaved off his beard—Anderson went to the armoire and drew out a new uniform, a Zouave suit that made Bill's eyes widen in both admiration and alarm. The uniform was eye-catching, but no one else in the brigade wore one.

"I can't wear this." Bill stepped toward the armoire, the glitzy outfit draped over his arm."

The chaplain blocked him. "Of course you can. At least for the ball. You can don the old uniform afterwards. Franny wants you to keep the frock." Anderson's forehead furrowed. "You can't say no. Those were her orders to me."

The chaplain took the uniform from Bill, who swathed himself in a quilt as Anderson laid the fancy outfit on the bed. "I don't have much of a choice, do I?" Bill grinned, admitting defeat.

Anderson shook his head. "It will go well with the fetching ball gown Franny will be wearing, as you will soon see."

Seventeen

A Wintertime Ball

The chaplain's Brougham buggy bounced along the carriage road toward Forest Hill. Seated beside Chaplain J. Monroe Anderson, Bill kept glancing fretfully at the new frockcoat and Zouave uniform that clothed his scrubbed body. He looked like one of those fancy Louisiana Tigers. With the coat unbuttoned, he could see the embroidered gray shell jacket, baggy white pants with blue stripes, and brogans that were pinching his big toes. He couldn't wait to get back into his comfortable boots.

The day and now the night had been infuriating—rainy one minute, dry the next, as unpredictable as the arrival date of Becky's next letter. Maybe she'd found someone else, and no longer wanted to express her love for him. If that proved to be the case, then Bill need not feel guilty for the debauched thoughts about Franny whirling inside his head.

The chaplain perched his arm on the sill, elbow pressed against the buggy window. A spattering of raindrops dripped down the glass. No patter on the roof, so the rain must be negligible. "Going to be a party for the ages," the chaplain observed as the buggy drew near the Hamilton mansion, its oil-lamplit façade visible through skeletal trees. "Back in the early fifties, I pastored the First Christian Church in Fredericksburg. Got to know the people. They've been through hell. Forced to camp out in fields beyond the town, living in tents in the freezing weather or sheltering in barns. Some lucky ones have been taken in by relatives or friends, but they're few in number. I went to one refugee camp to try to cheer them up. Little girls were crying to their mommas to take them home."

Bill grimaced. The Yanks were making war on civilians. "Those poor girls. I'm sorry." He wrapped himself in silence. What else could he say?

Buggies and carriages were lined up on the carriage road and in the Hamiltons' driveway, moving slowly as each unloaded partygoers under the *porte cochere.*

"Caught in the crossfire," Anderson said, nodding. "Now that the Yanks are in their winter camps on the far side of the Rappahannock, folks who still have homes have returned to them. Others... they'll be dependent on the charity of loved ones until the war ends." The lantern outside the buggy window cast an amber glow on the chaplain's face. "So glad Jane Hamilton and her daughter Matilda are holding this New Year's Eve ball. The people need it. Worst December in their lives."

The buggy cleared the tree line, providing Bill a clear view of the mansion. The brilliantly lit Forest Hill house lay atop a small knoll, surrounded by outbuildings. An army ambulance had stopped under the overhang where Army of Northern Virginia officers were helping gowned ladies from the conveyance. Lamplight blazed in all twenty-four windows.

"We've a few grand houses in Kenansville, but nothing like this," Bill said, his voice awestruck.

Anderson chuckled. "Wilmington has grander, but this one is impressive. The main house was built at the turn of the century. The ballroom was added later."

Bill rubbed his hands together. They were sweaty. "Lordy, I'm nervous. I feel like it's my first dance."

"Relax, Stamford. Remember, some of the people you'll see tonight are just glad to be alive." The chaplain toyed with his waxed mustache. "The Hamiltons took in refugees, but everyone had to flee to Belvoir when fighting erupted around the mansion. That's why Jane and Matilda were able to help nurse the wounded at Belvoir."

Bill fidgeted as the buggy wheeled closer to the portico. Just ahead, a general helped his lady disembark from another ambulance. Arm in arm, the couple disappeared into a double-door side entrance, the portal into the ballroom. A front-yard fountain frothed in the wintry air, chilly but not cold enough for snow. The noisy water cloaked Bill's growling stomach.

The general's lady wore an exquisite blue satin gown embroidered with white lace, a white petticoat peeking beneath the gown. Bill wondered: Would Franny look so divine? Under different circumstances, he might have already seen her gown. Franny's house hadn't fallen victim to Yankee cannons or the ensuing fire as Bill feared. The chaplain had planned to pick her up in Fredericksburg, except Franny was staying at Forest Hills helping decorate the ballroom. Bill would have to wait until he walked in. He pointed to the general's exquisitely toileted filly and giggled like a ten-year old. "Lordy, look at the size of her hoop! How in the world would we have gotten Franny into the buggy?"

The chaplain's scamp eyes twinkled with tomfoolery. "You're not a man of the world, are you? You've heard of carpetbags and trunks, right? We'd have brought the gown and her unmentionables in a trunk. Franny would have changed in Matilda's room." Anderson laughed. "Preened in her gown and sitting with us in the buggy... what a dreadful ordeal that would've been." He laughed some more. "You do have a sense of humor, Stamford."

Bill rolled his eyes. "So I've been told." He entertained a wicked thought. Those officers helping their ladies out of the ambulances ... later in the night the men would be plotting how to remove the gowns and sundry underthings.

At the portico, a Forest Hill servant garbed like an 18th century butler opened the buggy's door. "Sirs, welcome to Forest Hill." He bowed. "No ladies?"

"The ladies await us inside," Anderson answered, chuckling, letting the manservant help him step down to the flagstones.

Bill hopped down the steps, waving away the manservant's offer of aid. Another manservant stood at rigid attention at the portico's entrance. "Welcome, Reverend Anderson." Bowing, the manservant opened both doors, then gave Bill an inquisitive look.

"Private Bill Stamford, Eighteenth North Carolina," Bill said, thinking his title sounded paltry next to a general or senator.

"Nonsense, Bill," the chaplain spoke up. "Announce him as Private Bill Stamford, Eighteenth North Carolina, the Nightingale of Fredericksburg, and the special guest of Miss Franny Neale."

"Gladly, sir." The manservant stepped into the ballroom's foyer. "Chaplain J. Monroe Anderson of the Army of Northern Virginia and his friend, Private Bill Stamford, Eighteenth North Carolina, the Nightingale of Fredericksburg, special friend to Miss Franny Neale." The longwinded declaration embarrassed Bill.

A cold breeze blowing through the entryway into the foyer diminished and then disappeared entirely as Bill and the chaplain made their way past a grand stairway to the balcony. Anderson squeezed Bill's arm and whispered, "Prepare to see Glory."

The chaplain nodded toward the ballroom's grand archway. Glinting in firelight, Franny stood under the arch, draped in a satin gown with tulle, swansdown, and pearls. The gown's costly embroidery could have kept the Eighteenth oversupplied with enough hogs, chickens and steers for six months. Her diamond and ruby necklace could have paid for the provisions of the brigade for thirty days. He hardly recognized the girl he'd worked beside at the Belvoir. The simple hairstyle was gone, replaced with a fancy coil at the back of her head and silk roses twined into her tresses. He looked upon an angel come from the Realms of Glory.

Two officers—captains—shadowed her as she stepped toward Bill and the chaplain. She stopped and spoke in near-whispers to them, words Bill wanted to hear but couldn't. The captains' desire to monopolize her time would end in disappointment. Bill allowed a slight smile to crease his mouth.

The officers coveted her, but for this night she belonged to Bill. Afterwards? Only God knew what awaited them. A Blue-Belly bullet for Bill? Or another man's heart that might touch Franny's soul? On New Year's Eve, the aureolas of fire stayed silent, concealed within the fog of possible futures. She strolled gracefully toward him, her white slippers revealed fleetingly when the gown's hemline swirled above her ankles. No hoop... she meant to shock the older ladies and probably a few of the younger ones.

"I'm stealing him, Chaplain." Franny pocketed her gloves in a purse. "He's mine for rest of the night."

"I've brought him to you, Miss Neale, just as ordered." Anderson bowed, kissed her hand and went looking for Jane Hamilton.

On tiptoes, she let her lips touch his cheek. Bill swore his heart skipped a beat. "I picked out the Zouave uniform for you," she said softly and took his arm. "I left my dance card back in Matilda's bedroom. I'll dance with no one else but you."

After a side trip to the cloak room to stow his frockcoat, Franny led Bill into the ballroom. The light dazzled. He'd never seen a room so bright. Franny pressed against Bill's side as he glanced upward. Hundreds of candles shone from three chandeliers. Above them, a Michelangelo-like fresco of flying snow geese and Mallard ducks brought Bill to a stumbling stop.

Franny noticed his starry-eyed gawking. "Sometimes I sneak into the ballroom, sit and stare at the artwork. Painted by a Yankee way before the war. Rufus Porter, publisher of *Scientific American*." She rolled her eyes. "And no... I don't read it religiously."

"I've heard of him," Bill acknowledged, lowering his eyes from the ceiling to Franny's face. "Thought his murals could only be found in New England."

"The Hamiltons convinced him to take the train to Fredericksburg and paint the ceiling. Politicians can be quite persuasive."

"Young women too." Bill grinned.

Franny turned her gaze back to the ceiling. "I prefer the ceiling sculptures."

Following her eyes, he spied stucco sculptures of angels with tiny wings and cherubic faces. Bill had yet to pay heed to the walls, their mirrors and French tapestries of dancing medieval aristocrats. The light from the wall lamps and chandeliers reflected off the mirrors, and with the greenhouse-grown azaleas and primroses blooming in flowerpots along the walls, the ballroom smelled like a warm summer day.

"It's almost as if we're in a garden, not a ballroom," Bill observed.

Franny did an exaggeratedly formal curtsy. "You can thank yours truly and Matilda for the illusion. I had to convince Matilda and her mother, though. They were going to let their slaves have all the decorating fun. I said: 'All you kidding me? This ballroom needs the touch of these creative hands.'" Franny lifted her hands, her slender fingers dancing to imaginary music.

Lordy, he wanted to kiss her. Maybe it was the scent of the nearby primroses responsible for the seductive thoughts in his head. He wanted to slip his arm around her waist and pull her tight against him.

"I see someone we need to greet." Franny led Bill to a civilian, an older man dressed in a blue coat and white vest, with lavender pantaloons and gloves. The middle-aged gentleman lingered underneath the balcony, surrounded by an entourage of admirers. Two grandfatherly men stepped back as Franny and Bill approached.

"Good evening, Mayor." Franny extricated her hand from Bill's arm and curtsied, this time without the theatrics.

"Evening, Franny," the mayor replied, kissing her hand. He eyed Bill guardedly, as if unsure what to make of a private in a flamboyant Zouave uniform. Apparently satisfied, he offered Bill his hand. "Name's Montgomery Slaughter. I do some speculating in wheat and mill flour. And, as you heard, I'm mayor of this sad city."

Bill clasped the mayor's hand. "William Stamford, Eighteenth North Carolina, Lane's Brigade."

"Bill for short." Franny tapped Bill's shoulder. "Mayor Slaughter and eighteen other distinguished gentlemen of Fredericksburg were recent prisoners of Lincoln, confined in the Old Capitol Prison."

"I'm sorry for your ordeal, sir," Bill said neutrally, not sure what he should say.

"From August until the latter part of September, about sixteen weeks as guests of Lincoln. The worst time of my life... until the damned shells started falling on us." The mayor pointed to a band of young Confederate officers chatting with two young ladies. "Thank God for the Army of Northern Virginia."

"Bill's the Angel of Belvoir, Mayor." Franny clutched Bill's arm again. "I wanted you to meet him, not just hear his name bantered about."

"Ah, yes, the man you kidnapped to help nurse the wounded during those terrible days." The mayor sat down in one of the tufted leather armchairs arranged against the ballroom walls. "A bad back. One of the scars from my stay in Lincoln's prison. A few minutes' rest, and I'll be as good as new and ready to dance."

Franny brushed her hand up and down Bill's arm. "My swain for tonight practiced Tar Heel journalism before the war."

"She exaggerates, sir," Bill amended. "Just learning the trade from my papa."

"A worthy profession," the mayor said, his look revealing otherwise. "Most editors are patriots. A few write disloyal editorials. Not your papa, I'm sure, since he has a loyal son in Lee's army." His features softened. "I didn't mean to sound harsh. Time in a Yankee prison changes a man."

Bill nodded. "You're just as brave as any of the officers in this magnificent room. No chance Lincoln could break you."

After more small talk, the mayor excused himself and mingled. Franny did the same, introducing Bill to a whirlwind of faces and names quickly forgotten once the dancing began. All had spent months in Old Capitol Prison courtesy of Lincoln. Thomas Knox, a flower grower; James Bradley, a grocer and deacon in the Baptist Church; the Rev. William Broaddus, pastor of the Baptist Church and head of the female academy, and James Cooke, the town's best-known druggist. All frowned when they noticed Franny's gown lacked a hoop. Yet they didn't seem surprised, as if they'd come to accept her rebellious spirit. *A pretty face will melt a stern man's heart.*

A tittering feminine voice rang out: "Oh, Franny! Franny Neale!" Bill zeroed in on the voice, which belonged to one of three jammiest bits of jam huddled around a Confederate lieutenant with a villainous mustache. "Franny, who's the pretty gentleman?"

Franny guided Bill toward two tables overflowing with food where the surrounded lieutenant tried to keep up with the prattle of the gigglemugs. "Jody Knox, Leslie Bradly, Milly Cooke," Franny told Bill. "Daughters of three of the Old Capitol Prison lodgers. And their prisoner is Frank Broaddus, one of Fredericksburg's soldiers with the Army of Northern Virginia, and a suitor until I became engaged to a Tennessean."

Bill decided to allow Franny to volunteer her fiancé's name at her own pace. Still, the knowledge that she belonged to another took the wind out of his sails. Truly, this night must be a lark for her. Then again, that held true for him as well. "He doesn't seem eager to escape."

"Evening, Frank," Franny said, obviously amused by the look on the man's face, an expression that said *I want to be on the other side of the room.* "I know you've been hereabouts in Fredericksburg for well over a month, and you've not once been to see Momma. She's quite irritated with you."

"We fought a battle. Remember?" Frank's voice emerged low and cold.

"Oh, I remember." Franny swiveled her gaze from Frank to Bill. "I was at the Yerby house nursing the wounded. Bill"—she caressed Bill's jacket sleeve—"helped me. I thought I'd reward him with some dances at tonight's ball."

"Oh, how romantic!" Milly exclaimed, stirring a breeze with a flowery fan.

"Nice seeing you again, Franny," Frank said tightly. "And congratulations on your engagement." He turned to the three girls. "I must excuse myself." He laughed lightly. "More dance cards to sign." He grabbed a slice of lemon cake and ambled toward another band of young ladies.

"Don't forget to claim your dance with me!" Leslie reminded Frank, which he acknowledged with a flick of his right hand, fingers wiggling.

"Franny! You haven't introduced your friend," Milly chastised. She picked up a plate containing a slice of white cake with lemon icing and handed it to Bill. "Franny can be so possessive."

"Is he your Nightingale?" Jody asked, fanning herself furiously.

Franny raised her hand. "Ladies! Let my gentleman caller breathe. You're going to knock him into the table. Cake is to be eaten, not sat on."

Bill braced himself as his hip gently touched the cake table. "No harm done." He dipped a finger into the icing and tasted it. "Sumptuous. Got to admit, ladies, I'm tired of cornbread dipped in coffee."

"Indeed, ladies, he's my Nightingale. Bill Stamford. All mine tonight. He'll not sign another girl's dance card." A lighthearted laugh leapt from Franny's mouth. "Especially yours, Leslie."

"You're still sore over Frank Broaddus?" Leslie tapped the edge of her fan on Franny's hand. "Just one kiss. You weren't supposed to see it."

"But I did," Franny said, her tone saucy. "You deservedly got a black eye."

"Ah, Franny, you didn't come through unscathed. A split lip, right?"

Ignoring Franny and Leslie, Jody eyed a woman and a girl dressed in mourning gowns. She gasped, fought back tears. Failing, she sobbed quietly. "There's Donald Franks' mother and his baby sister Mildred. He was killed at Second Manassas. My first beau."

Her tears stunned everyone into silence. If not for Jody's sobs and the buzz of conversation coming from elsewhere in the ballroom, the silence might have continued. Except Jody looked heartrending, prompting Franny to spring away from Bill and hug her. "There, there, Jody." Franny sounded like a mother reading a nursery rhyme to her toddler.

Up in the balcony, the band played "Dixie," and Jody eased her weeping and wiped a hand across her face. A half-smile appeared. "I never noticed until now. There're so many black gowns in the ballroom."

Bill agreed, his eyes sweeping the ballroom. More than a third of the women wore mourning gowns. Irony bubbled to consciousness. At least no officer bore aureola flames. Of course, that didn't mean they still wouldn't die of disease in the weeks ahead or perish in battle in the spring. It's only meaning? The Gift-Giver hadn't let Bill see a manifestation since Daniel. But he couldn't escape a stab of guilt for being inside the ballroom with Franny while Daniel's remains rotted in a hastily dug grave. He'd kissed Franny; Daniel would never again kiss a woman. Bill knew what Kenny would say if he could read his morbid thoughts: "Lordy, possum, Daniel would want you to kiss her. Just don't tell him she has a fiancé. Daniel's a bit prudish."

Franny raised her voice. "They'll be playing a waltz soon. Men will flock around you in no time, Jody."

"And you, Franny, and your Nightingale will be a filly and a foal on the dance floor." Leslie chortled at her choice of words.

Her eyes still watery, Jody said in a shocked voice, "Leslie! You're so naughty."

"Naughty? I'm not the one with a fiancé in Tennessee and a new beau in Fredericksburg." Leslie's eyes twinkled as she regarded Franny. "In a way, I wish I were."

"War changes people. You know that, Leslie." Franny tucked her hand into the crook of Bill's elbow. "Sometimes in small ways, like the crinoline hoop and the white gloves I'm refusing to wear. Other times in bigger ways, like my decision not to allow my Nightingale to see in the new year without a chance to dance and forget the war for a night. I'm sure my Peter is doing the same this night."

Bill sighed. "Peter, eh? I envy him, Franny. He's a lucky man."

Franny cocked an eyebrow. "Bill Stamford, you're the lucky—"

At the archway, the manservant bellowed: "Presenting General Robert E. Lee, commanding general of the Army

Northern Virginia, and at his side, Helen Mayre, daughter of John Mayre." The room erupted into rebel yells. Instead of a waltz, the band played "Bonnie Blue Flag."

Lee strode toward Bill and Franny. Bill expected him to pass by and head toward one of the generals or colonels, maybe Longstreet or Jackson. Instead, he stopped in front of Franny. *Oh, Lord, please no aureola.* None appeared, and Bill breathed again. Stunned that the South's greatest general should be so close to them, Leslie, Jody and Milly stumbled backward several steps before regaining their balance. Their fans waved ferociously, creating enough air to foment a small twister.

"Ladies, please, I'm not a statue." General Lee offered the girls a tolerant smile, as if he'd seen far too many hero worshippers.

Lee looked the part of a hero... a tall, gray-bearded gentleman, the epitome of a dignified, quietly devout Christian. Still broad shouldered at fifty-six, he wore a uniform that didn't brag of his military rank. The only mark of his rank were the three stars on his collar. Without trying to look too obvious, Bill inspected Lee from his white hair down to his well-worn gray jacket and blue trousers tucked into his Wellington boots.

"Oh, you're not a statue, sir," Leslie gasped, stuttering. "Greatest man who ever lived... that's you, my general."

"Hardly," Lee answered. "President Washington, Benjamin Franklin and Wolfgang Amadeus Mozart... they're my heroes, ladies." Lee bowed to Franny. "Good to see you again, Franny Neale. Mary and I always enjoyed your and your mother's visits to our Arlington house."

Franny offered her hand, which Lee kissed. "You made a very fine gentleman farmer, sir. Hopefully, you'll soon be able to get back to growing things. I trust all is well with

Mildred. She was a wonderful playmate when we were children and a dear friend in recent years." Franny did the unexpected, at least to Bill. She abruptly seized both Lee's hands and kissed them. "I am so sorry to hear of Annie's death. She was five years older than me, so we were never chums like Mildred, but she was always willing to play board games with us."

"Little Raspberry has been gone for two months," Lee said in a subdued voice. "Thank you for your kind words. She always liked you, liked your spirit, your hijinks." The general gestured to her hands, still grasping his fingers. "Gloveless... you're a scandalous young woman." He grinned.

"No hoop either," Franny teased.

Lee fixed his gaze on Bill. "I want to thank you for the tender care you gave General Gregg. His loved ones have spoken highly of you."

Bill saluted. "Thank you, sir."

"I've an order for you, Franny Neale. Make sure your Nightingale has a wonderful time tonight." He bowed to her. "Regrettably, I see the mayor's summoning me."

The last tones of "Bonnie Blue Flag" faded, replaced by the droning sounds of fancy-garbed soldiers and civilians watching the mayor and General Lee step onto the stage at the back of the ballroom. As the two made their way up the steps, the band—an eclectic mix of middle-aged Fredericksburg musicians and the 26th North Carolina Regimental Band—began playing "Darling Nellie Gray."

Looking up at the balcony, Mayor Slaughter raised both hands above his head, signaling the band to stop the song. When it was quiet, the mayor cleared his throat and called out: "Now that General Lee has arrived, I want to take a moment to recognize some of the brave soldiers who routed the Yankee curs and sent them scurrying back across the Rappahannock." He announced a litany of names of generals, colonels, captains and lieutenants—Longstreet, Jackson, A.P. Hill, J.E.B. Stuart, Richard Garnett—so many Bill's mind drifted. He slanted his gaze and enjoyed something much more interesting... Franny, lovely in her hoopless gown.

Bill whispered into Franny's ear, "I hope he mentions the sergeants, corporals and privates."

"General Lee will," she answered.

And he did: "As we dance in the new year of 1863, we should remember the real heroes of the Army of Northern Virginia, the men who at this moment are in their winter-quarters huts tending to their fires and eating their suppers. Enough speechifying. Let's dance."

"Yes, let's dance," Mayor Slaughter echoed. "A warning to older folks like me: The young ones want to do a few *round dances*. I don't think we're going to corrupt Southern society by allowing an occasional waltz and polka. Our soldiers are risking their lives for our freedom from Lincoln's tyranny. Let's let them do some round dances. General Lee, please choose a lady as your dance partner for a waltz, 'Byerly's Waltz.'"

Lee descended the stage steps and marched straight to Franny. He regarded Bill. "May I borrow your lady?"

Nodding, Bill replied, "Please, sir, enjoy your waltz."

Bill could hardly believe his eyes. Franny was dancing with the commander of the Army of Northern Virginia. She was friends with a man who in all probability would someday be President of the Confederate States of America ...if Lincoln's ambitions could be thwarted on the battlefield and in Europe. He should be jealous, but honestly he just enjoyed watching the general and Franny dance. They both were graceful dancers, much better than his awkward exertions. At the song's conclusion, as folks clapped, General Lee returned Franny to Bill.

The general told him, "I've seen Franny at my Arlington house each summer since she was this high"—Lee held his hand at toddler level—"and this is the first time I've shared a dance with her. You'll discover her a splendid dancer."

"Bill Stamford, I've been waiting for this moment since we first met at the Belvoir." She nodded toward the tiled dance floor.

"Will you honor me, Franny, with this dance?"

"Of course," she said, eagerness in her voice.

Bill returned the cake slice to the table, and with his hand on her elbow, promenaded her onto the dance floor as the band struck up the "Prima Donna Waltz." They danced, their eyes only on each other. He blocked out everything else in the ballroom ...the state flags flying above their heads, the chandeliers, the red and blue bunting, the refreshment tables and tufted leather armchairs along the walls. His eyes never wandered from her heart-shaped face. His right hand nuzzled perfectly against her hip. The gown fabric tickled his palm. He interlocked the fingers of his left hand with hers. Their sweat mingled and trickled to their wrists.

"You smell good." She sniffed. *"Eau de Cologne Imperiale?"*

"You know your colognes. I wanted more, but the chaplain refused. Said I'd overwhelm your nose."

"Not possible. I can't get enough of you, Bill Stamford.

"Love your fragrance, Franny Neale."

"You should. It's the same as yours." She laughed, obviously delighted with his *faux pas.* "Citrus and lavender. Puts a soul in the mood for romance."

Even as the last notes of the waltz faded until only voices filled the room, Bill continued to spin Franny around the dance floor until they stopped in front of straitlaced Naomi Cooke. Naomi raised her voice to make sure Franny heard every word. "Loathsome! Prurient French taste. All the rage? Let the Yankee females do these filthy dances."

Next up for the band: the "Jenny Lind Polka." Bill reached out with his right hand and encircled Franny's waist, ready to try his luck with a polka. *Let the old lady complain*, he thought, ready to hug Franny close.

Franny spoke up, "The air's too stuffy. Let's walk in the gardens." There was a lilt to her voice, a coquettish quality.

He'd always forsake a dance to hold hands with a magnificent woman in a greenhouse garden. "It's cold, so we should get my frock and your fur."

"I'll race you," she said, giggling.

Eighteen

Wintertime Lovers

Swaddled in his army frockcoat, Bill shepherded Franny out of the coat room and through a side door into the greenhouse. Franny pulled her fur tighter around her, protecting skin from a chill wind. Bill wished it were he, not her fur, keeping Franny warm. He did twine his fingers with hers, and in return, she burrowed against him.

A solitary lamppost provided minimal light, perfect for couples sneaking kisses among the poinsettias, lilies, azaleas and primroses. Bill recognized one couple in a passionate embrace near a quiet fountain... Frank Broaddus and Nan Bradly. He opened his mouth to tell Franny about the two lovebirds, but she put a finger to her lips and hurried him toward the second and last fountain, two tiers with a Roman lady holding a basket of grapes. When they reached it, Bill pressed his body against her gown, crinkling the petticoats. They kissed once, twice, three times, each kiss longer, their touch more ardent. She stepped back, took his hand, and led him toward the exit. He expected to turn around and go back to the ballroom. Instead, Franny reached into her coat pocket and produced a key.

"It's to the front door of the overseer's cottage." She slipped the key into his hand and closed his fingers. "The house is vacant. The overseer fled when the bombardment started. No word from him. Seems he doesn't like the war so close."

Bill swallowed his doubts. The oil lamps in the main house provided enough light to see the cottage a hundred yards away. His plugtail pushed against his pantaloons. Not even beyond the greenhouse, and he was getting a bad case of loll tongue. He vanquished an uninvited thought about Becky, slipped his arm around Franny's waist and steered her toward the cottage.

The cold hit like an incoming shell. Raindrops and a few snowflakes fell, not many, but enough to make them dash for the cottage's porch. The key went into the lock's hourglass slot. Bill heard the click as he turned the key.

"Ready?" Franny asked, a sultry lilt to her voice.

"Nervous… and ready."

"That's what I like about you. Honest." Franny opened the door.

Beyond the threshold lay a narrow hallway and at its end a stairway. Murky light from the main house's windows crept into the hallway, revealing closed doors on either side of the corridor.

"Cold, like a tomb," Bill said, shivering. "We need a fire."

"Upstairs. We'll have one going soon." Franny took Bill's hand. "In the overseer's bedroom. The heat will warm our skin as we lie on the bed." His skin tingled as her heard her saucy words.

Bill let Franny lead him up the narrow stairs to the second-floor landing. At the top, she turned and waited, a silhouette barely visible in the shadowy light. Once he joined her, Franny stood on her tiptoes and kissed him lightly on the chin and lower lip, then led him into the overseer's bedroom.

Franny sidled to the bedroom window, pulled the blinds shut and closed the lace curtains. Kneeling at the fireplace, Bill loaded firewood from the rack onto the grate. He felt the touch of Franny's lips on the back of his neck as she put a matchbox in his hand. Soon, the fireplace provided just enough light for tender kisses and amorous hands.

"I detest petticoats," Bill said playfully, rising to his feet. He closed his arms around Franny and drew her close against his chest. Her petticoats pushed against his legs.

"Grannies invented them to keep their granddaughters safe from bad boys." She giggled.

A long kiss stopped her giggles.

"The poster bed's feather mattress looks inviting." His barely considered words somewhat shocked Bill. He expected some guilt, some thoughts of Becky. Nothing.

She lifted her hands to the back of her head and pretended to unclasp the gown's first hook. "No, you do it," she said.

Franny's scent whispered, *You could fall in love with this woman, Bill.*

He licked his lips. "My pleasure." Bill took off the fur, draped it over an easy chair near the fireplace. Maneuvering behind her, he unfastened the silk gown's hooks, kissing her neck after each uncoupling.

With the last hook released, the gown puddled at her slippered feet, and she stepped out of it. Resting his fingers on her shoulders, he tenderly turned her and ogled the camisole over her corset and petticoat bodice. No skin revealed so far, but his mind still entertained fairyland thoughts of what would soon happen on the bed. Bill cupped her chin and let his tongue tickle her bottom lip, then kissed her.

"Softly and tenderly. Savor these moments, my sweet boy." She brushed her fingers along his cheeks, over and over.

"You're my General Lee. I march to your commands, fair lady." The firelight brightened the room just enough so he could see the color of her eyes... pale yet vivid blue. Nonetheless, he wanted more illumination so he could savor all of her. "Don't wander."

Franny ran a finger down his frockcoat. "I'm going nowhere. Except to the bed when you're ready."

With a safety match, he lit a candle-lamp on the bedside table. "I can see the flowers, ribbons and lace in your hair."

"And I can see those eager fingers of yours."

He stripped off her petticoat bodice and watched her wiggle out of her camisole. Both lay atop her gown, where they belonged at that moment. Their tousled look encouraged—no, commanded—him to eye her corset with a hunger that could only be sated when it too fell at her feet.

More hooks and eye clasps... for an insane moment, he wanted to rip off the hooks, unlace the damn thing and throw it against the door. Slow and tenderly, she'd said. He wanted her naked, sweat glistening so he could lick it off. This time he'd hurry.

His finger and thumb slipped off the first hook and eye clasp. She took his hand and guided it back to the hook. "Like this. See?" She slid the hook off the clasp. "Get the corset off, and you'll almost be ready to storm my breastworks." She kissed the end of his nose.

"Your granny still living?" Bill asked in a sardonic voice.

"Yes. My momma's mother. Why?"

"If she only knew, she'd be on her knees in church praying for your soul."

Franny snorted. "If my granny had her way, I'd still be a virgin on my wedding night." She hooted at her words. "Granny's too late. I gave my fiancé a very special goodbye before I returned to Fredericksburg." She raised her hand to her mouth as Bill's curiosity turned to puzzlement. "I haven't really talked much about Peter, have I? It seemed silly to remain *pure* when we both knew he might not survive."

Bill curled his hand around the corset's next hook. "I've lain with Becky." Not the complete truth. But not a lie either. Just no actual wapping.

She chuckled. "So we're not virgins. Just one-timers."

Nodding, Bill finger-stepped his hands away from the hooks and eye clasps, and stroked some of the whale bone sewn into the cotton. *Oh, Lord, she's so beautiful.* He didn't care that she'd allowed this Peter to tip the velvet.

Bill let his eyes mate with hers as he undid the last of the hooks and tossed the corset atop her other things. Her eyes shone brightly, seemingly more brilliant than the fire and lamplight. She kissed his chin, then kissed her way to his lips. As she drew away, she kicked her clothes under the bed.

A cat's *I-ate-the-canary* grin on his face, Bill regarded her linen chemise. Beneath it, her breasts awaited his messy kisses. First, though, the two annoying petticoats had to go. He loosened the drawstrings, and keeping his eyes fixed on her, watched her hips sway as the petticoats dropped to the rug.

Franny stood languidly before him, only cotton drawers, linen chemise and stockings keeping his hands and lips from touching ivory skin. She sucked in an audible breath as he swept her into his arms and deposited her on the bed. Her knees bent as Bill tumbled onto the bed beside her.

"Bill! Your shoes! They're filthy. Get off the bed this instant!" She pushed against his shoulder. "Now!"

Grimacing, Bill rolled away from her and sat on the edge of the bed. "Sorry, Franny. Wasn't thinking."

"Take off your brogans, sweetheart." She slanted her right leg toward him and rubbed her toes against his back. "Take off your boots and uniform, and come to bed."

The boots, Zouave pants, shell jacket, and shirt dropped to the floor far more rapidly than Franny's gown and underthings. Body taut and cocked like a gun, he prepared to vault back into bed.

"No!" Franny held up a hand in protest. "I won't tolerate modesty. Off with those long johns. And it's getting chilly. Please add some logs to the fire."

"Lordy, you love to torture men." Moaning melodramatically, Bill slithered out of his long johns and tossed them and his uniform onto a rosewood chair at the foot of the bed. His feet cold, he fed firewood into the fireplace. The revived flames brought welcome heat to his skin.

"Turn slightly, please," Franny said waggishly. "Nice back avenue, Mister Stamford."

"Well, thank you, Miss Neale." The fire flared, heating his body even more, but not nearly as much as the sight of Franny lying on the bed in her chemise and drawers.

"You're welcome. Now you can come to bed and finish what you started."

Soon, Bill sat on his haunches on the bed, his eyes greedily feasting on the usually unseen curves of her body. She moved closer, dragging her fingernails across his bare chest, then raised a slippered foot up to his face. "Please, remove it... and the other."

"My pleasure." He didn't stop with the slippers, but slid a pink garter along her white stocking and slipped it off her foot. He brought the garter up to his nose, smelled and kissed it.

"And the other."

Fingers laced around the second garter, Bill eased it off Franny's leg and foot. He rubbed the garter against his face, then kissed it.

"Did you kiss your girl's garters?" Franny smirked.

"No." He put both hands at the top of her right stocking and rolled it down her leg, revealing ivory skin. "At last!" He stopped unrolling the stocking at her foot and kissed her knee, working his way up her thigh until his lips touched the lace trim of her drawers. "You're my Cleopatra."

"Well, my Marc Anthony, my toes are still clothed."

"That's easily remedied." He slipped the stocking from her foot and let it fall to the floor. Tickling her big toe, he kissed it, then ran his tongue across it.

"Much better than waltzing, don't you think?" She giggled.

"I need another test. Thank you, Jesus... there's another foot I can kiss." Bill removed the final stocking and kissed every toe.

"That tickles," she moaned.

Franny fluffed the pillows. Turning them into a backrest, she leaned back and raised her arms. "Don't you want to see my ripe fruits?" She kissed her right hand's fingers and pressed them against his lips.

"Lordy yes!" He lifted the chemise up her arms and above her head, watched it flutter to the floor. Gaping at her jutting breasts, he caressed their tips, took a nipple into his mouth. A moan of pleasure gushed from her mouth. Blood rushed to his groin.

Bill slipped his hand inside her drawers, felt her buttocks, soft and warm. "What's this?" His fingers touched the fabric of a pocket, undid its waist-string and pulled it away from her.

Her fingers closed around his, drew the pocket from his grasp. "Rubbers, sweetheart. You dig breastworks for protection. I use rubbers." She placed them on the side table next to the bed. "When it's time, we'll put one on your steed." She touched it, groaned in anticipation. 'You're certainly ready."

Fingers closing around her drawers, he yanked them down her legs and off her feet. "I'm a gal-sneaker." Bill rubbed the drawers against his cheek, then let them fall beside the bed.

Firelight and the table candle shimmered along her body as Franny opened her legs. No more need to imagine that *place* all men wanted to explore. Bill gaped at Franny's fairest flower. He kissed her along the insides of her thighs, looked up at her face. "I feared I'd die on the battlefield and never see this."

"I hope you plan to do more than look, Angel of Belvoir." She moved her hand in a slow circle across his chest, then caressed the back of his neck and spine. He tingled at the touch of her fingernails.

He slipped his tongue into her mouth, sharing intense kisses. His fingers stirred her coiffured hair. The strands rippled as the coil at the back of her head came undone. Flowers, ribbons and lace fell away, settling on the pillow beside her.

She purred softly, warm and inviting. Bill rolled atop her, crooking a leg across her hips. His hands followed the contours of her body… her thighs, her ribs, her breasts. Franny took one of his hands, brushed it through her downy spring-moss.

"Time to do some knocking," she said saucily, reaching for a rubber. Her eyes danced as she unrolled it over his steed. Desire coursed through him.

As firelight flickered on the wall above the bed's metal headboard, Bill and Franny made frenzied love. Drenched in sweat, they gyrated wildly. When they were spent, they lay in each other's arms, breaths tickling cheeks and necks. Her hand wandered to his ribs, finger-walked each one. "These moments wouldn't have happened if not for the war." Franny caressed his neck. "Papa would never have given you permission to court me."

"I know. I'm the son of a printer and newspaperman, good enough for most fathers. But not worthy in your dad's eyes?"

"Only a jurist or a large landowner." Franny snickered. "Like Frank Broaddus. And my fiancé." She snuggled closer and kissed him lightly. "You'd have needed permission from a floor manager to dance with me. And you would have been refused. Before the war, no couples could have waltzed. Only fit for the Frenchies. The war's not just killing and maiming young men; it's killing our way of life. We went to war to protect our state's right to keep our peculiar institution. Now we're debating arming slaves for use as soldiers. If we do that, we'd just as well stayed in the Union. Do I make sense? My girlfriends think I'm crazy for thinking such thoughts."

Bill felt like a character in a French farce. He lay next to a naked woman he'd just made mad love to a few moments earlier. Now, still twined together, Franny and Bill were discussing slavery and states' rights. Definitely bizarre.

Closing his eyes, he finessed his way along her chin and stroked her bottom lip with a fingernail. "Jeff Davis's already drafting white men. If things get desperate enough, he'll make the darkies soldiers. That means they'll be free if we win the war."

"The state governors will nullify anything from the Confederate government that frees slaves." Franny sucked on Bill's finger for a moment, then continued, "Remember the United States government before the 1789 Constitution? The failed Articles of Confederation? With no central authority over foreign and domestic commerce? States could do whatever they wanted, even nullify any central government law. The Founding Fathers went back to the drawing board and wrote the Constitution, the contract we walked away from last year. We're not very bright, are we? Articles of Confederation... the Confederacy."

Did those tar-and-feather words just gush from Franny's mouth? Bill decided he'd no choice but to fall in love with this spirited free thinker. She said what he'd been too spineless to say aloud... States' Rights and Nullification would undo the victories on the battlefield. "What happened to my Southern belle?" He laughed.

Franny slithered her right foot's big toe up and down his lower leg. "She read lots of books, and learned insidious ideas the rest of the South tries to bury. At the Yerby house, I saw you do wound care that most doctors would reject. After you left, I asked Doctor Straith about what you'd done for your captain friend. He said battlefield doctors were starting to try the same experimental approaches to prevent rot. There and then, I decided you were my soulmate."

"Soulmates? Yes!" Bill kissed her hard on her mouth. "My papa is wishy-washy, just like the Confederate government. He wants to help our darkies reach Yankee lines at New Bern. But he keeps coming up with reasons to delay freeing Malinda and Wilson."

"Malinda and Wilson will flee on their own." Franny toyed with Bill's chest hairs. "The slaves know all about our Mister Lincoln's Emancipation Proclamation. This war's turning our world upside down." She maneuvered her body so her left leg and breast rested against him. "Lordy, don't we make the perfect Southern couple? Prigging and then talking politics."

Sighing, Bill caressed Franny's back. "I figure I'm going to have to ask for your hand in marriage."

She choked, then laughed. "Wait until the end of the war. But we still have a problem... my fiancé and this Becky you adore."

"Seems insurmountable, doesn't it?" Another long sigh, then Bill brushed his hand along her leg.

"*C'est la vie.* Not often do the mists of time clear enough to see the future." She too sighed.

"Halos of fire."

"What?"

"Nothing." Bill coated her face with kisses as Franny caressed his buttocks.

"I don't hate Yankees." Franny traced his spine. "Before the war, I wanted to study at Cleveland's Oberlin College. Pursue a literary career, write great books, and share my love of Melville, Hawthorne, Emerson and Longfellow to wide-eyed students. Lordy, we Southerners are so provincial. I was open to marrying an Ohioan. The war got in the way."

Bill offered up a quote: "Happiness is as a butterfly which, when pursued, is always beyond our grasp, but which, if you will sit down quietly, may alight upon you."

"Hawthorne, and that's why I am falling in love with you, Bill Stamford." Franny clambered across him and sat on the edge of the bed. "We need to get back to the ball."

"They're probably thinking the worst."

"I don't care." She stood; her hair sheeted down her back. "The chaplain needs to get you back to your hut."

"I wish this night didn't have to end."

She twisted around, draped her arm across his shoulder and kissed him. "Maybe there'll be an encore. Someday."

"So what's the plan?"

"It took two servants to dress me in my underthings and gown. You'll have to do this time."

Nineteen

The Great Fredericksburg Snowball Fight

January was nearly spent, like the weary soldiers of the Army of Northern Virginia. While 1863 was a month old, at least two months of winter remained. Bill badly wanted to see fields blooming with wildflowers, even though warmer weather would mean another year of campaigning. Men with camp sickness were dropping like fruit flies in desert heat, except the temperature stood below freezing. Maybe marching would cleanse their chests and buttocks. Bill grimaced. Marching always ended with a pitched battle—artillery shells falling like a hail, mini balls filling the air as if maddened hornets.

Tuesday, January 28 was nearly done. No more drilling. Snow fell outside while flames gorged on logs in the hut's fireplace. The fresh fish, Nathan Pacini, sat on his bunk reading a newspaper just received through the mail from a Richmond uncle. He cursed, mostly under his breath but sometimes out loud and shrill.

Kenny stopped his favorite pastime… whittling. "What's got you foamin'?"

Nathan hurled the newspaper to the dirt floor. "These damned stories in the *Washington Daily National Intelligencer*. Outrageous!"

Kenny shrugged. "It's a Blue-Belly newspaper."

Sitting on a stool with his stocking feet propped before the fire, Charlie grinned. "Nathan reads the rag so he'll stay riled up against all things north of the Mason-Dixon."

Charlie and Nathan had buried their differences, although Bill suspected Nathan still considered Charlie a coward. Nathan would never say it to Charlie's face. The battering Nathan's mug had taken was finally disappearing, skin pale white again, not yellowish-brown. In Charlie's case, his better angels had won out, and he no longer hated himself for outrunning the rout. Next time, he swore, he'd not break even if it meant burial in a shallow grave. Bill didn't like Charlie's fatalism, but kept his opinion to himself.

"Of course, I'm riled up. It's that darky firebrand Frederick Douglass." Nathan retrieved the newspaper and jabbed a finger at a headline. "Damned darky's braggin' he persuaded Lincoln to issue his lousy Emancipation Proclamation. Douglass's the reason we're facin' darky regiments. He and his white pal, William Lloyd Garrison."

Nathan's angry words took Bill back to the overseer's cottage at Forest Hill. Franny had awakened his body and then his mind. King Cotton hadn't forced the English and the French to recognize the South and support the Confederacy's war aims. Lincoln and his Emancipation

Proclamation stood atop the high moral ground while Southern leaders wilted whenever they contemplated freedom for slaves who'd fight for the Confederacy. What a night... making love and debating the war.

"Not quite accurate," Bill spoke up, emboldened by the memories of New Year's Eve in the overseer's bedroom. "Garrison hates Douglass and Lincoln. He brags that he didn't vote in the last election." Being the son of a newspaper editor could sometimes come in handy.

"So one abolitionist is more radical than the other?" Nathan rolled his eyes. "They're both scoundrels. I'd send agents up North and kill the bastards. Then I'd blow up Oberlin College for educatin' darkies. What an abomination!"

"You know what's funny in all of this, Nathan?" Bill rose from his bunk where he'd been sewing a shell jacket button. "We're already considering what the abolitionists want. Our politicians are debating putting slaves in our armies. If we ask them to kill for us, we can't enslave them when the war's over."

Nathan scowled. "I won't serve with darkies. Won't fight with one beside me."

Bill headed for the door, opened it as he turned toward Nathan. "You may have no choice." He peered out the entrance. Snow swirled down from a gray overcast much darker than it should have been for the hour of the day. Bill couldn't see much beyond a sutler cabin across the way. A gust of wind slapped snowflakes against his cheeks, jolting him. Quickly, he reached toward clothing hooks nailed to the wall near the fireplace. "Snow's bad. Can't see a thing. Douglass could be leading a company of charging abolitionists down the street, and I'd never see them. At least until I heard them singing 'The Battle Cry of

Freedom.'" Freeing his frockcoat from the nearest hook, Bill donned it and headed into the snow. With Franny dominating his thoughts, he knew he needed a walk.

Since the New Year's ball, Franny and Bill had managed just one afternoon together. They'd taken a walk along Fredericksburg's church row, then through a park and the town cemetery. Again, their conversation had focused on secession politics. When Franny thought she'd get to enroll at Oberlin College, she couldn't wait to hear the tales of escaped slaves who'd crossed the Ohio River into the Buckeye State. "All I ever heard was how they were going to come back and murder us in our beds."

Around them that afternoon, buildings were in ruins—gaping holes in walls, steeples and chimneys toppled. The sight of block after block of destruction had dispirited Bill. "Your words, Franny, and the sight I'm seeing… they're so discordant." He'd locked his arm around her, tucking her close. "Lincoln's troops did this a month ago. I swear they want us to pay for the sin of slavery. How's that song of theirs go? 'As He died to make men holy, let us die to make men free, while God is marching on.'"

She'd stopped abruptly, enfolded Bill in a fierce hug, sought and found his mouth, kissing him as if she might never get to do so again. "I won't lie. I entertain doubts about this sad war. But I'll stay true to Virginia whatever the eventual outcome." Nearby, afternoon strollers had watched Franny plant yet another kiss on Bill's eager lips. War had numbed those who idly gazed. If anyone disapproved, they'd kept their thoughts to themselves.

"I fear we're the only two souls in the South who think like this," he'd whispered, caressing her lips with the tip of a finger.

"Just keep your head down and don't get killed."

"I'll keep my head, but the other… no guarantees there."

She'd gazed skyward, her expression stoic. "Then *You* keep him safe, Lord. Please."

Bill hadn't seen Franny since the afternoon walk.

He'd hoped to sneak off for a rendezvous, but the regimental officers kept the men busy. They didn't want to chance General Jackson riding by and seeing idle soldiers shuffling cards, rolling dice, and God forbid, brawling. Drill, drill, drill… all day, every day. In the morning, they'd probably drill, even in six inches of snow.

Out of the snowy mist, a voice sang out, "Go see her, boy." He turned to find Charlie hurrying up to join him. "They don't care, as long as you're in your bunk by midnight. I do it all the time."

"And someday a picket will shoot you dead."

Always on the prowl, Charlie excelled at finding a willing widow hungry for affection. At least once a week, he crept into the dwindling forest to give a green gown to his latest night flower in some barn on the outskirts of Fredericksburg. Just like Franny said, the war had made *proper* men and women eager for dalliances. Death, after all, might ask you to dance at the next ball.

There'd been no aureolas since Daniel's death… thank God. Bill found it way too easy not to think about them, especially since he dreaded the prospect of seeing one around a friend. If a mind had alleyways, he wanted the darkest one to conceal the aureolas. Yes, where light never penetrates, he reflected as one brave thought crept out from the alley: *Please, Lord, let Franny grow old.* Then he felt guilty… he'd not included Charlie, Kenny or even Nathan. No wonder God seemed not to hear his prayers.

Too cold to stay out in the squally snow, Bill and Charlie shortened the walk and hurried back to their bunks. The wind beyond the logs and chinks wailed, but Bill slept well, warmed by the fire. He always did when he allotted his waning moments of wakefulness to remembering the touch of Franny's chili-pepper body. Even with the snoring of Kenny and Nathan and the wind's howls, Bill had no trouble remembering Franny's every hair and pore.

Bill awoke to reveille and news that the officers had canceled drills. He made sure to mark the date in his head—Wednesday, January 29—so he'd remember it in the future. Drills were never canceled.

After slogging through snow drifts to the cook's cabin for breakfast, the bunkmates returned to the hut, settled around a roughly hewn table and drank pseudo coffee aging nicely in a coffee pot on the fireplace grill. Bill had a splendid view out the window the boys had commandeered from the ruins of a Fredericksburg building. Beyond the partly frosted glass, two privates were packing snowballs and trying to roll them into grander ones, their goal to build a snowman.

Charlie, Nathan and Kenny went out to help. Bill stayed in the hut, content to bask in the fireplace heat, a soothing sensation, but not blissful like the touch of Franny's fingernails. Let his bunkmates play in the snow; Bill would spend the day perched before the fire, enjoying the freedom of doing whatever he wanted.

Boots removed, he reached for one of Nathan's newspapers, the Washington paper, and began reading. Amazing how negative the newspaper editors were north of the Mason-Dixon. The headlines declared Lincoln a miserable failure, Burnside a nincompoop, and the war about to be lost. For Bill in the toasty hut, he could almost agree, but the Army of the Potomac soldiers across the Rappahannock undoubtedly disagreed. Except maybe about

Burnside's incompetence, that was. Fredericksburg had been a disaster for them.

A glance out the window elicited a laugh. The snowman lacked a head, and it appeared he'd never get one. Instead, his makers were embroiled in a snowball fight, ganging up on Nathan, four against one. One of the pitfalls of being a fresh fish. Never good to brag when you've yet to dodge a cannonball or heard the buzz of mini balls.

The door flew open, crashed against the wall. In the doorway, Charlie, his coat dusted with snowball debris. "Come on out, Bill. You got to see this."

Bill shook his head. "Coffee's still hot. Outside ain't."

Sniggering, Charlie barked: "If Franny stood here, you'd be in your frockcoat in an instant and out the door."

"She's prettier."

"Get out here, Billy Boy. You won't believe it."

Groaning like he did when ten and forced by Malinda to rise from his warm bed, Bill wiggled into the coat, tugged on his boots, and stepped out into the snow. Beneath his feet, he could feel the unevenness of the plank walkway. A white mantle stretched all the way to the river and beyond.

"Better than a carnival or freak show," Charlie claimed, acting as if he intended to snuggle into the frockcoat and share the heat.

"Stop that!"

"Yea, I know… only Franny—and Becky." Charlie chortled. "God help you if those two ever meet."

"Franny's marrying a Tennessee officer. I'll be marrying Becky if she waits for me. So there's no chance they'll ever meet, unless Franny invites us to her wedding."

Hard to believe… Charlie deftly shifted the conversation away from the women. "What you're about to see, Billy Boy, will be talked about into the next century. Long after States'

Rights and Nathan's temper are old hat, folks will be talkin' about how the Army of Northern Virginia spent this day. Yes, indeedy."

Beyond the huts, obscured by the black smoke belching from chimneys, Bill heard the roar of many men shouting and laughing. "Okay, I've bitten your hook." He strode toward the noise, passing the half-done snowman. "Let's see the commotion."

Atop the railroad track embankment, Bill and Charlie looked down on two Butternut battle lines closing in on each other under a gray but dry sky. As they marched, the combatants hurled snowballs. "Fire in volley," a sergeant bellowed just before a barrage arched toward him. Maybe two hundred men fought on a field peppered with tree stumps. The trunks and limbs were now the walls of the huts and firewood consumed to keep the men warm. And more would fall to axes before the Butternuts marched off to yet another spring campaign somewhere in Virginia, Maryland or Pennsylvania.

As snowballs flew and some of the men grappled, Bill recalled Burnside's three-day fiasco that had begun on Monday, January 20. Ready to chance another wintertime battle with the Army of Northern Virginia, the Blue-Bellies marched away from their winter quarters just as a drizzle turned into a heavy rain that lasted for four days. In the middle of the hubbub, one of Jeb Stuart's cavalrymen shared a story with Bill: "Just got back from the Rappahannock. Saw me the silliest sight. Wagons, horses, cannons bogged down in a quagmire of mud and drunken Yanks brawlin'." Eyeing the *snowball* battlefield, Bill smiled. Lee's men preferred snowball tussles, not mud fights. The Yanks were back in their winter camps, and according to Nathan's newspapers, Burnside had been fired.

A snowball whizzed by Bill's ear. Charlie slapped him on his back. "Let's join in."

Shifting slightly, Bill pursed his lips. "I don't know. Maybe."

Charlie took a couple of steps down the embankment toward the fighters. "More regiments are joinin' in. Officers are barkin' out orders. We got to join in, Billy Boy. Got to auger ourselves some Graybacks."

Near Bill and Charlie, more men from Company G slogged through the snow toward the railroad embankment and began scaling the manmade hill. "Form up, boys!" Sergeant Barnard bellowed, his roar echoing across the cold plain. "We're going to have ourselves a snowball war."

Bill elbowed Charlie. "Bully! Time to let 'er rip!"

Charlie actually did a jig and danced up to Sergeant Barnard. "Fall into line, Kurtz," the sergeant rumbled. "You too, Stamford."

Even colonels joined the fray, on foot rather than horses. Major John Barry of the Eighteenth and Colonel Clark Avery of the Thirty-Third decided on a flanking movement. With an unharmed tree line as cover, the two Tar Heel regiments crept past the snowball-tossing battle lines. Out in the field, the hooting and hollering men failed to pay heed to the distant tree line, its dark skeletal limbs and branches cloaked in snow and icicles.

"Like taking candy from a babe." As he marched, Charlie scooped up a handful of snow and made a snowball.

"Or taking a lass's virginity," Bill added, getting into the spirit of the moment.

"I've been a busy fella," Charlie deadpanned. "Don't reckon there's any virgins left in Fredericksburg."

Emerging from the trees, still undetected, the two regiments wheeled into battle lines and charged. Packed snowballs in each hand, Bill shrieked the Rebel yell. The sound erupting from his mouth mingled with a thousand more howls rumbling across the stubble of a crop field.

Thousands of unexpected snowballs pelted the Fifteenth Alabama. Under attack from two directions, the Alabamians retreated. Their officers hollered: "Withdraw! To the rear!" Most did. Some lost their tempers and bulled into the Eighteenth, throwing fists instead of snowballs. "Son of a bitch!" one Alabamian growled when two snowballs smacked him in the back of his head.

They came from the hands of Nathan and Kenny. Blood seeped through the Alabamian's coal-black hair onto his neck and collar. Bill's bunkmates had scooped up pebbles and sprinkled them into the snowballs. The Alabamian whirled and charged them like a derailed locomotive. His head slammed into Nathan's chest and both tumbled to the snow. Nathan flailed away weakly as the Alabamian drove his fists into the recruit's face, reopening old wounds delivered by Charlie. Nathan whimpered like a toddler given a spanking. "Stop, I beg you! You're hurtin' me!"

Together, Kenny and Charlie tossed the Alabamian against a farmer's check-bank. The fellow clutched his arm and moaned, "Son of a bitch! You broke it!" He wobbled to his feet, and shoulder drooping, floundered after his comrades.

Suddenly, Bill found himself on the ground, the air knocked out of him, fists pounding his back and head. A snowy pebble gnawed his bottom lip; cold dirt leached into his mouth and nose. Bill sucked for breath... futilely. Unexpectedly, the weight on his back and neck disappeared, and a voice boomed, "Fight's over, soldier!" Finally able to wheeze a breath, Bill flopped onto his side and saw a Fifteenth Alabama private raise his fist to strike Major

Barry. Noticing the single star on the officer's collar, the private dropped his clenched hand. The Alabamian grimaced as if he expected the executioner's axe to fall at any moment.

"Fight's over, soldier," Barry repeated, his voice matter of fact.

"Yessir. Got carried away." Expression contrite, the Alabamian saluted and took off running.

More than nine thousand soldiers engaged in the daylong free-for-all. Like a good army, they executed the proper maneuvers and tussled in the ankle-deep snow. Two soldiers were seriously injured and taken to the hospital. Some snowballers packed snow around rocks that were much larger than the pebbles in the snowballs Nathan and Kenny threw, virtual hidden mini balls. Bill shook his head. Always got to be some spoilsports.

As the *battle* drew to a close, Bill spied sleighs and their horses parked along River Road. Some of the citizens of Fredericksburg had come out to observe the shenanigans. Dark against the snow blanket and the bluish-gray horizon, the conveyances were far enough away that Bill couldn't make out the faces of their drivers and passengers. A fur-clad figure—a woman—waved frantically. "Bill! Bill Stamford!" Faint, yet loud enough for Bill to hear.

Could it be? Just the thought of her name seemed to chase away the cold breeze nipping at Bill's ears. Heat poured from his heart and warmed his body. Franny! She'd come out, hoping to get a few minutes with him—perhaps they'd slip behind the sleigh and do the bear.

Plodding toward River Road, Bill slipped his tongue between his lips and felt the bite of cold air on its tip. He swore he could taste the scent of her lips against his mouth. Perhaps they could decide on a location for a future rendezvous. Could he be so lucky? Why not? The day had been fair to middling so far. The snowfall fight turned out more fun that Bill anticipated. If only he could conclude the afternoon with a few precious moments with the girl he just couldn't get out of his mind.

Clad in a winter day dress and fur coat, Franny scurried to him, her boots leaving prints in the snow. He went to kiss her hand European style, but she brushed it aside and hugged him. "I'm sorry," she whispered as he felt something slide into his frockcoat's pocket. "Read it when you get back to the cabin." Tears dribbled down her cheeks and chin. "Don't look at it now. Please." She hurried back to the sleigh.

"Franny?" He shouted her name again, "Franny?"

She glanced back. "Forgive me."

Franny climbed into the sleigh, then looked straight ahead as the darky driver urged the harnessed horses toward Fredericksburg.

Bill didn't wait. Didn't follow Franny's advice. Reaching into his coat pocket, he plucked out a carefully folded sheet of paper and began reading: *I love you. Let me say it again. I love you, Bill Stamford. This is why this is so hard for me to write. I'd planned to end my engagement and battle for your heart with this Tar Heel woman you adore. But my fiancé is deathly sick. I've decided to go and nurse him. I leave by train in the morning. Will I end up marrying him? I don't know. But I can't break the engagement now. I'll never forget our night together. I love you, dearest one. Franny.*

He wanted to run after her, but the sleigh crested a ridge and disappeared. Balling his fists, he started back to camp. *Nurse him? Let him die.* Bill felt guilty for the thought.

Twenty

On The March Again

Sergeant Barnard's voice thundered: "Get your rations ready, boys! We'll march in the morning."

Bill's heart quickened. In a matter of days, he'd soon see another Season of Fire. More battles, more men praying and reading their Bibles, more men discarding their cards and dice. And maybe some with aureolas flaming around their bodies.

It had been a brutal winter encampment. Not enough to eat. And what the men did eat failed to sustain them. A few weeks earlier, Sunday, April 5, a foot of snow had fallen. At Eastertime! Soldiers were gaunt, eyes sunken with dark circles, bodies emaciated. Most of the trees around the camps south of Fredericksburg were stumps. More than ready to march away from Fredericksburg, Bill didn't care if he never again saw the town's toppled steeples and towers. Ugly reminders of Franny.

He'd gotten no letters from her. Not even a note saying she'd arrived safely in Memphis. Truly, she'd scratched his name off her dance card, removed him from her life. It was clear she intended to marry her fiancé. And if her nursing failed, if this Peter died, what then? Would she return to Fredericksburg and live her life as if that night with him had never happened? *Sweet Jesus... I've got to put her out of my mind.*

Over the last day, the boys yakked about nothing else but the coming march and what Lee's plans might be. Would the spring and summer find them heading back to the Shenandoah's golden fields and ripe orchards? Would the growling of their stomachs finally let up? Or maybe this new Union commander, Joe Hooker, would try yet another flank march? Bill exhaled a sigh of frustration, then laughed to himself. The Blue-Bellies were always so damned slow. They might eat better than the Butternuts, but they didn't march worth a damn. *Bellies too fat, always dragging the ground.*

Bill gazed around the cabin, his home since late December. Just one more night, and he'd say goodbye forever. They'd even built shelves where they kept their tin cups, plates, forks and knives. Bill had claimed a spot where he placed the book of poems he'd read to Gregg... next to Becky's letters and Franny's wretched note. Yerby had given the book to him. Sadly, he intended to leave it behind.

Charlie and Kenny blew through the front door like a spring thunderstorm. "Hey, Billy Boy," Charlie gushed, "I'm hearin' the Yanks are up at Chancellorsville."

"I 'member passin' the place back in the fall, on the way to Fredericksburg." Kenny sat on his bunk patiently whittling yet another piece of wood. "A plantation mansion at a crossroads, Orange Turnpike and Ely Ford's Road."

"That's less than twelve miles," Bill said, counting the distance in his head. He too remembered marching by the mansion.

Nathan looked up from his Bible. He'd been as quiet as a church mouse at a revival. "I'd heard the Blue-Belly curs might land below Fredericksburg."

Kenny laughed. "And refight the December battle? Not likely. Nobody wants to get whipped twice on the same battlefield."

"Yep, we're marching to Chancellorsville." Certainty resonated in Charlie's voice. "Nasty countryside. Thickets will tear clothes and bloody your face. Dark and forbidding place. A damned wilderness, that's what it is."

Nodding casually, Bill eyed Charlie, then Kenny. *How did those two chuckaboos learn those kinds of details? And they're almost always right. I'm the one who's going to be a reporter, not them.*

So far, Bill's last day in the cabin had been much like the others over the last five months. Belly grumbling, mind rambling, sometimes Franny, sometimes Becky. He'd once mentioned his byzantine thoughts to Charlie. "You consider this a problem?" Charlie had replied, incredulous. "I'd like to have two women in love with me."

"You don't have problems with women," Bill had retorted as he cleaned his musket. "You're sneaking off once or twice a week."

"Not the same, Billy Boy." Charlie had then talked about the widows he met in barns and abandoned farmhouses. "They don't even pretend to love me. But they do love the way they feel when I touch them. Billy Boy, they're so lonely. They miss their husbands."

Stripping off his boots, Bill wrapped himself in his blanket and rested his head against a pillow stuffed with his shell jacket and vest. As he turned his face toward the window, Bill heard Nathan stoke the fireplace, resurrecting the flames. Outside, the last of the streaks of orange were gone from the sky; inside, the bunkmates had eaten another measly meal, cleaned their muskets and packed their rations for a march. Now only sleep remained to be done. Of course, he didn't sleep, but again thought of the two girls who invariably kept away snores.

With Franny, he'd given up hope for a miracle. Lordy, how happy he'd be if he found her alongside the Orange Turnpike waving goodbye as he marched west to face the Blue-Bellies. He promised himself he'd look in the morning... just in case. He knew he'd be disappointed. She'd undoubtedly left for Tennessee in late January.

Yawning, Bill tallied his time in the army—seven long months. Somehow he still lived, despite Yankee bullets and camp disease.

Up on the shelf were just four letters from Becky. Some boys received a letter a week. At least she hadn't stopped writing. Just not timely, and no new socks or a shirt, both promised but not delivered. He rolled onto his back. The last letter... he tried to remember its arrival date. Two weeks ago? *Yeah, that Friday when the throat got scratchy.* Not entirely true, he conceded. The latest letter arrived this very day. And when he read it, the sore throat went away.

Since that first read, he must have read her letter a hundred times. Mostly newsy, but at the end quite affectionate. Becky couldn't wait to smear Bill's mouth with red ruse. Her words had brought a grin to his face. "Of course, I'll have to sneak the letter out without Momma or Papa wanting to read it first. They'd think I'm a fallen woman. Maybe I am, considering what I want to do to you when I see you again… alone." Words like that sure made it easier for Bill not to think about Franny. She'd even left ruse kisses along the edges of the letter. That's what he needed, just more of it.

Morning came with sunbeams sneaking past homemade curtains. First light tickled Bill's eyelids, prompting him to scrabble for his pocket watch he'd left on the floor next to his bunk. Just after six.

His packing done long before the bugler blew reveille, Bill ate a hot breakfast for the day's march and downed a cup of chicory coffee. He expected to be marching long before 8 o'clock, but it came and went with the Eighteenth still in camp. The chuckaboo who sometimes thought he knew more than the colonels and generals offered a theory. "Lee and Jackson must still be calculatin' where Hooker will attack," Charlie explained as he sat down next to his packed bedroll. "Our lines stretch from the fords near Falmouth to downriver from Fredericksburg. I figure Lee won't move until he thinks he knows Hooker's intentions. So we wait."

The waiting didn't last long. Lee must have figured out Hooker's intentions. Just before noon, the Eighteenth got its marching orders, the soldiers making their way along the Plank Road. Some Fredericksburg folks lined up along the road and waved; some clutched Bonnie Blue Flags.

A girl in a cotton dress with a skimpy petticoat—she looked no more than twenty—darted into the road and planted a kiss on Charlie's mouth. "Dodge them Yankee bullets, Charlie," she trilled, kissing him again. "I want to do me more bear huggin'."

"I'm always up for doin' the bear, Hazel, my bluebird." Charlie caressed her cheek.

Slowing her side-by-side walk, Hazel stopped and watched him march away. She blew kisses.

"Your bluebird got a sister, Charlie?" Kenny punched Charlie's shoulder. "Who likes to do the bear too?"

"She does, and she's just thirteen, so you'd better stay away from her!"

Near Charlie's bluebird, Franny's mother ran up to Bill. A man Bill assumed to be Franny's father stood alongside the road, arms crossed, mouth unsmiling.

"Franny loves you," Juliet huffed, out of breath. "My Franny's not thinking straight right now. Please, don't give up on her."

Bill shifted his rifle to his left shoulder, then took Juliet's gloved hand. "Ma'am, I want Franny to be happy and have a wonderful life, whatever the future holds for her." *Sweet Lord, he hated lying. He wanted her in his bed for the rest of his life.*

"Remember, she loves you." Juliet aimed a quick peck on his cheek and hastened back to her husband.

Had Juliet just given him some hope? She'd said nothing concerning Peter's health. For a reason? Did she expect Peter to die and Franny to dress in mourning clothes for the next year? Or had Peter recovered and convinced Franny to set a wedding date, with Juliet desperate to see it not happen? And why Juliet's fascination with Bill? Lots of questions, none with answers. Bill shifted the musket back to his right shoulder and kept marching.

Picking up the pace, he swung his gaze rearward. Juliet waved.

With dust clogging his lungs, Bill fell out of the column at Shiloh Church four miles west of Fredericksburg. He coughed and gagged until he vomited his breakfast and gobs of dust and grime. The planks should have damped down the dust cloud that inevitably accompanied armies, but many Butternuts had chosen the dirt beside the road.

The bitter winter of sickness and dismal rations left them anemic, their legs not up to the march on planks.

Bent over, Bill turned as someone's hand squeezed his shoulder. Done retching, he groaned annoyance: "Charlie! Don't you have something better to do?"

"I reckon you spewed most of your innards, Billy Boy." Charlie kicked dirt over the vomit.

"At least I'm breathing better."

"I've got better things to do than lose my breakfast, Billy Boy." Charlie eyed Salem Church, a steepleless, barn-like building two miles east of where the Orange Turnpike, Plank Road and a third road forked. "There's a farmhouse nearby. I know the oldest daughter. They used to live in the Smokies, but moved up here three years ago. Her pa's servin' with Early in Fredericksburg. She carries a torch for me. I paid her a visit in early April just to see how hot the flame burns." He patted his chest near where his heart beat. "It burns bright."

Bill swiped his hand across his face, cleaning vomit from his mouth, then rolled his eyes. "Not a good time to be sparking with an old love, Charlie."

"I know. You'll keep me safe, won't you, Bill? Give the officers a proper reason for my absence?" Charlie kept nodding as if he hoped jerking his head up and down would turn Bill into an accomplice. "Lots of boys are droppin' out and catchin' up later. Not holdin' up well after the awful winter. Tell 'em I'm pukin' my guts out and will catch up in a few hours. And I will... after I tumble sweet Jill."

Bill straightened his spine. "I'll do my best. You're a crazy man, Charlie. That's why you're my chuckaboo."

Charlie kissed the brim of Bill's slouch hat. "I'll give her a kiss for you, right on her fruitful vine."

"You're an incorrigible rogue, Charlie."

Like an oil lamp first ignited, initially dim then flaring into brightness, an aureola flamed around Charlie. Bill nearly fell back onto his buttocks, but managed to regain his balance.

Charlie bent and slapped his hands against his knees, not to vomit but to chortle. "Don't tell me you're getting sick again?"

"I'll be all right." Bill whirled away from the aureola, afraid he'd start crying. Somehow, he calmed his nerves, his trembles. "Be careful. I mean it! Be careful."

Completing a mock bow, Charlie sprinted away, hurdled a fence and beelined toward a coppice. Soon, trees swallowed him.

Numb, his musket cold in his hand, cold like Charlie's future, Bill slipped into the columns of the Thirty-Seventh North Carolina. His cheeks suddenly wet—and not from a shower—he looked up into the clear sky. *Why, Lord? No rhyme or reason. Months free of the curse… and suddenly it's back.* Men would face death in a matter of days, maybe tomorrow; men he'd come to know in the last months, but their ultimate fate remained known only to God. Not so Charlie.

Behind Bill, a voice jolted him from his thoughts. His eyes flared open as the curious voice inquired, "You're with the Eighteenth, right?"

Actually grateful to hear the voice, Bill looked over his shoulder. A corporal coated in dust. Vaguely familiar. The name Henry piqued at Bill's mind. "Yessir. Had to take an unscheduled break." He rolled his eyes. Second time in the last ten minutes. *Good God! Now Charlie. Why only my friends? How about an occasional stranger?*

Double stepping, the corporal marched beside him. "You look like you just saw a ghost."

"I hope not." Bill glanced at his shell jacket; no vomit residue drying on it, thankfully. Bill said nothing further, and soon Henry left him alone.

The curse lay like a grindstone on Bill's chest. Charlie might not die on a battlefield. He might soon become a corpse in a barn, shot dead by his farmhouse sweetie in a jealous rage. Maybe her momma catches them naked and doing the bear, and puts a gunshot between Charlie's eyes. Bill decided he'd not be stoic this time, not shrug his shoulder and accept Charlie's death. He remembered Daniel's last words: "Bill, you should have told me about the aureola." A French phrase came to mind. *C'est la vie. No! Not this time. I'm being shown this for a reason. Why... if not to change fate? I was a coward, didn't even try to help Daniel. This time will be different!*

Up ahead, gunfire erupted, musketry punctuated with cannon booms. Black powder clouds mixed with the dust haze. The rumor mill hummed into high gear, news traveling from soldier to soldier down the marching columns. *What a damned mess!* Somewhere behind Bill, Charlie and one of his sweeties were doing the bear as Hill's boys prepared to go into battle.

On a cleared ridge near two country churches, Zoan and Tabernacle, Anderson and McLaws' divisions battled Blue-Bellies. The butternuts drove the Yanks into a wilderness of shadows dark and deep. The reverberating sounds of battle persisted through the afternoon and into the evening. As the sky turned dark, the firing stopped as did the Yanks' push toward Fredericksburg. As the first stars appeared, Butternuts quickened their pace... just in case Lee and Jackson decided to make a final push and drive the Blue-Bellies into the Rappahannock.

No final push happened. No battle on Friday, May 1 for Hill's division. The men settled in on either side of Orange

Turnpike midway between Zoan and Salem churches. With darkness claiming the sky, Lee decided to renew the battle in the morning. Or so a weary Bill figured as he settled into his bedroll. He glanced around—all Thirty-Seventh boys. Not far away, a few stragglers still marched along the turnpike. He didn't spot Charlie. Bill would give him another thirty minutes, and if Charlie didn't show up, he'd go look for the Eighteenth on his own.

Parched, Bill reached for his wooden canteen as a familiar voice barked, "Billy Boy, you get lost? I do some naughty courtin', and you fall apart and can't even find the Eighteenth."

"Charlie, so good of you to remember you're in the Army of Northern Virginia."

"Couldn't leave as long as sweet Jill kept begging for more."

"So you left her contented, eh?" Bill rolled up and retied his bedroll, then slung it across his shoulder and rose to his feet.

"Not really. In the barn, we heard far-off thunder. A peek outside showed a sky clear of thunderheads. Knew it was time to catch up with you and the boys."

"Let's find the Eighteenth." Readjusting his bedroll, Bill stepped carefully, meandering among men preparing campfires as he made his way toward the turnpike. Behind him, Charlie tripped over a Butternut loafing on his blanket and mumbled an apology when the soldier cursed.

Once on the turnpike, Bill and Charlie shadowed the ragged line of makeshift camps and their cooking fires, hollering out: "Eighteenth North Carolina! Yell if you're with the Eighteenth!" Late April and early May can be a time of turbulent weather, but on this starry night a warm breeze promised pleasant sleeping, if Bill and Charlie could find the Eighteenth before sunrise and another day of marching or worse... battle.

They suffered through a good hour of fruitless searching, then Kenny's shout rang out, "Over here, runts!" Near the turnpike, as if he and Nathan knew their other two bunkmates would eventually show up, they cooked a sorry-looking soup of salt pork and dried beans over a fire. Well, not exactly. Kenny fretted over the cooking pot while Nathan jabbed his bayonet into the Virginia dirt, digging a grave for his dice and playing cards.

No aureola around Kenny or any of the others gathered around the cooking fires in the vicinity. Still, some would soon die; Bill just didn't know who. For whatever divine reason, only Charlie got the godly roll of the heavenly dice and the glorious aureola. Unless Bill could figure out how to cheat fate, Charlie would die... this very night, tomorrow, week from now, a month. Bill couldn't be sure of the time, just the certainty. He stole a glance at Charlie, who eyed Kenny's poor fare with relish. Doing the bear made a man hungry. Bill smiled, in spite of the gloom enveloping him.

"Smells good, Kenny!" Charlie shouted.

Kenny waved. "You've a bad nose. Nothin' from the army's food stocks ever smells good. Just edible. And not particularly healthy."

"Bitch! Bitch! Bitch!" Charlie joked as he advanced toward the cooking fire.

Kenny jumped up from the boiling pot and shook their hands, then hugged them. "We'd about given up on you two. Thought ya'll decided to finish the rest of the war on your porches in North Carolina."

"Kenansville? Not a bad idea. Actually, a splendid idea." Charlie dropped to his knees beside Nathan, who nodded while continuing to dig his tiny grave. "Nonetheless, I'm stayin' put. Got to make up for what happened in Fredericksburg. Even if we get flanked, I ain't movin'. Not till I hear the order to withdraw. Goin' to spit into the pretty faces of those three Greek ladies of fate." Charlie regarded Bill. "See, Billy Boy, I didn't sleep through the Grove Academy classes. Know all about the Fates."

Later that evening, Sergeant Barnard moseyed past the four bunkmates. "Lookee, our two deserters finally showed up. Damn! I was hopin' I could draft me a firing squad."

"Thanks, Sergeant." Bill's half-smile turned into a belch, drawing laughter from everyone but the sergeant. "I love you, too."

Barnard crossed his arms against his chest and grumbled, "Enough with all this lovin'. So why are you boys late to the ball?"

Bill offered up his polished fairytale, a fine story Herman Melville would appreciate. "I know I should have stayed away from it, Sergeant. Smelled good, tasted fine. Bacon I'd bought from a Fredericksburg freedman for a book of poems by Walt Whitman. Planned to use the Yankee book as firewood anyway."

Brows nearly met over the sergeant's nose with the ferocity of his scowl. "What's a darky doing reading?"

Shrugging, Bill took off his slouch hat and ran his fingers through sweaty, unkempt hair. "Some owners are peculiar. I guess the darky was fascinated by that land up north, Abolitionist Heaven, and wanted to read some of its poetry."

"Sergeant, I told him to throw it away." Charlie pointed accusingly at Bill. The finger waggled too much, like a finger of one of those melodrama actors favored by Wilmington's Opera House. "Any darky who wants to read a Yankee poet's up to no good. I wouldn't eat the bacon. Told him it was probably poisoned. My Billy Boy had a terrible time marchin'. Complained his belly ached. At Salem Church, he puked out his innards. I couldn't leave a friend in such dire straits, so I stayed with him under the church shade. The wretched soul lay on the ground cryin' for his momma." Charlie gave a rueful smile. "When he felt better, we got to marchin' again. Caught up fast as we could."

Barnard laughed without amusement. "That's quite a fancy story, boys. I don't believe a word. But I know you two pretty well. You're devoted to the Eighteenth. So whatever the real story, tell me after the war, especially if it involves two sweet darlin's." The sergeant started to amble away but stopped. "Get some sleep. We missed out on today's fight. That won't happen tomorrow."

Later, they drank sham coffee and ate the soup. No tents overnight. They slept under the stars, their muskets and rifles stacked. Just before the snoring began, the bunkmates talked of home and the people back there who no doubt said a prayer for them at the supper table and before crawling into bed.

For the first time, Nathan opened up about his wife, Ethel. "I've loved her since I met her at church when we were ten. Long hair the color of sun-kissed wheat and lips sweet like strawberries. We were goin' to have a big wedding after the war, but I wanted her to be my wife before I left for the Army. She gave in. I promised she'd someday get her big wedding." He gave everyone a wide firelit grin. "We did get to enjoy the marriage bed before I got on the train for Virginia. Just got a letter sayin' we're goin' to have a baby. I have so much to live for, don't I?"

Bill drank the last three swallows of still-hot coffee. "Yes, you do. A new wife, a baby on the way... as well as a huge wedding. When the war's over, I'm going to come by and meet your girl and the baby." Bill cast a quick glance at Charlie, sitting cross-legged across from the fire. As expected, no aureola. But there had been, and always soon before the person died. He wished he could talk to his bunkmates about aureolas, but they'd think him off his rocker. Better to keep it inside, in spite of Daniel's last words.

"You'll always be welcome in my house, Bill." Nathan drew his knees up to his chest and rested his forehead on them. A second later, he raised his head. "I know the elephant's comin' tomorrow." He held out hands that trembled. "God, I hope I don't let you guys down."

Charlie slapped Nathan's knee. "You'll do fine. I worry about the ones too full of bravado. Like the boy who brags he loves the circus, but when it comes to town skedaddles when the elephants get too close for comfort."

As the chatter—and nagging coughs—died down around the bunkmates, firelight talk turned to how Lane's Brigade would be used the next day. "Lordy, I hope we're not in a frontal assault," Nathan opined.

"Not Lee's style." Kenny picked up the pot and plates to take down to a nearby creek and wash. "Even if Bobby Lee contemplates it, Stonewall will talk him out of it. He'll say, 'Let me flank 'em.' Yep, that's what we'll do. We'll rout them. We'll hear them screamin' for their mommas."

Bill mulled Kenny's words. "The Yanks are brave men too; they just got lousy generals."

Nodding, Kenny rose to his feet, the cooking and eating utensils cradled against his chest. "That bravado thing, eh?"

Nathan kept silent, not raging about abolitionists, money grubbers or ape-faced Abe Lincoln.

"Well, at least we don't have any hard marchin'," Charlie said, grinning.

Later, as he lay on his bedroll, Bill heard Kenny return just before he slipped off into dreams of Franny in Peter's arms.

Twenty-one

A Hellish Flank Movement

Charlie was wrong. All Stonewall's men marched in the morning, thirty thousand strong. The bunkmates ate a quick, unappetizing breakfast, rolled up their bedrolls, and at seven bushwhacked through farm country toward the Plank Road. They trailed Rhodes and Colston's divisions, forcing Bill to keep company with a dust cloud.

Strange morning, for sure. No marching toward Chancellorsville and forming battle lines to turn Hooker's right flank. Instead they headed away from the town, first following Plank Road past Zoan and Tabernacle churches, the site of some of the previous day's fighting. Bill could see abandoned breastworks, dead horses beyond the trenches, some Blue-Belly bodies starting to bloat. Wetting a handkerchief, he held it against his nose until the bodies, both horse and men, were far to the rear.

The marchers swung behind Anderson's entrenched division and plunged into the thicket-infested woodlands. The sun disappeared, cloaked by a dense canopy, and the land became noticeably darker, a land of shadows. Near Catharine's Furnace, the column diverted onto Wellford Furnace Road, a dirt lane that led to Brock Road. Narrow but suitable for artillery, the road cut through thick woods that muffled sounds and kept Yankee eyes from seeing Butternut troops. Confined in winter camp near Fredericksburg since late December, Bill had come to know some of the roadway names in the Wilderness region. That's what happens when a Tar Heel boy becomes lovers with Franny Neale. The boy gets to know the places and the roads in her stories whispered between feverish kisses.

Emerging out of the woods, the Eighteenth plodded across a covered bridge spanning Poplar Run. The furnace could be seen from the intersection, a massive chimney tower surrounded by a complex of buildings. A few small fires burned, the remnants of cannon fire from the day before. The smell of charcoal hung in the air as ember fireflies danced around Bill.

Ahead, the lane forked. The troops marched past the junction road that diverted toward Chancellorsville. Their marching direction puzzled Bill. "I thought for sure we'd take the right branch."

"It leaves me curious too." Charlie tunneled through his beard and scratched his chin. "If we were strikin' the Blue-Bellies' right flank, that's the road we'd take."

"Damn! I've no idea why we just went left." Nathan verbalized the thoughts of Bill and Charlie.

"Me neither." Kenny glanced toward the dark woods. "With Stonewall, anything's possible. Even an attack in the Yankee rear."

"That would be audacious." Four words from Charlie, spoken with wonder in his voice.

So audacious it would result in Charlie's death? That fear howled inside Bill's head. Maybe he and Charlie should find a way to get lost again, miss the upcoming fight. *No, that's not honorable*, Bill reminded himself: Charlie's death doesn't have to be the result of a Yankee mini-ball. Instead, a rotten tree falling on him in this damned wilderness. Or a crotchety old farmer wanting to bag two deserters.

"I need to take a piss." Breathing around the unease in his chest, Bill left the column.

A tear leaked from his right eye. Soon, there'd be a flood, something his fellow soldiers didn't need to see. Once away from the lane, he found refuge behind a thicket, its plants flowering with white blossoms that would produce elderberries come June. Bill opened the floodgates and let tears gush down his cheeks. *That's enough. Wipe your face. Get back in line.* First, though, he leaned his musket against a stripling, unbuttoned his fly and let the urine flow. Just four aureolas in his life. Three died soon after the manifestations. Charlie's the fourth. *Why have them happen if I can't change things? Maybe Daniel's last words mean I can.*

He mulled his question. Would his chuckaboo's thread stay uncut if Bill managed to outfox Charlie's Fates? Put death off for another day... to when Charlie's rocking on his front porch with grandkiddies at his feet and his old-man's heart beats for the last time.

Honestly, Bill had no idea how to outfox the Fates' boyfriend, Death. He wiped his sleeve across his face and thought: *Probably won't get a chance. Death's like a thief.* He grabbed the musket's strap and shouldered the weapon.

Bill's muscles ached, but nothing like they would later in the day. The morning promised a day much like the one before it. Warm but with a canopy providing shade to help the Butternuts not wilt under the springtime sun. Even with the canopy and low humidity, Bill marched amidst many sick men. His own sudden hacking cough reminded him of that stark fact.

Back in the column, chest hurting from the coughing, Bill turned to Charlie. "Let's be vigilant, more than even Fredericksburg. We'll soon be in danger."

Squinting, Charlie gave Bill an odd look. "That's a given. Bullets will be flying. Cannonballs too."

"I know." Bill chose his next words carefully. "I just got a funny feeling. Like I said, Charlie, be vigilant."

Charlie chuckled, then nodded. "Sure."

"I mean it, Charlie. Tell me you'll be *extra* vigilant. Hell, run if you get in trouble. I just got a bad feeling." Bill decided on a little lie. "Happened while I was pissing. Got cold. Like death touched me. And your name popped into my mind. Please be vigilant."

Charlie grimaced. "Damn, Bill! You really are serious. That's a scary thing you just told me. Okay, I'll be vigilant. I promise."

"You both are crazy," Kenny said with a pie-eating grin mortared on his face. "And you're going to get trampled by the people behind you if you don't move faster."

A few miles beyond the furnace, they passed a brick mansion capped by two chimneys and surrounded by a meadow. In the driveway, slaves and white women loaded chests and trunks into several carts. Charlie hollered to the women, a matron and three girls, "We'll protect you, ladies."

The older woman shouted back: "Thanks, boys. My young'uns' safety comes first. We're leavin'."

Bounding out the front door and down the steps, a boy of maybe ten tore toward the graycoats, trailed by a toddler. "Let me join! Let me join!" the boy bawled.

"Me too!" the toddler screeched.

Their mother chased after them, her day dress swirling around her ankles. "Get back here!" She grabbed their hands. "You're not joinin' today or any day. Not until you're eighteen, and the war long over by then." A wide grin nearly hid her impish eyes as the breeze whipped a strand of gray hair across her forehead. "We'll be independent with Robert E. Lee as president."

"Pray for us, ma'am." Nathan doffed his hat to her.

"I promise." She tugged her sons toward the carts. "And you pray for my boys and girls, and for my oldest son, who's helpin' General Jackson find his way in these dense woods. Yanks were here yesterday searchin' for arms, shootin' fowls. Sometimes I hear the rattle of rifle fire. We're almost packed; might stay and see what happens." She shook her head. "Naw, goin' to leave. Why take chances?"

"What's your name, ma'am?" Bill shouted, trudging farther beyond her. "So we can pray?"

"Mrs. Charles C. Wellford. Evelina. My husband's a dry goods merchant in Fredericksburg and owns the furnace back there." She pointed to the tower jutting above the trees. "We left Fredericksburg to escape the fightin'. Looks like it followed us."

Bill pursed his lips. "I'm sorry. God's luck to you and your children, Evelina," he said, glad no aureolas had appeared around the woman or her children.

The buoyancy Bill felt in his legs after the piss break had vanished...,and he'd barely marched half a mile. Their weakness and the pain in his chest felt like God had shoved His hand down Bill's throat and yanked out his lungs.

Other Butternuts looked in comparable shape, if not worse. Like Bill, they marched as if slogging through a foot of snow, not a dirt lane on a rainless day. Faces pallid, they struggled to keep pace with the men in front of them. The columns were spreading out, a great gray serpent winding through the trees and thickets. Stonewall must not be happy, Bill thought.

"Close ranks!" officers hollered, pressing soldiers not to become stragglers. Anemic men suffering the quickstep could hardly be expected to march like they did in the early days of the war. They did the best they could, including Bill. He sucked in a breath, commanded: *Go faster, legs!*

Pine trees surrounded them. Low brush and brambles, some with white and pink flowers, grew around the trunks. In a different time without war, he'd pick some and present them to Franny. *Franny? What's wrong with me? Becky!* Trees had been cut and their trunks and roots removed to clear land for the narrow road. In places, logs had been laid one after another, creating a plank road. Too rough to walk on, so Bill shifted to the side. His boots kicked up tiny clods of dirt.

He badly wanted to take a spur-of-the-moment break, but pressed on. He knew officers would soon call a ten-minute halt. The boys, though, would be up and moving in five minutes. Something big was afoot; they didn't want to let Stonewall down. And they liked their nickname... Jackson's foot cavalry.

Finally, Colonel Purdie ordered the men to fall out near Poplar Creek. No need for dignity. Bill plopped to the ground. Musket on his lap and slouch hat on his chest, he lay back and closed his eyes. Sunlight peeking through the canopy stroked his forehead. Nearby, Poplar Creek gurgled, a soothing sound that promised sleep had the break lasted beyond ten minutes.

"I thought we'd be attackin' long ago." Bill opened his eyes at the sound of Charlie's voice. He could hear creek water sloshing down his friend's throat. Charlie corked the wooden canteen, then added, "The longer we march, the more interestin' this gets."

Colonel Purdie made his way among the resting men, encouraging them. Kenny called out to the officer, "What's Stonewall's plan, sir? I ain't no West Pointer, but I know what's not taught there, and that's dividin' up an army. General Lee and Stonewall must reckon this Hooker's a monkey."

Purdie stopped before Bill's splayed legs. "Can't tell you, soldier. You might get captured and spill the beans."

Kenny gave the colonel a skeptical look. "If I get captured, that means we've been discovered. No need for secrecy then."

Purdie frowned, but then let a grin swallow the scowl. "True, lad. I'll say this much. Some Yanks are going to soon get the biggest surprise of their lives."

Curiosity piqued, Bill decided the colonel might be in the mood to answer a question percolating since marching beyond the gray-haired lady and her kids. "A while back, Colonel, we passed a big old house."

"Yes, the Wellford house. The owner's teenage son is the general's guide. Both are patriots."

Bill rose to a sitting position. Somehow, it seemed disrespectful to talk to your colonel while lying flat on the ground. "Youngsters ran up to us to wave. Their momma had to lasso them. She says Blue-Belly cavalry paid a visit yesterday, so they know about this route."

The colonel folded his arms against his chest and harrumphed. "That was yesterday, Private. With our cavalry screening us, no one knows we're here."

End of conversation, Bill understood. "Yessir. That's good to know."

Up ahead, men were shuffling into the marching columns. The first wisps of boot-produced dust twirled about in the air as the Butternuts resumed marching. Bill could hear the colonel barking orders to his staff. The captains' response echoed along the lane: "Up, boys! Up off your butts! Plenty of day left for marchin' and a battle!" Groaning good-naturedly, the three hundred and fifty men of the Eighteenth resumed marching. Three hundred and fifty men? The number disheartened Bill. Organized at Camp Wyatt near Carolina Beach, the regiment had eleven hundred men at the war's start. Battle and disease had taken a toll. By nightfall, the numbers would drop even more.

Pushed by officers to keep up a fast pace, the troops tired easily due to the ghastly winter that had sapped their strength. They'd eat better when they could get their hands on crops and fruits. But that still lay ahead. Plodders at best, they tramped out of the wilderness and turned right onto Brock Road. The new route meant some marching out in the open, away from the wilderness. With no canopy to offer shade, men began to drop. The bunkmates tramped by stragglers congregated alongside the road, a few massaging their legs, some drinking from their canteens, others suffering coughing fits, even vomiting.

"Goin' to miss a fine battle," Kenny joked as they passed the exhausted soldiers.

"Candle to the devil, gigglemug!" one of the dog-tired Butternuts shot back.

"Coopered out," another whined, then coughed until his face turned red. When he could, he mumbled, "Just plain worn out."

Up ahead, next to a cabin with the roof caved in, they came across a fellow beyond *plain worn out*. Bare feet bloody, disheveled hat to his side, the long-haired Butternut lay in a heap where he'd collapsed and died. Men around Bill took a glance, then stared stonily ahead.

A redbird warbled, an unexpected sound as Bill eyed the fallen Butternut far from the arms of his wife and little ones. No bird songs would be heard tomorrow… just musket and cannon fire.

More gloom. Ahead, further corpses littered the land bordering the road. In the early afternoon, two miles into their Brock Road hike, they forded Poplar Run, crossing it for a second time. Bill dropped beside the water, and not only drank copiously, he drenched his face to remove dust and grime. *Sorry, Momma, I've tasted nothing better, not even your lemonade.* The rock-strewn creek signaled the beginning of another stretch of wilderness, just as wild and filled with impenetrable trees and brambles as the earlier tract. The Eighteenth took no more than three minutes to fill canteens, then resumed their march.

Nathan swung his head around and took a last look at the bridge. "The wood would make a fine cabin."

Bill cocked an eyebrow. "Naw, let's leave covered bridges alone. There'll come a time when everything's iron and steel, and folks will consider them treasures. Mark my words."

"Aren't you the poet, Billy Boy?" Charlie eyed the dense tree cover and the thickets bunched around the trunks. "Lordy, that's thick wilderness."

Near two o'clock, they scaled an unfinished railroad bed. "That's the same unfinished track we crossed back on the

Furnace Road, isn't it?" Nathan took off his hat and raked back hair he'd given up trying to keep combed.

"I reckon so, but can't be one hundred percent sure," Kenny answered. "We've done a flanking hike. Just like the colonel says, we're going to ruin a perfectly fine afternoon for some Blue-Bellies."

At the back of the column, behind Rhodes and Colston's divisions, Lane's boys marched into yet another dust haze kicked up by the soldiers ahead of them. Bill gazed up Brock Road, bordered on both sides by wilderness pines. Above him, the sky could be sunny or cloudy and about to shower a muddy rain. Who could know for sure? Not with the harsh pall.

Bill could taste the cloud, a chalk taste that would stay with him until replaced by the sulfur bitterness of black powder. As he licked his lips, Bill hoped the jungle-like wilderness concealed the dust cloud from Hooker's Yankees.

"I'll be glad to face Yankee bullets if it means the end of this damned dirt." Coughing, nose running, Charlie unstopped his canteen, dripped water across his face, and wiped it off with his hand. A smear of mud coated his face.

Bill trembled at Charlie's slapdash manner. Glad to face Yankee bullets? Crazy chuckaboo! Bill wanted to scream: "Be vigilant. God wants you dead." Of course, he didn't.

With Bill's pocket watch ticking inescapably toward the late-afternoon hours, the Eighteenth North Carolina came upon a road with a marker identifying it as the Orange Plank Road. They marched past it, continuing along Brock Road. Bill listened for any sounds of battle to his front. Nothing. *Lordy, I hope you're at your best today, General Jackson. And the Blue-Bellies a few cards short of a deck.* He hoped for both.

One more mile of marching brought the regiment to another intersection. Near tents set up to be a hospital, a road marker read: Orange Turnpike. A modern plank road, fit for the fast movement of artillery. Bill remembered the road from last fall's trek. The turnpike ran past the Chancellorsville mansion. Bill whistled a few bars of "Dixie," drawing a grin from Nathan. They were on the other side of the Union army—and if the silence could be trusted—still undiscovered.

At the intersection, within shadows cast by the backwoods trees, generals Jackson and Hill and their staffs motioned the Eighteenth forward onto the turnpike. "Hurry!" Jackson urged, gesturing like a Baptist preacher waving a Bible before his congregation. "We got 'em."

Near Jackson, a teenaged civilian nodded eagerly. The boy had to be Mrs. Wellford's eldest son.

Astride his blond chestnut, one of Hill's dapper staff officers led them through a maze of trees and brambles to their battle line next to the Thirty-Seventh. "Give 'em hell!" The staff officer waved his hat excitedly, then rode away. Soon the remaining regiments maneuvered from a marching column into a battle line spread out along both sides of the turnpike. In front were two more battle lines, Rhodes Division at the forefront, Colquitt behind them. The shadows lengthened inside the Wilderness, a sign the sun had begun to sink toward the western horizon. Precious daylight dwindled. It was five o'clock.

Charlie whispered, "Jackson's old game."

"Be vigilant, Charlie." Bill waited for the bugles, for shrill notes signaling *charge*.

Twenty-two

Like Chaff before the Wind

The bugles blew.

In front of Rodes' division, wild animals spooked by thousands of Butternuts burst out of the tangled woods into camps filled with Blue-Bellies cooking supper, playing cards and writing letters.

A volley of rifle shots rang out, then rebel yells that made Bill's skin crawl. To his front, Rodes' men charged, thrashing through dense thickets. Bill saw little, his view obscured by the undergrowth and the lengthening shadows of evening, twilight settling on the woods and fields of Chancellorsville. His hands, both grasping his musket, quivered as gunfire clattered somewhere beyond the thickets. For him, it turned into a battle of sounds, rifle and musket fire, cannon booms, eerie shouts and screams muffled by the foreboding surroundings.

Lane's Brigade saw no action in the initial Confederate onslaught, just the divisions of Rodes and Colston. Bill crouched with the other boys of the Eighteenth waiting for orders to advance. Last to arrive, they were in the reserve to be used to exploit a breakthrough.

At least Charlie still breathed. It's difficult to die when you're kneeling in the rear while others do the dying. But the night could still hold terrors and maybe Charlie's death. Bill's friend needed to stay vigilant… all of them needed to be wary. Orders would come soon.

As he listened to the sounds die down in the wilderness jungle, Bill knew Rodes' boys had swung to the left and attacked; Colquitt's to the right. Loud at first, the gunfire and shouts soon faded, signs the Butternuts were careening through the Blue-Bellies, a storm blowing the Yankees toward the Rappahannock.

Kenny caressed his musket's barrel as if fondling a lover. "The Blue-Bellies… they're chaff before the wind," he told Bill and the other bunkmates.

Darkness came and with it the orders from A.P. Hill. Stonewall wanted the two brigades held in reserve, Bill's Lane Brigade and McGowan's South Carolinians, to undertake a night attack in the ugliest terrain Bill had ever seen. Tangled, dense brambles that would become skin-ripping walls between trees, a close approximation to the African jungles Bill read about in geography books. Some lines of poetry came to mind: *Better angels of our nature… stay awake now, you're in danger.*

Later in the evening, the dashing figure of General Lane appeared before the troops. Mounted in his saddle, Lane rode along the plank road in front of the artillery, leading the brigade forward into the dense woods. McGowan's troops trailed. Soon, they reached the enemy's breastworks, empty now, the Blue-Bellies somewhere around New York City. Bill smiled at his attempt at humor.

Rampaged by Rodes' boys, the Union camps looked like a circus after crowds had departed. No Blue-Bellies to be seen, but lots of proof they'd been enjoying an evening of leisure when rudely interrupted by Stonewall's boys.

"Looks like some of the boys tried to take the contraband with them, especially beefsteaks and coffee pots," Charlie observed, harrumphing. "Running at the double quick ain't the way to do prosperous filchin'." Charlie glanced at a coffee pot on its side, its black contents soaking into the ground. "Lots of valuables dropped."

"More for us to claim." Kenny helped himself to an exquisitely made quilt.

Still riding along the plank road, Lane inspected his regiments as if he knew an order from A.P. Hill meant the boys would soon face a hailstorm of shellfire and mini balls. "Steady, boys," he shouted over and over again. "We're going to win Glory for the South." A brave man twice wounded during the Seven Days battles, Lane would be right there fighting alongside his lads.

Raucously, an artillery shell from a Confederate gun swooshed overhead toward the Yankee lines, barely discernible with brambles and trees blocking light from the stars and a near-full moon. A moment later, the Blue-Bellies returned fire, and soon no-man's land roared with cannon booms. Bill hugged the ground, just in case.

Near the bunkmates, Major John Barry bellowed, "Lie down, boys! Don't take chances."

Near the Eighteenth, at the edge of scrubby oaks, a voice rang out during a break in the cannon fire: "Brigadier General Lane? Do you hear me? Colonel Palmer, sir." The only Palmer Bill knew... Hill's chief of staff.

More shellfire, then Lane's voice near Bill: "Colonel, over here! Past the oaks!"

Colonel William Palmer, Hill's chief of staff, strode into view on foot and stopped no more than ten yards away. On foot himself, Lane met him and the two conferred amid the racket of cannon fire. Shells were shearing through the canopy, lopping off branches, turning them into spears. Canister balls crashed into the trees above the bunkmates, shaking the ground; twigs, leaves and branches rained down on Bill. Chest tight, gut so tense it made him queasy, Bill turned uneasily toward Charlie next to him, half-expecting to see a sheared-off bough jutting from his buddy's back. Instead, Charlie offered him a wicked little grin.

"I'm still here, Billy Boy," Charlie declared, brushing twigs and leaves from his tatty uniform. "Instead of me, you should be worried about yourself. You're bleedin'." Charlie's finger scooped up a tiny amount of blood from Bill's neck.

"It's nothing. I'm not the—" Lordy, Bill almost revealed the aureola to Charlie. He needed to be more circumspect.

The raining debris and shell fragments did little damage beyond cuts and bruises to Eighteenth soldiers. *Some good news for a change*, the future newspaper reporter thought.

Behind Bill, Lane and Palmer resumed shouting, trying to be heard above the barrage. Bill resisted the temptation to look. Better to make himself the smallest target possible.

"General Lane, General Hill wants to know why you've not formed your line as ordered," Palmer hollered.

Lane waited for a lull, and when silence returned, hastened a response, "Tell General Hill I can't move forward with this murderous enfilade artillery fire. If he orders it stopped, I'll advance. Union cannons are firing only because they are being fired upon. They'll stop if we stop."

Unable to resist, Bill peeked. He rolled onto his side and swung his head around just in time to see Palmer heading back to division headquarters. With a sigh, he rubbed his temples as though somehow that could soothe his spirit. Confederate cannon fire would either cease or General Lane would be relieved of command. Famous for his temper, A.P. Hill didn't tolerate officers who questioned his orders. Yet Bill had seen Hill kiss General Gregg on his forehead in the last hours of the man's life, a gesture that revealed a kind heart.

The Confederate cannon fire stopped. Not long after, Union guns grew quiet.

Still within earshot, Lane conferred with the Eighteenth's officers clustered around him. With orders dispensed, Lane departed while Colonel Purdie shouted to captains to put the Eighteenth into line on the left of the plank road, with its right resting on the road. Interesting—and terrifying—that a man born with the aureola curse should serendipitously hear the conversations of Palmer, Lane and Purdie. Or not as serendipitous as it appeared... God worked in mysterious ways, Reverend Sprunt preached.

In a silence broken only by the crunch of their boots, brogans and even bare feet crushing twigs and leaves, the men moved forward to their launch point, cursing as brambles tore their jacket sleeves and slashed skin. Expecting to charge at any moment, they didn't bother building breastworks. Enough moonlight sneaked past the trees to give Bill a peek at the brigade's alignment. The Seventh and Thirty-Seventh were on the right of the road, the Eighteenth and Twenty-eighth on the left. Colonel Avery's Thirty-Third Regiment moved forward as skirmishers.

Bill patted Charlie's shoulder. "Be vigilant, my friend."

"That's about the sixth time you've said that," Charlie grumbled, brushing Bill's hand aside.

Bill grimaced. "These shadows, the darkness, these deep woods… they make me nervous." *Wish I could tell you why, but I don't want you thinking I'm a lunatic.*

Immediately to the brigade's front were large oaks with little scrub. The Thirty-Third Regiment's skirmishers occupied the crest of a hill sometimes lit by muzzle flashes.

Bill kept his misgivings to himself. Although the terrain to his front didn't look as tortured as the land behind him, he knew the shadows could hide thickets so dense they could conceal more than enough Blue-Bellies to thwart the assault. He dreaded this charge.

Inexplicably, nothing happened. Butternuts stared at each other in the darkness, their faces dimly illuminated by the meager moonlight filtering through the trees. All wore expressions of puzzlement. Nathan looked like he needed to straightaway find a secluded spot to dump his last paltry meal. For Bill, fighting his aureola fears, this torture of doing nothing churned his belly. He closed his eyes and fought not to vomit.

A voice startled him. "Always worse when you expect to charge and you do nothin'," Charlie grumbled. "Just be vigilant, Billy Boy, eh?"

Bill blinked his eyes open. "Long night ahead. Plenty of time to get—" He left his thought unspoken. "Just be ready for whatever happens."

"Hate doin' nothin'!" Fisting his hand, Nathan punched the tree next to him. He yelped. "Sweet Jesus! Hope I didn't break it. Lordy, it hurts."

"That was stupid, Nathan," Kenny said, sniggering.

Making his way along the Eighteenth's line, Major Barry overheard the bunkmates' grousing. "Then dig breastworks. Beats punching tree trunks."

The first factual news came from Colonel Purdie, who followed in Barry's wake, warning the boys to be ready to charge at a moment's notice. "General Lane's gone to get final orders from General Hill. I expect him back anytime."

Five minutes later, Lane found Purdie still with the Eighteenth. Lane dismounted, handed the reins to a staff officer, then motioned Purdie away from Bill and the other bunkmates, but not far enough. Bill could still hear them. "Ran into General Jackson on the way to find Hill. I asked for orders. He pointed to the enemy and said, 'Push right ahead, Lane.'" The colonel shouted to the troops within hearing distance: "Listen for the bugles, boys!"

Bill listened. And listened some more. The bugles remained silent.

Among the thickets, insects buzzed but not as loud as the grumbling of Butternut troops. Kenny buzzed a tad louder than the others. "Getting damned late! We need to charge or forget it."

"This ditherin's goin' to get a lot of our people killed." The voice came from a soldier further down the line, a private named Milford who'd actually emerged alive from a winter-camp hospital.

Bill fixed his gaze on Charlie, which earned him a wisecrack. "There ya'll go again, Billy Boy, starin' like I'm one of them ghosties in a Dickens novel."

"No, Charlie, you don't have a chain hooked to your leg and your face ain't white enough." His own words brought a chill to Bill's skin.

Rumors were flying down the line faster than a signal on a telegraph wire. A Yankee officer waving a white flag had come up from the brigade's right between the skirmishers and the main battle line. Not sure in the darkness who'd he stumbled across, the Blue-Belly had wanted to know if the men he approached were friends or foes.

Growling his displeasure, Nathan snapped, "So what was General Lane's answer?"

Grinning, Kenny replied, "The general made him our prisoner. The fella was spittin' mad he wasn't allowed to return to his lines. I mean… it was a white flag, after all."

Nathan hissed a curse and muttered, "The good Lord must have been playin' the clown when he put half-formed souls in Yankee brains."

As if the Thirty-Third's skirmishers on the right of the brigade's line wanted to celebrate Nathan's droll words with fireworks, they opened musket and rifle fire at a horseman who drew too close to them. In answer, Union artillery and infantrymen unloaded on the Thirty-Third's hilltop position. In the dark, the firing sounded like a wild thunderstorm, except Bill knew otherwise. Not lightning flickering within the thickets and trees… muzzle flashes.

Charlie rolled his eyes. "Well, there goes the element of surprise."

"Maybe we'll stay put?" Nathan said in a hopeful tone.

"Sorry, Nathan," Kenny responded, voice stoic. "A.P. Hill's a charger."

As if Kenny had inadvertently become a herald for Hill, someone in the Eighteenth shouted out, "Make way for General Hill!"

"Talk about the devil," Charlie teased.

Like the Red Sea parting in Exodus, soldiers danced back, allowing Hill and his staff to ride through the Eighteenth's line and continue up the plank road toward the Thirty-Third's skirmishers, and somewhere beyond them, new Yankee breastworks.

Just beyond the Eighteenth's line, Hill swung around in the saddle. "Boys, fall back to those abandoned breastworks. No reason to take unnecessary casualties." He doffed his fancy hat and waved it. "Don't get settled in. We're still attacking."

Hill's orders were passed on by the brigade's officers and sergeants, and soon the men were withdrawing to the breastworks, slithering once more through the thickets, getting more slashes.

Bill's canteen bounced on his hip as he crouched behind the Yankee breastwork. *Well, that explains why we've not heard the bugles. Everybody's nervous tonight. Lane's about to order an attack, then Hill rides through our line.*

Bill heard axes beyond the Thirty-Third's skirmishers …the Blue-Bellies strengthening their breastworks. They were expecting an attack. *Great,* he thought, scratching his neck.

The fellow shoulder to shoulder with Nathan, Donnie Kelly, told the fresh fish, "I'm hearin' Lane ordered the Seventh forward, but had second thoughts. Some in the Seventh thought there were troops of some kind on our right." The racket among the skirmishers was loud, and Bill had trouble hearing Donnie but caught enough to get his meaning. "Lane sent out some scouts. They returned with some newly-captured Yankees, a Pennsylvania regiment that up and surrendered."

The night didn't feel right to Bill. Hill wanted to attack, yet he and his staff were out reconnoitering in no-man's land. Obviously, no attack while they were out there swallowed by the wilderness and the darkness. And Lane almost ordering the Seventh to advance… with Hill between the Graybacks and the Blue-Bellies? The night definitely had the feel of a train wreck about to happen. Bill darted a quick glance at Charlie and thought: *No, not tonight, my friend. The aureola can't have you.*

Nathan harrumphed his disgust. "So do we attack or not?"

"General Hill's out there," Bill reminded the recruit. "General Lane won't attack now. Hill will get trapped in the crossfire. This is plum crazy trying to fight in the darkness." He gave in to an overpowering urge to again remind Charlie: "Be vigilant."

Laughing, Charlie punched Bill in the arm. "Stop it!"

To the front, brambles and undergrowth crackled as if rustled by a gusty wind. Except there wasn't much of a breeze.

Bill expected to see Hill and his staff returning. With all the firing, the boys were jittery. Some caressed their guns' triggers.

Frazzled, Nathan croaked, "Someone's out there. Damned Yankees! They're attackin'!" He raised his musket and aimed toward the rustling.

Lunging past Charlie and Kenny, Bill grabbed the barrel and shoved it against the breastwork. "Hill's out there, damn it!"

Nathan craned his head toward the sounds. "That's not Hill. It's comin' from another direction. Blue-Bellies!"

Bill focused on the all the noises beyond the breastworks. One sound dominated. "All I hear are axes. The Blue-Bellies expect an assault, just as Charlie said. Going to be a messy business."

"Ya'll blind?" Nathan again raised his rifle. "Axes don't grope their way through thickets." This time no one stopped him. He fired.

"Lordy, Nathan, Hill's out there." Unease gripped Bill as strongly as the shadows cloaked the wretched terrain in front of him. "We can't be shooting at every noise. Please, please, make sure they're Blue-Bellies."

Thankfully, no frantic shouts rang out from the brambles, no "friends, friends! Don't shoot!" Maybe Bill's fears were overblown. He hoped so.

Up at the skirmish line, new firing erupted, a hullabaloo that made the situation even more muddled. Blood-red muzzle blasts from the Thirty-Third's muskets and rifles lit up pockets of the wilderness terrain. The hairs on Bill's arms and head prickled. An appalling thought roared into consciousness: maybe the axes were a ruse and Blue-Bellies were attacking, about to overrun the skirmishers. Smothering doubts, he raised his musket.

Thrashing sounds, shadows moving... swiftly. Hill and his staff were off to the left, hidden in the shadows. These galloping horsemen came from the right, charging toward the Eighteenth's line. Time seemed to stop, like that hushed moment between when a band stops playing a tune and the crowd breaks into applause.

A jumpy voice behind Bill bellowed, "Yankee cavalry!"

Out of the shadows, dark mists clinging to him, a cavalryman rode toward the breastworks, a short-barreled gun aimed at Bill... no Charlie. Or maybe just the shadows weaving weird patterns that briefly took on the aspect of a horseman? A red flame shot from the barrel—no time to debate its reality—and Bill reacted.

Taut as a loaded bow, Bill barreled into Charlie, ramming him into the soft Virginia loam.

"Fire!" that same jumpy voice behind Bill ordered.

Knocked off balance by Charlie's tumble, Kenny fell into Nathan and Nathan into Donnie Kelly... and like a game of dominoes, the pieces kept falling. But not before flames spurted from Butternut muskets, and wildly aimed mini balls shrieked into the shadows.

Bill's neck stung. He reached up, touched the skin. Wet, warm, blood. His first thought... the Yankee bullet. Then the doubts. Maybe Charlie's belt bucket or scabbarded bayonet reopened one of the thickets' slashes.

Still rubbing his neck, Bill peeked above the breastwork. In ghostly moonlight flittering among barely visible trees and brambles, oncoming horsemen—Graycoat officers—tumbled from their mounts. "No!" he wailed.

All along the line, encompassing all four brigades, gunfire roared. More Graycoats fell from their mounts.

One of the horsemen maybe sixty yards away cried out, "You're firing into your own men!"

Behind Bill, Major Barry responded, voice tight with anger, "Who gave that order? It's a lie! Pour it into them!" And more mini balls flew into the shadowy night.

Panting, Charlie scrabbled to his knees and grabbed Bill's sleeves. "Thank you, Billy Boy," he gushed, emotions overflowing. "You saved me, saved my worthless life."

Between the Confederate and Federal lines, voices in distress screeched for a litter.

A voice dripping with fury pierced the shadows and roared into the Eighteenth's battle line. "You've destroyed my staff." Bill knew that voice from the night in the Yerby house when he sat beside General Gregg and read poetry. A.P. Hill, there to comfort the dying Gregg, there to reassure him that old arguments mean nothing when it's time to cross the river.

Bill pushed Charlie away. "God help me! What have I done?"

"Done? You saved my life." Confusion reigned on Charlie's face.

Bill patted Charlie's cheek. "At what cost?"

Bill jerked his head to the side, glared at Barry. "That's General Hill, sir."

"He's right, sir," Sergeant Barnard echoed. "General Hill just rode up the plank road, passing through us."

The light in Barry's eyes dimmed. "God, no!" he groaned. "I didn't know." Fisting his hands, Barry smacked them against his hips. "I can't be everywhere!"

The ground beneath Bill rumbled. He ducked as a horse leaped the breastwork. As the mount landed, its rider tumbled off.

Barry squatted, turned the man over. "Dead. It's General Jackson's chief engineer, Boswell."

"Stonewall's chief engineer?" Charlie's voice quivered with confusion as if realizing the Eighteenth had shot innocent men.

"Bad night all around." *Not completely. A mini-ball headed for Charlie's head missed.* An unbidden thought taunted Bill. When the Fates are denied, the Lord requires another soul to cross the river, the way a substitute can take the place of a draftee.

A Federal battery unleashed an angry fusillade. Canister and shell shredded trees along both sides of the Plank Road. Bill lay flat as leaves, twigs and branches showered on him. The barrage thinned and silence returned, except for frantic voices echoing in the shadows beyond the breastworks. He craned his head for a look. Moonbeams cut through the shadows, revealing stretcher bearers carrying someone on a litter. Twice they dropped him as enemy bullets riddled a bearer. Determined not to falter, they carried the wounded man over the breastwork near Bill, who steepled his hands.

The man tilted his bearded face toward Bill. The Kenansville editor's son locked eyes with Stonewall Jackson. Blood seeped from a forehead scratch, staining his chiseled face. The general's bleeding left arm hung limply over the litter's edge. A litter bearer muttered, "You boys shot him. Three bullets, one in his right hand, two in his left shoulder. Pray hard for him, for his recovery."

Another unwanted thought stole into Bill's weary mind. Those three mini balls came from the muskets of Kenny, Nathan and Donnie Kelly, their aim thrown off when Bill threw himself against Charlie and initiated a near-comical game of dominoes... except this game had turned deadly. Coldness enveloped Bill. Perhaps he hadn't thwarted the Fates. They and their Master had been quite willing to trade other lives for Charlie. Except how could he actually be sure those mini balls that wounded Jackson were truly from the guns of Kenny, Nathan and Donnie Kelly? And Jackson wasn't dead... yet.

Bill thought of the infinitely small odds of those errant mini balls finding Stonewall Jackson. The balls that wounded Jackson somehow didn't get diverted by dozens of bramble bushes so thick they bogged down advancing soldiers, avoided second-generation trees fat with leaves, and through it all managed not to get slowed or even stopped by the jungle-like foliage. *As if God's hand guided them.*

Charlie was still alive; Stonewall Jackson, probably dying, and Bill felt numb as he stared into the blessed shadows dark and deep.

Twenty-three

A Shell Sliver Wound

Charlie could still die in the war, but Bill didn't think so. Without quite understanding all the complexities of what had happened, Bill had unintentionally traded Charlie's life for Robert E. Lee's right-hand general, Stonewall Jackson. Even more confusing, Jackson still lived, but Bill feared he'd die soon. Otherwise, why did Charlie still breathe?

Some might accuse Bill of muddled thinking. He knew better. Aureolas were strange creatures. Until Charlie, he'd never considered messing with one. Now he had, and General Jackson lay in a bed with three bullets in his body. Bill sighed. Now wasn't the time to be thinking of such things... it was first light, May 3, 1863, and the long-delayed charge would soon begin.

Even so, time remained for another thought or two. Not unexpectedly, Jackson's left arm felt the surgeon's saw.

He'd soon be on the way to a nearby mansion to recuperate—or in Bill's mind, die.

Not one to worry about the inexplicable, Jackson never wasted time debating the merits of dying in bed or on the battlefield… when God's chosen time came to die, he would die and not until then. Which opened a can of worms in Bill's mind. If fate decreed Charlie's death and God changed fate to save Charlie at the expense of Jackson's arm or more likely his life, then God could change his mind. Why else allow someone to see an aureola around a soon-to-die man if not to give that someone a chance to change fate? Big ideas could sometimes birth headaches. *Lord, have mercy, my head's going to burst. Oh, for a sip of laudanum.*

More than Jackson had been hurt… A.P. Hill as well. The Eighteenth's mini balls killed and wounded men from both generals' staffs. In the immediate aftermath, officers went along the line and reassured the men the shootings resulted from a deadly amalgamation of darkness and dense scrub. The men shouldn't blame themselves. Farmland years ago, the wilderness had reclaimed what farmers no longer tilled. That's where Jackson had lost an arm, a godforsaken land of nightmares. Bill grimaced… he'd just called the land around Chancellorsville forsaken by God. Had God deserted Jackson for the sake of Charlie?

In a sitting position, Bill lay against the breastwork wall, cursing himself for thinking too much and not getting any sleep. Near him, he heard snoring—Nathan and maybe Kenny. Not Charlie, though. Charlie eyed him curiously.

"What're you thinkin'?" Charlie yawned.

Dawn approached. In a few minutes, first light. Sunrays would creep above the horizon and chase away the remnants of darkness.

"Thinking about Franny's bubbies," Bill lied.

"Ah, your favorite subject." Charlie glanced up at the brightening sky through holes in the canopy. "I hope that girl realizes what she gave up and comes flyin' back into your arms. Lovesick chuckaboos drive me nuts."

Bill chuckled, then probed the slash on his neck. Bramble thorn? Or mini ball? Earlier, Charlie claimed a mini ball. "I *am* driving myself nuts, Charlie." Bill couldn't resist. "Be vigilant. Looks like we're finally going to attack some Blue-Bellies."

Awash in morning light, Major Barry meandered along the Eighteenth's portion of the line, meeting with small groups of melancholy soldiers. He stopped where Donnie Kelly and his chuckaboos tended a newly started campfire. "Eat some salt beef and cornmeal bread with your coffee, boys. If you don't, you're going to regret it. Going to do some charging this morning, make up for what happened last night."

Most lads close enough to hear Barry's words shouted out a cheer. Bill refused. When told the Eighteenth had fired on Jackson, Hill and their staffs, Barry had done nothing to stop the firing. The man should be tormented by nightmares. Bill left his thoughts locked in his head.

They ate quickly and assembled for the attack. The troops knew little beyond Barry's words. Cavalry general Jeb Stuart now commanded Lee's Second Corps. Bill wondered why A.P. Hill hadn't been named interim commander for the attack. Jackson's decision? Jackson and Hill did feud a painful amount.

Assembling didn't require much time or effort. They scrambled from the abandoned Yankee breastworks, formed lines and waited for the bugles. Just a few hours earlier, they'd formed a similar battle line, but the bugles never sounded. They'd waited behind the Blue-Belly breastworks as the night filled with shells and mini balls. And when the noises spooked the boys, they'd shot General Jackson. Bill grimaced; he just couldn't get the previous night out of his mind. A thought tickled his funny bone: Stuart should stay away from the Eighteenth; otherwise, he'd end up shot.

Finally, Sergeant Barnard provided news that sated the boys' curiosity. The Eighteenth would participate in a frontal attack on the Yank line immediately on the right of the Orange Turnpike, but not before Confederate cannons softened up the Blue-Bellies. Barnard joked, "We're goin' to blow them a thousand feet in the air, boys!" Bill turned away so Barnard didn't see his smirk. *No Blue-Bellies shooting at us when we charge, eh? Sure. They'll all be swimming across the Rappahannock.* Barnard wanted to perk up the boys, but bombast wasn't the way.

The barrage lasted thirty minutes. When the Confederate guns grew silent, the bugles blew.

Sunlight sifting through the leafy canopy heated Bill's face as he and the rest of the Eighteenth surged forward at the double-quick, beelining for a tangle of scraggy hickories and brambles. They'd pressed through the same wall of brambles twice during the night, tolerating the lacerations. Repeating the hellish movement in daylight proved nearly as bad, although the woody scent reminded Bill of a ham baking. Ahead of the brigade, skirmishers moved forward, guns at the ready. In the darkness, those same skirmishers were the ones who opened fire on some lost Yankees, triggering the mix-up that resulted in General Jackson's wounding. And to make the entire night absurd in Bill's mind, not one—not even Jackson—glowed with an aureola.

No Yankee gunfire ripped into the Butternut lines. Still, the Eighteenth's formation jumbled up as men tried to avoid the brambles. Impossible to march quietly, they made a racket as they thrashed through the gnarled wilderness.

Boom! Boom! The Confederate cannon resumed firing, supporting the advance, keeping Blue-Belly heads below the top of their breastworks and their rifles silent. Swoosh! Bill's heart rattled as he heard the thump of a mini ball shattering bone. Donnie Kelly wheezed and fell. Yankees perching behind their breastworks could still shoot blindly.

The Confederate cannon fire sparked a beehive of Blue-Belly fury. Shells and canister juddered into the tangled wilderness and toward the advancing Butternuts. A few found targets, their successes punctuated by wails and howls of pain. Near Bill, a canister load exploded, spraying lead balls and mutilating two soldiers. Bill knew those boys, Tommy Irwin and Sam Grogg, college fellas who loved to play checkers and yack about Poe's poetry. Smeared in blood not his own, Nathan staggered and retched his meager morning meal down his shell jacket. His face pale as a corpse, Nathan wobbled back into the tattered line as shells continued to shear the canopy, raining down iron and wood slivers.

Bill skirted a bramble bush, but not before its thorns slashed his shell-jacket sleeve and slit skin along the back of his hand. Feeling the warm seep of blood, Bill looked down at his musket's trigger and his beet-red hand. The sight reminded him of the paint on his lead toy soldiers. Up ahead, the wilderness seemed to be thinning. Through a gap in tree branches, a steepled building seemed to hover on a ridge way off in the distance.

Above Bill and Charlie, a shell plummeted toward the mutilated canopy and burst. The concussion's fiery wind knocked them to their knees. Searing pain exploded in Bill's back. As a waterfall of dazzling red pounded his brain, Bill crumpled into soft soil. Moist, musty dirt filled his mouth, nose, even his eyelids. Somehow, he managed to suck in raspy breaths. *No! You'll not scream! Not when you saw brave men die silently at the Yerby House.*

Through the pain, Bill heard weeping. Spitting out dirt, grinding his teeth, he grunted, "Not dead."

Charlie kissed the back of Bill's head. "Oh, God, Billy Boy! Your poor back... it's gapin'. Ain't bleedin' bad. Not sure why. Lordy, you ought to be dead."

Spitting out more dirt, Bill strained, "Help me up! Can't just lie here. Could be days until I get help." Bill tensed, preparing for even worse pain.

Growling, Charlie secured Bill under the armpits and lifted him to his knees.

Bill screamed, then panted: "Stop! Hurts! Goin' to faint if you don't."

"Got to get you to your feet even if you bleed more. Stay here... you die."

Above the canopy, shells still exploded, although none near them. *Thank God*, Bill thought. *Something's going right.*

Die? That infuriated Bill. "Fuck you, Charlie. Get me on my feet. Now!" Sweating profusely, vision blurred, spots dancing in front of his eyes, Bill fisted his hands and waited for another stab of scorching pain.

He felt like a voodoo doll getting lanced with Bowie knives. Straining to stay conscious, Bill glanced at his feet. Boots were firmly planted in the soil.

"Take a step," Charlie ordered, clasping Bill's shoulders above the wound. "I just love springtime walks." Laughing sourly, he lugged Bill back toward the breastworks.

The noise of a cannonball's passage got louder and louder. And from the raucous sound, coming right at them.

Charlie wrenched Bill to the side, and the cannonball bounced past. Again, Bill screamed. Pain throbbed as if his spine had been scrunched and tossed into a trashcan. Tears rained down his face and blotted his shell jacket.

"Sorry, Bill. Couldn't let it hit you."

Wheezing breaths, Bill coiled an arm around Charlie's neck and clung to him. "Carry me if you have to." He focused on Charlie's face, trying to bottle the pain.

Bill lessened his focus on the agony surging from his back to eyeball the brigade's advancing regiments, enveloped by a black-powder cloud that twined around trees and bramble bushes. Behind gaps in the ragged battle line, men lay strewn in grotesque positions, some with the backs of their heads blown off, others their faces maimed. He wondered if Kenny and Nathan were among the dead or the wounded wailing for their mothers. The regiments closed the gaps, pressed on toward the Union breastworks.

"What did you say, Charlie? A springtime walk?" Bill huffed a laugh, then grimaced. More strewn Butternuts lay closer to them, most of them moaning. One or two lay in their path. "Only way to the field hospital is to walk. Can't get the back fixed standing here." Bill offered what he figured must be a ghastly smile.

Charlie nodded. "We'll do it ten steps at a time. Ten steps, a thirty-second break, ten seconds. At the breastworks you can catch your breath."

Bill's legs wobbled and his head spun as he walked those first ten steps, then rested for thirty seconds. "Holy God, my back feels like it's on fire. Is it burned badly?"

"Really won't know until we get you to the field hospital and cut away your jacket and shirt. Both are burned through and your skin... it's cooked along the edges. The wound's a ticket to Kenansville. You're a lucky man, Billy Boy."

"Not as lucky as you." Bill grunted, then began the next ten hesitant steps.

Charlie's chatter helped dim the pain, Bill discovered, as he completed his second set of steps. "I wasn't touched by even one sliver of that shell," Charlie said, wonder in his voice. "And I was standing next to you."

Through the knifing pain, Bill spat, "What if I told you God wanted you dead last night, but I saved your worthless hide?"

Charlie laughed, his hoots competing with the artillery's noisy off-tone concert. "I'd say you're mad as a hatter."

When they reached the breastworks, Bill decided to press on rather than take a longer rest period.

As Bill teetered into the next step, Charlie squeezed his friend's elbow. "You sure? You look terrible."

Certain Charlie wouldn't let him fall, Bill trudged onward on the planks of the Orange Turnpike toward the Second Corps artillery, the guns lined up on a knoll maybe two hundred yards away. "Gaping holes in the back will make a man look terrible." Bill turned serious. "Still not bleeding?"

"Just a little." When a shell exploded about a hundred feet away, Charlie twitched and bumped against Bill. "Tell me about Franny."

"Trying to get my mind off the pain, eh?" Bill glanced at the mini-craters caused by the shell's jagged fragments. "Franny's got hair that gets kissed every morning by the sun. That's why it's so blonde. At that ball"—Bill paused to clear his throat, catch his breath—"not a strand was out of place. Lordy, Charlie, I wanted to make love to her in front of everybody."

Away from the deep canopy, a clear blue sky above them, Charlie squirmed at the sight of Bill's wound. "You're doin' fine, Bill, keep tellin' me about Franny."

"The eyes of all the men at the dance were fixed on her when we promenaded into the ballroom. They all wished they could replace me. In the overseer's cottage, I had her... I better stop now."

"Yes, you should. I'm much too respectable to hear about your liaison's sordid details." Charlie feigned solemnity.

Bill managed a feeble cackle. "Respectable? With the ladies? Did the sun shine in the night sky?" Up on the ridge crowned with cannons, a horseman headed down the slope. Bill watched the officer's approach as he returned to his memories of Franny on the night of the ball. "She didn't wear a hoop. See what war does to young ladies?"

The horseman reined in his Morgan in front of Bill and Charlie. As if the shells flying overhead were raindrops, not weapons of death, he swept a bandana across his forehead. "Hospital tents are a quarter mile back, beyond Union fire. I'll get some stretcher-bearers. Be back in a few minutes." He galloped away, the Morgan's hoofs clopping on the planks.

Without prompting from Charlie, Bill resumed walking. Each tentative step sent jolts of pain lancing through him. "Where was I?" he mused, willing the pain to subside. "Oh, yes, Franny's gown. Peach colored. Embroidered with lace flowers. I'm boring you, aren't I?"

"Just a little bit. But tell me more." Charlie secured his grip on Bill, whose voice sounded brittle.

The memories were getting harder to summon. Pain played a stingy gatekeeper. A few he mustered: their kisses in the Hamiltons' greenhouse garden, the walk beneath the aurora sky—and then the artillery officer reappeared with stretcher-bearers. "Hallelujah," Bill whispered, grateful he could soon lie down.

They placed him on his side atop the stretcher, careful not to let the wound grind against the canvas. Bill closed his eyes while the bearers took him on the jerky trip to the field hospital. As the ride deepened the pain, flashes of vivid colors danced in his mind, like a painter splashing watercolors on a canvas.

Well, you made this bearable, Franny.

The jarring ended. Bill knew it meant they'd reached the hospital tents. He opened his eyes. A surgeon bearing a somber expression leaned over him. Once Bill's shell jacket and shirt fell away, cut by one of the bearers, the sawbones assessed the wound, deciding if Bill could be saved. "No injury to the ribs or spine or he couldn't have walked this distance," the surgeon said to himself. "Little bleeding. The heat must have cauterized the wound." The sawbones nodded to the stretcher-bearers. "Take him to the surgery tent. Need a closer look."

Grim work still to be done, the sawbones dashed toward the tent.

"Doc?" Shouting, Charlie flapped his arms above his head. The surgeon glanced back toward the stretcher, an annoyed look on his face. "In case you don't recognize him, Bill here helped tend to General Gregg in his last hours. He's the Angel of Belvoir."

The doctor returned with morphine. Bill sighed as if he'd just been gifted George Eliot's *Adam Bede*. He sighed again when the morphine chased away his pain and eased him into a wonderful sleep.

Twenty-four

Under a Surgeon's Scalpel

"He's coming around."

Bill knew the voice, just couldn't place it.

He struggled to open his eyes; they seemed glued in place. When they snapped open, he blinked, startled by the brightness. Lordy, he wanted to drift back to sleep, but slumber eluded him. He lifted his right arm and rubbed his eyes. Gradually, the face that belonged to the voice came into focus—Bill's chaplain friend, Monroe Anderson.

"Howdy, Chaplain." His words emerged scratchy and hoarse. Bill swung his gaze outward past the chaplain, and saw a tent of cots filled with groaning and sleeping men, all swathed in bandages, most bloody. "This can't be Heaven, else Heaven looks awfully like Chancellorsville."

The chaplain grinned. "No, not Heaven. Just a hospital tent for some of Stonewall's convalescing soldiers."

"The surgeon didn't cut off my back, did he?" *Terrible joke. Should have kept that thought in my head.* Bill lay on his side. Not overly comfortable, but far better than on his back, on his wound. He didn't want to think about trying to sleep. Or sitting in a chair. The morphine must still be working… the pain throbbed, but no worse than a coffee spill.

"You still have your back, my friend." The chaplain surveyed nearby cots and the soldiers on them, all without limbs. "Doctor Straith tells me you're a lucky man. Once he got a look, he found the dorsal integuments torn away and severe muscle lacerations, but no injury to a rib or your spine."

Bill strained to arch an eyebrow. "Dorsal integuments? Speak English, Chaplain."

"A well-read man like you needs help with some words?" Anderson shook his head, a pretend look of incredulity blooming across his face. "Your back has a hole five inches wide and six inches long. Dr. Straith extracted a shell fragment lodged in the muscle a fingernail from the spine. Some burning, but not bad, the doctor says. Stretched nearby skin for a graft and stitched you back together." Anderson held up a sliver-sized shell fragment. "He extracted this. A real beauty, eh? Cauterized the veins. Allowed you to walk almost to the cannons."

"Please tell me they've been washing bandages and surgical tools in boiling water?" Bill waited to hear the bad news. With the wound located in the back, he couldn't do his own cleaning and bandaging. Rot seemed inevitable, fated. *My favorite word lately, it seems… fated.*

"Yes, Bill, Doctor Straith's not from the Dark Ages." Leaning across Bill, the chaplain took a gander at the bandaged wound. "The war offers opportunities for experimentation. He's trying to reduce wound rot. It's why he gave you bromine."

A woman's voice, one Bill immediately put a face to... Juliet Neale, Franny's mother. "You've had him to yourself long enough, Chaplain. My turn." Bill heard her footsteps and then saw her face as Anderson moved aside. "Hello, soldier-boy. I'm going to be your nurse. I promise I won't leave your side. Franny will skin me alive if I do."

Lordy, never realized how much she looks like her daughter. Older, but still beautiful. Always a stylish woman, even when wearing a gray cotton dress with a calico print and white apron. No one could call her a wilting blossom. Blood spotted her dress below the apron.

Bill squeezed her offered hand. "Mrs. Neale! Ma'am, you shouldn't be here. There's a battle nearby."

Juliet harrumphed. "Why not? There was a battle near Mr. Yerby's house, remember? That didn't stop me. And anyway, I hear the Blue Devils are on the other side of the Rappahannock, whipped like usual."

"What day is this?" Uncertainty quivered Bill's voice.

"Tuesday, May 5th. You've been asleep since Sunday." Juliet swept damp bangs from his forehead.

"So we prevailed?" Bill whispered a prayer for Charlie, Kenny and Nathan, that the three came through the battle not just alive, but without a wound.

Behind Juliet, the chaplain spoke up, "Your friend Charlie plans a visit. He can give you the particulars."

"Charlie's alive!" *That was stupid to say.* Stonewall was wounded, many on his staff and A.P. Hill's staff were dead. To keep Charlie breathing, God had required a sacrifice, which meant Stonewall would soon die. Nothing else made sense.

Juliet brought over a chair and sat. The chaplain stood behind her, hands on the backrest spindles. "As soon as I heard you'd been wounded, I telegraphed Franny. She *ordered* me to stay by your side. Can you believe it? Ordered her momma? That's my daughter, especially when she's in love."

The pain had crept again into his back, like lion's teeth nibbling at his wound. "So she's thinking of me?" He squirmed in bed, hoping movement would ease the pain. It didn't. Two pillows cushioned the side of his head, about the only part of his body comfortable. "I would never have made it off that battlefield without Franny's face pictured in my mind."

"She couldn't say much in a telegraph missive. She did ask me to kiss you." Juliet leaned closer and kissed him on the cheek. "I know she'd have kissed you way differently." Juliet grinned.

Bill stared at his fingers. One hand he could maneuver; the other lay tucked beneath his body, cramped. "So is she going to marry the fellow? I love fairytales. Do I believe in them? It's hard, Mrs. Neale. I understand why Franny rushed off to nurse him. He's her fiancé, after all." Come-true fairytales didn't feel farfetched when a man got bedeviled by aureolas.

Juliet frowned, a sad look in the hospital tent's low light. "Franny didn't expect another man would awaken her heart. Peter's her safe choice. The oh-well choice, if all she wants is a warm hearth and a walnut sofa with only her sitting on it. Peter will end up a state legislator puffing on a cigar, stuffing his pockets with ill-gained money. He'll spend all his evenings cooped up in his office drafting legislation for his business cronies. If she follows her heart, she'll snuggle on the couch with you and discuss emancipation or perhaps the women's vote. Peter would tell Franny to shut up and knit." The only light in the tent came from two oil lamps positioned on each end. Shadows played on the walls and on Juliet's face as she kissed Bill again, this time on both cheeks. "Her kisses, not mine."

Bill maneuvered his right arm from out under his side. Free of the constriction, blood flowed once more and the prickly numbness disappeared. He flexed his fingers and entertained sweet thoughts concerning Franny. "It's odd. Without this war, I'd have never met Franny. Things happen so fast in war. A whirlwind romance for us, then she's racing off to take care of a fiancé and maybe marry him."

Shadows shifted; Bill turned his gaze to where a nurse entered the tent and picked up a dark lamp. Light flared inside the lamp, and she carried it to the cot next to Bill. "I'm sorry to wake you, Corporal," she told the soldier. "You need to drink this medicine. Then you can go back to sleep." Juliet and the chaplain blocked Bill's view of his neighbor, so he didn't get to see the soldier drink the concoction. The corporal said nothing, though Bill heard the gulp-gulp of the medicine streaming down his throat. Moments later, the nurse exited the tent and the shadowy light returned.

As if the nurse performed a holy rite, Juliet remained silent until the soldier drank his medicine, probably for pain. Only then did she respond to Bill's words about Franny. "She told me about your Becky. In my last letter, I told her she needs to come back into your life and file a claim, not just hand you over to a woman she hasn't even seen. I can't live her life. She has to make the choice." Juliet leaned back in the chair and rested her hands in her lap. "I've a question for you, Bill. Where do you want to convalesce? At the Hamilton house in Fredericksburg, a short trip by buggy? By troop train to the convalescent wards at Chimborazo Hospital? Or by train to your home in North Carolina?"

Bill didn't need to mull over Juliet's question. "Home, of course. Kenansville. Let my momma look after me. Do some recruiting for the Eighteen while I'm there. I hear the fever has run its course in Wilmington. I'll sign up some fellas there for Sergeant O'Rourke."

Juliet kissed him on the forehead. "One more from Franny," she said, laughing as she rose to leave. "I'll pass on Kenansville to the head nurse who oversees placement in convalescent hospitals and homes. Soon, you'll be back in the arms of your Becky." Unthinkingly, she scratched her nose. "I'll be writing Franny and including some choice words. She needs to make up her mind rather quickly, or she'll lose you forever."

With the chaplain in tow, Juliet made her way toward the tent's door. As if watching her leave sent a distress signal to Bill's back, the pain suddenly spiked. A young nurse entered the tent just after Juliet and the chaplain exited. Sucking in a deep breath for courage, Bill forced himself onto his elbow as the wound protested his action. "Nurse?" He shouted louder. "Nurse! Please. I need your assistance."

She rushed to him. The woman might be pretty; he couldn't be sure, not in the dim light, not with her hair in an austere bun and her body clothed in a grim black dress and bloody apron. "Don't do that!" she scolded. "You'll tear your stitches."

He lay back down and let his head settle into the soft pillows. The pain didn't subside. "Please, Dover's powder for the pain? Coming up on me like a locomotive." Bill knew it would do the trick… opium and ipecac.

"Of course. I won't be long." A coy smile curved her lips.

Soon, she returned with a tin cup of tea and a bottle of Dover's powder. She mixed the tea and powder and he drank, grimacing as the bitter mixture slithered down his throat.

"Thank you, miss." He reached out and with the tips of his fingers brushed her hand.

"They call you the Angel of Belvoir." Again, that smile.

She wants to get to know me better. Drowsiness washed over him like a wave at Wrightsville Beach. He tried to return her smile, but fell asleep.

Bill woke up thinking only two hours had passed since he took the pain medicine. Juliet informed him otherwise... a whole twenty-four hours since he had drunk the Dover's powder tea. Juliet sat in the chair as before, her hair encapsulated in a black bonnet. Two eye-pleasing fellows stood nervously behind her—Charlie and Nathan. Delighted to see them, Bill at first failed to comprehend the obvious. His stomach burned, and not from a lack of food. *Kenny too*? He feared the worse, but hoped there'd be a silly explanation for his friend's absence.

Still drowsy, Bill massaged his eyes, hoping the vigorous buffing would clear away the cobwebs. Thinking more clearly, he coughed, lubricating his dry throat. "Kenny?" *Please let it be girl-chasing or guard duty or even a minor wound.*

"Kenny didn't make it." Charlie's voice, grave, cracking. "Fell on the battlefield."

Bill really wished he could roll onto his back and stare up at the top of the tent, stare beyond it, beyond the sky, beyond everything between himself and Heaven. Except he couldn't, literally and figuratively. A wall of pillows kept him from rolling over. And God kept him from seeing Heaven, but not aureolas. "These are terrible, terrible days."

Nathan sidled around the chair and stood next to the cot. "Be glad you weren't there, Bill. Our charge won the Yankee breastworks, but we couldn't hold them. The Blue-Belly artillery proved too murderous and their counterattack forced us to retreat." He touched his neck, fingered a scab similar to the one Bill sported, the result of a near-miss of a mini ball rocketing toward Charlie's forehead. "Took this in the retreat. We lost our colors. Colonel Purdie's dead, shot through the forehead. Only one field officer's fit for duty."

Hands shaking, Charlie gripped the chair's finials. "I did my normal snoopin', Billy Boy. Just the Eighteenth alone... thirty killed and ninety-six wounded. I didn't run. Saw all the horror. The woods were on fire. Shells, muskets and cartridges were explodin' in every—"

Nathan's voice quaked with tension, "God, they were on fire. The wounded were screamin'. Beggin' us to get them away from the flames. Kenny was out there. He was tryin'—"

"Enough!" Juliet sounded like a schoolteacher who'd just caught a boy and girl sneaking kisses. "Just a day ago Doctor Straith dug a shell fragment from Bill's back. He needs rest."

"No, let them speak," Bill told Juliet. "I want to hear about Kenny."

Sighing, Juliet nodded.

"We couldn't help Kenny or any of 'em." Nathan wiped a sleeve across his eyes. "I tried. Just too hot, Bill. Had to watch them burn up. I don't ever want to see this place again."

Horror in his voice, Charlie added, "In 1900, I'll be havin' nightmares about those men."

Outside the hospital tent, rain fell, drops splattering on the sloped roof. It sounded soothing.

Nathan glanced at the ceiling, listening to the rain, then said, "At the end, when the woods were burnt over, we linked with Colquitt's boys. There we stayed until Monday. If the fires of hell ever go out, Hades would look like that battlefield... embers, ashes, charred oaks, half-consumed bodies."

This time more forceful, a still-vexed Juliet pointed to the exit. "Boys, I know Bill's glad for your visit, but we've some hard work ahead if he's going to catch a train for home in a week or two. Come back tomorrow. I know he'll enjoy another visit." She stood and kneaded her apron. "But please... not so gloomy."

Bill surprised himself. He painfully scooted into a sitting position. "Please, let them stay."

"Excellent! I was going to help you sit up, but now I don't have to, Bill Stamford." She edged to a small table beside the cot. On it... a bedpan. "We've some business to attend to, boys. And after that, I'll be taking him for a walk. A warning, Bill. It won't be easy. Your legs will feel like noodles."

"Bedpan?" Charlie's voice crackled with sham fear. "We're leaving."

Twenty-five

Train Ticket for Home

Bill glanced at the ticket dated May 19, two weeks since waking up in a convalescent tent. The destination: Warsaw, North Carolina. Mrs. Neal—Juliet, Bill kept reminding himself—and Chaplain Anderson waited with him in the Fredericksburg depot near the swinging door to the loading platform. On this fine spring morning, the depot windows were portals for a welcome breeze that stroked Bill's face.

Near the ticket counter, the schedule board said the eight-in-the-morning train to Petersburg was running one hour late. Not bad, Bill reassured himself. Some trains ran even later. He wondered why the depot master bothered trying to post a schedule. At Petersburg, Bill would change trains and head south to the Tar Heel state aboard a train operated by the Wilmington & Weldon Railroad, twenty-some years old but not as trusty as prewar days. Two years into the war, rail service had become haphazard. With all able-bodied men in Confederate armies, maintenance had gone to hell. Locomotives broke down frequently. Rickety tracks constantly derailed trains. Bill's trip home promised to be tortuous, especially with the bandaged hole in his back. The constant pain could be managed with canteen water and Dover's powder… as long as the train didn't run off the tracks.

"Won't be long, Bill," Juliet observed, shifting her handbag from the bench to her lap. "Soon you'll see your family. Don't think even once about the war. Just concentrate on getting better."

"You better tell Charlie not to write any letters to me." Bill released a wary chuckle, not wanting to irritate the wound. "Charlie's a newsy guy. If I read his words, I'll know all about the war."

Juliet opened her handbag and extracted a mirror. The walk from the carriage to the depot had left her hat and hair in disarray. "You may think about General Lee and the boys once in a while. Just not constantly." She grinned.

Bill nodded as he digested Juliet's words. "Don't know how much time I'll have to keep up with war developments. There'll be a constant line of visitors coming by the house to pay their respects. And trips to visit Becky."

Mirror in hand, Juliet adjusted her hat and swept a graying strand away from her forehead. "Franny's throwing away her future."

Bill shrugged. "What will be, will be."

"He'll make some trips to Wilmington," the chaplain reminded Juliet. "Bill's expected to recruit."

"Poor Wilmington," Bill said, fidgeting as a twitch in his lower back nagged at him. "I'm sure you've read the headlines. Yellow fever decimated the town. I cringe at what'll greet me."

"Bill, you should go to church this Sunday." The chaplain looked down at the floor as if in deep thought. "Pray for those lost in the yellow fever epidemic. Pray for your friend Kenny. And pray for a fellow named Bill Stamford. Give thanks that he too didn't die on the battlefield."

"The Lord has gotten a bushel of thank yous from me over the last two weeks, Chaplain." What Bill didn't say... a bushel of pleadings for God to lift the veil hiding the purpose of the aureolas. General Jackson had died a week after the wounding... and Charlie still lived. When it came to revelations, the Lord preferred silence. Frustration and growing anger gnawed at Bill. *Lift the shadows, Lord.*

A few days before, the soldier in the bed next to Bill had cried out, "No! General Jackson's dead. Please, God, let it be a lie." He'd been reading the May 11 edition of the *Richmond Daily Dispatch*. Enraged, he'd slammed his stump against the mattress until it bled. As the nurse cleaned up the mess and put on a new bandage, the soldier continued to weep. "Lord, you can have my other leg, even my arms, just let this be a damned false rumor."

The soldier let Bill read about Jackson's death. *We have this morning to announce the sorrowful tidings of the death of Lieut. General Thos. J. Jackson, which took place at the residence of Mr. Thos. Chandler, near Guinea Station, at fifteen minutes past three o'clock yesterday afternoon. We can partly anticipate the deep gloom which this announcement will cast over the whole country, with whose fortunes he was so closely identified, and by which he was regarded as one of its first and ablest defenders.*

"A penny for your thoughts," Juliet said, scooting in her floral summer dress to face Bill.

In the distance, a train whistle blew. Bill reached for his carpetbag and wheezed in pain.

"Go slow, son," the chaplain reminded Bill. "Don't give the hole in your back a reason to complain."

Gingerly, Bill clutched the bag by his fingertips. He'd packed light …one change of civilian clothes, a new uniform provided by the chaplain, and some toiletries. The chaplain's advice fresh in his mind, Bill stepped toward the loading platform, taking care not to bump against anyone heading outside to watch the train roll in. "The whistle means I'll soon see familiar Duplin sights—strawberries ripe for picking and muscadine vines weighed down with grapes." He offered his friends a twisted smile. The carpetbag pulled and tugged at his wound.

Noticing Bill's pain, the chaplain took the suitcase and turned it over to the darky porter. Julia snagged Bill's arm and together they walked to the passenger carriage. He showed the convalescent pass to the porter.

Juliet kissed Bill's cheek. "Your heart's going to flutter seeing your Becky. I hope my daughter wakes up before it's too late. Ultimately, I want you to be happy, Bill Stamford. Pick the girl your heart desires. My wish for you? To someday have grandchildren arrayed around your feet as you rock in your rocking chair, even if their grandma is your Becky."

Going up the steps into the carriage jarred his wound, but he tolerated the twinge of pain, and soon passed through a car filled with soldiers resting on stretchers. In the next car, he sat beside a window and leaned forward. He almost touched the backrest of the seat in front of him. As the train chugged away from the depot, Bill glimpsed Juliet and the chaplain. They waved, hands gyrating wildly. Juliet shouted, "I lied! Marry Franny!"

Maybe ten minutes into the journey, a sergeant from the Thirteenth South Carolina wobbled down the aisle, eyeing the empty seats. He plopped beside Bill. The sergeant shook Bill's hand with his left one. His right arm had been left in a pail next to a surgery tent at Chancellorsville. The bandage over the stump needed changing. Soaked with blood.

"Name's Willy Arnett," the sergeant prattled, gabbing as if the flood of words would keep his pain bottled up. "From Lightwood Knot Springs, South Carolina. We're known for our fine trees and sawmills. Our lumber makes the prettiest houses in the South. John Calhoun use to say he'd only build with Knot Springs' wood. Did I tell you we're also renowned for our kilns? Your momma's flowers are probably potted in a Knot Springs' pot. Take a look at the bottom—"

Bill had to interrupt or they'd be in Richmond before he could introduce himself. "Bill Stamford. From Kenansville, North Carolina."

"Not familiar with the town. What's it near?"

"Wilmington." Bill braced for an account of the sergeant's visits to Wilmington.

"Ah, Wilmington." Scowling, Arnett fumbled with his canteen, failed to unstop the cap. "Having some difficulty. Could you?" Bill unplugged the opening and handed the canteen back to the sergeant, who took a long swig. "Medicine makes my throat dry. Now where was I? Wilmington, one of my favorite towns. Nothing's as beautiful as the waterfront at sunset, tall masts painted in shades of red. I once saw the actress Laura Keene on stage in the new Opera House… a grand time for me. Not so grand for the town's citizens now, eh? Hundreds dead from yellow fever. Ain't just soldiers doin' the dyin'."

"My sweetheart's letters have ghastly accounts of the fever. Heartbreaking." Bill capped the canteen and returned it to the sergeant. "In the summers, she normally stays with a cousin in Wilmington. With coffins filling up, she and her cousin's family stayed with relatives in a nearby town, Burgaw. She says the fever has spent itself, so I'm not worrying. Going to do some recruiting there."

The sergeant slipped the canteen into a haversack and sighed. "It's warming up. Be careful. Yellow fever likes muggy days and nights." He examined his dressing. "Damn! Blood's leakin' through. It was doin' fine. Doc liked the look of the pus. Bet it's startin' to putrefy. Goin' to Chimborazo for more treatment. At least I'm not on a stretcher."

The turtle-crawling trip south to Richmond proved dull and uneventful. Not one derailment. Probably the most carefully maintained section of rail in the South, the line from Fredericksburg to Richmond carried the wounded needing nursing care to the sprawling Chimborazo Hospital. No one wanted to see a troop train run off the rails and tumble soldiers already wounded in battle or struck down by camp sickness.

At the Main Street depot, with its domed clock tower, stretcher-bearers hopped aboard and carried the soldiers to ambulances for the short journey to Chimborazo. Sergeant Arnett gritted his teeth as he rose to leave, then said, "Watch out for the fever, Private Stamford." Bill stayed on the train as soldiers and some civilians boarded for the trip to Petersburg.

This time a mother and toddler sat beside Bill. Bobbing on her momma's lap, the girl sneaked silly-face peeks at Bill. "Quit botherin' the soldier, Sue," her momma admonished.

The child ignored her momma. On her knees on the bench beside Bill, the child gazed up at him until he surrendered and acknowledged her gawking stare. "Hey, soldier fella, a bad Yankee hurt you?"

"Yep, Sue. He thought I was dead. The Blue-Belly was hungry for some Tar Heel meat." Leaning on the edge of the bench, Bill raised his right arm and pointed down at his back. "He started chewing. Left a big hole in it. Some other Butternuts came to my rescue. Filled the air with mini balls humming like honeybees. Scared the Yank all the way back to Washington."

Her eyes grew huge. "The Yankee was a cannibal?"

"Yep, the fella had a hankering for some Tar Heel grub, and I was the closest morsel." Bill tweaked her nose. "But don't worry. Only a few Yankees like Tar Heel meat. Most go for a well-cooked mule steak, tender in the middle."

Her momma laughed sourly. "Oh, Sue, he's joshin' you. I hope." She maneuvered the girl back onto her lap. "We've been to Chimborazo visiting Sue's papa. Lost an arm and a leg. I want him home, but the doctors say he needs to stay longer. He's carrying a fever and the stump's festerin'. Sue and me... we've been doin' heaps of prayin'." She straightened her bonnet. "You've got all your arms and legs."

Bill knew what she needed to hear. "Shell fragment in my back. Quite a hole, I'm told. Hard as I try, I can't see it." He laughed. "A mirror might do it, but not really sure I want to see it."

Usually a short hop to Petersburg, the trip took three times as long as prewar days. Twice the locomotive had been forced to stop while a slave crew repaired track. The first time, the white overseer found the patchwork deplorable and made the darkies redo it. After the second time, the supervisor let the train pass over the repaired section. "Damn useless slaves," the conductor mumbled as he moved past Bill. "Substandard work, probably deliberate." At the Petersburg depot, Bill bid adieu to the toddler and her momma, and headed for another track where the North Carolina-bound train took on wood for the boiler.

As Bill weaved along the aisle and tottered toward a window seat, he plopped onto the cushioned bench. His momentum unchecked, he slammed into the backrest. "Oh, God!" he grunted, pain unsettling his belly and rattling his teeth. Immediately, he scooted to the edge of the bench and looked down at his feet. He kept staring at his brogans, willing the pain to wane at least a little bit.

A shadow flickered across Bill's face. A fancy-pants gentleman took a seat beside him. "You okay, soldier?" Concern furrowed across the fellow's forehead.

"Wound's acting up." Bill turned toward the older man. He knew the gentleman saw a face twisted into a Mardi Gras mask portraying agony. "It's feeling better." Little chance the fellow believed Bill's lie.

"A back injury?"

Bill nodded, drew a long breath and released it slowly. "The back didn't take kindly to getting slapped against the seat."

"Let's see if this helps." The gentleman stepped into the aisle and flagged down the conductor. Bellowing steam, the locomotive surged forward, its noise drowning out the fellow's words. The conductor hurried away but soon returned with two pillows. The nattily dressed chap tucked the pillows between the backrest and Bill's wound, and quickly sat before the wobbly train knocked him against Bill. "Looks like we're on our way. Name's Abraham Watkins Venerable."

The pillows looked soft and capable of cushioning his back without sparking pain. Bill leaned back into them with excruciating slowness. He waited for a spasm of pain. It didn't happen.

He'd heard of Venerable, a C.S. Representative from the North Carolina Eighth Congressional District. Sometimes being the son of a newspaper editor came in handy. He shifted to get more comfortable. "Representative Venerable, I'm delighted to meet you, sir."

Venerable doffed his bowler hat. "I'm returning to Oxford for a soldier's funeral. And you must be returning home to convalesce. A wound suffered at Chancellorsville?"

"Yes, Representative. Returning to Kenansville. Name's Bill Stamford."

Sitting beside the politician, Bill felt like a hayfoot seeing the big city for the first time. The lawmaker wore a tweed suit, spit-and-polished boots, lavender gloves, the green bowler, and a walking cane with a carved dog's head. Venerable smelled fashionable.

Bill smothered a smirk as he thought of Venerable's first name. No doubt the Representative had become an expert at dodging snide remarks from fellow politicians in Richmond… *Honest Abe Venerable.*

"Kenansville, eh? I know the town." Venerable raised his cane from between his legs and used the dog's muzzle to scratch the skin beneath his Van Dyke beard. "A flourishing town of farmers. A few years back, I inked a turpentine deal in your hometown. The town fathers took advantage of the new railroad just a few miles away. They realized they were no longer slaves to wagon-freight rates."

Bill watched the politician return his ornate cane to its rest position. "Yessir." Sighing, Bill wished the politician would shut up.

Venerable glanced at the pillows cushioning Bill's back. "Glad you survived. So sad that we lost our great hero, Stonewall. The Yanks must be celebrating, smelling the fragrance of victory in the Northern air. Won't happen. Not with the great Lee at the head of the Army of Northern Virginia."

"So true. General Jackson can't be replaced. Still, we'll manage." *Damn aureola.* Bill gazed up at the carriage car's ceiling as if he could see God on his throne enjoying his handiwork.

Venerable plucked a stack of correspondence from a satchel bag and dropped the letters in his lap. "My work never ceases. Constituents asking for help—a son in a Yankee prison, a father needing a pension for time served with Beauregard, a widow wanting help getting her husband's remains brought home from the battlefield." He fingered the edge of the topmost envelope. "It's been a hard couple of weeks in Richmond. Been to one funeral already and headed to a second one. Thousands turned out for Stonewall's funeral. Now I'm bound for Oxford for the funeral of my best friend's son, killed at Chancellorsville. Shipped him home in an ice coffin."

Just inside the Tar Heel border, Venerable debarked at the Weldon depot. Worn to a frazzle, Bill shuffled to the Wilmington and Weldon's train to Wilmington and boarded. He collapsed into a seat in the passenger car closest to the wood tender. The train chugged south to where it stopped for the night in Rocky Mount. With the first wisp of darkness cloaking the landscape, lookouts couldn't see well enough ahead to warn the engineer if the tracks were buckled or separated. So Bill took a room at a three-story hotel next to the depot. First, though, he directed the depot's telegraph operator to send a message to the Warsaw depot... just in case his father still waited to pick him up. *Train late. Stop. Spending night in Rocky Mount. Stop. See you tomorrow.* He strolled to the hotel and ate a meal, then slogged upstairs to his room.

Later, he lay on the bed, his belly against the mattress. Thinking of Franny, Bill found himself kissing the pillow, imagining its softness as her lips. He'd soon see Becky, yet Franny monopolized his thoughts, the woman who'd soon marry her Tennessee officer. Her momma might think Franny would ultimately choose Bill, but he couldn't build his life around *mights* and *maybes*. Anyway, the tick, tick, tick of the alarm clock soothed the edges of his restless mind, promising to lull him to sleep.

Ring… ring… ring. He flipped the alarm-clock switch, stopping the tiny ringing bells. Sunrise light streamed through the window, dim but sufficient to allow him to read the clock face: six o'clock. Bill palmed soapy washbasin water onto his face and other areas, then toweled off. Pulling up his butternut pants, he slipped on his shirt, shell jacket, brogans, and slapped his slouch hat on his head. Glancing at the wall mirror, satisfied with how he looked, Bill stepped downstairs for breakfast. His supper and now breakfast easily won the claim of best food he'd tasted since eating at Becky's house months ago. Even the hospital food had been better than the grub in winter quarters and on the march to Chancellorsville.

A detachment of Homeguards got on the train along with Bill. They were there to safeguard the train in case Union raiders attacked. Once in a blue moon the old men would get to fire their antique rifles at the backs of Union Cavalry riding off after wrecking track. New Bern had been under Blue-Belly occupation for more than a year, since the Neuse River city had fallen to General Burnside. Yes, the same general who'd gotten his butt whipped by General Lee at Fredericksburg. Whistle blowing, the train twitched into motion. Like the night before, the locomotive wheeled along at turtle speed so lookouts could scan for bad track.

Not long after Bill boarded, a civilian sat beside him, a gentleman in wrinkled traveling clothes who promptly began snoring. Apparently, the hotel failed to provide a good night's sleep for the frumpy gentleman. More likely he'd imbibed too much warm Old Forester whiskey. Yawning, the fellow—who looked well over fifty—opened an eye. Bill had been staring out the window, counting the farmhouses. At the sound of the yawn, Bill glanced at the gentleman, who eyeballed a middle-aged guardsman toddling up the aisle to a seat at the front of the carriage. The guardsman joined three others, all armed with smoothbore muskets old enough to have been fired at the Barbary pirates.

In a voice kept low so only Bill could hear, the unfashionable gentleman said, "He's got to be older than me. Likes playin' soldier, just like the other old boys with him. But if Union Cavalry shows up, he and his chuckaboos will run for their lives. Nothin' but a feel-good move by the railroad and the gents in Raleigh."

"I'm fine with them aboard as long as one doesn't accidentally shoot me," Bill quipped, grimacing at the harsh touch of the cushioned backrest against his dressing. First, the sight of Warsaw, then home to his own room… that's what he needed. A wound cleaning, new bandage and some time on his belly would do wonders for the pain.

Standing, swaying as the train juddered, the gentleman removed and crumpled his coat. "Lean forward, soldier. Maybe this will help ease the discomfort." He slid his makeshift pillow between Bill and the backrest, and resumed sitting. "Name's Lawrence Baylor. From Clinton."

"Bill Stamford, Kenansville."

"Pleasure to meet you. With the Thirty-Eighth?"

"No, sir. Eighteenth, out of Wilmington."

"I hope you get to feelin' better soon. Chancellorsville?"

"Yes, Mister Baylor, a shell fragment." Bill decided he needed a couple of days where no one asked him about his wound. He yearned to sit at his mama's dining room table hearing about the springtime adventures of Mark and Laura.

Baylor's easy-going voice jerked Bill from his thoughts. "You've seen the elephant, soldier. What do you think we should do about New Bern? It's become a real irritant for Governor Vance. They're always out and about destroyin' track and making a general nuisance of themselves."

Just thinking of an answer seemed to chase away the twinges. "I leave the strategy to the generals and politicians. Ultimately, the governor will need to work out an arrangement with President Davis and *borrow* a few Tar Heel regiments from the Army of Northern Virginia."

"I agree, Private Stamford." Baylor's easy-going voice turned harsh. "Homeguards, even the Regulars down in Wilmington, won't get the job done. Need bloodied boys like y'all."

Bill shook his head. "Not me, sir. At least not for a few months. I've some healing to do."

Baylor stepped off the train at Goldsboro. Bill hated surrendering the man's suit coat. It had made for an excellent pillow. Just four more stops, then Warsaw. When no one boarded and took up the seat beside him, Bill sprawled on his stomach, forehead resting against his hands. Relaxed for the first time since waking up in his Rocky Mount hotel room, he listened to the locomotive's chuff-chuff-chuff as the train rolled toward Dudley, forty minutes away. In prewar days, it'd be a twenty-minute jaunt.

In Dudley, a businessman boarded, and the train crew took on mail posted for Wilmington, then set off for its next stop, Mount Olive. Almost home, Bill sighed. Just Faison and then Warsaw. At Faison, schoolgirls and a chaperone boarded for a trip to a Wilmington academy and a poetry recital. One read her poem aloud to Bill, who oohed and aahed in a sweet way, earning a blush. The girl, Patsy, plied him with questions about his army adventures, and of course, his wound. Luckily, no twinges as he gave her a tame version of the battle. No mention of how Butternuts and Blue-Bellies burned to death.

As the train wheeled through Warsaw, Bill gawked at the grocery and dry goods stores, two-story houses, the bank, Methodist and Baptist churches, the feed store and City Hall, all arrayed along Front Street. His belly warmed as he took in the view, almost like rolling a piece of hard candy in his mouth and tasting its cherry flavor. The locomotive didn't slow down fast enough for Bill. He'd put up with the pain just so he could leap from the passenger car's top step onto the platform, give his momma a hug, shake his papa's hand, and tousle his siblings' hair. *Let me smell Duplin air.*

Agonizingly, the train rumbled up to the loading platform. A few families and individuals waited to step aboard for trips to Magnolia, Rose Hill, Duplin Roads or maybe farther south to Burgaw or Wilmington. Then he saw his family... and someone else, an angel with raven hair partly covered by a floral bonnet. Attired in a green cotton day dress, Becky jumped up and down on the platform, waving wildly. Seeing him gazing through the window, she eagerly blew him kisses. Lordy, he wanted to forget the pain and hold her so tight she'd feel his engorged manhood pressing against her. Then guilt soaked him like a spring rainstorm. Charlie, Nathan and the soldiers of Lane's Brigade could very well be on the march, heading for battle and perhaps death... without him.

Twenty-six

A Turn for the Worse

Bill nearly leapt from the train. Instead, he gingerly stepped down and hastened toward his family and Becky. His momma cupped his face and kissed both cheeks. "Oh, you're so thin. And pale. Thank God you're home."

Wearing a printer's apron, his papa shook his hand. "Oh, hell with it," Clarence exclaimed, and kissed Bill on the forehead. "Yes, thank God you're home. We'll make you well."

Bowing to Becky, Clarence drew back, allowing her to fly into Bill's arms. Hugging him, she gushed, "I kiss better than I write—"

Bill yelped a wail. His back radiated pain. "Stop! Hurts!"

Becky stumbled away from him, shock on her face. Her hands flew up to her mouth. Green eyes widened in alarm.

"Sweet Savior! I'm such a fool! I knew you were wounded. And still I hurt you! Forgive me!"

Mouth scrunched, Bill forced the pain into a corner of his mind. He shortened the distance between them. Curling his hands around Becky's hips, he tilted his head toward hers. "Pain can't stop me from kissing your mouth." He kissed her three, four times, each lingering longer. After the last one, he sighed. "Our kisses... just as I dreamed." Lordy, Becky smelled fine... *Eau De Cologne...* just like someone else wore.

"Did I surprise you?" She did a little dance and giggled. "You had no idea, did you? That I'd be here."

Bill could see it in her eyes: Becky didn't care that Bill's momma and papa hovered nearby. Propriety could go to hell. The two women in his life were so much alike, Becky and... no, he wouldn't mentally voice her name. She belonged to her Tennessee officer.

Swaying, their jumpiness obvious, Mark and Laura ran up to Bill, but stopped short of actually hugging him. He chortled and said, "A Yankee shell popped me in the back. Hurting some, but nothing I can't handle long as you don't squeeze too hard." He waved them forward and cautiously hugged them, then ran his fingers through both mops of hair.

Becky snuggled against Bill's side, locked her fingers around his arm. "I'm staying at your house. Going to help your momma nurse you."

Grinning like a possum eating persimmons, Bill patted Becky's hand. "You'll be much nicer than the nurses at the field hospital. Hard to tell if they were building buggies or fixing men. Your touch will be heavenly."

Bill's momma took his free arm, and the two women escorted him through the depot and out to the stables where the carriage awaited them. Back on the platform, his papa picked up Bill's carpetbag, and with Mark and Laura tagging along, joined them. Everyone climbed into the Dibble surrey, a black four-seater with cushioned red seats. His momma and papa sat in the front seat with Mark between them. In the back, Laura nuzzled between Becky and Bill. With papa handling the reins, they set off for Kenansville, traveling the Warsaw-Kenansville Road.

Even with the Kinston-made surrey's springs, the ride tortured Bill's back. He leaned forward, trying to protect himself, but every rut sent jarring pain through his body. Becky noticed and kept babying him. "Even when you heal, I'm not letting you go back to the army."

Grimacing as the buggy hurtled past a rut, Bill rasped, "No choice… unless you want me shot for desertion."

His momma planted her elbow on the front seat's backrest and looked rearward. "Desertion?"

"Don't worry, Momma. Becky wants to baby me for the rest of the war."

"Baby you?" Becky challenged. "Better than more holes in you."

"Let's see me healed, and then we can start worrying about the war." Bill changed the subject. "Papa, why are you handling the reins? Where's Wilson?"

"The state and the railroad commandeered him." Clarence maneuvered Peanut to the side of the road to avoid a deep rut. "He's on one of the work gangs fixing rails. Sleeps in a tent on the outskirts of Warsaw. I've been trying to get him back, but no luck so far. I need him. Hips aren't good. Can't afford a handyman."

"Maybe I can help out." Bill caressed his father's back.

"I won't hear such silliness." His momma glanced at Bill. An adamant look ruled her face. "You're doing nothing that could undo the surgeon's work."

Warsaw's downtown looked *tired*. The war hadn't been kind. Most of the able-bodied men wore gray and butternut and served the cause. No longer spry, the old ones failed to keep up with the town's repair needs... painting, road upkeep, slapping on new roofs. Slaves worked with the armies—not soldiering, of course, but repairing rails, digging inside the mines, building gun emplacements, stuff that freed up white soldiers to fight the Blue-Bellies. Bill straightaway noticed the stark storefronts... no dresses and gowns, no ladies' hats, saddles, stoves, pianos, sewing machines. The war effort took priority over everything. For a Wednesday afternoon in mid-May, the sidewalks should look—if not busy—at least occupied. Bill smiled at the term *occupied*... like New Bern in 1863. Not even a soul seen going into Kelly's Tavern to wet a parched throat.

The trip turned smoother once beyond Warsaw. Not as many hoofs and wheels digging into the dirt. Had they taken the road up to Clinton, they'd be traveling on a plank road. In rain, buggies, wagons and carriages seldom bogged down on a plank road. Bill leaned out the window. Just a few clouds. No chance of a rainstorm.

Icie Belle asked Mark, "What's your favorite song?"

Mark spit out a swift answer. "Ma," he said, "you know 'Dixie' is my favorite."

"Well, start singing it, and we'll join in. A carriage ride has to have some singing." Icie "Belle slipped her arm around Mark and squeezed him against her.

Clearing his throat, Mark sang out: "Oh, I wish I lived in the land of cotton, old times they are not forgotten..."

The others joined in. Becky sang the loudest. She stretched across Laura's lap and held Bill's hand. He raised her hand to his mouth and kissed it, earning a hooray from Laura. Becky tickled the end of Laura's nose. "Your turn, Laura. What do you want us to sing?"

Barely eight, Laura puckered her lips in thought. "I want to hear 'Lorena.' Nothing like sweet love."

Becky patted Laura's pink dress above the girl's knees. "You and I... we'll start it off together. Okay?"

"Yes. Ready, Becky? One, two, three. 'The years creep slowly by, Lorena. The snow is on the grass again'…"

Everyone joined Laura and Becky, even the mare Peanut, who whickered as they sang. At the end, Bill again rustled his sister's hair. "Lordy, I'm so glad to be home."

"Well then, let's sing it," Clarence said, and began singing "Home Sweet Home." "Mid pleasures and palaces though we may roam, be it ever so humble there's no place like home…."

And so it went, song after song for more than an hour. The music seemed to tame Bill's pain. He sang, just happy not to be obsessing on every thump and jolt. Or fixated on his army possums, aureolas and why Daniel and General Jackson were in graves and Charlie still breathed. *Lord, you ever going to lift that fog in my mind? I'm still waiting to learn if it's a gift or a curse? Or am I demon—*

"I'm sung-out tuckered." Becky playfully tugged on Laura's ear. "Let's play a game instead. Let's count how many barns have the new North Carolina state flag. Sound fun?"

Laura clapped, glee engulfing her face. "Oh, yes. Lots of farmers are painting them on their barns. You'll play, won't you, Mark?"

Not keen at all, Mark shrugged guardedly. "I suppose so. Nothing better to do."

"Well, let's make it worth your while, Mark." A hint of mystery crept into Becky's voice. "If we manage to count twenty barns with flags before we reach Kenansville, I'll take you and Laura to Frankfurter's Drugstore for a bag each of lollipops, peppermint sticks and penny hards. I'm not hearing enthusiasm from—"

"I see one!" Laura shouted, pointing to a barn bordered on one side by a tiny scuppernong vineyard. "And it has a flag."

Bill grinned. "One down, nineteen to go." *Lordy, so nice to smell the air of Duplin, not the black powder of Chancellorsville or the poop pits of Fredericksburg. Too damn many memories of faces I won't see again. Dear God, don't let me see another aureola until I'm on my deathbed, and I see—*

"No! No! No!" Mark shook his head forcibly. "I haven't seen any candy in Frankfurter's in months."

"Mama, no candy?" Laura tugged on Icie Belle's sleeve.

"I'm sure Mister Frankfurter's has some candy hidden away for very special occasions," Icie Belle reassured her daughter. "If not, I'll bake Grandma's Eggless, Butterless and Milkless Cake... if you two win Miss Becky's game."

Laura clapped. "Don't pout, Mark! Look for barns with flags. I want cake!"

"Not pouting," Mark grumbled. "I'm playing your silly game, Laura."

By the time they reached Kenansville's outskirts in the late evening with the sun tickling the horizon, Laura and Mark had counted twenty barns that displayed the Tar Heel state flag. "We get candy," Laura sang.

"Probably cake," Mark muttered.

"We'll go see Mister Frankfurter tomorrow afternoon." Becky swung her gaze from Laura to her soldier-boy. "Maybe Bill will feel up to going with us?"

"I'll do my darnedest." Bill continued to fight a tendency to lean back against the seat. Instead, he perched his hands on his knees and scooted forward. Only a bit farther and he could rest on his bed... on his belly, of course.

They wheeled through the downtown, passing the print shop alit with flickering light. "Dale's working late," Clarence observed as he guided Peanut toward Seminary Street and the family's house. Two years into the war, Kenansville bore the same weary, dingy look as Warsaw—peeling paint, rutted roads, sparse storefronts.

Alongside the buggy, the family cat, Indy, raced them to the house. When Peanut turned into the driveway, Indy tore toward the front door, no doubt hoping to lap up a bowlful of milk. While Clarence took horse and the surrey to the stables, Icie Belle, Becky and the two youngsters escorted Bill into the house. Malinda had prepared a light snack …tea, cornbread, frizzled beef and stewed fruits from the cellar. Bill sat at the dining table and took a bite from the beef. His belly roiled; nausea washed over him. The on-and-off pain combined with the buggy ride had left him with a beaten belly. "I'm sorry. I can't." He looked away from the food. "I know it's wonderful, Malinda. It's been a hard day. Back's complaining."

His momma and Becky went to his aid as Mark and Laura looked on in frozen shock. "You can eat later when you've had time to rest." Icie Belle's voice shook with worry. Together, the two women helped Bill up from the table and, shooing Indy out of the way, assisted him to the stairs.

He hardly noticed the sundry things of home that he'd fixated over during the winter months inside the hut—the paintings of grandparents on the wall, the lamp with the frost white cranberry shade, the art-glass windows overlooking the stairway. So much Bill wanted to breathe in and touch that would have to wait until morning. He did feel the touch of feminine hands as he negotiated the staircase.

At the landing, he heard Laura at the foot of the steps, her voice strident. "Please, Bill, be okay. I don't like being scared."

Shadowy light intensified the lines of dread etched on Laura's face. "Don't worry, little one. I'll be fine." With his momma and Becky supporting him, he tottered toward his childhood room. Malinda waited inside.

"Help me with his uniform," Icie Belle instructed Malinda. "I need to look at his wound." His momma eyed Becky, who bobbed beside the dressertop, shaking fingers cloaking her mouth. "Please, Becky, get the roll of Doctor Day's Surgical Tape and the bromine bottle from the top drawer."

Bill sat on the edge of his childhood bed as his momma and Malinda removed the shell jacket and vest. Malinda did the nitty-gritty while Icie Belle gave the orders. Both concentrated on not irritating his wound.

A gasp... then Bill flinched. A gasp, but not from him. This time his momma. He gazed over his shoulder. His momma and Malinda blinked huge eyes as they stared at his wound. "You're leaking like a sieve, son." Icie Belle patted his shoulder. "This is going to hurt. Shirt's stuck to the dressing."

Bill didn't know who did the yanking. It didn't matter. Hurt worse than pulling a tooth. Just seven when the dentist had jerked the tooth from the gum, Bill had squealed and then cried. This time he didn't yelp when the shirt ripped from bloodied skin, but his eyes moistened. "I'm acting like a baby," he muttered.

Rushing to Bill's side, Becky set the surgical tape and bromine bottle on the quilt, and hovering over him, stripped off his hat and kissed the top of his head. "No, you're not! It hurts. Men are silly when they act like cold statues." She ran her fingers through his hair.

Now topless, and with the evening wind blowing through the open window into the bedroom, Bill shivered.

"I'll start a fire," Malinda said, sidling to the fireplace. "I washed the linens as you taught me, mistress. In a steamin' hot washbasin. They ought to be dry as a bone. As soon as the fire's poppin', I'll lickety-split downstairs and get them."

Standing helplessly in the doorway, Laura spoke up, "I'll get the cloths, Malinda. I want to help."

"Thank you, baby," Malinda tossed the bloody shirt into the fireplace.

"How does it look?" Bill chewed his lower lip, waiting for his momma's answer.

"Got to get the bandage off, then I can tell you." His momma steadied her breathing. "Sorry, son. Can't risk ruining the stitches. Going to go slow and careful. Expect some pain."

"Just do it, Momma."

Sudden pain flared, like a cat-whip biting into skin. Just as quick, it dulled. Before Bill could wipe away sweat beading on his forehead, the pain flared again. And so it went... pain... brief lull... pain... brief lull, over and over again.

"Shit! Ruined a stitch," Icie Belle bristled.

"I'll live," Bill strained. "For the pain, worse going slow, Momma."

"It's almost off," Icie Belle reassured him. "No more stitches lost, I hope." She laughed sourly.

More pain... and then Icie-Belle sighed loud enough to send a curious mouse scurrying for cover.

"Oh, Bill, sweetheart!" Becky settled on the bed, scooting beside him. "No wonder you didn't want to lean back."

"Don't like what I'm seeing." Icie Belle traced a finger beyond the edge of the wound. "Doctor Iuppenlatz needs to see this. Sweet Jesus, I wish he lived closer than Wilmington."

"I'll rouse Dan Wright." Clarence's voice, coming from the doorway. "He'll be glad to open the telegraph office and send a telegram to Iuppenlatz. The doctor will catch the Early Bird and be here by early afternoon."

"Damn! Ghastly?" Bill frowned. He'd spoken a curse word in front of his momma and Becky. Then again, his momma had said one too.

Icie Belle held up the blood-soaked bandage for her son's inspection. "Here's the lowdown. Ended up with two broken stitches and more festering than I wanted to see." The downstairs front door closed with a bang. "That's your father and Mark headed to Dan Wright's." She handed the bandage to Malinda for disposal.

The family's longtime slave dropped it into an empty trashcan between the bed and side table. "Baby, you've gone and ruined a perfectly nice bandage." Malinda grinned the smile that had chased away bad dreams and tummy aches.

Steepling her fingers as if in prayer, Icie Belle appeared to stare at every sweaty pore on Bill's face. "Sweet Jesus, you've only been away for seven months. You're skinnier than a chimney sweep." Her hands shifted to her hips. "As soon as Laura returns with the linens, I'll clean and dress your wounds."

"I'm useless. When I look at your wound, I start to faint. What a terrible wife I'd make for you, Bill Stamford. Thank the Lord your mother's here." Becky buried her hands in her face.

Bill snuggled against Becky's shoulder, took her hand. "Don't be so hard on yourself. Momma was a nurse in her younger days. Anyway, I'll be fine. I'm so much luckier than the other boys. They've lost arms and legs. And that's not the end of it. So many ended up dying. Just like General Jackson and my bunkmates, Kenny and Daniel." Hand cupping her chin, he turned her face so her lips lay inches from his mouth. "I love you, Becky Powell." He kissed her full on the mouth.

Wiping away tears, Becky sniffled, "I don't deserve you."

Unwanted thoughts seeped into Bill's mind. Franny would nurse him without squeamish thoughts, but she'd chosen to return to Tennessee to nurse another soldier. Squeamish or not, Becky nuzzled against him, not Franny. "I want you. No ifs or buts allowed."

Icie Belle cleared her throat, reminding her son and his sweetheart they weren't alone in the room. Becky's face reddened; Bill chuckled. "Soldiering makes a man pine for his darling, Momma."

Footsteps in the hallway interrupted his momma's response. Bill's papa and Mark returning from Dan Wright's house? Too soon, Bill decided as Laura breezed into the room toting Malinda's clean linens. "Bill," she gushed as she handed the linens to her momma, "don't forget the food's getting cold down in the dining room." Laura must have been eavesdropping on her father's discussions, for she added, "Too much scarcity to let food go to waste."

Bill rolled his eyes. "Do you even know what scarcity means?"

Laura shook her head. "No, but Papa uses it when he talks about the bad times."

"These are hard times, child," Icie Belle agreed, setting the linens on the bed beside the surgical tape and bromine bottle. "Just like the song says: Hard times, hard times come again no more. Many days you have lingered around my cabin door." Icie Belle caressed her son's cheek. "With the blockade, not much cargo gets in. No Paris dresses, Austrian violins, German dolls. And even if they did, with the inflation we couldn't afford them. Each month the food shortages get worse as farmers try to supply our armies, but my canning and our garden keep food on the table. We've Bill home with us, and we should all say a prayer of thanks."

Bill whispered a prayer… not for himself, but for his momma and her God-given nursing talents. And another thought crept into his mind: *Lord, I thought maybe you wanted me to save Charlie's life. Yet you took away another. A fair exchange? Charlie continues to deflower women, and you take General Jackson to Heaven to fulfill your own enigmatic purposes.* He stifled a bitter laugh.

Malinda boiled water over the bedroom fireplace. When the water cooled to allow Icie Belle to dunk her hands without scalding them, she dipped a cloth and cleaned the wound where the graft's stitches had loosened or ripped free. Icie Belle drizzled a compound solution of bromine over the wound, especially pus areas and where broken stitches provided an entryway for grime and sweat, something she'd learned as Doctor Iuppenlatz's nurse before she married. Bill twitched when the bromine touched the wound; the solution stung, but not like when Icie-Belle had removed the old dressing. Satisfied with her handiwork, she bandaged the wound with a gauze dressing and surgical tape, gifts from Dr. Iuppenlatz.

Icie Belle pointed to the dresser. "Becky, please return the tape and the bottle of bromine to the top drawer." Bill's momma pinched his ear. "Don't put a shirt on yet. Relax on the bed. Stay on your belly or side. Please, no pressure on your back. We'll see what Doctor Iupplenlatz says in the morning. Becky will keep you company until you feel like coming downstairs. Don't think you have to join us, son. Feel free to sleep for rest of the night. It's been a hard couple of days for you."

"Yes, Momma. But not as bad as the day the shell fragment burrowed into my back."

When everyone had left, Bill lolled on his side and gazed at Becky, remembering the night when she lay beside him inside her papa's house. As the pain dulled to an annoying tingle, he enjoyed feasting on her hourglass figure, from the top of her raven-black hair to her leather boots with the gold-tinged embroidery peeking out from under her day dress.

She tucked the corners of her mouth into a bewitching smile. "Lordy, you've had a miraculous recovery, Bill Stamford. I do believe you've decided to make me your stewed fruit."

The pink tint of sunset colored the bedroom window. The last of the day's sunrays strained to make their way into the room. Those that did pushed back the growing darkness and created a halo-like effect on Becky's face. *Thank God it isn't the real thing.*

"Sweetheart, light the dressertop's lamp." He patted the mattress next to him. "Then take off your boots and lie beside me. Please."

Her eyes ballooned. "No! Not after your momma just cleaned and dressed your wound. You're mad."

Again, Bill patted the mattress. "Trust me. I'll do nothing to ruin Momma's handiwork. Those cold winter nights at Fredericksburg, all I had were my memories of you snuggled beside me."

Smiling, she stroked her bottom lip with a long fingernail. "No credit for the fireplace? Or maybe on really cold nights, you and your friend Charlie shared body heat?"

"You know you want to join me. If I get too rambunctious, stop me. You can always tatter: 'Icie Belle, Bill's agitating his wound and my bubbies.'"

Harrumphing, she sat on the edge of the bed and tugged off her boots. "I'll go no further until you take off your shoes, mister."

"Brogans. They're called brogans." He rose to a half-sitting position on the bed and gasped in pain as he reached for the shoes.

"Stop!" Standing, Becky strode toward the closed door, but stopped well short of it. "Just as I feared. You're going to undo your momma's work."

The stage actress Laura Keene couldn't have done a better job, Bill figured. He needed to look contrite... and in a convincing manner. Otherwise, she might open the door and head downstairs... and he just as well get the bottle of Dover's powder from his carpetbag and let it ease him into sleep. "I'm sorry, Becky. Please stay with me."

She returned to the bed. "Let me remove the brogans." Untying the shoes, she slipped them off his feet, then wiggled her nose. "You need fresh socks." Once her adept fingers slithered the socks from Bill's feet, Becky kissed the big toe of each foot. "When a woman kisses a man's feet, that's true love."

Not done, Becky sat on a cane chair next to the armoire, unlaced her boots and removed them, along with her silk stockings. Raising the day dress to her knees, Becky jiggled the toes of her right foot.

Bill blew her a kiss. "If it weren't for the hole in my back, I'd get you out of that pretty dress and your underthings faster than Jackson marched us around the Yanks at Chancellorsville."

She tsk-tsked. "You could try. Remember, the room's barely beyond the top of the stairs, and your papa could stop by to see how you're doing."

Dover's powder looked better to him. "I know. Still makes me sad. I've wanted to hold you naked in my arms since my birthday celebration."

"That's for our wedding night... if you ask me, and if I accept your proposal."

"Are you daring me to ask? I will. Right now. Are you ready?"

Rolling her eyes, she rose from the chair. "My papa will have a fit. We hardly know each other. Let's do some courting first." On the balls of her bare feet, she stepped to the bed and settled in beside him.

Her breath tickled his neck and lips. Warm, sweet breath, like the stewed fruit she'd been eating earlier in the evening.

Gritting his teeth to prepare for possible pain, he squirmed closer until they nearly touched. Propped on his elbow, he kissed her, and when she opened her lips, his tongue brushed hers. "Little Bill's coming to life." Bill took her hand and rubbed it against his pants' crotch.

"Naughty boy. Not so much pain now, eh?" Friskiness gleamed in her eyes.

"Love vanquishes even pain."

A sigh of victory on his lips, Bill maneuvered his hands along the contours of her body, her thighs, her ribs, her breasts. Cotton clothing separated his fingers from her smooth ivory skin, but soon—when he healed—he'd find a place where they could make love. Maybe the Purcell House in Wilmington? He'd need to stay overnight when he took his recruiting trip. Lordy, how he wanted to tip the velvet with her.

Yes, he'd ask her to agree to a romantic rendezvous. "Soon, when my wound heals, I'll embark on a recruiting trip to Wilmington. Please tell me you'll accompany me." He hoped that in the lamplight she'd see the mischief brimming in his eyes. "I'll set up on Front Street and you can sit next to me. What patriotic Southern boy could resist a chance to fight for Dixie with you smiling at him? Afterwards, we'll hold hands and walk along the riverfront, then have a bite to eat at Purcell's."

Licking her lips, Becky said in a silken voice, "Yes. I'll spend the day with you. And whatever else you're concocting in your head." She laughed coyly.

Damn, he liked playing these love games. "Whatever else?"

Her forefinger traced the edge of his upper lip. "You just put my hand against your tallywag. So I expect you're not as innocent as you appear, especially with that adventurous tongue."

Innocent? Not anymore, Bill thought, not since that night with Franny in the overseer's house. These minutes belonged to Becky, he chastised himself, then shut Franny away in a mental jail cell deep in his mind. "You sound like you want to be just as adventurous. The less clothing, the better."

And she claimed those minutes, batting her eyelashes at him. "Indeed. I've wanted you free of your clothes since that night you slept in my brother's room. Heavens, I hope you haven't forgotten?"

He jerked his hand to his mouth as if in shock. "Forgotten? Those memories got me through many cold, ravenous nights."

Kissing him gently, she caressed his cheeks with probing fingers, then ran them through his hair. "Heal quickly, sweetheart. I can't wait until we escape to Wilmington."

With the scent of her hair pleasing his nostrils, Bill let his gaze wander to his chestnut dresser and the objects on the dressertop, all illuminated by lamplight. Buttonhooks, combs, shoehorn, cuff links, a pocketknife. Undisturbed for the past months, they held little interest for him. It was the toys of his childhood that drew his gaze... toy soldiers painted in bright colors, the Bilbo catcher, yoyo, and his favorite, a wooden clipper ship. He was home, a beautiful woman lying beside him.

Unexpectedly, Franny escaped her jail cell and threatened to spoil a wonderful time. He closed his eyes and she appeared, naked, twisting her blonde hair over one shoulder, smiling mischievously. *Go away. You made your choice when you ran off to your Tennessean.*

Scowling, Bill kissed Becky's face fiercely, then cupped a breast through the cotton fabric of her dress, corset and chemise.

"Decided not to wait until Wilmington?" She sighed. "But you know what would happen? You'd pop another stitch or Laura would walk in."

"I know." He clambered over her and went to the armoire. "I'm feeling much better. Let's join the others." He put on a shirt, then turned to find her behind him. Encircling her waist, he drew her against him. "Damn! You feel good. Maybe I'm being too hasty."

"No. I don't think so. I know kids. Laura or Mark will be in soon." Becky pushed him away, sat on the bed and put on her stockings and boots.

Sitting beside her, Bill slipped on his brogans. On the other side of the door, someone hightailed it up the stairs. "Bill! Becky! Come down! We're going to play checkers."

"See?" Becky tickled his kneecap. "We'll be right there, Laura."

Lord, I do believe you just revealed a Great Truth. A man's mind can rest on the assurance that a nice pair of bubbies will always win out over aureolas. At least for a while, aureolas and the maelstrom of emotions they engendered vanished from Bill's mind.

Twenty-seven

A Time for Healing

"I'm not playin'. Plain and simple. It's a Yankee game." Mark's friend Durham Poindexter twisted his face into a sourpuss mug. "I'm goin' home. The rest of ya'll should too. Don't be a bunch of scalawags."

"You're the spoilsport, Durham," Mark shot back. "You're coming up with a poor excuse because you ain't as good as the rest of us. You're always the last one picked."

Face reddening, Durham squeezed his fist, as if he intended to take a swing at Mark.

Bill stepped between the two boys. "Durham, it's our game now. We claimed it as booty. They lost it at Chancellorsville. Not just the battle. Baseball too."

Durham mulled Bill's words. His worn boots toed the loose soil, kicking up a clod. "That makes sense. Let's play ball. Enough prattle."

Agreeing to umpire the pickup game, Bill chose two team captains and held a draft. Mark captained one team, Durham the other. Nine players each, enough to field two teams. When all the players had been chosen, Bill waved Mark's nine onto the field, open parkland near the Beverett Spring behind the courthouse. Barrel covers became first, second and third bases as well as home plate. Bill eyed Durham. "You've a minute to come up with a striker order."

"I need more time," Durham protested.

"Okay. An extra minute." Bill crossed his arms against his chest and whistled "Yankee Doodle."

"That's an awful song," Durham wailed as his teammates stared at him, waiting for the striker order to be announced.

To the west, the sky looked ominous, filled with roiling hammerheads. Normally, Bill would have sent the youngsters scurrying to their homes, but Mark had been eagerly awaiting the game. Against his better judgment, Bill decided to let the game go on until the first lightning bolt streaked across the sky. The rumble of far-off thunder he could live with, but he'd not risk the boys' lives. Hopefully, they'd get to Bill's house before rain gushed from the clouds.

"General Lee won that song too for the noble cause. It's booty." Bill swiveled his gaze from the storm clouds to home plate. "Time's a wasting. Striker up!"

"You, you and you… you bat one, two and three," Durham blurted. "Kevin, you're up. Then Terry Waller and Steve Welch."

Kevin was a plump boy. In a year or two, he'd lose the weight and take on the athletic build girls like to ogle. Bill searched his memory… Kevin was the baby brother of Caleb Best, killed at Second Manassas.

Kevin smashed a liner down the third base foul line. Roger Burris, who'd lost a brother at Malvern Hill, held out his arm to snag it and hollered when the ball bounced off his fingers. "My hand's broke!" he whined, staring at his fingers, already inflamed. The left fielder tossed the ball to the second baseman, keeping the hit to a single. Bill called timeout and examined Roger's hand. Beet red and swollen, but no bones broken. Players needed to wear a glove larger and more padded than ones designed to keep out the cold. Bill could make a million dollars if he patented one and found a partner to build a factory, someone like Louis Froelich who'd just built a sword factory in Kenansville.

Thunder rumbled in the distance as the game progressed into the late innings. With the last of blue sky surrendering to onrushing rainclouds, a striker hit a popup to Mark's shortstop, Jeff Kurtz, Charlie's brother. An ace, or runner, at second base barreled into Jeff, knocking him off balance as he tried to catch the ball.

"You can't do that!" Jeff protested, shoving the ace, a boy everyone called Peewee Huck. Peewee shoved him back. Soon, the two boys were biting, kicking and slapping in the dirt.

Like a sergeant intending to break up a fight between privates brawling over the winnings of a poker game, Bill strode toward the belligerent pair. Tensing in case a jab of pain flared from his spine, Bill separated the two boys—but not before an errant punch hit him… thankfully in the belly. All the twisting and the wrenching to keep the boys from resuming their fight drew angry protests from Bill's back… not bad pain, but still teeth grinding. They were feeling more pain than him; he had both by their hair.

"You're out for interfering," he said crankily to Peewee. "You got to give the fellow a chance to catch the ball."

"No, I don't," Peewee pouted.

"That's the rules." Bill thrust out his arm and gestured toward the print stop and telegraph office.

"I don't like the rules." Peewee glared at Bill.

"I'm going to walk over to the telegraph office and send a telegram to General Lee." Bill pursed his lips thoughtfully. "He'll order a regiment down here to knock some sense into you, Peewee Huck. I've got a hole in my back, a gift from a Yank. It gives me the right to say you're out and order you off the field."

Peewee gulped. "I'm sorry, Bill."

Tree root-style lightning flashed across the sky, followed by thunder that sounded like a cannon discharge from down near the courthouse. "Game's over," Bill barked. "Time for some hard candy and cake."

When Becky had taken Mark and Laura to Frankfurter's Drugstore, the expedition turned up a cache of lollipops, peppermint sticks and penny hards in the storage room. Becky bought the candy and convinced the kids to hold a neighborhood party where they and their friends could enjoy the treats. Malinda promised to bake one of Grandma's Eggless, Butterless and Milkless cakes. Icie Belle sent out invitations with a date of Tuesday, June 10. By mid-June, daylight lasted until nine o'clock, plenty of time for a baseball game and a party afterward. As more thunder rumbled and the first raindrops splashed him, Bill was glad he'd ended the game.

On the walk to the house, Bill reflected on how smoothly his healing had gone since Doctor Iuppenlatz's visit nearly three weeks before. Nightmares had ruined Bill's first night home. Cockroaches spewed out through the broken stitches, the wound festering in rot. All night long he dreamed of the bugs, perhaps engendered by the brew of blackberry tea and Dover's powder that tamed the pain. One roach glared at Bill. Surrounded by a halo, the roach spoke, its voice gravelly. "I am Thomas Jackson. God's will be done on

Earth as it is in Heaven. HIS will… a life for a life. And a change in fate." Bill didn't sleep another wink that night.

The nightmares never returned after the Wilmington doctor's visit. His words brought relief, ending Bill's fears that infection and eventual gangrene would bring fever, the sweats, and in the end, death. Bill remembered Iuppenlatz's words: "Most excellent work by your mother. I'm going to leave you in her capable hands. Bromine and even iodine should help keep rot at bay. A cleaning and a fresh dressing every night. No exceptions." Later, after a snack, Bill's papa led the good doctor downstairs and out the door to the family surrey for the ride to Warsaw and the train back to Wilmington.

Becky wanted to be on hand for the kids' party, so Bill's papa hitched up the surrey, picked her up at the Warsaw depot and returned to Kenansville. Umpiring the game, Bill hadn't seen her arrive until he spied the house as the jabbering ball teams made their way up Lodge Street. Sitting ladylike on the front porch swing alongside Bill's momma, she tossed a wave as soon as their eyes met. He quickened his pace and regretted it… a stab of pain in his back. He'd actually forgotten about the wound. Healing nicely, according to Doctor Iuppenlatz, but Bill didn't need to pop a stitch by acting like an ancient Olympic runner. He slowed.

Even in a summer dress with a narrow hoop, Becky rose easily to her feet and flounced toward the porch steps. A red petticoat peeked out as she descended and rushed toward Bill, a savor-the-moment smile flitting across her face. Her third visit since returning to her Duplin Roads home on May 23, she skipped the last few feet separating them, displaying even more petticoat. As sprinkles dampened the red roses on her teardrop hat, Becky rushed into Bill's arms and smothered him with kisses. Near them, Peewee Huck groaned, "Disgusting! Cooties!"

"You didn't think so, Peewee, when you tried to kiss Sarah Craig," Mark kidded, finger-flicking Peewee in the back of the neck.

"Ouch! That hurts!" Peewee whined, then raced Mark for the front steps.

Reluctantly, Bill let his lips drift away from Becky's cider-smelling mouth. "Lordy, I love doing the bear with you."

"See how good I'm getting not rumpling your wound?" She took Bill's hand as they walked along the brick walkway up to the porch steps.

Inside, each boy found a slice of cake, a lollipop, a peppermint stick and two penny hards on his plate, and alongside a glass of switchels, Bill's favorite drink as a kid—water, apple juice, vinegar and molasses. Bill's momma made sure the boys understood the hard candy came as a gift from Mister Frankfurter. Bill chuckled silently. Not so much a gift, but a trade... the candy for some free advertising in the *Gazette*.

Only ten years old, and with a devil-may-care temperament, Durham winked at Becky as she brought a pitcher of switchels to the table for refills. "So you're Bill's jammiest bits of jam?"

Becky smacked him hard on his head. "Jam? Where did you learn that turn of phrase?" Dawdling in his sleeping basket amid old towels, the cat Indy caterwauled in concert with Becky's voice.

Durham smiled innocently. "In the latest serial runnin' in the *Weekly Standard*. The hero's lass was the jammiest lady in California. But I reckon you're prettier." Lightning lit up the dining room windows, brighter than the soft light of the oil lamps. Several second later, thunder rumbled.

A stern expression fixed on his face, Bill growled, "Trying to steal my girl, Durham?"

"Me?" Durham giggled. "Might try... in ten years when I'm older."

Becky stooped and whispered into Durham's ear, "Why, thank you, Durham. You're trying to butter me up. What do you want?"

Durham swung his gaze between Becky and Bill. "Maybe another slice of cake? If it's okay with Mark's momma?"

Icie Belle scrutinized the crumbs on Durham's plate. "Malinda, give that growing boy another piece." She ruffled Durham's hair. "So who won the game?"

"My team!" Durham shouted. "Bill made me the team captain, and we did darn well for only playin' once."

At the end of the table, Laura and best friend Nola snickered, and then Laura bolted to her feet and filched the slice of cake right out of Malinda's hand before she could give it to Durham. Sticking out her tongue at Bill, Laura goaded, "Durham wants his new girlfriend to serve him the cake. Don't disappoint Durham, Becky."

Settled beside his papa on a love seat beneath the dining room window, Bill broke into a half-moon smile and gestured to Becky. "Don't disappoint your new boyfriend, Becky."

"Disappoint sweet Durham?" Becky gamboled up to Laura and took possession of Durham's new plate of cake. "Never." Dancing to Durham's side, she placed the cake beside the crumbs. Winking at Bill, Becky kissed Durham on the cheek and pinched his ear. "Anything for my new boyfriend."

Still lounging in his basket, Indy raised his nose and sniffed, but evidently wasn't a fan of sweet cake. He whined his displeasure over the food offering, then rolled on his side and slept.

Rolling his eyes, Clarence rose from the love seat. "I need some fresh air. Care to join me in the garden, Bill?" Again, lightning flashed in the windows, followed by thunder.

As they walked toward the mudroom, the kids' raucous voices faded, allowing Bill and his papa to hear the rain gusher pound the roof. "The garden looks out of the question," Bill said casually.

"The library then," Clarence amended. "Better anyway. I can lock the door."

A turn of the skeleton key and the door lock clicked. With the rain, overcast sky and an evening rapidly becoming night, little outside light found its way into the library. Weaving through the shadows, Clarence lit an oil lamp on one of the room's small round tables and turned up the wick, chasing away the shadows. He sat on the red velvet couch between bookcases containing tomes by authors with last names from R to Z. Settling beside his papa, Bill twisted around so he could prop his left leg on the cushion... and keep his wound away from the backrest.

"Why the privacy, Papa?"

Clarence filled two glasses with muscadine wine from a decanter on the end table beside the couch. He passed one to Bill. "I want to bring you up to date on my efforts to get Wilson returned to us. We have to be careful. These times are crazy. Mobs are burning down newspaper offices of editors who write anything that smacks of treason, and treason nowadays is a very loose term. About anything fits."

Bill sipped the sweet wine, not at all like the rotgut stuff the soldiers drank on the march from the Shenandoah to Fredericksburg. "But lock the library door in our own house?"

"Loose lips, Bill, and I don't mean the kissing kind. I can't chance Mark and Laura and some of their friends poking their heads in to see what we're doing. I can't have them blabbering about Wilson. Gossip spreads faster than a fire consuming a newspaper office."

Bill sipped more wine. "We're not talking about freeing Wilson, just getting him returned to us."

"You got to remember how the fanatics think, son." Clarence stared at the wine in his glass as if it held hidden knowledge. Sighing, he drank several swallows. "Wanting him back means I'm not a true patriot, not dedicated enough to the cause. I should be willing to make sacrifices like them."

Bill nodded. "You have. Me. And the hole in my back."

"Mobs have short memories." Clarence patted his son's knee. "I've been corresponding with Owen. Normally, he'd not intervene over a slave, but I told him my health's failing, and I need Wilson back at the house."

Owen Kenan owned not just one of the largest houses in Kenansville, he also owned thousands of acres of plantation fields along the Northeast Cape Fear River. Wealth enough to make him one of North Carolina's representatives to the Confederate Congress in Richmond.

"You lied to Mister Kenan about your health?"

"If only I had." Clarence sagged. The grimace wiped away a half-hearted smile.

Bill twitched, spilling wine on his shirt. "What happened, Papa?"

"I don't want your momma to hear what I'm about to tell you. Agree?"

Bill almost refused. In the end, he nodded. "You're scaring me."

"I've been abnormally tired lately. Even the short walk to the print shop has me panting for breath. Worst yet, I've been getting chest pains. I fear this old ticker"—Clarence slapped his chest—"wants to give out. That's why I need Wilson back. I'm barely able to keep up with my newspaper and print-shop duties. I just can't do all Wilson's chores too."

"I can. I'll help you at the print shop and at home." Bill downed the last of the muscadine.

"You'll soon be going back to General Lee's army." Clarence scooted forward on the couch and rested his hands on his knees. "Bill, I'm going to sell the *Gazette* to the publisher of the *Wilmington Daily Journal*. He's looking to have his own newspaper fiefdom."

"You can't keep that from Momma. You're going to have to give a reason." Bill swung his leg to the floor and wiggled to the edge of the couch.

"The sale won't occur for a month or two. I'll tell her then." Clarence drained his wine glass and set it beside the decanter. "When Owen learned of my illness, he told he'd do all in his power to get Wilson released to me. I'm hoping to get him back in a few weeks." He reached into his vest pocket and drew out a letter. "It's from Governor Vance. He's says my request is being evaluated. With Owen's recommendation, he doesn't expect any roadblocks."

"Poor Wilson and Malinda!" Bill exclaimed, realizing his papa's deteriorating health would put any plans for freedom on ice. "Wilson's not young, yet has been forced to fix track from sunrise to sunset and sleep in a tent at night. And now we're going to tell him and Malinda we can no longer help them reach Yankee lines."

Regret and grief flickered in Clarence's eyes. "Sometimes we have to face hard facts. Even without my bad health, I don't see how Wilson and Malinda can reach New Bern. They'd end up hung from oak trees. Yankees on our doorstep... that's the only way Wilson and Malinda will ever see freedom, I fear. Slaves have been running away from their masters and following the Yankee armies. I've read accounts, but haven't printed them in the *Gazette*. Don't want to rile up the firebrands."

"Horrible times. God's angry at us and the Yanks." A stark thought crept into Bill's mind as he recalled the talking cockroach. God wanted to alter His grand plan and he used Bill. One life saved, another one taken. The world stays in balance. But General Lee loses his best general. *You got your way, Lord. You can take back your aureolas.*

"God has found us wanting. Our sins are great." Clarence picked up the decanter and refilled his glass. "More for you, son?" When Bill offered his glass, his papa topped it. "I've another matter to discuss, something I'd like to put in the next *Gazette*. Some news about General Lee and the Army of Northern Virginia."

"Bad news?" Bill studied his father's face for clues. Nothing. Hell, he'd been clueless about his papa's declining health. Everyone had. His papa could keep secrets better than most men.

"No. At least not yet. Just news. What it means remains to be seen." He took a swig of the wine. "They say muscadine's good for a man's heart. I hope so."

"So what's Marse Robert up to?" Bill looked up at the ceiling. He no longer heard rain spattering the shingles or thunder. "The library's getting stuffy, Papa. Don't think it's raining anymore. Let's go back to our original plan... the flower garden."

No one in the rowdy dining room noticed Bill and his papa slip out the French doors into the garden. "Lee's on the move," Clarence said, stooping to smell a pink rose. "Any idea where he's going?"

Outside, the clean air smelled of roses, blue irises and lilies. In the distance, lightning lit up the dark clouds, but

Bill heard no thunder. A sprinkle now and then landed on his head. "My thoughts… they'd better not end up in the *Gazette's* columns or in the Raleigh or Greensboro newspapers. Agree?" Bill traced a finger along the petals of a blue iris. "Don't need General Lee furious with me."

"Won't go beyond us two. I promise." Clarence flicked a raindrop from his cheek.

"It's speculation anyway… based on what I've heard other soldiers say."

Tilting forward toward the iris Bill had just finger-brushed, Clarence inhaled its fragrance. "Truthfully, I'm nervous about printing anything controversial. Just like what I said in the library, print anything negative about Jeff Davis or how the war's going, and soon furious folks are burning down the newspaper office. My fear? We will win the war, but lose our democracy."

"All this worry isn't good for your heart, Papa." Reaching into a pants pocket, Bill drew out his childhood Laguiole knife, cut away the stem of the blue iris, and handed the flower to his papa. "Dissent's the first liberty lost in war, isn't it?"

"They'd rather burn than build." Clarence brushed the iris against his nose. "It's such a pretty blue. I'm going to bring it to your momma." Annoyed, he wiped another raindrop from his face, this one from an eyebrow. "Too bad politics can't smell as nice as this iris. Up in Richmond, politicians won't discuss what needs to be discussed… making slaves soldiers. Fight alongside us, help us win, and you're forever free and equal. That's what the politicians should be preaching. Instead, more and more of the darkies are running to the Union armies. And we keep getting weaker and weaker. No one can get past the fear of a slave insurrection. Nat Turner, John Brown. By the time the politicians wake up, what's left of our armies will be surrendering. But I can't print that uncomfortable truth."

Bill laughed. "No, I wouldn't."

Clarence slipped the iris into his shirt pocket. "So what's Lee going to do with his army?"

Grabbing his collar, Bill rearranged the fit of his shirt. The wound had begun to itch. "Papa, Lee's got to get to a place where the men can eat decent food. The rations are pitiable. We're going to have to live off the land in the good months. That means the Shenandoah."

"Nothing bolder?"

Bill mulled his papa's question. "General Lee only knows bold. Like you said, the South needs a victory to win European recognition and to convince Lincoln to give up the fight. My best guess? He'll send the boys into Maryland, force Hooker back into the Washington trenches." Bill squeezed his papa's shoulder. "Remember, if you print any of this, don't use my name."

"I'll mention the Shenandoah. Nothing more."

Bill could hear giggling inside the house, noisy but not loud enough to mute the chirping crickets and the frogs croaking in the fountain's pool. Above him, a half-moon shone through thinning storm clouds, its beams dancing among the flowers. Knowing Lee had sent his columns marching northward, Bill gazed at the candlelit windows of neighbors' houses and felt gratitude for the tranquility of Kenansville. *Lord, don't let the war steal it.* That he felt no guilt for not marching in those columns surprised him. Someone called out his name, Becky searching for him. Soon enough he'd be back with Charlie and Nathan and playing dice games with God. But until he stepped aboard the train bound for Virginia, he'd enjoy Becky's kisses and meals with his family.

Twenty-eight

A Chance Meeting in Wilmington

Bill strode across the train-loading platform into the modern depot, an edifice that signified Wilmington's status as North Carolina's most populous city and busiest port. The station had also come to symbolize the Wilmington and Weldon Railroad's near-miraculous recovery from a disastrous 1840s fire that destroyed the older depot, roundhouse and mechanic shops. All had been rebuilt, bigger and better.

With three railroad companies serving the city, Wilmington in mid-June 1863 boasted nearly ten thousand citizens, or did until yellow fever filled a thousand graves in Oakdale Cemetery. General Yellow Jack should have decimated the city, but as Bill sauntered through the main entranceway onto Front Street, he saw a metropolis teeming with citizens out to make a tidy profit while aiding the Southern cause. Their masts black against an azure sky, blockade runners bobbed alongside Cape Fear River docks. Longshoremen swarmed the decks, unloading war supplies and luxury items or taking on cotton and naval stores bound for European markets.

Inhaling the smells of turpentine, horse manure and the dead fish floating in the river, Bill made his way toward the headquarters of the Cape Fear Military District under the command of Major General William Henry Chase Whiting. He laughed aloud as he thought of the general's fancy name. No wonder Whiting preferred the moniker W.H.C. Bill would have scalped his papa had the old man given him such a hoity-toity name.

Boarding the train in Warsaw at eight in the morning, Bill had arrived in Wilmington at noontime. When the train stopped in Teachey to pick up passengers, Bill wished Becky could have joined him in the passenger carriage. Sadly, she still slept in her bed. Their rendezvous wouldn't happen until the next day. She'd come up with a fanciful story for her father—cousin Sharon planned a day of adventure in Wilmington for the girls. Uncomfortable with Becky's lie, Bill nonetheless understood her reasoning. Her father believed in the strict rules of proper courtship, and having his unchaperoned daughter doing bear time with Bill in Wilmington didn't fall within those guidelines. Bill grinned like Charlie had just before he headed off to meet one of his buttered buns. With luck, Bill would soon enjoy far more than bear time with Becky Powell. He slipped his hand into his vest pocket and felt his pocket watch. *Lord, instead of aureolas, make my watch speed up.*

Making his way along the plank sidewalk, Bill passed the Purcell House at the Market Street intersection. He almost stepped into the hotel lobby to get a room, but decided to put it off until he had spoken to General Whiting or an underling. Bureaucracy had a way of bedeviling a man. Bill wanted to set up a station near the headquarters and do some recruiting starting in the morning. He figured it would take most of the afternoon to get an ad put in the *Daily Journal* and make arrangements for a band to play some patriotic airs. His stomach rumbled at the thought of all he had to do. General Whiting, newspaper ad, the band, hotel room, then a meal in the Purcell House. Its food had a fizzing reputation. He'd never tasted any of the menu's dainties, but planned to later in the day… and with Becky sitting across from him on the morrow.

Two women in flowery summer dresses strolled toward him, one middle-aged with gray ringlets curling out from a green taffeta bonnet, the other not much older than Bill, wearing a straw hat adorned with freshly cut red roses. "Good afternoon, Private," the older woman said in a prim voice. "Fine weather we're having."

The younger woman offered Bill a coy smile gone so fast he wondered if he'd seen it. Her saucy eyes danced before returning to a blank look when the older woman glanced at her.

"Ladies, tell everyone you know there'll be a band concert tomorrow at General Whiting's headquarters." Bill tipped his slouch hat to them.

"Splendid!" the older woman remarked. "We'll be there if the rain stays away."

The two women and Bill shared the sidewalk with soldiers, stevedores, shopkeepers and an overdressed gentleman who stepped into a lawyer's office next to a dentist. Bill looked to the right, along Market Street down to the Cape Fear River. Obscured by a tavern's awning, the

Daily Journal building nearly escaped his notice. With the newspaper office barely a stone's throw away, he decided to buy the ad now and not wait until later in the day. Whirling, Bill headed down Market Street toward the river. The dockside smell grew more pungent as he drew near the newspaper office and the market house. Water Street smelled of too many chamberpots, of hemp and pitch from the shipyards across the river and the docks on the town side. Two masts jutted above the warehouses. They belonged to a sleek blockade runner.

Before secession, Bill's papa brought him to Wilmington on New Year's Eve to see fireworks light up the night sky. Through the decades, the downtown suffered ghastly fires, but launching pinwheels from the west side of the Cape Fear kept hundreds of yards of water between the skyrockets and the downtown. The fireworks outing included a stay in a downtown hotel overlooking the Market House. On New Year's Day, he peered through a slit in the window curtains and saw so many slaves he rubbed his eyes to make sure they were really there. His papa explained. "They're getting their contracts renewed. The slaves have been leased by their owners to construction firms. Who do you think built the Opera House, Bellamy Mansion and the Wilmington and Weldon depot?" Just thinking about the stench of all those slaves huddled together set Bill's healing wound to tickling.

Two men, one a graybeard, the other younger and missing a leg, slouched on a bench in front of the newspaper office reading the latest edition. Above them, the *Daily Journal* sign creaked in the light breeze.

"Afternoon, soldier." The graybeard rearranged the horn-rimmed glasses on the end of his nose. "From Fort Fisher?"

Bill shrugged. "I'm with Lee. Eighteenth North Carolina, on four-month furlough. Shell hole in my back. Going to do some recruiting over the next few days. Want to be my first signee?"

The graybeard fiddled with his cane propped against the bench's armrest. "Last I heared, Jeff Davis don't want sixty-five-year-olds."

The one-legged former soldier growled. "Fought with the Sixty-First, Army of the Tennessee. Got this"—he gestured to his stump—"to prove it. Proud of my service, but I'm done with it." The crutch leaning against the shopfront buttressed the ex-soldier's words.

Bill repressed a sigh. "War's not done for me. I'll be going back in September."

The miniature bell above the entryway tinkled. Door groaning open, a heavyset woman dressed in a black dress shuffled from the newspaper office. Bill doffed his hat and bowed. "My sympathies, ma'am," he told her.

The odor of ink and grease permeated the *Daily Journal*'s reception room. A comely young woman, likely the publisher's daughter, smiled as he stepped up to the counter. With so many men in the armies, more women stood behind counters trying their best to keep the economy creaking along. Even with the conscription law exempting many men holding jobs indispensable to the cause—railroad and river workers, telegraph operators, miners, druggists and teachers—the women were still needed. Bill rolled his eyes. Loopholes riddled the law, allowing corrupt politicians and their bootlickers to evade the draft. At forty-six, his papa had escaped the draft, although that might change. Politicians had tweaked the law and made the cutoff age fifty.

Bill fished his furlough paper from a pocket and handed the document to her. "Need an ad in tomorrow's *Daily Journal*. Big, so it catches everyone's eye. At least a quarter page. I also need it in poster size." Grimacing, Bill realized the girl had just waited on the woman in mourning clothes, there to pay for a small display ad thanking friends for their kindness in the wake of her soldier husband's death. *What a juxtaposition!* His mood turned sad as he handed her a Confederate government IOU.

Crumpling it, she tossed the paper in a trashcan. "No need for an IOU, soldier. Patriotism still lives at the *Daily Journal*. We're doing our part to win the war."

He almost said her family would soon own his papa's newspaper, but decided not to share that revelation. "Starting a nation from scratch isn't easy. Things will get better."

The girl tapped her fingers on the counter, her emerald-green eyes thoughtful. "Big mistake Davis made putting an embargo on cotton in the early months. The Brits and the Froggies don't need our cotton as bad as he thought. Every day inflation gets worse. Beef's now two dollars a pound, bacon's five dollars, and coffee's almost eighty dollars. I saw a wonderful gown for the Summer Ball... five hundred. I'm going to wear an old one."

Bill eyed the scene beyond the back window... the Cape Fear and the city-side moorings. "Cotton's being loaded aboard that blockade runner."

She shot a glance over her shoulder. "It's the *S.S. Cyren*. My father thought the embargo would work, said so in editorials." Frustration scrawled across her face. "But the Europeans won't recognize us nor intervene. No need with a surplus of cotton in their textile warehouses. Enough to keep their mills running until they found a replacement, cotton from India and Egypt." She reached into a drawer and brought out several sheets of brown paper. "What do you want the ad to say?"

His eyes drifted from a wall painting of a printing press and sweaty laborers to the paper on the counter. "Hand me a sheet and a pencil, and I'll show you."

Again reaching into the drawer, she emerged with a thick pencil, then slid it and the paper across the countertop to him. "Write away, soldier. By the way, name's Tanya Gleeman, my father's the *Daily Journal's* publisher."

No way around it… he'd soon learn if his last name piqued a memory tucked away in her mind. "Nice meeting you, Miss Gleeman. My name's Bill Stamford. I'm from Kenansville."

Her right hand cupped her chin. "Oh! I'm so sorry. Your family owns the paper in Kenansville."

He couldn't help smiling at her discomfort. "No reason to say you're sorry, Tanya. Papa's choice to sell. And if the new owner's nice as his daughter, it'll be in good hands."

"Thanks for the kind words. I've seen some of the editions. Excellent newspaper."

Pencil in hand, Bill scribbled down his thoughts, drawing a rough approximation of the display ad he hoped to see in the *Daily Journal.* He finished within minutes, and handed the rough draft to Tanya. "That was fun. Maybe your father will hire me after the war?" He chuckled.

She studied the draft, tracing her fingers along the pencil marks. "Definitely. You're good, Bill Stamford." No flirtatious smiles or saucy eyes. All business, this woman. Tapping the pencil against her lower lip, she pointed to a headline. "I'll put woodblock artwork in it. Something patriotic. Something about soldiering. Crossed Rifles with a kepi and a bugle. I guarantee you'll like it."

Bill took a final look at his creation. At the top, in big lettering: Join The Eighteenth Regiment. One line down, lettering still extra big: Your New Country Needs You. Next, the words a tad smaller: Come To The Rescue. And the last headline: Three-Year Enlistment With $100 Bounty. Then in small letters: Cape Fear Military District Building On Market St., Thursday, June 25; Friday, June 26; Saturday, June 27. He handed it back to her. "Build it."

"I'll have it typeset and ready for tomorrow's newspaper. Stop by at six o'clock and I'll have a proof for you."

Bill headed for the door, stopped. "Oh, I forgot. I want to hire the community band. Who should I see?"

"Aren't you the lucky man? Next door. Wright's General Store. Bob Wright plays the saxhorn. Not much advance notice, but Mister Wright's a patriotic man. He'll help you out."

Lucky? The man who sees aureolas? "Hope you're right."

She was. Wright turned out to be a sixty-year-old man with a flaming-red beard down to his belly button and a personality more bubbly than a sixteen-year-old girl at her debutante ball. Even with the short notice, he volunteered for all three days, two hours of music per day. Bill intended to bill the Confederate government for the band's performances, but Wright refused the money. His son, a captain, served with the Twentieth North Carolina.

Whistling "When Johnny Comes Marching Home," Bill proceeded to the Cape Fear Military District headquarters where he got the go-ahead to set up a recruitment station for the next three days. Next, he paid for a room at the Purcell House with a War Department IOU note. When Bill said three nights, the clerk didn't look happy. The proprietor would get paid eventually if the CSA prevailed… not a certainty with the economy a shambles and the central government shaky.

With time on his hands before he needed to return to the *Journal*, he ventured down to Water Street, passed a whorehouse bursting with loud piano music, and walked into the Worth Tavern for a mug of warm ale. He preferred his ale with a chunk of ice, but didn't think the proprietor would have blocks of ice stored underground. Taking a seat at a corner table near the counter, Bill leaned against the backrest and didn't worry about irritating the wound. The spot provided a view of a wall painting depicting a blockade runner eluding a Yankee ship. A matronly waitress in a prim brown-and-white dress partly covered by a green apron approached Bill. "From Fort Fisher or Fort Caswell? Or attached to headquarters?" She flicked cornbread crumbs from her apron.

"From the Army of Northern Virginia, ma'am," he told her. "On furlough, recuperating. Took a shell fragment in the back. If you know any boys with spunk, tell them I'll be recruiting at district headquarters for the next three days. Trying to get the Eighteenth Regiment back to full strength."

She frowned, understanding what the recruitment drive portended. More names on the casualty lists posted on bulletin boards all over southeastern North Carolina. She scratched at sweat-dulled hair that had escaped her white bonnet. "I'll mention the news to our customers. What can I get for you this fine June afternoon?"

Bill changed his mind about a mug of ale. Instead, he inquired, "How about a glass of rum punch?" He needed something sweet—rum, sugar, oranges and lemons.

"We don't get that very often." She gave his shoulder a motherly squeeze. "But for one of Lee's own, you'll soon have the rum punch on the table with a chunk of ice. That's right. We've some ice hidden away underground. My husband owns the tavern; we look after soldiers who do real fightin'."

At a nearby table, a striking woman in her mid-forties stood and wove her way to the bar where the tavernkeeper's wife mixed the rum punch for Bill. Both eyed him, then the dark-haired, dark-eyed older woman leaned across the counter and whispered something to the chubby younger woman. Nodding knowingly, the wife moseyed to Bill's table, the mug of rum punch cradled in her hand. "As soon as you finish this one, a second one will be speedin' your way, compliments of Mrs. Rose O'Neal Greenhow." The barkeep's wife waved to the older woman, who snuggled against the counter as if she owned it.

Bill spit out the rum punch as Rose Greenhow headed his way, a glimmer of a smile ghosting across her face. He'd heard of her exploits. Newspapers credited the Wild Rose with helping the South win the First Battle of Manassas. She'd turned on her charms to worm information out of Yankee officers. Before the battle, Rose supplied General Beauregard with crucial information about Yankee troop movements. Bill's back didn't complain when he rose and bowed. "Thank you, Mrs. Greenhow. I'm honored to meet our most indispensable spy."

"The honor's mine," Rose answered, resting her hands on the finials of one of the table's chairs. "You've bled for the South, took a shell fragment for me and other patriots. May I join you, sir?"

He motioned her to sit. "Ma'am, I apologize for not recognizing you. I should have. I'm a humble fellow. I seldom get to walk among elevated personages."

Twittering a light laugh, Rose settled into the chair across from him. "Oh, don't exaggerate."

Austere, with her hair parted in the middle and tied in a bun, she hardly looked a seductress. In the dim light inside the tavern, her olive skin appeared delicately flushed with color, so different from most women who never let sunlight tan their skin. Exotic regardless of her unstylish coiffure and old-school day dress, she knew how to get members of the Yankee Congress and diplomats to blather into her ear at dinner parties. Men always underestimated women.

"Nelly," Rose addressed the barkeep's wife, "I've reconsidered the rum punch for my new friend." She gave Bill a questioning look.

"Bill. Bill Stamford," he told Rose.

"Instead of the rum punch, I'd like my favorite drink. One for me. One for Bill."

Soon, Nelly returned with two dark red drinks. "Just how you instructed me to make them, Rose. Even some cracked ice." Nelly raised her index finger to her mouth as if signaling everyone to be extra quiet. "But say nothing to my husband. He's tight with the ice. No more than one servin'."

Rose raised her drink to her mouth and sipped. "Nelly Shook, I'm sure Mister Shook would gladly surrender more of his ice for the Wild Rose of the Confederacy." She licked droplets of the drink from her lips. "Wonderful. I do love my whiskey cobblers."

"As always, you're right." Nelly trilled a high-pitched laugh. "My husband's proud as Punch that you love our little place." She regarded Bill. "Not your rum punch. Punch the puppet." Still chuckling, she retreated to the bar.

Rose tapped his glass with a fingernail. "Please try it. Brand new drink created in New Orleans last year. Old Crow whiskey mixed with fruit and sugar, and served over cracked ice."

Bill took two swallows. "I'm done with rum punch. I've a new favorite. Old Crow Cobbler. Delicious. I'll have to share the recipe with my father and mother."

Rose sipped more of her drink. "Please do. Whiskey Cobbler, or Old Crow Cobbler as you call it, needs more fans." She paused, watching him drink his Old Crow Cobbler, grinning when he sighed melodramatically. "Nelly says you were wounded by a shell fragment." She bore an expectant look, hoping to learn more.

Since the wounding, Bill rarely shared the gruesome details with anyone, but Rose Greenhow sat before him. "At Chancellorsville. During a charge. A shell blew apart above me. An inch either way and I would've died on the battlefield."

"God spared you. Now you must learn His reason." Her eyes gleamed earnestness.

"Spared me? A soldier in the Eighteenth North Carolina?" He reached for his drink, but left it untouched.

Startlement scrawled across her face. Rose understood. "It was an accident. The darkness, artillery fire, musket sniping. It was bound to happen. I'm sure General Jackson believed that night to be God's terrible will."

God's will? Bill remembered his harried efforts to thwart Charlie's aureola's will. He changed the subject. "I don't live in Wilmington. My folks live in a small town north of here, Kenansville. My papa's a publisher and printer." His shoulders slumped. "I could've enlisted in a Duplin County regiment, but my buddy Charlie chose the Eighteenth, so I did too. Bad move, eh?"

Her eyes ballooned, then flickered amusement. "Uhoh. My name will appear in newspapers again... not that I'm against the fame. I've booked a blockade runner to Liverpool, me and my daughter Little Rose. Hope that bad luck of yours ain't catching. Not with us having to outrun all the Union Navy ships."

He raised the whiskey cobbler in a salute to her and her daughter. "To a speedy, safe trip to Liverpool." He sipped, relishing the taste.

"Why thank you, Bill." Rose raised her glass in a salute and drained it. "What you did is much braver than outrunning a bunch of slow Yankee ships. Marching into a hail of shells and bullets."

Bill proffered a sheepish smile. "Can't have chuckaboos thinking you're a coward or wandought. So you keep charging until the Yankees get routed or you get wounded or killed. Sorry to say... no glory in war."

"You're right. No glory." Rose glanced at the ceiling fan. No movement; the waterfront breeze had calmed. "But life will turn hellish if we're ground under Lincoln's heel. We can't let that happen. We're protecting our way of life."

Fire lurked in her eyes—passion and fanaticism. Bill could never share his doubts about the war. Women like Rose dreaded talk of tapping into the last remaining manpower reserve—slaves, almost four million of them. Discounting women and children, there remained a manpower reserve of more than a million potential soldiers—if politicians could bring themselves to offer freedom. On the warfronts, they were building fortifications, digging latrines and hauling supplies. Still others were working in the mines, factories and railroad yards. If not for the commandeered slaves, the South might already be under Lincoln's heel. If he suggested letting them fight for their freedom, she'd probably report him to General Whiting, and he'd end up in the stockade. No, he'd limit the chitchat to pleasantries.

His mind made up, Bill told her, "I'd make a lousy spy."

She fiddled with a single strand of hair that lay along the edge of her forehead. "Helps to be a lady with wit. I've often been told I'm a great conversationalist."

"You are," Bill concurred.

Rose waved her hand dismissively. "Men like to hear themselves pontificate. Especially politicians, military officers and diplomats. They write me off, think I'm only good for dinner parties, much too airy to remember anything of substance. After First Manassas, they don't think that anymore."

A gang of boisterous stevedores dripping with sweat erupted through the entrance, eager to wet their tongues with cheap ale. Bill watched the hullabaloo for a moment, then swung his gaze back to Rose. "I read about your tribulations in the *Richmond Dispatch*, ma'am. Don't think I could handle imprisonment. I'd definitely not be the trooper you were. How many months?"

"Five months under house arrest, then four in that military prison on Capitol Hill." Rose too glanced at the stevedores, waved to one who blew her a kiss. "Awful time. Little Rose and me were treated like common felons. The Confederacy treats Federal prisoners far better than Pinkerton treated me."

Bill scooted his chair forward, bumping his belly against the table's edge. Elbows splayed on the tabletop, he raised his voice above the stevedores' racket. "You're with friends now, ma'am, in a country that loves you, respects the sacrifices you made." He sniffed her orangey perfume, a welcome change from the intense smell of tobacco, ale and stevedore sweat.

"Thank you, Bill." She touched one of his elbows, still splayed on the tabletop, then gestured to the stevedores. "They're loading my ship, the *Cyren*. When I get to London, I'm going to mingle with aristocrats, maybe marry one. I'll have them begging Queen Victoria to recognize the Confederacy, even send troops to fight alongside us, just like the Frogs did at Yorktown. I'll do the same in France, get the Blue Bloods to entice Napoleon the Third to join the war."

"You're going to be a very busy woman." Again, he drank in her perfume, a reminder of Franny, no longer part of his life.

"I'll be writing my memoirs too. I intend to bring back lots of gold to help you and your soldier friends win Southern independence. Every night I pray to the Good Lord to help me do my duty to Him and the South." Rose scooted the chair back and came to her feet. "It's been splendid meeting you, Bill. I need to get back to Little Rose. I've a free black servant girl looking after her. Don't be surprised if you do see Little Rose and me tomorrow. I feel like doing some recruiting for the Eighteenth."

Bill rose and bowed. "Be glad to have your company, Rose."

She said her goodbye to Nelly, mingled with the stevedores for a minute, then strolled to the door.

His heart suddenly thumped in his chest, as if dwarves with hammers were smacking its chambers. Bill sucked in a jittery breath that never managed to slither down his throat. He dug his nails into the table. As Rose opened the door, admitting sunlight, an aureola enveloped her, subduing the sunbeams, seemingly lighting up the room. The stevedores ogled Rose, oblivious to the golden light spilling out around her. The door closed, and Rose O'Neal Greenhow was gone.

Twenty-nine

Lovers' Thespian Tour

The open window in Bill's hotel room allowed the night breeze to cool him as he lay on the four-poster bed. Every night his mind ran faster than a prewar locomotive. So much for Bill to fret about in the early days of summer 1863. The Army of Northern Virginia and his chuckaboos on the march somewhere in the Shenandoah Valley or Maryland. Charlie hadn't written. Probably too busy fondling his latest dollymop's diddeys. His family, facing shortages that would only get worse as fewer and fewer blockade runners escaped the Yankee Navy's dragnet. And adding to the hard times wearying his mind… the aureola blazing around Rose's body.

Rose Greenhow had sat with him in the tavern for almost an hour, sharing her whiskey cobblers. Not one flicker of an aureola flame. God, or Satan or the Fates themselves, had waited until Rose left the tavern to light her up like a ballroom chandelier. At Chancellorsville, Bill had somehow managed to stay the hand of Death targeting Charlie. His best chuckaboo still breathed. Not General Jackson, the sacrificial lamb required in the place of Charlie. That was Bill's theory, though he couldn't be one hundred percent certain. Only God—and maybe Satan—knew, and they weren't whispering answers into Bill's ear.

Rose? Should Bill try again to stay the hand of Death? If yes, who might get hurt by an unforeseen ricochet, like General Jackson? Forever and again, Bill had wrestled with the quandary plaguing him since his cousin fell from their granddaddy's tree. Why reveal the aureolas unless a highfalutin' SOMEONE meant Bill to make a difference? He mumbled into the coolness of a mid-June night: *What am I to do, Lord?*

No burning-bush answer filled the hotel room with light, but Bill made a decision anyway. If Rose and her daughter turned up at General Whiting's headquarters, he'd say his night had been interrupted by a nightmare that left him unable to sleep for rest of the night. "You died in it, Rose," he'd tell her. "Please, for my peace of mind, be extra, extra careful in the days ahead. I've heard dreams can be messages from God. Remember the Bible's Daniel and the dreams of Nebuchadnezzar?" His warning would probably go over Rose's head. But if he told the truth? She'd think him a maniac or demon-possessed.

Borne by the cool breeze, voices of people finding pleasure in the saloons and brothels of Water Street sailed through the window and tickled his ears. Streetwise dollymops cuddling up to blockade-running sailors, garrison soldiers eager to ride the rantipole with toffer girls, all having a gay time, just like Bill in twenty-four hours. Soon... his *melting moment* with Becky.

Bill still slept mostly on his stomach and his side. His wound healed nicely, yet his momma continued to keep it rot-free with bromine and a fresh dressing every few days. Too many soldiers were dying weeks, even months, after suffering wounds. During his Wilmington outing, Bill hoped to visit Doctor Iuppenlatz for a thorough cleaning and new dressing. He feared leaving a filthy lint pressed against his wound for three or more days could undo his momma's hard work.

Yawning, he took a gander at the room's alarm clock. He'd set it for six o'clock, more than enough time to eat a breakfast, set up his recruiting station, and get to the railroad depot to greet Becky at nine. A headquarters lieutenant had agreed to man the station while Bill did the bear with Becky at the depot.

Worn out, his body spent after the day's dawn-to-dusk workload, Bill shut his eyes and tuned out the voices. Instead, he mentally recited poetry. He chose Emily Dickinson, not caring she was a Massachusetts woman.

Nobody knows this little Rose.
It might a pilgrim be.
Did I not take it from the ways
And lift it up to thee?
Only a bee will miss it,
Only a butterfly,
Hastening from far journey...

Like ether administered to him before his shell-fragment surgery, Bill drifted off to sleep, the poem's last words left unspoken on his lips: "Ah, Little Rose, how easy for such as thee to die."

The alarm blared. With sunlight streaming through the window, Bill perched on his elbow and fumbled for the off switch. When the alarm went silent, he lay on his side feeling the breeze against his face, then shifted to a sitting position. *Finally, I'll make love to Becky, and wipe Franny from my mind.*

Courting Becky hadn't turned out the way he anticipated. How could anyone know what lay ahead in a time of war? He rose from the bed and glanced at a wall mirror. Turning slightly, he examined the dressing. No blood; he was holding up so far.

Sighing, he splashed washbasin water on his face, slipped into his clothes and made his way down the steps for breakfast.

Not like his momma's fare, the hotel's hoecakes, salt pork and the fake coffee nevertheless filled his belly. Before heading out the door, Bill left instructions with the front desk. Hip pressed against the counter, he told the baldheaded clerk, "Have a bathtub ready in my room when I return at eight tonight. Filled with hot water."

Soon, he had his recruitment sign tucked under his left arm. The morning sun warmed his neck as he set up his makeshift recruiting station at General Whiting's district headquarters... desk, chairs, Bible, easel for the poster, and a surprise, an Eighteenth flag sewn by the wife of Major George Tait. After seeing the recruitment ad in the *Journal*, she had brought the flag to the headquarters ten minutes before he arrived.

Bill no sooner sat down when a pimply-faced kid with baby fat ambled up to the recruiting station. He beamed. "I want to join up, see the elephant."

Big enough to be eighteen, the fellow didn't look the age in the face, more like thirteen or fourteen. Bill eyed him sternly. "When I swear you in, you'll have to keep your hand on the Bible. If you're not eighteen, you'll be lying not just to me but to the Lord. Are you eighteen?"

He nodded eagerly. "Yessir. Newly minted eighteen."

Opening the Bible, Bill slid the Holy Book along the desktop to where the boy stood, wobbling on cornstalk legs. "Put your right hand on it, Hayfoot."

Arm quivering, the boy warily dropped his hand onto the Bible, the Book of Mark. "I'm ready." He didn't sound like it, Bill thought, maintaining his stern mien.

"What's your name?"

"Gary Douglas, sir."

Bill pointed to the Bible. "A simple oath, Mister Douglas. Swear that you are eighteen or older. Say: 'I, Gary Douglas, of sound mind and body, do hereby swear on this Holy Bible that I am at least eighteen years old and eligible to serve with the Eighteenth North Carolina Regiment in the Army of Northern Virginia.'"

Guilty eyes darted between Bill and the Bible. "I, Gary Douglas, of sound mind and body, hereby swear on this Holy Bible that I am at least… that I am at least… that I am—"

Bill harrumphed. "Well?"

The boy's shoulder sagged. "I can't. Momma raised me to be an upright man, a good Christian man. I'm not eighteen, sir. I'm fifteen. I don't care about the bonus. What good's a bonus in this inflation? I just want to help the Tar Heel state and our new nation… and kick those Blue-Bellies out of New Bern."

Gripping the boy's hand, Bill raised it away from the Bible. "It'll be 1866 before you can join up. God help us if the war's still going on, son. But if it is… I'll gladly swear you in then."

Sighing, Gary eyed the Holy Book forlornly. "Sure you couldn't cheat a tad for me?"

Sweat ran down Bill's back, dampening the wound's dressing. He removed his shell jacket and hung it on the chair's finials. "And have your momma scalp me? No way! Stay in school. Become educated. We're going to need smart men to run the country after the war and save our devastated economy." Bill squeezed the boy's shoulder. "Now get on home."

"Yessir." Shoulders slumped, the boy headed south on Front Street toward the porched houses beyond Nun Street. Soon, he disappeared among men in dapper suits and straw hats, and women in rainbow colored summer dresses and their servants pushing baby buggies.

Bill wiped sweat from his forehead. The sun gleamed in a cloudless sky so blue it belonged in a fairytale book. Birds black against the sky squawked as they winged across the Cape Fear. Only the sound of footsteps drawing near could yank his eyes away from the sky. A man with muttonchops and blue eyes as striking as the morning's sky marched up to Bill's desk, a newspaper clutched in a hand.

"Where is she?" Mister Muttonchops' voice dripped with annoyance.

Bill cocked an eyebrow. "You'll have to be clearer, my friend."

Muttonchops jabbed a thumb at the newspaper. "It's right in here. Says she'll be in front of General Whiting's headquarters helping lasso recruits. See!" He opened it to a below-the-fold ad on page two that shared space with a news story about President Jefferson Davis. "Meet Rose O'Neal Greenhow, spy extraordinaire, Heroine of First Manassas. Well, I'm here and she ain't. I want to kiss her hand and join up. You put that ad in the paper, soldier boy?"

Bill reached for the *Journal.* "Ah, let me get a closer—"

"I'm here, boys." Rose strolled up to the desk and proffered her hand to the prospective recruit, who kissed it with elation. The other cradled Little Rose, her daughter. Reaching into a roomy handbag, the Heroine of First Manassas plucked out toys for Little Rose. "You can play in General Whiting's office. He's at Fort Caswell today."

Little Rose gathered up her pickup sticks, chalkboard, jacks and a book titled *Forest Pony and Other Tales*, and disappeared into the headquarters building.

Eyeing the suddenly reticent complainer, Rose slid the topmost recruitment form from Bill's stack and waved it in Muttonchops' face. "Cat's got your tongue? The South and General Lee need you. Make that kiss mean something, sir." Rose slapped the form down in front of him, alongside a pencil. "Sign here." She pointed to the dotted line at the form's bottom. "Bill will let you know what comes next."

Bill swore him in, a fellow with the odd name Dingus Runion, and told him to be at the Wilmington depot on Monday, September 28, at nine in the morning, the date for returning to Lee's army. He'd take all the recruits with him.

"This is going to be a fine day for recruiting," Bill told Rose as he and the spy settled into the side-by-side chairs behind the desk. "Thanks to you, Rose."

"Ah, here's your band marching up the street." Rose peered north toward the Market House. "They're playing 'The Rose of Alabamy' for me." Her face wore a look of delight.

Guilt hammered at him. He needed to warn Rose, but even his earlier *nightmare* plan sounded hollow as the band played and folks gathered for the concert. She'd laugh at him. Beware of a bad dream? She'd pat his shoulder and make a joke about scared boys hiding their heads beneath their pillows. He couldn't mention the aureola. She'd haul him to a Baptist pastor for an exorcism. But to do nothing… unacceptable. Later, he'd come up with a credible plan.

A line of would-be recruits formed in front of the desk, almost all with a wife or sweetheart standing with them, a few with rambunctious children. The war manifested two kinds of women: the fervent patriots who grew more zealous as war fortunes worsened, and those like Becky and Franny who privately questioned the war's aims, yet supported it. When a freckled, redheaded fellow, maybe twenty-one, reached the front of the line, he entertained second thoughts. He turned to his wife, who had a baby in her arms. "I need to think about this more," he told her, voice shaky. "You've just had the baby. I should be here with you. We can revisit this later."

The wife stamped her foot. "Ya're goin' to get drafted anyway. Do your duty!" Her riled voice upset the baby, who began crying. "Shush! Your papa's being obstinate."

Scowling at him, Rose slid a recruitment form to the edge of the desk and tapped the paper with a pencil. "Sir, all good white men need to enlist, not dodge their service. If you men don't do your duty, the government in Richmond may do the unthinkable—give guns to slaves. You cannot allow that to happen. Never forget Nat Turner!"

Bill picked up the recruitment form and thrust it toward the redhead. "What are you going to do, Peckerwood? I worried too. Left behind a sweetheart."

As a jumble of emotions flitted across his face, the reluctant recruit took the pencil and signed his name. Bill swore in the fellow and told him to be at the depot at the appointed time.

"When you're an old man sitting on a rocker watching the Confederate Independence Day parade, you'll take pride in your service to the country," Rose said, then kissed the infant on the cheek.

As the band played, more and more men signed up, far more than Bill thought possible… all due to the patriotic fervor of Rose O'Neal Greenhow. During a break in the music, Bob Wright, the general store owner and saxhorn player, greeted Rose and Bill.

"It's an honor to make your acquaintance, Mrs. Greenhow," Wright introduced himself. When Rose offered her hand, the saxhorn player kissed it. "I've written a new song that honors your presence in our sad city."

Smile gone, Rose grimaced, knowing from Richmond's newspaper headlines what had transpired in Wilmington a year earlier. She sidled around the table and gave Wright a sisterly kiss on the cheek. Around them, everyone clapped and cheered. "That's why it's so important you and your band are here helping my friend Bill recruit for the cause we all will support to our last breath." Rose curtsied to Wright. "Thank you for the honor, kind sir. Please, what's your song's title?"

"It's 'My Old Wilmington Home.' If you will excuse me, Mrs. Greenhow, the band will now play the song for the first time ever." A sheepish smile curved Wright's lips. "I apologize. A small lie. We have practiced playing the song."

As the band played, Bill felt a tap on his shoulder. He turned in his seat and looked up. It was Lieutenant Leroy Sieffenbach, a smile and amusement monopolizing his face. "It's ten minutes after ten o'clock," the lieutenant said. "You intend to pick up a young lady at the depot, right?"

Sweet Jesus save me! The morning had been so hectic Bill had lost track of time. Ten minutes after ten? Becky could very well be in the depot tapping a heel in frustration.

Rose whirled around, turning her back to the band. "A sweetheart?" she exclaimed, her voice nearly as loud as the music. "You're keeping secrets from me, Bill Stamford."

"A little secret," Bill conceded as the music faded. "I wanted it to be a surprise for you and for Becky. But I need to skedaddle. I'm running late."

Rose harrumphed. "Don't you dare bring Becky here! Show her the mansions on Second Street and tour the Opera House, magnificent as Washington's Ford Theatre. Let people see a filly and a foal, eyes only for each other. I'll get a bushel of recruits for you. My promise... a bushel."

Donning his shell jacket, Bill sped away, no pain in his back, as folks cheered the band.

The lieutenant shouted, his voice outmuscling the cheers, "You're in trouble, Stamford. Give her a bushel of kisses. She's probably in line to buy a return ticket."

Bill dashed by a stable. If he could have harnessed a horse to a buggy in three seconds, he'd have prodded the horse into a gallop and wheeled to the depot... and God help any cigar-puffing old men too slow to get out of the way. But no buggy, no horse, just his feet and his fear of what Becky would think of him. Panting, he rushed into the depot's main hall.

Becky perched on a bench, staring at the floor. Bill advanced toward her, steps hesitant. *Look apologetic*, he reminded himself. His footsteps echoed, boots spanking the tile. She looked up and fixed her gaze on his face. A farmer's grin spread across her mouth. No anger lines etched her forehead. Instead, her eyes brimmed with joy.

"I'm so sorry I'm late." He hoped she saw remorse in his eyes. "Time got away from me. It's been a busy morning signing up the fopdoodles."

Standing, Becky blew Bill a kiss. "I knew you were busy recruiting. Thought you might be even later." She wrapped her arms around his wiry frame and kissed him full on the mouth. Her hand caressed his bandage. "Your wound giving you any trouble?"

"Almost no pain. Sometimes I forget it's there."

She pinched his cheek. "So what's your plans for the day? I know what we'll be doing tonight." Her saucy eyes danced.

He gawked at the graceful way she guided him toward the double doorway and Front Street. The scent of her *Eau de Cologne* transported his mind to his hotel room and the image of her naked body atop the bed, beads of sweat glistening on her breasts and belly. The night couldn't come quickly enough. Barely beyond the depot portico, her sweet perfume retreated before the smells of the waterfront—tar on the riggings of docked ships, pitch coated on the hulls, riverside turpentine stills, cotton bales stacked on the wharfs. The heated air stank like the riverbank mud and the sooty smoke belching from smokestacks and chimneys. Bill had grown used to Wilmington's perfume. Becky rubbed her nose.

Bill never grew tired of the waterfront view, the tall masts jutting above the warehouses, the church steeples and courthouse tower on Third Street. Across the Cape Fear, billowing gray clouds rolled in from the west, swallowing blue sky, bringing more collar-drenching humidity. Thankfully, no lightning flashed inside the clouds. Perhaps it wouldn't rain.

"Ignore the clouds," Becky instructed him. "It's going to be a fine day. You never did share your plans."

Bill swiveled away from the river and tucked an arm around Becky's waist. "Have you ever been inside the Opera House?"

Becky burrowed closer as they walked along the Front Street sidewalk. "Once, just after First Manassas. For a performance of *Major Jones' Courtship*. Saw George Bailey on stage. He's very handsome, but not a looker like you."

"Well, thank you, Miss Powell." They crossed the Grace Street intersection, scurrying between a lickety-split buggy and a slow-moving wagon heaped full of tin goods. "I thought we'd sneak a gander at the Opera House, take our own private tour."

"I thought you were going to recruit this morning and afternoon." A hot breeze swirled through an alley and tousled Becky's hat, its flower design similar to her dress's floral scheme. Curling her lower lip, she fixed the headwear's skewed look.

The alley's breeze proved an irritant for Becky, but Bill basked in its relief. Hot but still a welcome touch. "I've some stand-ins... a fine lieutenant and someone I'm going to introduce you to later. When you meet her, you'll get the vapors, but I'll catch you."

Blazes! Now I'm going to obsess on that bloody aureola. Just think about how fun it's going to be disrobing Becky. He winked at her. *Maybe I can first try out the aureola dream on her. Will she believe me? If she does, perhaps the two of us can convince Rose to take extra caution. Lordy, I just want to think about loving her tonight... not this stuff.* He caressed her back.

She playfully slapped his forearm. "You're so melodramatic. A secret, eh? You must expect me to beg you to tell me." She poked his ribs. "Guess what? I'm going to let it stay a secret. Just to annoy you."

Turning, they headed east on Princess Street. Two blocks ahead, the colonnaded Opera House and City Hall dwarfed the two- and three-story buildings around it. Before the war, the theater had hosted dozens of performances by some of the best actors in the South and even the North. He'd seen a couple. Since the spring of 1861, the Opera House seemed even busier with performances almost every night. People wanted to get their minds off the war—the casualty lists, the disabled soldiers tottering on crutches, the ridiculously high prices.

He held the door open for Becky and they entered through the theater's side entrance. A dandy with a horseshoe mustache and a white suit greeted them from inside a ticket booth. "Howdy, folks. We've a play tonight perfect for you, soldier. *Virginia Cavalier.* It's the rage in Richmond."

Bill and Becky traded coy glances. They knew what they planned once the sun went down. "Thank you, but we've other plans," Bill said politely, kissing Becky's hand. "My sweetheart's from Duplin County, and I'm hoping to give her a tour of the Opera House before I return to General Lee's army. May I?"

The dandy exited the ticket booth. "You're with the Eighteenth North Carolina, right? One of our local boys." Bill nodded. "Get wounded?"

Again, Bill nodded. "Shell fragment. At Chancellorsville."

Becky gently stroked Bill's bandage, making sure the ticket agent saw her doing it. "My Bill's not the complaining type. Healing went slow at first, but he's doing much better now. I promise we won't disturb anyone."

The dandy hung a sign from the ticket booth: *Out To Lunch.* "Tell you what... I'll give you my personal Gold Coin Tour."

Dressed as one of the villains in a Captain G.W. Alexander play, the ticket agent bowed to Bill and Becky, then kissed her hand. "Name's David Gutteinstein, jack of all trades. Do a bit of everything for the company... sell and collect tickets, work as a flyboy, run the lights, stand in for the stage manager. Even act some, usually the villain. And you folks are?"

Becky took the lead, "I'm Becky Powell and this fine soldier and gentleman is Bill Stamford."

"Pleased to meet you both." Gutteinstein ran his fingers through his hair, then pointed to the set of double doors directly ahead. "We'll take a look at the auditorium, the parquet seats and the dress circle. The entryway… notice that it's framed by Grecian pillars with the customary triangle at the top. Nothing like being awed before you even see the main stage."

"The first time I came here, I decided to become an actress." Becky grinned broadly. "The thought still appeals to me. Maybe I'll give it a try someday, if I can't get my writing published." She tucked her hand in the crook of Bill's elbow. "My beau and I are like two halves of a delicious pear. He wants to be an author too."

Gutteinstein laughed. "*Sweet* lovers, eh?" He swung his gaze to the proscenium main stage and its wide-open curtains. "Perhaps one of your beau's plays will someday be performed on our stage." He led the couple down an aisle into the main auditorium. Sunbeams streamed through arched windows, flitting among the goliath chandelier's tear-shaped crystals. "We're privately owned, so we're able to book road shows even with the war. This stage's always busy, as I'm sure you already know, Miss Powell."

"Please, call me Becky," she insisted.

"I will, Becky." Gutteinstein scratched his elaborate mustache. Bill half-expected to see the man's lunch fall out. "I pinch myself every time I walk into the theater. I'm so lucky to work here."

"Any farm boy who steps into this place will think a piece of Heaven just descended." Becky's ogling gaze wandered from the stage to the two back balconies.

Gutteinstein leaned against a first-row chair. "The darkies doing the construction thought the same when they finished painting the walls and columns." He eyed the ceiling. "You won't see a grander chandelier, not even Ford's Theater in the Yankees' Washington. Notice how it's suspended from the cantilevered beam over the top of that grand box. At Ford's, the box is set aside for monkey-faced Lincoln and his horrid wife Mary."

Yawning, Bill folded his arms against his chest. "I'm itching to see the stage machinery."

"I'm itching to tell you about the equipment," Gutteinstein chuckled, leading Becky and Bill to stage right.

Once in the bowels of the stage, barely lit by small windows, Gutteinstein pointed upward into the murkiness. "See the fly galleries three stories up? The central scenes are lowered from them. The drop curtain is raised and lowered by two flymen. Notice the gaslights inside the sconces? They're the floodlights. The flymen control all the stage machinery. The ropes, the pulleys and sandbag counterweights move the scenery."

"I don't see a prompter's table." Becky stepped away from Bill and Gutteinstein, and slipped into the shadows. "Who's giving directions to the actors and the flymen?"

Mulling Gutteinstein's narratives, Bill half-heard Becky's words. At that moment, the war seemed a million miles away. The Opera House and its make-believe plays seemed more real to him than the world beyond its doors. Becky's dress swished as she sidled up to him.

"It's there." Gutteinstein urged them toward a narrow stairway. "Concealed by the end of the proscenium. The stage manager can talk with the orchestra leader in the pit with a speaker tube. At the rear of the boxes is the governor that controls the stage and house lights. Quite a production, isn't it?"

Bill had never climbed stairs so constricting. He kept both hands on the metal railings as he ascended in the semi-darkness. Twice he brushed against Becky's hoopskirt as she climbed ahead of him. At the top, Becky strained, "Lordy, felt like the walls were squeezing in."

"Your eyes will adjust." Gutteinstein opened the nearest door and lit a gas lamp on a dressing table. The light revealed an actress's dressing room.

Becky fingered a silk costume hanging in a wardrobe. She turned to Bill. "I could be wearing a costume like this on stage someday." Grimacing, she kneaded her own dress. "Not likely. Not in these hard times."

"You can be whatever you want to be, Becky Powell." Bill caressed the back of her neck. "The war will end. You'll be free to pursue your dreams. We'll knit our dreams together."

Becky nuzzled against him. "Knit our dreams… nice turn of phrase."

Go ahead, Franny. Go ahead and marry your damned Tennessee officer. Don't need you in my life.

Gutteinstein stroked the golden curls of a wig on the dressing-room table. "Did you notice the sign on the dressing-room door? Sally Partington, the Toast of Richmond. She's ending her performance tonight with a salute to the Confederacy and singing "Southern Soldier Boy," written by Captain Alexander. The captain's quite the rogue. A pirate at the beginning of the war, now the commandant of Castle Thunder. He's making the worst of the Blue-Belly prisoners beg for mercy." Gutteinstein began singing, and Becky joined in: "Yo ho! Yo ho! He's my only joy. He's the darling of my heart, my Southern soldier boy."

"Lordy, that's awful," Bill wisecracked. "The voices, not the words."

"Always got to be a critic in the audience," Gutteinstein groaned.

"Well, *Virginia Cavalier* did get less-than-stellar reviews in Richmond." Becky grinned evilly, but then turned serious. "The song's so beautiful and sad. When we're dust in our coffins, people will still sing it."

"Here in Wilmington, the play does have the lovely Sally Partington, which means the garrison will keep coming back." Gutteinstein's chortle echoed in the room and beyond. "But perform in a century? Not likely."

Back at the ticket booth, Bill and Becky thanked David for his tour, then headed outdoors into a day ruled by gray clouds and mugginess. Not far from the entrance, in an alcove providing privacy, she closed her arms around his neck and drew him against her breasts. Her mouth pressed against his lips, and he felt the tingle of her kisses.

When finished, she said playfully, "I know you'd like to take me to your hotel room." She gave him a saucy look. "But there's lots of daylight. Back to recruiting, eh?"

"And where you'll learn my secret," he teased.

"Yes, that secret." She rolled her eyes.

Thirty

A Sting of Pleasure

The mid-afternoon crowds were still robust, although not the ones in line at the recruitment desk. That crowd had dwindled to just a handful waiting for Lieutenant Sieffenbach to sign them up and swear them in. Dozens stood or sat on sidewalks, porches, buggy seats, watching, sometimes cheering as the band played songs that made everyone sentimental for a simpler time. Becky tickled Bill's palm as she joined her voice with others singing "Aura Lee."

As the music faded, Bill led Becky to the desk and its stack of recruitment forms. Rose eyed Becky. "Bill, my new friend, I can see why you skedaddled."

Bill clasped Becky against his side. "This is Miss Becky Powell of Duplin Roads. Without her to sustain me at

Fredericksburg and Chancellorsville, I don't think I'd have survived."

Becky disentangled herself from him and groaned. "Shame on you. I suspect you were eyeing every beauty in Fredericksburg."

She was closer to the truth than she knew, Bill thought, smothering guilt before it reached his face. Just one beauty... Franny, now in Tennessee and out of his life forever.

"Private Stamford is quite right, Miss Powell," Lieutenant Sieffenbach spoke up, rising to properly greet Becky. "Your beauty could sustain any man going into battle."

"Men! So full of hot-air praises." Rose laughed lightly as she too came to her feet. "Just this once I'm going to concur with your sweetheart and the lieutenant." She swung her gaze to Bill. "When I reach Europe, I'll meet no woman in London or Paris who will outshine her. You, sir, are a lucky man."

Bill knew he sported a pleased look. "Becky, this is Rose O'Neal Greenhow."

Becky's chin dropped to the sett-paved road or at least it seemed so to Bill. Disbelief reddened her face. She perched her hands on her hips and replaced the look of amazement with a play-glare. "I concede you sprang a grand surprise, Bill Stamford. I didn't expect this." She curtsied to the older woman. "I'm sure many young ladies have told you this. You're my hero, Mrs. Greenhow."

Rose embraced Becky. "Please, call me Rose. No need for formalities."

Becky kept shaking her head. The curls beneath her hat swirled back and forth, a look Bill found alluring. Becky reached for the famed spy's hands. "Rose, you give hope to all young women like me."

Rose grinned. "I'm glad to have been of service to womankind."

"When I was just this high"—Becky leveled her hand at her waist to indicate height—"I loved reading books about grand adventures. Only it seemed to me it was always the boys doing the adventuring."

Rose nodded, her mouth pinched into a sour expression. "I remember reading children's books and thinking, 'Not even one heroine to take on pirates and bandits.' We need women authors. Maybe you, Becky?"

"I'd like to write. And I also have another dream… the stage." Becky tapped Bill's shoulder. "I predict this one will someday be an author. Ink runs through his body, not blood."

Rose gestured to a storefront across the street, its proprietor sign almost hidden by the band—Wainwright's Books. "I have a prediction, too. Both of you will write novels about thrill-seeking girls. Becky, yours will be about a young girl who helps a Confederate general whip the Yankees. Bill, you'll place your Southern heroine in Revolutionary War days."

Becky looked toward a little girl holding the hands of her mother and father as they waited for the band to play another tune. "I believe in your prediction, Rose. You've shown little girls anything is possible."

"It can't happen soon enough for me," Rose agreed, sliding her arm around Becky's waist. "Come. I want you to meet my daughter, Little Rose. She's playing inside headquarters."

Bill settled into Rose's chair and watched her and Becky disappear into General Whiting's building. *I should have tried out the dream on Rose. Never the right time, eh? Bill, you damned fool, you're letting the aureolas rule your life.*

What's the worst that could happen? She rolls her eyes at you? Sieffenbach thinks you're off your chump? Bill looked away from the HQ building to the recruit line—just two fresh fish. Both signed up, and soon Lieutenant Sieffenbach and Bill were alone. Even the band had marched away after an adieu speech by Bob Wright.

The lieutenant jabbed Bill in the side. "She's a fine woman." He pulled out his pocket watch. "Soon be four o'clock. She must be famished. Delight her with an evening candlelight dinner at the Purcell House. Then retire"...he winked..."and tip the velvet."

With the musicians gone and nearly everyone else with them, Bill and the lieutenant carried the desk, recruiting forms, and Bible into the headquarters building, along with the easel, poster and the Eighteenth battle flag. Once everything went into storage for the next day, Bill approached Becky and Rose, who sat on chairs chatting as Little Rose sprawled on the floor sketching a farmhouse. "Lieutenant Sieffenbach thinks I've been remiss by not walking you to the Purcell House for dinner." He offered his hand.

"About time, Bill Stamford," Rose said in a feigned stern voice. "For putting up with you, the lady deserves a candlelight dinner."

"Lots of daylight left, yet no recruiting?" Becky beckoned toward the front door and the empty sidewalk and street beyond.

"Tomorrow's another day," Bill said casually, folding the table legs. "The band's gone. The crowd's left for home and dinner. A good day for the Eighteenth, though. Thirty-eight recruits. Time for some courting."

Rose opened the door for them. "Yes, sweep this girl off her feet."

Becky took Bill's hand. "I've eaten at the Purcell House. "I can't say with whom. Don't want you to get jealous." A few steps down the plank sidewalk, she whirled and gave Rose a goodbye wave.

We both have secrets, Becky, Bill thought, his mind returning to wintertime in Fredericksburg and Franny Neale.

Bill returned his errant thoughts to the proper girl. "I'm the only one who has your heart now, Becky Powell."

Harrumphing, Becky cuffed the back of Bill's neck. "Cocky, isn't he, Rose?"

Rose had nearly closed the door, but stopped and craned her head through the entryway. "A Confederate soldier's never unsure of himself."

Bill chortled and shouted, "Can I expect to see you tomorrow, Rose?"

Rose blew a kiss to Bill and Becky. "No, my dears. I've an engagement in Columbia. Little Rose and I will take the eight o'clock Wilmington and Manchester train and won't be back for two weeks. When we return, we're to set sail to England. I hope to see you again, but if I don't, these blown kisses will have to do."

Rose closed the door, and Bill realized he'd lost the chance to warn her. He nearly rushed back into General Whiting's headquarters, but decided a *dream* warning now would leave Rose wondering if she'd befriended a lunatic. And no doubt Becky would think the same. The night could turn out cold and lonely if Becky fled back to Duplin Roads.

"Please be careful, Rose," Bill whispered, the words meant for him only. "The Confederacy can't afford to lose you." His mind wandered for a moment. "Like General Jackson."

"What?" Brows knitted over Becky's nose.

"Nothing. Just thinking aloud. About tonight."

"Aren't you the devil?" Becky slipped her hand into the crook of Bill's arm. "Swear I heard you mention Rose and Stonewall Jackson."

"Really? You need an ear trumpet." Bill guided Becky into the Bank of the Cape Fear and up to an open cashier. He'd been wired two hundred graybacks to cover the next three days… until he returned to Kenansville. In the spring of 1861, the cost of a hotel room, meals and extraneous outlays could have been covered by twenty dollars. "Richmond just keeps printing more graybacks to pay for the war." He slid the wad of paper into a money clip and stuffed it into a pants pocket. "If the war doesn't end soon, it'll take a wheelbarrow of graybacks to buy a mug of beer."

Nodding, Becky reflected, "I envy Rose. She's to help the Confederacy in London and Paris over the next year. I wish I could be with her and Little Rose." She sighed. "I wonder if she needs an assistant." She noticed Bill's hangdog mien. "Don't worry. I'm kidding. No Paris and London for me."

"Don't talk like that!" Bill grabbed his chest as if he's been wounded. "Thought I'd taken another shell fragment, this time to the heart."

Becky pecked him on the cheek. "You've a thick chest. The fragment would bounce off."

~ * ~

Beyond the Purcell House window near Bill and Becky's table, the sun hung low in the western sky, casting a ruddy glow on the Cape Fear and the ships moored along the docklands. A teenage waitress lit two table candles that shone, flickering light on Becky's face. The evening breeze blew through the restaurant's windows, turning a ceiling fan's blades.

Becky unbuttoned the top two buttons of her day dress, allowing the cool currents to tickle her neck and a sliver of her chest. "We women let men dictate what we wear. Ridiculous that on a hot day like this we dress like it's winter. My sweat could flood the Cape Fear."

Imagining what he'd see if she unbuttoned more of her dress, Bill ran a finger along his fork's prongs. "The Frogs have it right. Less material, more skin. Bosoms need freedom."

Giggling, Becky said saucily, "Sure you want to eat? Sounds like you'd like us to retire to the bed."

"I'm going to need fuel for what lies ahead." Bill watched the waitress deliver a plate of what looked to be venison to a dandy, probably one of the *Virginia Cavalier's* actors, his evening coat unfastened to reveal a silk vest and a cravat tied as an ascot.

Bill nearly jumped out of his seat when Becky caressed his upper leg. "We better keep your engine stoked," she said impishly.

"Naughty girl." He stroked the top of her hand as she massaged his inner thigh. Their tickling game ceased abruptly when the waitress approached and handed out menus. "Miss, what's the gentleman eating at the next table?"

"That's venison, sir," the waitress said, her voice bubbly. "Shot this morning near Castle Hayne. The blockade's bad for the South, but not quite as dire here, the East Coast destination of blockade runners." She held a jutting finger to her mouth. "A secret... a tiny portion of the foodstuffs bound for the troops miraculously end up in some of our restaurants. I won't say which ones." She grinned roguishly. "Let me recommend venison, field peas, cornbread, sassafras tea and strawberry pie. The strawberries were just picked in Castle Hayne."

"Sounds delicious." Becky poked the toe of a lavender boot between Bill's pants leg and skin. "I'll have the venison. Bill?"

His groin came to life as Becky's boot caressed flesh. "Ah, ooh, eeh... venison for me too." *Lordy, how can I eat now? I'd rather race her up the stairs to the bed.*

Bill's druthers came true. They gobbled down the food and sprinted to his room, an accomplishment in a crinoline skirt, even one with a narrow hoop like Becky's. They barely heard the front-desk clerk screech, "Private Stamford, your bath has been prepared." And only Bill saw a moustached gentleman in a black frockcoat, fawn trousers and small bowtie emerge through the front entrance and scrutinize the young couple racing up the stairs. A look of concern scrawled across the fellow's face, but Bill paid little heed to it. The bathtub and bed beckoned.

At his lodging door, Bill fumbled in his pocket for the skeleton key, finding it nestled behind the wad of graybacks. Once in the lock, the key turned easily, and the door groaned open. Becky moseyed to the tub, ran a hand through the water. "Oooh... that's nice and hot." A feisty smile winged his way. "I've never taken a bath with a man."

"Nor me with a beautiful woman. But that's about to change."

"Your wound, Bill?" She enclosed her arms around him, her fingers softly tapped the bandage.

Sometimes, though not as often as in late May and early June, he'd turn wrong and feel a jab of pain. Often, he'd forget about the shrapnel hole. Sleeping on his back or belly no longer seemed unnatural. Or perching on the end of a chair. The wound hadn't even been an inkling in his mind when he asked for a hot bath. "I'll keep my back above the water."

Becky scoffed, "I've heard enough older girls talk about their wedding night. The two of us in the water… I hardly think you'll be able to protect your back." She shivered. "It creeps me out to think how revolting that dressing will get."

Sighing, he splashed the bathwater in frustration. "You're right. You take a bath. I'll wash you. Soap your skin. Run this washcloth"—he fingered a white one left draped on the tub's edge—"over your back, your belly, your breasts. Give you kisses as I do it."

She cupped his chin, kissed him. "Water's getting cold."

Unfastening her hat, he stroked its scarlet tie-ribbon, then let the flowery thing fall to the bedcovers. He smelled her hair, a lemony fragrance. Ah, *Eau de Cologne Imperiale*, just like… Bill refused to think about another night when another girl let him remove her clothes. Tracing his finger along her lower back, he drew back and admired the blue-striped summer dress and its shamrock print. "Four-leaf clovers always mean good luck."

"For both of us, sweetheart." Her voice was smooth, seductive, yet its tone hinted at a deep sadness, something Bill didn't understand.

He ascribed it to a figment of his imagination as he finger-walked his hand down the bodice of her dress. "In our winter hut, I'd lie on my bunk and remember how you slipped into bed beside me. Lordy, how that memory sustained me during the dark times! I love you, Fr… Becky." He had almost said Franny. Thank God she'd thought he was clearing his throat. *I'm an idiot. No better than a damned Corinthian.*

She took his hand, shifted it to her shoulder. "Time to untie the hooks. Their hidden, but I'm sure you can find them. You're an adventurous man."

Inhaling the scent of *Eau de Cologne Imperiale*, Bill began unfastening the hooks. "So I've been told." The touch of her bosom proved a distraction.

"Slipping, are we? Fingers getting sweaty?" She chuckled an amorous laugh.

Growling, he freed the last hook at her waist and breathed, "Done!" He slipped the dress below her shoulders and freed her arms, then let the bodice slump below her waist. A cotton top, cut off at her midriff, covered her corset. Unable to resist, Bill danced his fingers along the lace fringe, touching skin at her decolletage. Tilting his head, he kissed her skin.

Purring, Becky swung her arms around Bill's upper back, above the wound, and squeezed her breasts against his chest.

Sweet Jesus... she's done this before. Suspicion ran rampant in his mind as he maneuvered the cotton top over her head. *One of her cousin Sharon's friends? While in need of comfort and under-the-cover kisses?* He didn't care. The war had done this to everyone. Why worship stupid conventions when a mini ball or shell fragment could put a soldier in the ground?

Charlie! Lord, forgive me for forgetting about him and the others. I know what he'd say. You and Becky tip the velvet, Billy Boy. Don't worry about me and the boys. We're in God's hands. If he calls us home, we'll take the journey on His celestial road. Bill dropped the corset covering atop her hat. "The bath's going to get cold. Time to pick up the pace."

Again, Becky tittered a skin-tingling laugh. "Cold? The brazier's fine." Below the claw-footed tub, the coals in the brazier still burned red hot.

"Good. I can savor every minute." His eyes settled on her azure-blue corset, a French design meant to drive soldiers mad with passion. The ruffled lace barely covered her breasts, revealing ample cleavage. Her father would keel over blue-faced dead if he saw how she'd clothed herself beneath the summer dress. Bill wondered: Did the middle-aged man truly believe his daughter planned a visit with her cousin? If not, they both would have some explaining to do. Bill caressed the ivory skin between her breasts. He intended to marry the girl if he survived the war. He'd faced shells and bullets... an angry father hardly seemed worth losing sleep over. Anyway, Becky's papa needed to enter the modern age. The starchy times were coming to an end, leveled by the war. "Lordy, Becky girl, you're beautiful."

"Thank you, Bill Stamford." She wiggled her hips. "Oh, I'm having some difficulty with this dress. I do believe I'll need the help of a strong man." She took his hands in hers and pressed them against her hips. "Forward... charge!"

Kissing her neck, he sashayed the dress past her hips and let it pool at her feet. She pushed him away and stepped over the mound of material. Shrugging, she gestured to it.

He gathered the dress in his arms. "Where would you like your knight to put the dress, Miss Powell? On the bed?"

Her eyes flared. "I think not! We'll soon be on that bed. Use the wardrobe."

Gladly her servant, he hung the dress in the armoire and wheeled. She stood beside the tub, her bare arm draped over it, her fingers moving through the bathwater. He feasted on her figure, on so much delightful skin. God, he wanted the wound gone so the two of them could immerse themselves in the water and play. "Now to remove the corset and chemise."

"Please hurry. The water calls and I'm getting cold." She sucked in air, then let it out with a come-hither moan.

Hurry? He unlaced her corset as he sprinkled her face with kisses. Once free, the corset slipped between his body and hers until he snagged it. Soon, it lay on top of everything else on the bed.

"I'm sad. Only this thin bit of material left," he said, fondling the chemise.

"Not quite. You're forgetting my drawers. When you get to those, you've nearly reached the Promised Land." Becky dipped her fingers into the bathwater again and flicked droplets onto Bill's face.

He giggled as if ten again. "I should drop you into the water since you apparently love it."

She raised her hands to her shoulders as if planning to remove her chemise. "I'm going to jump into your arms, but not until you've removed my last two garments. Then you can introduce me to the inside of the tub."

They kissed passionately. After the first few kisses, he moved his lips slowly away from hers, then grazed her chin and her neck with new kisses. He breathed onto her skin and let her scent arouse him. As he skated his fingertips along her shoulders, he felt her hands caress his back, even the dressing, as if saying she loved all of him, including his wound. Instead of a prick of pain in his back, he sensed a rush of pleasure in his loins. Bill slipped Becky's chemise straps down her arms.

Holding his breath as the chemise rumpled at her feet, he fixed his gaze on her breasts. King Solomon was right. They were like fawns, twins of a gazelle. Were all men like him, easily seduced by the swell of a woman's bubbies? He lowered his head, licked her right areola. Her moans tousled his hair.

Dropping to his knees, Bill jerked her drawers down to her high-heeled boots. Arms wrapped around her just below her buttocks, he carried her to the bed and onto the pile of underthings. He straightened her legs and slid the drawers off her boots, then loosened the boot-lacings. Still, he had to tug to get the boots off her feet. Just stockings… all else on that God-designed body was pale ivory skin ready to be massaged by rosemary-scented soap. Off came the stockings, and he kissed her toes, just like he had Franny's feet.

"Oooh… that tickles," she groaned.

Franny, get out of my mind. He might be irritated, but his hands were gentle when he picked Becky up and lowered her into the bathwater. Like a painter, he wanted to stare and remember every wet pore of her breasts, then stare through the water at her fairest flower between her thighs. Except the sun had set and shadows lurked in every nook and cranny in the room.

"Get out of that uniform, Bill Stamford," she ordered. "Then you can do all the soaping and kissing you desire."

He slithered out of his shell jacket, shirt, pants and long johns far faster than it took him to remove Becky's dress and underthings. No wonder women were fainting all the time. They were buried under a mountain of clothing even in the heat of the summertime. The temperature had to be in the seventies even at seven o'clock in the evening.

Naked with a woman for the first time since New Year's Eve, he lit the room's sole oil lamp and lugged a rug across the room to the tub. Stooping, he clasped her chin, his intent a kiss. He hesitated. Lamplight had exiled the darkness into the corners of the room and under the bed, armoire, desk and end tables. The flame burning from the lamp's mantle shone out from its glass shade, revealing her body. Legs drawn up to her chest, Becky moved a soaped washcloth in a slow circle across her breasts. Over and over again. "You like?" she said.

"Like? I could drink in your beauty for the rest of my life." *Unless a Blue-Belly ends it too soon.* Shifting to his knees, Bill took the washcloth from her hands, but not before letting his fingers linger against hers.

She leaned back against the tub's frame. "Have fun. But remember... I love kisses."

As they smooched, he noticed she wanted to drape a hand across his shoulder, but wavered. His wound. She feared water droplets might drip from her fingers and leak into the wound. Instead, she caressed his chest. He looked down, watched the droplets fall from her fingertips and trace rivulets to his belly. Taking the washcloth, Bill tenderly washed Becky's breasts. He paused as an idea manifested itself. His fingers relaxed, and the washcloth sunk to the bottom of the tub—alongside her inner thighs.

"It's between my legs," she said, her eyes inviting him to play the ultimate tickling game.

"Just where I hoped it'd be." Bill nudged his hand between her thighs and reached for the Palmolive soap. The bar slipped from his fingers. She grabbed his bold hand and held it against her downy spring moss.

"Sweet Jesus... I'm all spoony over you," she said in a tight, sultry voice.

Again: *She's done this before.* Who was he to judge? He'd been with Franny, might be with her now if she hadn't skedaddled to Tennessee to take care of her fiancé. If it weren't for the war, both would be in a rigid courtship, every minute supervised. Soldiers were dying, and so were the strict courtship rules. Had Death's scythe claimed this other man Becky had been with sometime over the last few months? Is that why he'd received so few letters? *Stop it! Just make love to her. Enjoy the moment... before you go back to the army.*

Becky bent forward. "Do my back." She stroked his chest as he shifted to reach her back.

He held the soap so that his fingertips would caress her back as he moved his hand in a circular motion. Later, he fished the washcloth from the soapy water and washed and rinsed her back.

"I'm frustrated, sweetheart," he told her. "I want to be in the water with you. Washing each other, kissing."

"You're not fooling me, Bill Stamford. I know what you want. A docking in this bathtub."

"It was a thought."

"It'll happen soon." She eyed the bed, then lifted a leg out of the water and wiggled her toes. "You've ignored my lower extremities. Please remedy immediately, dear man."

"I kissed your toes. What else do you want?"

"It's a good beginning." She swung her leg so it rested on the edge of the tub. "More kisses and then the soap and your fingernails. They felt so good on my back."

Her words engorged his truncheon. He was ready to fish her out and do some tupping, dripping water or not. She noticed, raised an eyebrow, and then maneuvered so her toes could touch it. "I can't stand it, Becky. The bed, please... the bed." He knew he must sound like a frantic boy begging to open his Christmas presents.

"I guess I shouldn't deny you any longer." She returned her leg to the water and rose.

Droplets dripped from her breasts, arms and her belly. "My poor legs will have to wait for another time."

"I'll massage them on the bed." He winked and reached out to lift her out of the tub.

She waved him away. "Get the towel."

Snatching it from a bedpost, Bill draped it over his shoulder and returned to the tub. Becky stood beside it. Perfection. She moved closer, dragging fingernails across his chest. He pressed the towel against her skin, followed the contours of her body, her breasts, ribs, thighs, her legs. Tasting a droplet fresh from her body, he spun her around and kissed her neck, then began toweling her back. The towel dropped to her buttocks, and in response she gyrated, pressing them and the towel against his loins.

"You're a dangerous woman, Becky Powell. And not just for giving me a bad case of loll tongue. I'm starting to think how nice it would be to wake up beside you for the next fifty years."

"No getting serious, Bill Stamford. I do know a few naughty words. It's time for prigging, not rings and preachers."

"Then let's get to prigging." Bill dropped the towel, and as Becky giggled, plopped her on the bed on top of her underthings.

"Not on my chemise and things!" Becky heaved them off the bed. Her drawers landed on one of Bill's feet.

He kicked her drawers against the wardrobe. "Last obstacle removed."

Hopping onto the four-poster bed, Bill mounted her. Her legs wrapped around his hips.

Their docking wasn't what he expected, not like the night with Franny when fireworks exploded inside his head. But Franny was with another man. Maybe the next time, when Becky could touch a scar and not a dressing over a wound. Then their prigging would leave both spent, their passion exhausted. He should apologize. Instead, he chose silence.

They'd both been reluctant to uncap their emotions, their passions, especially Becky. She'd been afraid her nails would rip off the dressing and dig into his wound. There would be other nights when he and Becky could let their passions melt the bed... if the Good Lord let him survive the war.

They lay side by side, his breath stroking the skin beneath her lower lip, hers rustling his whiskers. Her hand draped his hip, her fingers gliding to his belly, tracing circles around his belly button. She kissed him, whispered, "I love you."

He knew he wouldn't find a better time. Yes, she'd told him not to be serious, but that was earlier when she'd been fervent for his truncheon.

Bill caressed her cheek. "I don't have a ring yet. So maybe I shouldn't ask, but I'm going to anyway. I want to spend the rest of my life with you. In your arms. I should be on my knees, but lying beside you is much better. Please be my wife."

"Oh God, Bill!" Grief flickered in her eyes, powerful in the lamplight, the same look he'd barely detected earlier in the evening. "You've ruined the best moment of my life. Any other time but this, I'd gladly be your wife. But not now, not when the world's collapsing around us."

He shivered, as if their heated passion had never occurred, as if the fireplace flames produced ice, not heat. The bathtub, the bed, their clothes puddled on the floor, the armoire containing her dress... all looked cold and ugly.

You're a fool, Bill. She just gave you the mitten. He rose to a sitting position and sat cross-legged. "But you just said you loved me."

"I do. But it doesn't mean I'll marry you... not while the war's raging."

"Then there's a chance? After the war?" He could feel the grimace distorting his facial features. "When you know I won't be in a box beneath a gravestone etched with Lee's flag?"

"That's not what I mean." She looked hurt. "I want away from this madness. If you weren't in the army, I'd ask you to run away to Europe with me. But I won't ask you to desert. You'd come to hate me."

"You're going to Europe?" He figured he looked just as hurt as she did.

"I've spoken to my father." She rose to a sitting position directly opposite him and sprawled a leg across his lap. "He's willing to pay for the tour and even study at a university. I think he wants me away from you. You'll never be good enough for his daughter."

"He's the one who told me I had to join the army to court you." Bill growled under his breath. "I thought he liked me." A disquieting thought snoozing in his mind wormed its way to consciousness: The chap walking through the hotel's front door knew Becky and her father. *He'd only seen her back. No way had he known the girl with me was Becky.* Bill dismissed the thought.

Becky shook her head. "He did, until he realized the courtship could get serious. Now if you'd been the son of a railroad baron ..."

"I don't want to lose you." He rubbed her leg, barely touching the skin.

Her toes tickled his belly. "I expect you'll be married when I return, but if you're not, I intend to be a reckless woman and chase after you." She leaned forward and kissed him lightly on the lips.

"Yet you continue to kiss me?"

"Yes, and I fear you don't understand me at all." Again, she kissed him. "I hate this war. It's destroying everything. We're not going to win. But we'll continue fighting until all that's left are smoking ruins and long lines of hearses."

She'd spoken aloud his fears; her words were not all that different from what Franny had said after their lovemaking. The South's women were turning against the war. Well, not all of them. Some remained firebrands, like Rose, Belle Boyd and Antonia Ford. Poor Antonia was still a prisoner at the Old Capitol Prison, caught spying. "I understand. I'm disappointed. When do you leave? Will I see you again?" Bill wanted to cry.

"I don't know. When Rose and Little Rose leave for England. I want to go with them. Maybe convince Rose to let me be her assistant. That way I can meet some interesting people." She scooted closer, pressed her breasts against his chest. Pinching his cheek, she retreated. "When they return, I'll stay. Do my studies, maybe get stage training or try some writing at the feet of Caroline Norton and Margaret Oliphant."

Two bleak words burrowed out of Bill's mind. Rose's aureola. And a terrifying thought took flight: what if Becky died alongside the spy? A halo hadn't flared around Becky, a good sign. Maybe. Others—like Kenny—died without aureola manifestations. That's what made Bill's curse so exasperating, so inexplicable. Sometimes he just wanted to hate God.

Bill could try to explain the aureolas, ask her not to sail with Rose and Little Rose. He wasn't naive. She'd think the war had mangled his brains. No one would understand the aureolas, not even a girl who'd shared a night with him. So instead of a warning, he promised to pray for Becky's safekeeping every night. "I'll be worrying about you the whole time you're there," he told her.

"And you'll never be far from my thoughts, Bill. You're the one who will soon return to the Army of Northern Virginia."

He nodded, acknowledging that his recuperating time at home was growing short. No more thoughts of aureolas for the moment, he decided. With his mood dark and sardonic, he nettled her. "How are you going to survive over there without your servants?"

Her face pinched into an annoyed scowl. "Everyone will have to get used to a life without our servants. Lincoln's Emancipation Proclamation has made sure of that." She tapped his kneecap. "Lincoln has promised them freedom, and I'm promising myself freedom. Father's blind. I've been seeing a difference in Andalea since before Fredericksburg. She knows our military victories are pyrrhic. We grew up together. I taught her to read. Now she won't look at me, looks over my head when she speaks. All the darkies scent freedom in the air. Since New Bern."

For an insane moment, Bill wondered if he should mention Wilson and Malinda. He'd just asked Becky to marry him, and although she'd turned him down, he still trusted her. "Papa wants to free Wilson and Malinda. Not sure if it will happen. You already know Wilson's been seized to repair track, and even if Papa gets him back, he's afraid a mob might hurt Momma, Mark and Laura and burn down the print shop. Hell, Papa's not even sure how he'd get them to Yankee lines in New Bern."

Outside, the gas streetlights were lit up, their bright globes visible through the window. The window was ajar, allowing the breeze to keep the room cool. That breeze was needed. Bill was sweaty from their lovemaking. He could see beads of perspiration on Becky's breasts and belly.

"I'm getting cold and it's too late to take a train back to Duplin Roads," she said, as if she'd read his mind. "We're stuck with each other. We can snuggle under the covers if you want. If not, I'll understand."

Thirty-one

A Yankee Cavalry Raid

Bill lay in his childhood bed on a warm night in early July. Outside, a light breeze tousled the branches of an ash tree and wafted through an open window into his room. He rested on his back, right arm under a feather pillow that cushioned his head. Always, he felt safe inside this room, surrounded by the toys and games of his boyhood. No nightmares here, just dreams of leaping into the air and flying like the birds. One had just awakened him; he and Franny flying over Kenansville, holding hands.

Sadness washed over him. He'd lost Franny to another man; truly, had she ever been his sweetheart? A brutal truth revealed... Bill was the other man, sleeping with the fiancé of a Tennessee captain. And when this officer became deathly sick, Franny rushed to his side. He'd heard nothing from her, not even one letter, so he assumed Franny had married her captain. At least he had Becky, the Duplin girl he'd met and kissed just before he joined General Lee's army.

Except Becky too had deserted him, rejecting marriage for the whirlwind life of an American expat, hobnobbing with European aristocrats, actors and authors. She intended to flee a Dixie civilization headed towards ruin. And it had become unbearably worse for her since that night they spent in the Purcell House. Her brother Howard lay in an anonymous grave somewhere in the Shenandoah Valley, lost to a sniper's rifle.

No hope now of Bill saying goodbye to her before the blockade runner made the dash past the Union ships blockading Wilmington. He'd just gotten a note from Becky's father: "You are forbidden to call on my daughter." Terrifyingly, Louis Powell had learned of their dalliance in Wilmington, perhaps from that chap in the Purcell House who'd given Bill that look of concern. Could he have been an associate of Becky's father at the Wilmington and Weldon? Then again, her papa could have learned of the dalliance from Becky's cousin, Sharon. Bill didn't think his life could get anymore nightmarish, even for someone cursed with aureola visions. Howard dead, Becky sailing out of Bill's life, and Franny married to another.

Perhaps two more hours until first light, Bill estimated. *Get those two women out of your head,* he thought. As Tennyson wrote, 'Tis better to have loved and lost than never to have loved at all.'

Yet another woman bedeviled his mind... Rose, his newest aureola soul. He could have tried to save her from her fate, but hesitated. Again, ruled by his fears. He'd tried to save another aureola soul, his friend Charlie. Bill succeeded, but God had exacted a terrible cost—General Jackson's life, or so Bill believed. The Lord allowed Bill to change one man's fate in exchange for another soul. *You've made plain to me one of your Godly Truths, Lord. How can I try to save Rose's life when it might mean Becky's? She intends to be on that blockade runner with Rose.* His mind should be racing like one of the prewar passenger locomotives, but Bill sensed those thoughts gently drifting away into unconsciousness. He yawned as a wisp of breeze brushed his forehead. "Sleep… sleep… sleep," he whispered as he felt the willowy threads of slumber soothe his mind.

"Wake up, Bill! Wake up!" His papa's voice, agitated. Clarence clenched Bill's shoulder.

Still on his back, proof his wound was responding to his momma's ministrations, Bill spit out a loose feather perched partway on his lower lip and mouth.

Beyond the window, flames arched into a rose-tinted sky. The smell of ash permeated the air inside the room. He coughed, shook his head, struggled to rout the cobwebs in his brain. "Papa? What the hell?"

"Get up!" His papa wrenched the quilt off Bill's body. "Yanks are burning the sword factory."

Bill shuddered as if the house had been struck by lightning. *Sweet Lord! The war's finally come to Kenansville!* He rose stiffly from the bed. The skin around the healing wound barely protested.

"Guess this is the way the New Bern Yanks decided to celebrate their Independence Day." Clarence let out a pleased chortle. "Well, I know what will headline the *Gazette's* front page."

Clad in his long johns, Bill tiptoed to a washbasin and splashed water on his face. "How the hell did I sleep through this?" He headed for the armoire. "Hear any firing?"

"Wilson said he thought he heard musketry." Clarence handed his son a towel.

"Wilson?" Bill patted his face with the towel. "Wilson's back?"

"Got back a few hours before the Yanks showed up. Looks like my friendship means something to Owen Kenan. Wilson showed up at the front door with a pass to Kenansville signed by Governor Vance." Clarence grinned. "At least we have some good news."

"Malinda must be pleased as Punch." Bill stepped to the armoire and opened the double doors. "How close did Wilson get to the factory?"

"When he realized Yanks were about, he scarpered away. Expect our Homeguards let loose a volley and hightailed for Teachey. The factory's a good two miles off, probably the reason we didn't hear anything." Clarence slapped his son's hand away from the butternut soldier's pants hanging in the armoire. "Lordy, Bill, don't wear your uniform. They'll shoot you dead."

Bill let his arm drop to his side. He could wear civilian garb. But the Union cavalry could shoot him as a spy. Wear his uniform… get shot or captured. Wear civilian clothing… get shot by a firing squad if the Blue-Bellies become suspicious of a young man who should be in Lee's army. He slipped on civilian pants and a shirt. "The Blue-Bellies won't stay long, Papa. Our troops are probably on the march from Magnolia. They'll be retreating back to New Bern."

Clarence edged to the window, eyed the flames out on the edge of town beyond Owen Kenan's mansion. "I'm going to tuck you away in the storm shelter by the shed. Conceal you under debris, tree limbs, lumber, even rusted gardening tools. If the Yanks come further into town, I don't want them finding you. Hopefully, they'll see all that rubble and be too lazy to move any of it. The mayor wants to surrender the town, so I'm going to go with him and the town council out to the Yank camp."

Bill joined his father at the window, studied the smoke column with distaste. "Sorry, Papa. I'm not going to hide out in the shelter like a coward. I think it's best to be out in the open. I'm going with you, Mayor Whitehead and the councilmen."

Astonished, hands on hips, Clarence backed away from Bill. "That's madness."

Bill drew the curtains. "I've a plan. Much better than burying myself in a hidey-hole under rubbish. I'll act like an imbecile with a mental age of a four year old. I can do it, Papa. I'll take one of Laura's old ragdolls, act like I'm possessed." Bill smothered a sour laugh. That wasn't far from the truth. If his papa knew Bill still saw aureolas, he'd definitely think Bill lacked a return ticket to sanity.

"The storm shelter's safer." With most of the light in the room gone, thanks to the drawn curtains, Clarence's face revealed nothing.

"Trust me, Papa. I can make this work. Truly. Right out in the open." Bill shrieked a ghastly laugh, like a young girl getting murdered. "See what I mean?" He repeated the crazy-man cackle.

Bill's momma, Mark and Laura barged into the room, all wearing their nightwear. "What in the world?" Icie Belle exclaimed, her feet bare.

Clarence sighed like an eighty-year-old man, not someone in his forties. "Your son's trying to convince me to let him go along to visit the Yankees."

"Heaven's no!" Icie Belle wagged her finger at her oldest son. "I didn't nurse you back to health to see you captured by Yankees. I want you in the storm shelter."

Bill hugged his momma. "I'll be fine. I survived a shell fragment an inch further up my back would have killed me." He caressed her cheek. "This will be easy. I've been bedeviling you and Papa all my life. Now I'm going to bedevil some Blue-Bellies."

Clarence and Icie Belle sat on the unmade bed. Mark leaned against the dresser. Laura propped her hip against her momma's legs. "Don't think he's going to listen to reason, dear," Clarence said, scowling. "He's headstrong. We're just going to have to pray a lot."

Mark jumped up and down to get his parents' attention. "I'll sit on him." A smirk ballooned across the boy's face.

"My wound will start bleeding and then you'll feel guilty." Bill tweaked his kid brother's overly large nose.

Rolling his eyes, Mark sighed in disgust. "Okay, I won't sit on you." The boy dug into his right pocket and showed Bill a penny. "You're going to need luck. Here's my good luck penny. It'll keep you safe." Mark handed the coin to Bill.

Flipping it in his hand, Bill let the coin come to rest in his palm, then rubbed his thumb across its face. "Oh, the Yank Cavalry will love seeing this... a U.S. 1859 Indian Head penny." He slapped it down on the dressertop next to the clipper ship. "Now everybody out. I'll be downstairs as soon as I finish dressing."

Alone once more, he buried his uniform in the clothes chest at the foot of the bed, under winter clothes and older toys he hadn't used since he was a toddler. Soon dressed in a frumpy sack suit, his tie badly tied, vest misbuttoned, a tattered straw hat on his head, Bill headed downstairs to the dining room where three strips of crisp bacon, buttered cornbread and a fruit drink awaited him.

Once seated at the table, Bill looked past the stairs to the French doors leading to the garden. Seated on the bench overlooking the roses, peonies and daylilies, Wilson and Malinda cuddled and kissed like teenagers. Bill laughed. "When do you think they'll notice I've come downstairs?"

Icie Belle scooped up a strip of bacon from her son's plate and ate it. "I can't bring myself to disturb them. Malinda didn't think she'd ever see Wilson again. Thought the railroad and the army would work him to death."

"Both have had those *got-caught-raiding-the-cookie-jar* smiles since Wilson got back." Clarence turned his gaze to Bill. "Especially since he told her about the Yank Cavalry north of Owen's place. Of course, she already knew… hard to miss all that smoke."

Swiveling in her chair, Icie Belle patted her husband's leg. "Freedom's in the air, along with the smoke, eh?"

Still standing, Clarence leaned down and kissed the top of his wife's head. "I should write a letter to the Yankee commander at New Bern and thank him for the raid. I just need to turn my back. Wilson and Malinda will be gone tonight."

"Probably every slave in Kenansville." Bill tried the buttered cornbread and grinned as it melted in his mouth. "Happening all over the South, I hear. Tagging along with the Emancipator's armies." Grimacing, he tapped his fingers on the table. "Think one of them will betray me?"

"Not Malinda or Wilson." Icie Belle clenched her fists as she stared out the French doors.

"Others will, though," Clarence said crankily. "A way to butter up to the Yank cavalrymen. Turn in the wounded Confederate soldier." He sighed. "We'll be safe until nightfall. That's when the darkies will flee to the Yankee camp."

Bill stabbed his fork into what remained of the cornbread. "If the Yanks discover my ruse, they'll be plenty annoyed."

His papa squeezed Bill's shoulder. "That's why we have to sneak you out of town tonight. I'm sure one of the farmers between here and Duplin Roads will take you in. Probably shouldn't use the buggy. Too big; might be seen by a Yankee picket."

"If nothing else, I'll walk." Bill rolled his eyes. "I've walked all over Virginia. Duplin County won't be a problem. Moon comes up after midnight, so I'll be able to see, if it's a clear sky. If no moon, I'll march between the shadows." He drained the fruit drink with several long gulps.

Icie Belle ran her fingers along three days of growth on Bill's cheek and chin. "You need a shave."

"No, that's the way I want him. Too bad he doesn't have a real beard. Proper spittle needs a proper beard." Clarence turned to Mark. "Get me the shears. Your brother's hair's too neat. I'm going to give him a wackadoodle look."

Laura giggled and jumped up from her chair. "No. No! Let me!" Still tittering, she danced over to a china dresser and produced scissors from a top drawer.

Bill shifted to a chair away from everyone. His papa went to work, chopping up his immaculate coiffure. "Be prepared, Bill. I'm going to treat you like you're Kenansville's greatest embarrassment."

"Don't overdo it, Papa." Bill distastefully eyed the hair on the floor. "Better to show some love to your oddball son. Remember, you chose to look after him, not put him in an insane asylum."

Bill and Laura walked upstairs together, she to give him one of her tattered ragdolls, he to retrieve Mark's lucky penny. While his papa hitched Peanut to the buggy, Bill headed to the garden. "Glad you're back," he told Wilson, who'd aged a decade since being seized by the government for the Wilmington and Weldon. Bill steered his arm toward the column of smoke. "Expect I might not see you two again once it gets dark." He winked.

Wilson looked shyly at his tattered boots. Malinda burst into tears and hugged Bill fiercely, then leaped back. "Oh, your back, sir. I hope I ain't hurt it."

"No, Malinda. It's about healed up. Stitches out. Everything's fine." He held his arm up to his face and wiped away tears. "Stay safe you two." Bill turned and proceeded to the stables.

"When the war's over, look us up in Cleveland," Wilson said, his voice choking. "That's where we be goin'. Lots of freedmen up there."

~ * ~

Bill and his father met Mayor Whitehead and the five councilmen at the steepled town hall, a grand building for a town of six hundred and fifty people. Two hitched buggies were parked along the curb. The mayor and council waited alongside the buggies, beneath a morning sky filled with scattered clouds and the menacing smoke rising from the sword factory a mile west of the Kenan mansion.

Seeing Bill flummoxed Whitehead. Not just his presence but how he dressed—his scruffy look, vest and shirt covered with breakfast stains. "Didn't expect to see you. Got a death wish?" The mayor shook his head in disbelief. "You look terrible, Bill."

Nodding, Bill laughed. "Like my simpleton disguise, Mayor? For today, I'm the boy who never grew up, taken everywhere by his papa."

"You look like you hacked your own hair in the middle of the night." Whitehead rested a callused hand on Clarence's buggy. "Not sure the Yankee commander will buy it." The mayor smiled in surrender. "Ever done any actin'?"

"No, but it's worth the risk, Mayor." Bill gazed toward the billowing smoke, filled with embers. "I want to see the camp, look at their numbers, what our reinforcements from Magnolia will face."

Whitehead whistled. "Son, that's going to take a superb job of actin'. Pull it off, and I'll recommend you to Wilmington's Opera House managers."

Clarence leaned an elbow on the front seat's side handle. "No one but me do any talking when it comes to Bill. Less chance of a slipup. Bill will do his part splendidly."

A councilman sniggered. "Just like he and the Duplin Roads girl fooled her father? Quite the scandal."

Bill groaned, then shrugged. "Thought she loved me. Live and learn. Won't be a repeat performance, at least not with her." Everyone laughed, relieving the tension.

On a day that once meant afternoon church picnics and evening fireworks, the three buggies wheeled down Duplin Street and onto the Warsaw Road. At the Kenan house, the dignitaries passed slashed telegraph wires and wrecked telegraph poles strewn along the road.

Dozens of slaves—gardeners, stablers, maids, cooks, sculleries—congregated in the Kenan front yard, awestruck balloon eyes fixed on the smoking ruins. Some no doubt entertained subversive thoughts: Come nightfall, should they run away to the protection of the Yank cavalrymen? Owen Kenan lodged in Richmond near the Confederate Congress. His wife Sarah, their twenty-year-old daughter Annie, and Owen's sister Mary and husband Chauncey Graham were not outside, but probably lurking at windows peeking at the Yanks. The houses of the planter class could burn just as hot as a sword factory. If the Yanks needed provocation... Owen's sons served as officers in the Army of Northern Virginia.

Eyeing the Kenan slaves, Whitehead scowled. "Come darkness they'll be begging the Yanks to take them to New Bern."

"Lincoln can have them," Councilman Theodore Farrior growled.

Maybe half a mile beyond the Kenan house, Yankee pickets stopped the buggies. Whitehead bowed from his seat. "I'm the Kenansville mayor. The rest here are town councilmen and the newspaper editor."

Bill held out Laura's ragdoll. "Kiss Missy, blue fellow." Cackling, he dribbled spittle.

Looking skyward, Clarence rolled his eyes. "He's my wackadoodle. A tree stump's smarter than that boy."

"Jumpin' off tree stumps good nanty narkin'." Bill giggled like a toothless harridan. Whitehead had to calm his buggy's horse.

The clean-shaven sergeant barked, "Keep your imbecile under control!"

"He'll behave himself," Clarence promised, fixing dispirited eyes on Bill. "Right, son?"

Lips twitching, Bill saluted carelessly in the Yankee manner. "Aye, sir!"

Whitehead offered the sergeant a grim smile. "We're here to surrender Kenansville, Sergeant. Please escort us to your commander."

The sergeant took off his black cavalry hat and waved it back toward the smoldering ruins. "His name's Major Jacobs, Rebs. Follow me."

The sergeant and his men wheeled their mounts and trotted toward the factory ruins. "Giddyup," the mayor urged his horse, and the buggy jerked to life. Clarence, Bill and the council trailed in their buggies.

Black smoke hung over the remains of the factory's four buildings. Explosions shook the ground, and Bill even felt them aboard his papa's buggy. Maybe gunpowder or fuel for the machinery inside the buildings, Bill theorized. A plume drifted toward the downtown. Debris—burnt wood bits and red-colored particles of paper floated in the air as if tossed by a parade crowd run amok. Ash and embers settled slowly around the buggies as they wheeled toward the skeletal ruins. He tasted the ash and clamped his mouth shut, making sure the queasiness in his belly stayed there.

As his papa's buggy drew close to the cavalry camp, Bill resumed kissing the ragdoll, pouring spit over its button eyes. Doll lofted up to eyelevel, Bill spied Major Jacobs and his staff maybe a hundred yards from the ruins. Near a tree line, a work party of runaway slaves toting axes and sledgehammers loitered, waiting for the heat of the fires to die down so they could wreck machinery.

Bill nibbled on the ragdoll's grubby shoulder as he kept his eyes on the major and began to make out his facial features... a coarsely clipped mustache, a much better trimmed goatee, and a mole separating his right eyebrow into two fragments. An aide uncapped a canteen and poured water into Jacobs's cupped hands. The major splashed the water on his face and wiped away the soot with the back of his hand. Taking off his wide-brimmed hat with a flourish, he let a fleeting breeze stir his hair, neatly parted in the middle. The major cut a fine figure, a future Yankee politician if he lived through the war.

Major Jacobs and his staff spun toward the sound of the approaching buggies, their iron-shod wheels whacking the granite setts. As if slogging through snow, the major tramped through the ash toward the buggies. He brushed ash from both shoulders as he eyeballed the politicians. "What can I do for you gentlemen on this glorious day, our Union's eighty-seventh birthday?"

Everyone stepped down from the buggies, even Bill, who tumbled to his knees. The ragdoll squirted from his hand as he sprawled and tried to scramble to his ungainly feet. Gritting his teeth, Clarence stooped and brusquely dragged Bill to his feet. "My simpleton son. I saw no harm in bringing him along. He loves his toy soldiers and wanted to see real Yankees."

A hand's shadow draped Bill's face. "Here, let me brush some of that dirt and ash from your shirt and pants." The major's voice… kind and gentle, not what Bill expected. "I've a brother like you. His name's Stevie. His momma loves him dearly."

"I do too," Bill stammered, slobbering on his boots. "I mean my momma. Not Stevie. I might love him if I met him."

The major picked up the ragdoll, dusted it off and handed it to Bill. Frowning, the officer reached into a pocket and produced a handkerchief, which he used to wipe spittle from Bill's chin. "I can tell you're a fine boy."

Bill jiggled his finger at the ragdoll. "Missy! Missy, you bad girl. Tripped me, bad girl." He pinched the ragdoll's face. "Bad, bad girl."

Clarence spread his hands wide in capitulation. "I try to give him a good life, Major. He helps me at the newspaper office. I taught him to set some type, his name."

Whitehead strode forward and bowed as if the major were King Leopold of Belgium. "The man with the imbecile… he's the town's newspaper editor, Clarence Stamford. I'm the mayor, Wiley Whitehead. The others are on the council. We're here to surrender Kenansville. We promise you no opposition, and hope you'll burn no more than the sword factory."

"We only destroy military targets, Mayor," Jacobs said dryly. "As long as no one shoots at us, no families will be driven from their homes, no structures burned."

Bill maintained his simpleton mien, letting new spittle drool down his chin. *Lordy, I actually like the major. Has a loving heart for stunted souls. And gets no joy from burning people's homes.*

A hundred yards beyond the buggies, six prisoners of the Seventh North Carolina Cavalry crouched on the ground, some looking dismally at the Kenansville folks, others staring at the ruins. A few days ago, Bill had visited the Seventh's camp just outside Kenansville and chatted with some of the cavalrymen. He recognized one of the prisoners. Their eyes locked, a glimmer of a smile ghosted across the POW's face, then the faint smile vanished as he turned and stared at the burnt buildings. Bill knew his fellow Confederate wouldn't give him away.

Jerking on his father's sleeve, Bill yapped, "Daddy! Lookee! Greybacks! They don't look happy, Daddy."

Jacobs and his staff laughed heartily. "Not a bit happy, not since we sneaked in during the darkness. Do you like to watch rabbits hopping?" Bill nodded eagerly, pressed the doll against his chest and clapped. The major continued, "Well, the Greybacks scattered like scared rabbits. They hopped right out of here. Left behind most of their horses, their weapons and these six slowpokes. Not a good Fourth of July for the Confederate States of America."

Bill agreed, but thought he had the means to shorten the Blue-Bellies' sojourn in Kenansville. He estimated the Union horse soldiers as a force about the size of a battalion. The pennants and flags barely flapping in the wind identified them as cavalrymen with the Third New York Cavalry. Company F of the Seventh North Carolina Cavalry numbered about eighty men. Jacobs' force of about four hundred Blue-Bellies outnumbered them nearly five-to-one. The commander at Magnolia needed to know those numbers as soon as possible. If the Confederate commander sent an undersized force, Jacobs would bloody their nose yet again.

Clarence propped an elbow on a buggy wheel. "Have you heard anything about Pennsylvania? Telegraph lines are down, so I've heard nothing fresh."

The question drew a wicked little grin from the major. "No news, eh? Somebody cut the telegraph wires? I wonder who? Must be a hard-case fellow who done it. Someone like me." Again, Jacobs grinned. "Here's a flash. Been a battle at a crossroads town. Gettysburg. Don't know much more, except Lee's retreating and our boys hold the high ground." Jacobs swung his gaze to the factory, still burning but not as intensely as earlier in the morning. "So you want to surrender? I accept, and declare martial law. No one out after dark. What is it you folks like so much? Oh yes, mint juleps. So stay in your game rooms, play checkers and drink those mint juleps. And when you wake up tomorrow, we'll be gone."

The Town Fathers didn't stick around, but headed back to the downtown, glad the Blue-Bellies would be gone by the next day. As the buggy clanged along the road, Clarence reined Peanut into an easy-going trot, then eyeballed Bill. "Well, you pulled it off."

"Not really, Papa. I'm sure forces are on the way to intercept Jacob's men. I'm going to ride to the Magnolia garrison tonight and tell them what I know about Jacob's people. Make sure the reinforcements don't charge into a trap." Bill leaned partway out of the buggy and looked back at the smoky ruins. "As soon as the sun goes down, white folks won't venture out and risk a bullet to the head. Darkies... they'll run to the Blue-Belly campfires. Some will tattle on me, so I'll need to be heading away from Kenansville anyway."

"I know, but I'm still going to worry about you."

"Going to keep off the roads, bushwhack through the countryside."

"Moon's going to be nearly full tonight."

"Pray that it's cloudy."

Clarence's mouth pinched into a scowl. "If you're caught, Major Jacobs will be roiling mad over your deception."

"Then I'd better not get caught." Bill stretched his legs out on the floorboard as the house came into sight.

Thirty-two

A Moonlit Ride

Bill's momma hugged his father as soon as they ambled through the front doorway. Worry quivered her voice as she relayed, "Malinda and Wilson are gone. Didn't even wait for darkness."

"You knew they'd leave." Clarence mussed Icie Belle's hair.

"But not this early. It's not dark." She nodded in the direction of the window, the field across the road glowing in the late afternoon sun. "A son-of-a-bitch could take a shot at them."

Bill gulped. He'd never heard his momma use profanity. "Wilson and Malinda made their decision, Momma. They think they can get to the Blue-Belly camp safely, cut through woods, shy away from houses. With leaves thick on the trees, a farmer out in his field won't see a thing."

Clarence kissed Icie Belle, then drew back. "It's not like the old days. They won't be hunting runaways with dogs, not with the Yank Cavalry less than two miles away and the town under martial law. Wilson and Malinda will soon taste freedom in New Bern."

"More slaves are following the Blue-Belly armies." Bill plopped down on the entrance-hall loveseat. "Their bands play a new song: 'The Battle Hymn of the Republic.' I'd hear their voices floating across the Rappahannock. They thought they were bedeviling the boys."

"Thank God Wilson took the decision away from me." Clarence settled beside Bill, his shoulders slumped, face ragged-tired. "I know it sounds cowardly, but I truly worried a mob might burn down the *Gazette* building, even torch the house."

"Wars bring out the worst in people," Bill muttered, rubbing against the backrest to dispatch an irritating itch. The more things head south, the more the fanatics stop seeing reason. Even with slaves rebuilding tracks, toiling in factories and mines, digging entrenchments, we're still drowning in inflation. Ever think God's using Yankee armies to punish us?"

Clarence twirled his right index finger at Mark and Laura. "Anything you hear tonight doesn't travel beyond this house, understand? Ill-thought words can get people killed."

Mark and Laura's eyes ballooned with fright. "We understand, Papa," Laura said.

"People get riled up easy nowadays," their momma said tightly. "People do bad things they'd never do in peacetime, like burn out their neighbors."

"A word misspoke could get Papa shot," Bill told his brother and sister, his words hard as the staircase railing.

"We'll be careful," Mark promised.

Clarence stood, stretched his tired bones, and then headed for the front door. "Need to groom Peanut. Hope the Yanks don't consider a walk from the house to the stables breaking the curfew." He laughed sourly.

Rising, Bill took a step toward the staircase. "Now that Wilson's gone, you should hire an old codger to help out in the stables and the gardens."

"With inflation gone amuck, I'll have to pay with free meals and a place to sleep." Clarence grinned. "Not a bad idea, actually. I'll put an ad in the *Gazette* and see who bites." Bill's papa shut the door behind him. His steps could be heard as he made his way along the cobbles to the stables.

Bill took two steps up the stairs, stopped and looked back. "Time to change into my Lexington-Concord duds for tonight's Paul Revere ride." He stomped up the stairs.

At the entryway, his mother's vexed voice rose, "Paul Revere ride? What nonsense is this?"

His papa couldn't calm his mother, not with him in the stables getting Peanut ready for the midnight ride. Bill would have to do it. "Come upstairs, Momma. I'll explain as I change."

Bill ushered his momma into his room. He nearly shut the door, but noticed Mark and Laura dawdling on the top step. Squinting his eyes, he glared at them.

"Please don't say curiosity killed the cat," Mark challenged.

"No way," Laura snorted, then proclaimed, "I like Indy. He's a nosy kitty, but not daft."

A smile replaced Bill's scowl. "Come on in. You'll be listening through the keyhole anyway." He waved them in.

Icie Belle gestured to Laura to sit beside her on the room's lone couch, then eyed Bill. "First you act like you're off your head, and now you're sprouting nonsense about Paul Revere and some sort of nighttime ride."

"Momma, I got to warn the garrison in Magnolia. Don't want them walking into a trap. The Yanks got a sizable force here. With telegraph lines down, I suspect the Magnolia commander's in the dark about troop numbers. The Seventh got routed badly, not sure if he's getting accurate reports from them. I have to do this, Momma." He slipped out of his slobber-stained vest and shirt and tossed them onto the bed.

"I didn't do all this nursing to see you shot for some hare-brained scheme of yours. Let the damned Seventh"—she cussed again—"give him the bad news."

He rolled his eyes. "Momma, I'm going to have to wash your mouth out with soap." Sidling to the armoire, he donned a blue buttoned-up farmer's shirt with a banded collar. Dark blue would blend with the night. "My plan's to take a roundabout route, stay well away from the Yank camp. There won't be a Blue-Belly cavalryman within a mile."

"You be careful with your wound," Icie Bell warned, her mouth pursed. "Peanut's going to give you a jarring ride, not at all like a buggy."

"Stitches are out, Momma. Nothing's going to happen." Leaving the sack suit hanging in the armoire, Bill chose black cotton Duckins pants and a brown four-pocket leather vest. He fit a straw hat atop his badly cropped hair, ran his fingertips along the wide brim that would prevent severe moonburn. He groaned at his pun, thankfully left unsaid.

"Why are you groaning, big brother?" Mark scratched his lower lip and chin.

"I had a crazy thought... why cowboys wear hats at night."

"And?" Laura said.

"To keep moonbeams from burning their foreheads," Mark postulated.

"Good guess," Bill added, strapping on his holstered 1851 cap-and-ball revolver.

"Come on, kids. We've harried Bill enough." Icie Belle, Mark and Laura rose from the couch and beelined for the doorway.

"Keep it open, Momma. I won't be long." He sat on the edge of the bed and cleaned his boots.

"We'll be in the game room." Ice Belle herded Mark and Laura toward the stairs.

"Don't worry, Momma. Nothing's going to happen," Bill shouted. Unlike his aureola curse, he thought grimly as he listened to their footsteps descending the stairs. Rose Greenhow was probably somewhere in the Atlantic, maybe going down with the blockade runner. And possibly Becky and Little Rose as well. *Lord, if you're not going to let me understand, take this curse away from me.* Bill grabbed his Hawken hunting rifle from where he'd stored it in a corner of the armoire and returned downstairs.

Stopping in the downstairs hallway, he squinted at the man-height mirror and admired his outfit. He'd look fine for a cattle drive out West, except he lacked chaps. The outfit meshed perfectly for the ten-mile, late-night ride to Magnolia astride Peanut. An hour buggy trip during daylight, the moonlit trip would take at least twice as long, especially since he planned a roundabout route with bushwhacking across wild landscape and farmland. Bill intended a gentle pace; he didn't want Peanut coming up lame.

Laura and Mark didn't look up from the game table when Bill breezed into the room. He joined them, playing checkers for several hours, then challenged his papa to a chess match. Later, Bill wolfed down a meal of salt pork, cornbread... and beans from the kitchen garden, and a Carolina Red June picked fresh from the apple orchard.

Past midnight, the cobbles lit by lantern light, Bill and his papa made their way to the stables. Peanut had been saddled and looked ready for the ride. The horse nickered as Bill approached. "Tired of pulling the buggy, Peanut? Ready to do some real riding?"

"Bill, your momma's worried sick." Clarence scratched Peanut about the neck. "Please be extra, extra careful."

Bill let his palm rest on his father's hand. "Papa, you know how some soldiers know when their time's up? I don't have that feeling." Taking a long breath, Bill climbed into the saddle. "Remember when I was a kid, and I told you about the halo after Jenny died?" Clarence nodded, a puzzled look jumbling his facial features. "I've been having them again, including Charlie. But Charlie's alive. I changed his fate, although things didn't go perfect, didn't bang up to the elephant. I saved Charlie from a mini ball, but I think it set up a course of events that led to General Jackson's death." Bill shrugged. "I guess what I'm trying to say... it's not my fate to get wounded, captured or die tonight. I think I'd feel it in my bones. I don't need a halo to know when Death becomes my companion."

Armed with the pistol and rifle, Bill rode out, a three-quarter moon hovering in a sky filled with scattered clouds. A humid breeze failed to stem sweat dribbling down his forehead and back. Moonbeams provided sufficient illumination to see the terrain ahead, but they'd also make him and Peanut visible to Blue-Bellies riding picket duty... on alert for a nighttime attack by the garrison at Magnolia. So he reined Peanut south through Kenansville, away from the burnt sword factory and the Yankees.

Just beyond the Baptist preacher's house, Bill left Routledge Road, guiding Peanut toward Limestone Road, trampling crops growing in fields. These were crops planted by farmers without slaves, like most of the small farms around Kenansville. Come dawn, the farmers would be mad as hops when they saw Bill's damage. He leaned forward and told Peanut, "Old Boy, I'd get a punch in the nose if one got close to me."

Bill didn't keep Peanut on Limestone Road for long, but cut through more fields to the Teachey-Kenansville Road. He contemplated staying on it all the way to Magnolia, but that would add several miles to his wee-hour jaunt. Instead, he bushwhacked through hard-scrabble farmland, a copse and some swampy land, his goal the Magnolia-Kenansville Road. During the day, mule teams hauling metals traveled the road to the sword factory and transported weapons back to Magnolia.

As the noises of the night composed a spontaneous concert, Bill found himself thinking about the Union Cavalry major and his words about a battle up in Pennsylvania. "Don't know much more, except Lee's retreating and our boys hold the high ground," Jacobs had told Bill's papa. Bill had been home for six weeks, and he'd heard nothing from Charlie. As if his buddy had died and the generals failed to put his name on the casualty lists his papa tacked to the bulletin board.

Charlie wasn't much of a letter writer, so maybe he couldn't be bothered keeping Bill up to date on the army's spring and summer actions. No doubt hundreds, maybe thousands, died at Gettysburg over the last few days. Did Charlie's putrefying body lie among the dead? Just because Bill had outwitted fate at Chancellorsville didn't mean God didn't get the last laugh at Gettysburg. Sweet Jesus... Bill wanted to get back to the house and see a letter from Charlie on his bed.

A shot rang out. A bumblebee whizzed by, coming closer than Bill liked. He slid off the saddle and plunged to the dirt between rows of cabbage. Someone had seen the silhouettes of Peanut and him and taken a bead. A Blue-Belly picket on patrol? Lily-livered Homeguards looking for some easy glory? A farmer doing his Southern duty and trying to kill a damned Yankee?

The moonlight dimmed as if God put his palm in front of Earth's little sister. A bank of clouds, Bill realized as he reached for his saddle-holstered rifle. He couldn't stay and wait for the shooter to move closer and maybe put him in a coffin. Now he had the darkness as an ally, but for how long? Soon the wind would nudge the clouds, and the moon would shine freely again. If the shot had come from a cavalry patrol, they'd pounce in no time. Rising to his feet, he thrust his boot into the stirrup and stopped cold; the moon peeked out. Bill dropped to his belly, hunting rifle by his side.

Cupping a hand to an ear, he listened. No horses approaching, a good sign. Or not. The cavalrymen could have left a man behind to tend to their horses. If so, they were creeping forward on foot, using a nearby orchard or the cornstalks as cover. A voice ran out, one with a Southern drawl: "Drop your motherfuckin' guns, Yank. Got my rifle pointed at your damned forehead."

Bill obeyed. Good chance the shooter might not miss this time. He buried his face in the loam to make the smallest target possible. Warily, he tilted his head and spit out dirt. "Not a Yank. Bill Stamford from Kenansville. On furlough from Lee's army. Trying to get information about the cavalry raid to the Magnolia commander."

"Stand up slow. Leave your damned guns in the dirt. Hands behind your head."

Rising awkwardly, rifle and the pistol left in the dirt, Bill kept his hands clasped behind his neck.

Two older men advanced, both maybe fifty. Homeguards, just as he suspected.

"He ain't in uniform, Ralph," one of the chuckaboos blurted. "Yankee spy?"

"No, he ain't," the foul-mouthed one mocked. "I know him. Not good, though. The Duplin Roads hussy, Becky Powell, he's the one who tickled her laycock. A gigglemug fellow if there ever was one."

Both looked shifty and furtive, slouch hats pulled down almost to their eyes. In no hurry to find their buddies, the absconders were probably scouting hen houses when they noticed the silhouette of Bill atop Peanut, the old nag trotting toward Magnolia-Kenansville Road.

"Enough about my love life." Bill allowed his arms to drop to his side. "You're delaying me from reaching General Evans in Magnolia. That damned shot you took, not jemmy. In fact, plain stupid. Blue-Belly cavalry's probably on the way to check it out."

"He's got a point, Gavin," the one who'd yet to utter a cuss word said, darting glances at shadows that might hide Yanks.

"I ain't sure, Levi," the foul-mouthed buffer said crankily.

"I am, Gavin." Levi hugged himself. "It's darker than a closed coffin. Moon's behind the clouds. I say we skedaddle."

Stooping, Bill picked up the rifle and pistol. "You've two choices, fellows. Go with me to Magnolia or skedaddle."

They skedaddled.

Not knowing how close to Magnolia Blue-Belly scouts might venture, Bill decided to avoid the Magnolia-

Kenansville Road. It'd only been a few minutes since the Home Guard shirkers had taken a shot at him, and sounds seem louder, shriller at night. Guns holstered and mounted again, Bill kept to the farm fields, grateful that clouds still cloaked the moon. Near the roadway, lamplight beamed from a farmhouse window. The gunshot had awakened the family. Too far away to see for sure, Bill had no doubt the farmer and his wife were peering through the glass. If they had seen him, no one ventured onto the porch.

Stroking Peanut's neck, Bill mulled the actions General Evans might take. The routed Seventh North Carolina Cavalry had likely fled to Magnolia and described Jacob's force as mightier than the Army of the Potomac. Evans would think the Blue-Bellies much tinier, maybe too tiny. Anyway, Bill doubted Evans would have reinforcements marching on the Magnolia-Kenansville Road for a counterattack. Such an attack would have occurred long before darkness. Bill thought troops from the Magnolia garrison might be on the way to Warsaw to block the Blue-Bellies and force a fight. Or if Evans was worried about losing the railroad maintenance yard, he could have his four companies of infantry and four artillery pieces in the breastworks around Magnolia, waiting for Jacobs to attack. Whatever Evans' plans, Bill wanted the garrison commander to know the actual Blue-Belly numbers.

More than halfway to Magnolia, Bill led Peanut onto the Magnolia-Kenansville Road. As he closed in on Magnolia, he didn't worry about Union scouts, but a trigger-happy Confederate picket patrolling the dirt road at four in the morning. What should have been no more than a two hour-trip had taken him nearly four hours. He neared Magnolia as the first pink streaks of morning daubed the horizon.

Off to the right, the Wilmington and Weldon Railroad's repair shops took up acres of what had once been farmland.

Nearby sprawled the tent city of slaves who kept the tracks maintained. Until the last few days, it had been Wilson's home. To the left of the road, troop huts dotted the landscape. That the repair shops even existed in tiny Magnolia was due to Wilmington's yellow fever epidemic. The railroad magnates didn't want to risk another outbreak, so they moved their repair operations up to Magnolia, fifty miles to the north. The same story for a Wilmington businessman, Louis Froelich, a Bavarian immigrant; he'd moved his sword-making factory to Kenansville. Safe from the fever, Froelich had just learned there were other ways to bring production to a halt.

Near the huts, pickets stopped Bill at a roadblock. Thinking him a farmer, they didn't expect to get a brisk order. "Take me to see General Evans. I'm from Kenansville. Sword factory's been burned by Yanks."

The head guard, a corporal, wisecracked to his partner, "Another country bumpkin wants to give advice to the general."

The second guard, a private, snickered, "We know about the Yanks, farmer. Nothing you can say the general don't already know."

As the guards watched slack-jawed, Bill took off his vest and shirt, revealing his wound. "Shell fragment took out a chunk of my back at Chancellorsville. Been recuperating in Kenansville. I've been in their camp, seen their numbers. I think the general might want to see me." Bill donned his shirt and vest, then tucked his shirttail inside his pants.

"Eighteenth North Carolina?" The head guard scratched an eyebrow.

"Company G. And yes, I saw General Jackson shot." Bill wouldn't say anything further, though thoughts of aureolas and the Fates of Greek mythology warred in his head.

"Sad about General Jackson." Removing his kepi, the head guard ran his hand through his mussed hair. "Got to ask. How come the Yanks didn't shoot you? Being so young and the right age for soldierin'. They had to be suspicious."

"Went to the camp with my papa, the town's newspaper editor. Pretended to be a simpleton, a three-year-old in the body of a man. The Union major has a simpleton brother, it seems. He didn't question the disguise."

The corporal nodded. "Follow me." He took Bill to a grand three-story house complete with gables, tower and an elaborate garden a stone's throw from the railroad tracks. Only a railroad magnate would have the cash to build the magnificent house impressive as Fredericksburg's mansions.

"My papa's house would fit in one corner," Bill remarked as they rode toward the mansion's stables.

"My father's too," the corporal confessed. "One of the railroad's directors, A. J. DeRosset, Jr., owns the house. Mister DeRosset turned over his home to General Evans." He directed his gaze to Peanut. "I'll have your horse fed, watered and brushed down."

Evans' staff appeared amazingly informal even for a Confederate one. No one buttonholed the corporal and Bill at the front door. They walked in, moseyed past the grand hall and continued strolling until they heard voices coming from a room, which turned out to be the library. The voices belonged to General Evans, his staff and company commanders. They hadn't bothered to shut the library door.

"Claiborne's troops are on the way to Warsaw." Bill knew the officer talking was the general by the chicken guts—gold braiding—on his cuff. Evans sipped Essence of Coffee from his tin cup. "They left just before dawn and should—" Evans whirled at the sound of Bill's and the corporal's boots. "Yes?"

The corporal stepped forward. "Sir, I thought you'd be interested in this fellow fresh from Kenansville." He gave Bill an inscrutable look. "He's with the Army of Northern Virginia. Don't know his name, though."

Bill saluted the general. "Private Bill Stamford, Company G, Eighteenth North Carolina, home on furlough recovering from a shell-fragment wound." He fidgeted, swaying from foot to foot. "I've been to the Yankee camp at the sword factory, sir. I've some numbers for you."

Evans gestured to a chair next to a decanter of wine and glasses. "Sit. You look like you're about to drop."

As if the word *sit* had magical properties, Bill abruptly felt tired. His back ached as if he hadn't used its muscles in months, which wasn't far from the truth. Bill wilted into the chair and reached for the wine. His hand trembled violently. Grimacing, he placed both hands in his lap. "A battalion size force. Under command of a Major Jacobs, a New Yorker. It routed the Seventh North Carolina Cavalry. Not sure where rest of the Blue-Belly force is. Probably Warsaw."

The general nodded. "Yes, Warsaw, Stamford. I expect Jacobs' force is headed back to Warsaw to join up with the rest of the New Bern troops. Claiborne's on the way to Warsaw. If the Yanks are stupid enough to linger, we'll give them a whipping. Expect all we'll find are twisted rails and destroyed telegraph lines."

"So you haven't gotten anything new on a battle in Pennsylvania?" Bill propped his hands on his kneecaps.

"Not since July second. I know it's frustrating. We'll have the lines repaired soon enough. "So you were at Chancellorsville?"

Bill tried to keep his face expressionless. He came up short. "Yessir. Great victory for the Confederacy. Not so great for the Eighteenth North Carolina. Mauled on the third day, but maybe it's deserved after what we did to General Jackson."

Evans harrumphed, lit a fat cigar and puffed. "Hogwash! Don't go placing blame, Stamford. I understand it was dark with lots of mini balls and cannon fire. Sometimes we can only say two words: *God's will.*"

Bill swallowed hard. Had the Lord chosen the general to trumpet the truth behind the damned aureolas? Bill groaned inwardly. Of course not. Aureolas were like Siamese twins or a baby born with three arms or six toes. He had come out of his momma's womb with the aureola curse. No rhyme or reason to it. It just *was*. God's will... always unfathomable. He'd go to his grave without answers. "Those are kind words. Thank you, General Evans."

"Just telling you it's the nature of war. Probably not that much different when Lucifer and his fallen angels made war on God." The general eyed the door when an orderly dashed into the room with a telegraph message.

"General Evans, sir, the telegraph's repaired—at least for now. Just got a message from Warsaw." The telegrapher hurried to hand the message to Evans, saluted and departed faster than he'd arrived.

Evans glanced at the message's scribbled words. "Nervous fellow," the general observed, looking up from the sheet of paper. "I can barely read his words. Says a train of fourteen empty cars just left Warsaw for Magnolia with Yankee cavalry seen in the distance. There's a woman aboard, desperate to get out of Warsaw. Wanted to go to Kenansville, but there were some Yankees in the way."

Evans unstopped the decanter and poured Bill a glass of wine. He drank in breathless gulps. The wine lubricated his throat, but left him wearier. "It's been a long night, sir," Bill said numbly, unable to smother a yawn.

"Plenty of unused rooms upstairs, Stamford. Get yourself some sleep. I'll have breakfast ready when you awake. One of my staff officers, Captain Sam Bradford, will show you to your room."

"Thank you, sir. Glad I could be of service."

Thirty-three

A Face from Bill's Past

Thunder? A summer storm?

No, not thunder. Knuckles rapping on the closed bedroom door.

Bill rubbed his eyes as he slowly banished the cobwebs of sleep.

He'd been on his belly, his usual position since the shell fragment had torn a hole in his back. Bill didn't need to stretch out that way, but habits are hard to break. Turning on his side, he looked across the unfamiliar room at the door. The movement left Bill disoriented, like the time he explored a cavern with just a candlelamp for light.

More insistent knocks on the door. "Private Stamford! Bill Stamford!"

Light flitted through cracks in two window blinds, revealing pricey furniture—two armoires, a secretary desk,

411

reading chair, loveseat, bookshelves, and an elaborate dresser and mirror—too grand for Bill's family.

"Bill Stamford! Wake up! A friend's here to see you!"

Shaking his head, Bill rose to a sitting position on the strange bed. *What the hell?* Then he remembered. DeRosset's mansion in Magnolia. A crazy moonlit ride through fields, woods and lowlands. The Blue-Belly cavalry raid, flames consuming the sword factory, two Homeguards firing at him.

He scratched a shoulder, then reached under the bed and pulled out his boots. "I'm coming! Patience, please."

The clock on an end table read nine in the morning. He'd arrived at first light on Sunday, July 5. Was it now July 6? "What day is it?" He knew he must sound ridiculous.

The voice on the other side of the door chuckled. "It's still July 5, Bill. You've barely been in bed."

He forced his feet into the boots, then reached for his straw hat on the reading chair. "So if I've been barely asleep, why are you bothering me? You've ruined a fairytale dream."

Again, the male voice chuckled. "You should be so lucky to dream any fairytale that has the beautiful woman down in the parlor as your Cinderella."

His ears perked. Cinderella? *A woman downstairs who wants to see me?* Ambling to the dresser, Bill cupped washing-basin water and splashed it against his face. A shock, but one he needed. "You say there's a woman who wants to see me?" His first thought... Becky. Maybe she'd defied her father and come hunting for him. Maybe her brother's death made her reconsider his marriage proposal. Then again... he'd not gotten one note, one postcard from her. As far as he knew, she could be aboard the *Cyren* with Rose and Little Rose on the way to Liverpool. She'd defied her father... not to marry Bill but to flee to England.

"Yes. She came on the train from Warsaw. Once she learned you were upstairs, she was insistent we wake you."

So who wanted to see him? Forcing weary muscles to move, Bill made his way to the door and opened it.

Captain Sam Bradford stood in the doorway, right arm braced against the wall. "Had you not come out, *I* was all set to take your place, show the sights of Magnolia to your blonde friend, meagre though they are."

"The only blonde I know is in—"

"Well, here she is," Bradford interrupted. "I guess she got tired of waiting in the parlor."

Disbelief exploded in Bill's head, like the fireworks that burst above Kenansville when North Carolina seceded. *Sweet Lord above, don't let this be a mirage.* Hands clenched, Franny lingered in the hall, maybe fifteen feet from Bill and Bradford. Just like he remembered her, yet different somehow. She wore a pale white-and-aqua summer dress without a crinoline, hem scandalously short, revealing green high-button boots. Her hair had changed… shorter, more curls. A straw hat adorned with red silk roses partly covered the curls, but what Bill could see sent shivers down his back. Lordy, he wanted to toss the hat to the floor and run his fingers through her tresses.

"Please, don't say you hate me," she said, her face fraught with worry. "I'm barely keeping myself from crying."

"Hate you, Franny? Never." His eyes settled on how the traveling dress clung to Franny's body. Not just no hoop, not much in the way of undergarments either. Franny would be cool later in the day when the heat and humidity straitjacketed the afternoon. "Not even if you're Mrs. Peter Hamberton."

She regarded him with quiet amusement. "I'm not Mrs. Peter Hamberton, nor do I ever plan to be. Only one man can have my heart, and I think you know who he is, Bill Stamford."

With a rueful twist to his mouth, Bill prodded, "Let me hear you say the name."

Franny twisted a curl around her finger. "Better yet, let me show you." Skipping, then running, Franny flung herself into Bill's embrace. Her arms closed around him, pressing hard against his healed wound. No pain. Burying his face in her curls, he inhaled a faint rose scent from her favorite hair wash. She sprang upward and wrapped her legs around him, revealing silk pantaloons. Her mouth sought his, pressing against his lips, seeking the touch of his tongue. As he returned her kisses, she groaned, "Sweet Lord… I'm not too late."

Captain Bradford cleared his throat. "I do believe I should make my retreat. Give you two some privacy." Bowing, he headed for the stairs.

"I can't believe you're here." Bill suspected he wore a look of incredulity.

"I intended to look for you in Kenansville, but there were some Yankees in the way." She rubbed her cheek against his skin. "So I came to Magnolia hoping to hire a ride to Kenansville, and heard some officers say a fella with the name Stamford was sleeping upstairs. I'm a lucky woman."

Bill backtracked them into the bedroom. Franny kicked the door shut with her right boot as her tongue gatling-gunned every pore on his face. "Yes, lucky. Becky's running away to Europe," he said between kisses. "She's out of my life."

"Good! I don't want to hear her name ever again. Just mine. Say it! Franny!" Releasing the pressure against his hips, she let her legs slide to the floor.

"Part your lips, sweetheart." Bill nestled his mouth close to hers without touching and said, "Franny," then blew his breath between her lips.

"Your *Franny* just reached my heart," she said, her voice sultry.

Sighing, he cupped her face, slid his palms along her cheeks. "It's been torture thinking I'd never again feel the touch of your body against mine."

Franny wormed her fingers between his shirt buttons and found skin. "I had this traveling dress made special for this trip. The seamstress took in the skirt to accommodate just a petticoat and pantaloons. I see so many women suffering in the summer heat." She grinned, stroking her bottom lip. "I'm not being entirely truthful. I wore the dress and scanty underthings for another reason." Franny unbuttoned his shirt's top two buttons. "So it doesn't take you an eternity to strip me down to skin." She unbuttoned the next button. "It's lickerish time."

Their clothes came off far faster than at the overseer's house. It became a race, with his shirt, her dress, chemise and hat flying through the air, landing on the dresser, end table and the floor. They left his pants, her pantaloons and their boots for later. "Those beauties"—he eyed her breasts—"I need to feel them against my chest." He hugged her tight while she rubbed against him.

"On the floor, Bill Stamford," she ordered. "It's time for those boots to come off. Before you crush my toes."

"Crush? You still have your own on, and flowery things they are."

"We take turns, mister. Yours first. On the floor. Now!"

Bill chuckled as he sank to the floor planks, legs extended, back erect. With her back to him, Becky settled on his lap and began tugging on his boots. He leaned forward and massaged her breasts.

She tossed the first boot across the room, banging the door. She stroked both his hands as he continued to gently squeeze her breasts. "I was so afraid you no longer loved me," she said, her breaths rapid.

He held up his remaining boot for her to remove. "I never stopped loving you, Franny. I just didn't understand your silence. I kept waiting for a letter saying you were married."

She yanked off the boot and let it join the other. "I'll explain. Later."

Urged on by her insistent hands, he settled against the floor planks and brought Franny with him so that her back lay against his chest. Kissing her neck, his face buried in her shortened hair, he continued titillating her breasts. "I swear I've the nymph Calypso in my arms."

"No, just the woman who'll make a house into a home and birth our children." She rolled off him, then loosened his belt and twisted his pants off. "Oooh, look who's not wearing long johns."

Bill sighed, in love with Franny's words. They would make beautiful babies. "My turn. I've seen enough of those boots and pantaloons." Bill pondered tossing her onto the bed, but chose to slide her buttocks toward him. The stylish green high-button boots came off her feet with just a little tugging, then her stockings. Her toes so kissable, he couldn't resist and began with her left foot's pinky.

"Stop it!" she said half-heartedly, giggling. "It tickles!"

Tempted to keep his tongue jiggling, Bill regretfully eased the torture. Well, not regretful for long. Scooping her into his arms, he carried her to the rumpled bed. Skimming her pantaloons past her legs, he draped them on the headboard's ornate center post. "Now what?" he said, beaming.

She scooted beneath him, wrapped her legs around his hips and maneuvered his penis toward her vagina.

Unexpectedly, she snaked a leg away from his hip and pressed it hard against his chest. "Damn! I've no horse sense. Bad timing I know, darling, but would you get a rubber from my reticule?"

Their lovemaking frenzied, they drenched themselves in sweat. The bedsprings squeaked; the frame grumbled but didn't break. Both cried out as their flood of bliss washed over them. She shrieked, he gasped, and it was over, both of them spent, both sharing a final glow of long, wet kisses.

Bill rolled off Franny and lay beside her, his left hand on her hip. In turn, she draped her hand across his hip and moved it in a slow circle. She purred softly. His fingers wandered along the contours of her body to her breasts and neck, then roamed past her lips to her eyes, both closed. As he stroked both eyebrows, those wonderfully expressive eyes opened and regarded him.

"Ah, yes, the explanation I promised," she said, sounding wistful. "As you know, I left for Tennessee to help Peter recover. When his health improved, he wanted me to marry him and not wait for the war to end. I nearly did. I nearly married a man I don't love. Mother adores you, Bill. She told me to follow my heart. So here I am." Franny slithered her arm past his waist and skimmed her fingers along his fresh scar. "Peter's a boring man. He wanted a wife who would look pretty clinging to his arm. With him, I couldn't have my own life. He didn't want to hear my thoughts. So I came to the man who does."

"I try not to be boring. I seek out new ideas, just like you do." Bill tickled Franny's nose. "I felt sorry for myself when you left for Tennessee. An intriguing future vanished."

"Well, I'm giving it back to you." Her tongue caressed his lips.

He let her tongue slip between his teeth. They kissed until sated, and then he said almost timidly, "Becky did seek adventure and new ideas, but they didn't include me. She hated the war, decided to flee to Europe. No place in her life for a soldier of the South. So soon she'll walk the streets of London and Paris." *God, I hope so. Don't let Rose's aureola claim her too. And show mercy to Rose. Mercy, Lord, mercy for them.*

"Fine with me," Franny said petulantly. "She can walk the streets of Dublin, Berlin, Vienna, Warsaw and Moscow—as long as she stays away from my man."

"Same with Peter."

"You won't ever have to worry about him, sweetheart." She hooked her right leg over his hip. "I told Peter that after the war when we were married I wanted to travel beyond the Mason-Dixon, and visit places made famous by the North's great writers and poets... Walt Whitman, Ralph Waldo Emerson, Nathaniel Hawthorne, Henry Wadsworth Longfellow, Emily Dickinson. He laughed at me. Called them literary pretenders. Said that as long as I went by Franny Hamberton, I'd never walk on land north of the Ohio River. Bastard!"

"I tried to put you out of my mind, Franny. Tried harder than you'll ever know. As soon as I saw you in your beautiful dress, I knew I'd failed. And thank God I did!" Bill kissed a breast. "So did I hear you correctly? You intend to have my children?"

"Yes. And carry your name... Franny Stamford." As he shifted his mouth to her other breast, she fussed, "I won't leave this bed until you ask me to marry you."

Bill looked up from her bosom and rolled his eyes. "Pretty sure of yourself, aren't you?"

"You've forgiven me. So yes, I am." Franny stroked an ankle with her toes. "We're so alike. Adventurous bookworms. I know... it's an odd combination. But perfect for us. So yes, my sweetheart, please ask me to marry you. I took a risk coming here… and now I'm so close to having my dreams fulfilled."

He rubbed her ring finger with his thumb. "I don't have an engagement ring."

Taking his hand, she kissed each finger. "Easily solved. My carpetbag's down in the drawing room. I brought along my Grandma Newton's engagement and wedding rings. She left them to me, so we do have rings for our marriage ceremony." She tapped Bill's chin. "I'm not getting off this bed until you promise to make me your wife."

He twirled a finger around a nipple's areola. "We should wait until after the war. I don't want you to be a widow." Franny's areola reminded him of the time Becky explained the difference between an areola and aureola. He decided to never again call God's radiant light an aureola. Halo only.

"Hogwash!" Franny rose to a sitting position and drew her legs up to her chest. "I'm not going to be a widow. I've a plan, and it begins with us getting married within a few weeks, maybe sooner, in Kenansville. All I need to get it rolling is a simple question from you: "Franny Neale, will you marry me?" She groaned. "Don't you want to marry me?"

"God, yes, Franny! I want to marry you." Bill caressed her cheek. "So say yes. In Kenansville before I have to return to the army in September. I love you, Franny. I want to spend my life with you writing and reading books together. Sharing adventures above the Mason-Dixon, across the sea in Europe, on camels visiting the pyramids in Egypt. One word, Franny… *yes*."

"Yes!" She kissed his eyes, the tip of his nose and finally his mouth. "In your church before this month is out. When we go downstairs, you can put Grandma Newton's engagement ring on my finger."

"Gladly." Kneeling on the bed, he kissed her kneecaps. "I want nothing kept secret between us. I've barely said anything to anyone since my cousin Jenny died when we were eight."

Franny leaned an elbow on Bill's shoulder. "I've no idea what you're talking about."

"Just listen. This isn't easy for me." He fiddled with his fingers, staring at them as he mulled his words. "I see halos around people." Bill held up his hand. "Listen and then ask your questions. Just before Jenny fell from a tree, I saw a halo around her. I don't see them often. The next time didn't occur until I was sixteen, when Charlie and I got into a fight with some toughs. A halo blazed around one of them, and he drowned a day or two later."

"Why are you telling me this, Bill?" Franny hugged herself.

"So you can back out of the marriage if you think I'm crazy." He sighed and pursed his lips.

"Writers, even would-be writers, are a tad peculiar." Franny draped an arm around Bill's shoulders and snuggled against him. "I'm marrying you, Bill Stamford. So you've told no one else about these halos?"

"Momma and Papa know. When I was eight, they took me to our preacher. He didn't see how God would give anyone such a gift, so he said I was possessed by a demon. He did an exorcism. I thought it had worked until that damned fight."

Franny dropped her hand from his shoulder to the bedspread, then rested it on his leg. "Poor Bill. You've been in battles. You must have seen hundreds of halos."

Bill shook his head. "Just three more... my friends Daniel and Charlie, and Rose Greenhow."

Franny's eyes ballooned. "I'm so sorry, Bill. Daniel's the friend who passed away in the Yerby barn, right?"

Bill nodded. "Yes, the night we met."

"Your buddy Charlie died?"

"I don't know… I don't think so." Bill threw up his hands in frustration. "Charlie's the first one I tried to keep alive. I knocked him out of the way of a mini ball. He fell against the fellow next to him, wrecking the man's shot. Ever play dominoes? Men kept falling against their buddies, ruining aims, just as General Jackson and his staff rode toward us. Franny, I'm the reason the general got shot. He's dead because of me."

"Oh, Bill! You can't be sure." She grabbed his hands and nestled them against her breasts. "You just told me you're not even sure Charlie's still living."

"That's because he's a lousy letter writer. The next day the shell fragment shredded my back. Charlie got me to the field hospital. God gave Charlie to me at the worst moments of my life. His price? General Jackson. I feel the truth in my bones, Franny. I was his instrument to change the outcome of the war." Bill kissed the palm of one of her hands. "This can never go beyond this room. Right?"

"Your halo secret is safe with me. I'll always be at your side to listen to your fears… and help you find meaning in the gift."

He laughed bitterly. "Gift? It's a curse. Like now… Rose Greenhow. I didn't warn her. Let her sail away to Europe. And Becky's with her. If the ship's to sink, Becky could die with her. I'm so confused. If I try to save someone, something just as bad happens to someone else. A life for a life. God works in mysterious ways. I do know this… He always requires a sacrifice when it comes to changing his Book of Life."

"Perhaps the Lord's done with you, Bill. He got his pound of flesh in General Jackson. Of course, we can't know for sure."

"Then why Rose Greenhow?"

"I can't give you an answer." Franny rose from the bed, walked to the dresser and checked herself in the mirror. "I'm marrying a deep thinker. I think God laughs at deep thinkers. Sometimes we want answers He keeps to himself. Do we have free will? The halos say *yes*, right?"

Bill nodded. "I think God sent you back into my life."

"So maybe that's the message from God to you? When you see a halo, do what your heart tells you to do. I figure God has allotted Charlie his three score and ten. Stonewall and the Confederacy? With them, he's not so kind. Keep in mind, you don't just have this halo gift. You've a literary gift as well. In the novels you write, explore why God gave men free will. And for a precious few, the gift of seeing halos." Turning her gaze away from Bill, she assessed the condition of their clothes strewn all over the bedroom. "What a mess. Folks are going to see how wrinkly our clothes are and know what we've been doing."

Rising from the bed, he ambled to the armoire, clutched her shoulders and kissed her. "You never revealed your plans to keep me alive and in one piece. Whatever you're plotting, I won't shirk my duty."

She danced her fingers on top of his fresh scar. "I don't expect you to, sweetheart. You'll still serve the cause, but in Richmond, not with the Army of Northern Virginia." Stooping, Franny retrieved her pantaloons and silk stockings. "When I returned to Fredericksburg, I ran into a friend of ours, Chaplain Anderson. He told me about your wound. Another fraction of an inch and you would've been dead. Happenstance? Or God's plan?" She laughed lightly. "The chaplain is a good friend to have. He has important friends in high places."

Bill did some tracing of his own, from the skin between her breasts to her belly button. "You've been doing some heavy-duty plotting. Nathaniel Hawthorne would be envious."

"You've given your pound of flesh to the Confederate cause. They can't have another pound. The chaplain has arranged an army job for you in Richmond. Up your alley." She handed the pantaloons to him. "You can dress me as I tell you more."

Dressing Franny wasn't as fun as unrigging her. But it did give him a chance to mull over her plans. The chaplain had arranged a job for him in the War Department working directly with Secretary Seddon. She assured Bill that Seddon would appreciate his talents with the pen and in the newspaper office. He'd become Seddon's new press secretary, liaison with the Richmond newspapers as well as newspapers elsewhere in Virginia and other states. The old one had wrangled a transfer to General Lee's staff. Bill would write the War Department's dispatches on battles and military-related items Seddon wanted disseminated. Bill had been ready to put up a fuss, but he actually liked the idea of the job. He'd get the big picture of the war, and someday when governments turned battlefields into monument avenues, he could put the experience to good advantage writing novels, short stories and poetry.

"When do I see Seddon?" he asked, buttoning and lacing her dress.

"After we're married and after the honeymoon."

"Honeymoon? In war?"

Wriggling her toes, she slithered into her right boot. "Why not? Seddon likes me. Europe's out of the question. I'd be afraid we'd run into Becky, and I'd end up in a hair-pulling free-for-all. Got to be someplace closer. Hot Springs, Arkansas?"

Bill half-gagged as he watched Franny don her left boot. "A recent story in the *Gazette* says the place has been the site of partisan fights and hangings."

"Hey, I'm kidding. Too close to Tennessee and Peter." She ran a hand through her truncated curls. "I hear Wilmington's Opera House is quite renowned. Unlike most places, it's still pulling in famous actors and actresses. Maybe we can see a show and later make a hotel bed squeak."

As long as it's not the Purcell House. He then said aloud, "That would make a splendid honeymoon. After the war, we can consider a grander one, maybe in Egypt. I'd like see the pyramids."

Almost dressed, Franny set Bill's farmer hat atop his head, then Bill did the same with Franny's fancy one with its silk roses. She snagged his arm, ready to be escorted downstairs.

"We should pay our respects to General Evans." Bill patted Franny's hand. "In the mood for a Wilmington and Weldon Hansom cab ride to Kenansville? With the Union cavalrymen around Warsaw burning track and telegraph lines, the Magnolia-Kenansville Road should be safe."

"A romantic cab ride? Sounds divine." She leaned against him and pecked him on the cheek. He escorted her out the door, and they proceeded to the staircase's top landing. They could hear the drone of voices down below. "Think they'll have any slaves left to drive the Hansom? I hear they've been flocking to the Union armies like flies to honey. The news of Lincoln's Emancipation Proclamation puts joy in their hearts."

"We'll learn soon enough." They stayed moored to the landing, not wanting anyone on the ground floor to hear their talk about the Peculiar Institution. "My family's two slaves fled yesterday," he whispered. "We knew they'd leave for New Bern. Papa turned a blind eye. Wilson and Malinda couldn't resist, not with the Blue-Belly cavalry just up the road on Kenansville's outskirts. If all the darkies have run off, the railroad can find a disabled veteran willing to drive us."

"I love you, Bill, but please don't call them darkies. I hate that word. They're men, women and children."

Lordy, he deserved her scolding. "I promise. Never again."

"Do you think your parents will like me?" Franny rested her free hand on the wrought iron bannister. Any other woman, North or South, would have worn gloves. Not Franny. She valued freedom, not just for slaves but also freedom from grim conventions that forced women to wear straitlaced dresses and underclothes.

"Definitely. They'll come to love the woman who braved the dangers of a Yankee cavalry raid to tell their son how much she loved him." Bill urged her down onto the first step.

She giggled. "Why don't you present us to General Evans? You know... introducing the future Mr. and Mrs. Bill Stamford. Lordy, I love the sound of that coming off my lips."

Meet Michael Staton

A retired journalist, Michael Staton lives in Henderson, Nevada, where he enjoys Black Mountain views of the Vegas Strip and the stunning desert landscape beyond the glittery lights of the valley. He honed his writing craft as a newspaper reporter at newspapers in Ohio, Florida and North Carolina.

Other Works From The Pen Of Michael Staton

The Emperor's Mistress - Teenaged Stealth is an artful thief with an attitude. Hired to burgle an exiled mage's villa, she tangles with Derrius, an apprentice mage of revoltingly noble birth. Trapped by political upheaval and their own antipathy, Stealth and Derrius undertake a mission to avert civil war.

Thief's Coin - In the river town of Opal, as the traveling players in Balthasar's Dream Palace perform, sorceress Illisandra Zayla's spymaster Jarn Sork captures Prince Derrius Hextor and imprisons him in a tower in the middle of the River Dolor. The prince's lover, the thief Stealth, must employ her cunning to outfox Sork and rescue Derrius, even though she knows her effort might result in his death.

Assassins' Lair - An amnesic girl wandering the streets of a border city holds the key that will decide the fate of the Setor Empire. Plagued with dreams about a queen who commands magic, the girl will soon learn that her body has become the vessel of a tormented soul.